"In addition to a smart mystery, readers will enjoy humorous takes on running a church, owning a dog, and dealing with father-daughter angst. The clever structure, remarkable dialog, and subplots result in a wholly satisfying read."

—*Library Journal* (starred review)

"Packs a considerable punch. . . . Readers will look forward to seeing more of Bear, with his formidable intellect, tart sense of humor, and resolute sense of justice." —*Publishers Weekly*

"Well-delineated characters, including the self-deprecating hero, drive this first-person account, which is strengthened further by the perceptive examination of family relationships and the portrait of the life and work of a minister." —*Booklist*

"Bear is a wonderful amateur sleuth." —*The Mystery Gazette*

"Extremely readable with great characters that you love and hate (even when it comes to the 'holiest'). In addition, the author certainly teaches readers about the vibrant attitudes, policies, loyalties, and entertaining attitudes that dwell in the Lone Star State. It will be very interesting to see this series continue. Enjoy!" —*Suspense Magazine*

"[A] warmhearted and clever detective story."
—M. C. Beaton, author of *Hiss and Hers*

continued . . .

SAFE
FROM HARM

Stephanie Jaye Evans

BERKLEY PRIME CRIME, NEW YORK

THE BERKLEY PUBLISHING GROUP
Published by the Penguin Group
Penguin Group (USA) Inc.
375 Hudson Street, New York, New York 10014, USA

USA / Canada / UK / Ireland / Australia / New Zealand / India / South Africa / China

Penguin Books Ltd., Registered Offices: 80 Strand, London WC2R 0RL, England
For more information about the Penguin Group, visit penguin.com.

This book is an original publication of The Berkley Publishing Group.

BBERKLEY® PRIME CRIME and the PRIME CRIME logo are
trademarks of Penguin Group (USA) Inc.

Berkley Prime Crime trade ISBN: 978-0-425-25346-5

An application to register this book for cataloging has been submitted to the Library of Congress.

PRINTED IN THE UNITED STATES OF AMERICA

10 9 8 7 6 5 4 3 2 1

Cover photographs: *Storm Clouds* © Dudarev Mikhail/Shutterstock;
Trailer © Lara Solt/Dallas Morning News/Corbis.
Cover design by Judith Lagerman.
Interior text design by Laura K. Corless.

This is a work of fiction. Names, characters, places, and incidents either are the product of the author's
imagination or are used fictitiously, and any resemblance to actual persons, living or dead, business
establishments, events, or locales is entirely coincidental. The publisher does not have any control over
and does not assume any responsibility for author or third-party websites or their content..

For Richard Allen Box.
He knows why.

Acknowledgments

Malice Domestic awarded me their 2010 William F. Deeck-Malice Domestic Award for Unpublished Writers—the award and the organization have made such a difference in my writing career. Harriette Sackler and Arleen Trundy have been invaluable mentors.

Trevor Pinkerton and Father Brian Barron gave me invaluable information on converting to Catholicism. Both were generous with their time. Jo's feelings are her own, but I couldn't have gotten it right without their help.

Captain Stuart Denton of the Sugar Land Police Department answered endless e-mailed questions and finally agreed to meet me for lunch so I could ask all my questions at once. I'm sure he thought that would make the e-mails stop, but it didn't and he patiently continued to respond. The man has some great stories!

Sarah and Gabe Cortez helped me with questions regarding the Houston Police Department's policies, and about Texas gun law. Sarah, author of *How to Undress a Cop*, one of my favorite books of contemporary poetry, remains a writing mentor forever.

George Copeland (author of *Leverage*, my new favorite noir novel) and Bill Enyart (who takes my son Charlie hunting and has kept the boy from shooting off a body part, thank you, Bill) coped with many tedious questions regarding firearms. George has made the serious mistake of promising to teach me how to shoot various guns. One of us is looking forward to that.

Samira Fitts, one of my spiritual heroes, allowed me to use one of her stories.

Carol Dilley and Pam Allan have been invaluable allies in getting out the word about *Faithful Unto Death*, the first in the Sugar Land Mysteries—I am so grateful to them both.

Anne Kimbol, John Kwiatkowski and McKenna Jordan of Murder By the Book (the very best mystery bookstore I have ever had the privilege to linger in for hours and hours and hours) have been so supportive. I can never repay them. In fact, none of us in the mystery community can ever repay them.

Thank you to Karla Hodde of Katy Budget Books, one of my favorite independent booksellers. She hosted such a fun reading for me—cookies and tea, too! And I got to make a bloody handprint for their wall.

With *Safe From Harm*, I had the assistance of two of The Berkley Publishing Group's finest editors, Faith Black and my own beautiful Shannon Jamieson Vazquez. Unless you have ever had the help and attention of a truly brilliant and committed editor, you cannot know how they transform a book. I had two. I thank them from the bottom of my heart.

By the grace of God (there's no other way to explain it) I am represented by Janet Reid of FinePrint Literary Management. There isn't a better agent on earth. There can't be. I am her devoted fan forever and ever amen. If she ever needs a kidney, I'm her girl.

I am so grateful to the many readers and reviewers who contacted me. You can't know how encouraging I found your words and support.

Dwain and Barbara Evans and Lisa and Michael Nicholls are always there for me—questions regarding real estate, Houston history, whatever I need—they are there.

Drs. Hank Venable, Tim Sitter, Fae Garden and Adam Garden, Les Schoppe, and George Boyle assisted me in my fictional murders. Thank you, all.

The Pinkertons, the Phelps, the Sitters, the Marnoys— these couples hold me up with their stories and advice and encouragement.

Jay, Christina, Evans and Charlie, Adam, Larissa, Mackenzie and David, you feed my heart and forgive me my failings. Thank you.

Always my thanks to my husband, Richard Box. He puts up with more than any man should be called to. Janet Reid says Richard is the perfect writer's spouse. She's right. He's that, and so very much more.

Prologue

No one was there when she let herself into the dark house, the preacher's house, her friend's house—she was alone, alone and empty, and there was only this house where she could come, when she wanted, if it was empty, if they were gone, she could come and let herself in with her key, it was her key, it was. Her key to this house.

She dropped the key on the floor.

The dog was a dog and he didn't care. He was used to her visits and he came and pressed his head against her side and walked with her to the kitchen. She didn't put a light on. She didn't need to. She knew the house.

She straightened the frame of the family portrait when she passed. Too dark to see it and she knew the faces anyway. The mom, dad and older sister, tall and blonde and blue-eyed, and the slight, dark youngest sister who wore a secret smile. No place in the picture for another sister, who could be dark or blonde, whatever they wanted.

The cool, dark kitchen smelled of, what? Bergamot. Earl Grey, maybe. Names she had learned here in this house. Her hand found a mug in the sink and she touched her tongue to the rim, then tilted the cooled tea into her mouth. Milky and sweet and smoky.

They had had tea. The family had sat around the table, and they had drunk tea, together, like a family, sweet, milky tea like a family in a book. She drank the tepid tea dregs from the three cups, rinsed the mugs and put them in the dishwasher.

The fridge was filled with cartons of milk and juice, a Ziploc with carrot sticks, another with celery, plastic containers filled with blurred mysteries. She rested her head against the cool, polished steel and looked for a long time. She pulled a container out and popped the top. Cookie dough. She scooped some out with a trembling finger and tasted it. Ginger. With lemon. She gave the dog a pinch of dough. She carefully sealed the carton and put it back in and chose another. This held a vegetable casserole that had started to fur. She dumped the contents into the sink and ran the disposal. Rinsed the plastic carton out and put it in the dishwasher, too.

She wiped the counters down and the smell of the cleaner made her gag. She leaned over the sink and waited; nothing came up. She stayed that way a minute, resting her hot cheek against the cool granite. The dog snuffled at her ankles and she stood. Rinsed and dried the sink. Dropped the dishtowel into the basket on the floor of the laundry room. All without turning on a light.

The bed in the parents' room was made, but mussed. Someone had taken a nap without moving the bedspread. She smoothed the wrinkles, and tucked in a sheet corner that peeked out from under the spread. She tried a spray of the mom's perfume. Spritzed her wrists and rubbed them together and then sniffed. It smelled clean, astringent. She sprayed a little at the base of her throat, too. She put a hand down for the dog to smell and he sneezed, then licked her hand and nudged his head underneath it. She rubbed the velvet of his ears.

In the dark family room, she drew her hand over the backs of the couch and the chairs, feeling the rough and the smooth. She sat in the preacher's chair and the leather creaked. His Bible was open over the arm of the chair and she picked up the heavy, limp book, the cover as soft as the dog's ear, and turned a few of the whisper-thin pages. The pages crackled under her fingers. She couldn't see the words in the dark. She found the frayed ribbon that marked his place and tied a loose knot in it. A message, if he could read it.

For a long time, she sat there, the dog resting his big head on her knees.

The stairway was lined with the daughters' pictures, shadowy and vague in the dark. One blonde head, then one brown head, then the blonde again, and then the brown, the girls in the pictures growing younger as she climbed the stairs to the room where her old friend, no longer a friend, slept each night.

The room glowed dimly from the big goose-shaped lamp that held a five-watt bulb in its expansive belly, the light on, day or night. There were trophies in the bookcase and dried corsages on the bulletin board that held dozens of pictures of the dark-haired girl with her friends, her family, her guy. A pair of worn-out toe shoes hung from the end of the ballet barre fixed to one wall. Clothes spilled from a dresser drawer. Twin brass beds stood side by side, a homemade quilt draped over a brass rail. It had the alphabet appliquéd on it. For the letter *J* it said, "J is for Jo," and there was a little girl in a pinafore and a bonnet, carefully stitched in.

She wanted to sleep here tonight. She wanted to take a hot bath with pink bath salts and a bar of soap that would float if it slipped from your wet fingers. She wanted to dry off with a thick, white towel, and put on pajamas, cotton ones, laundered thin, with flowers sprinkled over the top. And elastic-waist bottoms that came all the way down to her toes.

She wanted to curl up with the quilt on the little brass bed. The mom would bring her a cup of tea, hot and sweet and milky. The mom would read to her. "In the great green room, there was a telephone, and a red balloon, and a picture of—the cow jumping over the moon . . ." The mom would smooth her hair off her face, and kiss her right *here*, the exact spot the tear had reached. And hear her say her prayers. And tuck her in.

She wanted to lie down on that soft, warm bed, and close her eyes, and go to sleep.

And never wake up.

One

Annie Laurie and I had long since finished dinner at Gina and John Redman's house. It had been dusk when we arrived and now it was full dark out on their back porch where we'd all eaten Gina's wonderful dinner by the light of oil lamps. The Gulf Coast of Texas had at last cooled and the October night was brisk for an alfresco meal, but John had called ahead to warn us to dress warmly. In jeans and sweaters, we were comfortable and the dinner had been a delight. Our older daughter, Merrie, was back at Texas Tech, starting her sophomore year, our fifteen-year-old, Jo, was at a friend's. It was nice to have an adult evening.

It was time to go, but we were enjoying the conversation, and the excellent pinot noir, and the companionship of really good friends.

As a preacher, I get plenty of dinner invitations. Preachers, like politicians, are treated like dignitaries, even if, in my case that would be a minor dignitary. A dinner invitation from the Redmans, though, was not a command performance; it was a privilege. John and Gina are both close to sixty, more than ten years older than me and Annie Laurie, more than fifteen years for Annie. But the age difference has never affected our relationship. The Redmans had welcomed us to our new congregation from the beginning. When I found that John had played football for Texas A&M, a rival of my own alma mater, the

University of Texas, that sealed it. John liked to joke that he had played running back, a brain position, whereas I had played offensive lineman, a brawn position, but we both know that without my position, his position would be turf jam. I'd gotten my nickname, Bear, from playing offensive lineman—my real name, Walker Wells, sounded too leisurely for a guy who was powering two-hundred and fifty pounders off their feet.

My cell phone pinged to tell me I had a text message. It was from Jo, our youngest daughter. The message said, "Come home." Nothing else. Not a lot of information there. Just enough to make a dad worry.

I called Jo's cell, but she didn't pick up. I called the house and let it ring until the voice mail picked up. Did it again. I told myself everything was fine. Jo was fine.

I handed my phone to Annie Laurie so she could see Jo's text, and we made our goodbyes, accepted a bag of Gina's homemade rolls, said the next time was our turn and got in the car. Annie Laurie pushed the Call button six times every minute of the ten it took us to get home.

The house was dark, as we'd left it, except for the lamp on the foyer table. Our Newfoundland, Baby Bear, wasn't there to greet us and Jo didn't answer when we called her name. My heart was cinching up inside me and I put a hand out to keep Annie Laurie back, but she pushed past me and ran up the stairs to Jo's room. I was on her heels.

Jo sat cross-legged on the floor of her dark room. Baby Bear sat next to her and leaned his heavy, hairy frame against Jo's thin back. His breath came out in little whistling cries and his tail made anxious, uncertain sweeps. He glanced from me to Annie Laurie and gave a pleading yowl, then pushed up firmer behind Jo and panted in her ear.

Jo's waist-length hair was loose, and tented over the body of the loose-limbed girl she rocked back and forth in her arms.

The girl's long, lanky legs stretched out awkwardly, and her head lolled against Jo's shoulder, her eyes open and sightless, the pupils like pinpricks. It was Phoebe Pickersley, Jo's friend who had not been a friend.

As my fingers dialed 911, my head started saying, *Please God, please God, please God* without any help from me.

Annie dropped to her knees and put a hand against the girl's throat. Her fingers searched. She said, "Oh, my Lord." It was a cry.

I knew God had said, "No."

As I spoke to the 911 operator, Jo looked up. Her eyes were clear and wide and there were no tears. She pushed her mother's hand away.

"She's not dead, Mom," Jo said.

"Okay, sweetheart." Annie's voice was squeezed tight.

"She's *not*, right?" Jo is at that halfway age where she wants us to fix things, even when she knows we can't.

"All right, Jo." Annie cleared her throat. "Daddy's going to put Phoebe on the bed, okay?" Annie Laurie stroked Jo's hair back from her face.

I disconnected, having told the dispatcher everything I could. On an impulse, I texted James Wanderley, a local detective I knew who'd once told me he'd like to shoot me. He didn't mean it. I don't think he meant it.

I said, "We shouldn't move her . . ."

Annie gave me a sharp look. "This is Sugar Land, Bear, not *CSI*."

I didn't think it mattered where we were, but I crossed to Jo and gently lifted Phoebe from her arms. The girl was clammy, pale, and as light and boneless as a dead kitten. Light enough to crush your heart. Phoebe's eyes stared and her bluish lips opened when her head fell back against my arm. Her open mouth was stained a deep purple, like a child who'd been eating popsicles, which made the alterations she had made to her body seem all the more like mutilations. Phoebe's short hair was dyed black, but natural blonde roots showed beneath. Dime-sized gold circles rimmed the holes in her earlobes, holes large enough to stick a pencil through. There was a gold ring through one nostril, another through an inky eyebrow. Her navel was pierced, and circled with a tattoo—a snake swallowing its tail. Her toes had black polish on the broken nails, and her bare, white feet were chafed and raw and scratched. It was those cold feet that did it to me. Poor thing, I thought. *Poor, poor baby girl.*

But mixed with my horror and compassion was a guilty gratitude that Phoebe was not my child.

I laid the dead girl on the bed next to Jo's. I straightened her arms and legs, and smoothed back the short, black hair that framed her empty face. I drew her lids down over the blank eyes and closed her mouth. There was a quilt folded over the brass headboard, one my mother had pieced before Jo was born. It looked soft and warm and I draped it over this lost child and tucked it around her cold, white feet.

Annie Laurie knelt before Jo, her arms around Jo's neck, her fingers combing through the silky mass of Jo's hair. Jo clutched her sweatshirt to her and kept rocking. Annie murmured and cajoled, trying to get Jo out of the room. Jo used her mother's shoulder to get to her feet, my tiny dancer clumsy and awkward. Jo reached a hand out, unseeing. Baby Bear laid his muzzle in the open, expectant palm, and followed as Jo drew him with her. She stumbled out the door and across the hall to the bathroom, and I heard her running water in the sink before puzzle pieces clicked together in my head and I threw myself across the hall and into Jo's bathroom.

Jo had a Dixie Cup of water in one hand, and the other raised to her mouth.

I snatched Jo's hand away and pried her fingers open. Two

orange tablets. I picked them up and slapped at my pockets, searching for my glasses.

Annie Laurie, behind me, said, "Give them to me, Bear."

Jo slumped against the wall.

I handed them to her and cradled Jo in my arms, holding her like the baby she'd once been, still was.

Annie Laurie sighed and passed the tablets back to Jo.

"Acetaminophen. Generic."

I felt an internal collapse of relief and pressed my face into the back of Jo's warm neck and breathed in my child's salty smell.

The doorbell rang; there was a pounding; the bell rang again. I sat Jo on the toilet seat and ran downstairs to open the door to the EMS men who would be able to do nothing, nothing, nothing . . . except take Phoebe away.

And I knew in my heart that while some would grieve for the loss of this heartbreak of a girl, there were some who would not be sorry at all. There were some who would be glad Phoebe was dead. I wasn't counting Jo.

Jo hadn't meant it when she'd said she wished Phoebe was dead.

Two

Imet Phoebe's father and stepmother two years before I met Phoebe. Mark and Lizabeth Pickersley-Smythe. "Smythe" pronounced so that it rhymes with "writhe." Make of that what you will.

More than two years ago, Mark and Liz and their twin baby boys had joined the church I serve as minister. Mark and Liz were in their early forties which made them old to be starting a family, but with all the wondertechs working on fertility, it wasn't unheard of.

Mark had the easy grace of a natural athlete, too, and though he hadn't played college ball, it was only because an injury stopped him. He'd had the offers. I knew because John Redman told me. In the first couple of months after they joined, I had about fifty women in my church tell me Mark was a good-looking guy, in more detail than I cared for, and the oldest of these could have been my grandmother. She's the one who told me that Mark looked "So fine, I could eat that boy with a spoon." I didn't need to hear that.

Lizabeth was different. All that came effortlessly to Mark had clearly been labored for in Liz. Even with the adjustments I suspected a surgeon had made, she wasn't a beauty. Some might call her handsome. I don't know. She just didn't fit together well. Her button nose didn't fit the strong bones of her face—and her eyes were on the small side. Just as she didn't have her husband's looks and grace, neither did she have his way with people. She could get people to do what she wanted them to—she was aces at that, but she couldn't make them like her. And looking back with all I know now, I know Liz was lonely. That maybe she had always been lonely. I felt uncomfortable and edgy around her, and instead of taking the time to know her, to understand where those words were coming from, I avoided her. I failed her in that way.

At the "get-to-know-you" session in the new members' class, Liz told us she had gone to work at a failing packaging company (which meant they made cardboard boxes if I understood right) straight out of grad school. Within three years she was running it; in ten, she owned it. She sold to the big boys months before the economic free fall that left a number of church members with half the retirement funds they had had months earlier. She got married and had the twins, and bought a house in the Sweetwater neighborhood. Homes there start at a million and a half; when she told us what their neighborhood was, she was telling us how much the house cost. And there was nothing about how *they* got married, and *they* had twins and *they* bought a house. I'm not saying the pronoun thing meant all that much. It was interesting, that's all.

"Now it's time to enjoy the life I worked for," she ended brightly.

It was one of the more self-congratulatory speeches I'd heard, and I found Liz off-putting right there at the beginning, but Lizabeth's frank and unself-conscious enjoyment of her achievements went some way toward disarming me. Finally one other brave soul in a skirt and cardigan spoke up.

"I guess I'll go next. My name is Melinda Turnipseed, and yes, that's my real name."

There was relieved laughter all around. Nobody else in the

circle said more than they had to, including Mark, who said only that he'd met Lizabeth through work and was glad to know us. He had a soft, self-deprecating way of speaking that didn't match his expensive suit. Lizabeth's eyes were on him, bright and approving and possessive. She gave a nod when he'd finished, the kind you'd give a well-coached kindergartener. For all her off-putting ways, though, I have to give Liz credit, too. Liz labored for our church.

––––––––––

Lizabeth took to church volunteer opportunities like a CEO with time on her hands, which is what she was, and if she was high-handed in her dealings with the other volunteers (which she was), she was also effective. Shortly after the Pickersley-Smythes had placed membership, I'd begun to hear stories from Rebecca, my secretary.

"Your new couple, the Pickersley-Smythes . . ." Rebecca over enunciated the complicated last name—everybody did. It wasn't a name that rolled off the tongue.

". . . they're stepping on toes." Rebecca had tapped on my door and walked in without waiting for an answer. I was working on my sermon, but I looked up. She stood in front of me, her arms crossed over her bosom.

Rebecca stands about five foot five, but she's got the bosom of a six-footer. Since she's slim-hipped and slim-legged, I never feel like there's quite enough surface area tying her to the ground. She looks precariously balanced.

"Let me clarify," Rebecca said. "*She's* stepping on toes. Lizabeth. I only hear good things about Mark."

Mark played golf with the men's golf fellowship and tennis with some of the die-hard tennis players, and both groups had reported that he could sub as a pro at the Bridgewater Country Club. He was that good.

"So, whose toes?" I asked.

"Katherine isn't heading up the bookstore ministry anymore."

"She's not?"

"No," Rebecca said, "Lizabeth Pickersley-Smythe is. She said we were paying too much for the books, and selling them for too little. She has a contact who can get them for us cheaper."

"Uh-huh," I said. "And how's that working out?" I highlighted a scripture that clarified the point I was trying to make in Sunday's sermon.

"She *can* get the books cheaper, and it's too early to tell if we can sell them for more than we were."

"Weren't we selling them at our cost?" I thought the idea was to get helpful books and CDs and DVDs into people's hands.

"Lizabeth did a big sell on how profits from the bookstore could help fund our food distribution program; then she called for a vote—something that has never been done at a bookstore ministry meeting. Everyone was so wound up that she carried the day. Katherine e-mailed this morning to say she was stepping down, due to scheduling conflicts."

"But you don't think Katherine quit because of scheduling conflicts." I pushed away from the keyboard.

"I think Katherine decided that any schedule that included Lizabeth meant there was going to be conflict." Rebecca pulled aside one of my guest chairs and sat down. Rebecca almost never sits down in my office.

"What do you want to tell me, Rebecca?"

"A couple of things," she said.

"Yeah?"

"I don't want you to think I'm gossiping."

Rebecca doesn't gossip. I have a lot of respect for her judgment. When there is congregational news she thinks I should know, she tells me, and only me. Even though Rebecca actually attends the Baptist Church across the freeway, not our church, she hears more than I do. Now, the way she goes about telling me things, that's something that could be improved on. She's a tad circuitous.

"All right." I shut my laptop.

"Okay." Rebecca settled in her chair and adjusted the back cushion. "Well, Lizabeth has reorganized the church kitchen, which I think has needed reorganization since long past. But Lizabeth didn't say a word to anyone. She must have checked the kitchen out at the last Ladies' Bible Class luncheon, because two days later, Lizabeth shows up and by the time she left, around five or so, the kitchen was done. Every lid without a pot got thrown out. Mismatched Tupperware, gone. Those grills that fit the old stove but don't fit the new? Gone. A place for everything and everything in its place.

"That woman cleaned around the fridge handle with a toothpick. I saw her do it. I was about to get myself a grapefruit seltzer and there she is, she takes a toothpick, puts it in her mouth and nibbles the tip so it's frayed, then dips it in a mayonnaise jar lid where she's poured Pine-Sol, and careful, careful, she cleans all around the fridge handle where the handle meets the door."

"With mayonnaise and Pine-Sol?"

Rebecca leveled her eyes at me.

"Bear. It was a clean jar lid. She was using it like a little bowl. One she could throw out later. And she has laminated a how-to sheet, how everything is supposed to be cleaned and stored, put it in a magnetic frame and put it front and center on the freezer door. And she's labeled every single drawer and cabinet in the kitchen. 'Paring knives and peelers.' That's a for-instance."

"So, that's a good thing, right?"

I was looking for the problem here. I mean, Lizabeth wasn't smoking in the girls' room, or anything, right?

"Yeah, it's a good thing, Bear, everything Lizabeth puts her hand to is done well. That's who Lizabeth is."

"Okay . . ." I said.

"Thing is, she's not exactly a team player. It's not like she doesn't ask for everyone's input, but that's all for show, like some kind of management ploy she learned in grad school. She takes in all the ideas, points out their pros and cons—and she's great at this, Bear, leaves each speaker feeling heard and appreciated— then she does a recap, calls for a vote, and, surprise! It's Lizabeth's idea that wins the vote, hands down." Rebecca slapped the top of my desk for emphasis.

"But her ideas *are* voted on . . . ?" I asked.

"I just said so," said Rebecca.

"And her ideas are best?" I linked a couple of paper clips, added a rubber band to the chain.

Rebecca stared at me long enough for it to get uncomfortable. Then she got up from her chair and headed out of the office.

"Right. Whatever, Bear. I'm letting you know you've got a barracuda swimming with your guppies. Do what you want to about it."

So even back then I knew that Liz was a force to be reckoned with.

I just figured there had to be room in the church for the overcontrolling.

Then that overcontrolling woman had an out-of-control teenage stepdaughter dropped in her life. Turned out, Mark had a daughter from his first marriage. This was a surprise because no one I'd talked to had mentioned either an ex or a daughter.

Two years after Mark and Liz joined our congregation, Jenny, Mark's ex-wife, died, and Phoebe came to live with Liz and Mark and the three-year-old twins. Phoebe moved in with

Mark and Liz the same month I got shot—not my fault, in spite of what some people had to say about it—so it was a few weeks before I met her. That business on TV where the guy gets shot and he bounces right back up, ready for more action? Not so much. It was Annie who told me about the new addition over at the Pickersley-Smythes.

"When I married Mark I did *not* bargain on having his scarecrow of a daughter come to live with us, I can tell you that." That's what Annie told me Liz had said to her. Get what I mean about the things that come out of Liz's mouth?

"What did you say back?" I asked Annie Laurie.

"Not a thing. I stood there gaping like a gaffed fish, Bear—I couldn't get my jaw back in place. That girl's mother had just died and she has come to live with her dad, and Liz acts like she's just learned she struck a bad bargain."

It wasn't a good beginning, and it didn't get better.

My first look at Phoebe was when Jo, my youngest, brought her home after school. I wouldn't have called Phoebe a scarecrow. But I understood why Liz had.

I was home that April day, still recuperating. I had been back at the church office and in the pulpit within three weeks, but I wasn't yet back at my old schedule, so that afternoon I'd been in our front yard giving Baby Bear some air when a fire-engine-red Ford F-150 jacked up on monster tires came to a sedate stop in front of our house. I knew that truck. It was Alex Garcia's. Which meant that Alex had driven Jo home from school. I didn't like Alex driving Jo anywhere—she was just fourteen, though until recently, Alex had been driving Jo all over the place. That was something Alex and Jo had not shared with me and Annie, or he wouldn't have been. Alex was sixteen and a junior while Jo was only fourteen and a freshman. We'd found out that Jo had been sneaking out her second-story window to the garage roof where she would drop into the backyard and slip out the back gate to meet Alex. I wasn't happy when I found out about it. You're hearing the understatement, there, right?

When I finally released Jo from being permanently grounded (do you know private citizens are not allowed to buy those ankle-bracelet things they put on at-loose criminals?), I had stipulated that Alex could drive Jo from the high school to our house—that was a journey of all of one-half mile, and it was on residential streets, no stoplights and only two stop signs. The concession still made me feel like an appeasement monkey. But a man's got to have some peace in the house.

On this particular day, Jo hopped out of the truck and dropped to her knees to greet Baby Bear who acted like he hadn't seen her in a year, and said, "Hey, Dad! This is Phoebe Pickersley. Her parents go to our church."

A long gangle of a girl descended from the passenger side. She clambered out backward, her booted foot feeling for the running board, and then turned to face me.

This was Phoebe.

There's my Jo, a tiny five feet two inches, slim as a sprite, in jeans and a T-shirt, her dark hair flowing to her waist, and Alex, closing in on six feet, blond, blue-eyed and tan, and then, next to them, stood Phoebe.

Phoebe was nearly as tall as Alex. She was breastless and skinny in a boneless, sexless way, an impression enhanced by her short, choppy haircut and the black dye she had covered it with. I knew it was dyed because she had about an inch of pale, blonde roots showing. Phoebe was fighting the androgynous look with heaps of makeup. Her nose and one eyebrow were pierced, and a constellation of tiny silver earrings rose from her earlobe and up around the auricle of her left ear.

She had big blue eyes and a weak chin and round, red cheeks—a childish face. That made her piercings seem especially brutal. Her clothes were like nothing I'd ever seen before.

I don't even know how to describe them—like a smashup between a biker babe and an elf, maybe. With her long, skinny limbs and exotic coloring, she looked like a tropical insect set down in suburban Texas.

I wrenched my eyes off Phoebe and bent down to kiss the top of Jo's head.

Jo said, "She's Mark Pickersley's daughter, Dad. Her mom died, and now she lives with her dad and stepmom. Lizabeth is where the 'Smythe' comes from, but Phoebe doesn't use that."

This girl was the same age as my two. I said, "Ahh, gee. I'm sorry, Phoebe. That's hard, to lose your mom and then have a move on top of that." Wholly inadequate. Any words would be in the face of that kind of loss. "So, are you at Clements with Jo and Alex? What year are you?"

Baby Bear had given the new girl a thorough smell inspection and now did Phoebe the courtesy of inviting her to play Steal the Sneaker. He did this by pulling at her bootlaces.

Phoebe took hold of Alex's arm to keep her balance and waggled her foot, trying to shake Baby Bear off. "I'm a junior. I'll go back to Torrance to take my finals, but I have to finish the year at Clements. Dad doesn't want me driving back and forth, and Liz says she doesn't want Dad commuting four hours a day to take me and pick me up. I'm only putting in days here. I can't have any more absences or they'll, like, make me repeat my junior year. They're making this huge concession since Clements is in a different district." She gave her left foot another little kick. Baby Bear was pleased with her encouragement and gave a play growl, mouth full of laces and butt in the air. "I wanted to stay at Torrance. I could have, too, if my dad had let me stay with Grandpop DeWitt. He moved into my old place. That's what I should have done."

I said, "Torrance High School?" Torrance High School is close to Hobby Airport—forty minutes away if there wasn't any traffic, but we're talking Houston and its outskirts—there's always traffic. Mark really could spend close to four hours a day driving if he had to drive Phoebe to and from school. And Torrance isn't only miles away—it's a world away from the green and affluent campus of Clements High School. Torrance is, at best, a struggling high school. According to a *U.S. News & World Report* article, it's a dropout factory. It serves a population that has never been given much voice in Houston politics, and I couldn't imagine anyone with options choosing to send their kid there. For a man who lives in a million-dollar house to send his daughter to Torrance—I couldn't see that. It made me reassess what I knew about Mark Pickersley-Smythe, above and beyond the whole hyphenated-name thing.

I said, "Huh," because nothing better came to me.

Phoebe nodded, sucked her cheeks in and looked over my head.

———

"I was in the magnet program at Torrance. Science and mathematics. Top of my class." Now Phoebe was gazing into the thicket of azaleas at the corner of the house.

Okay. I nodded my head. Jo and Alex had abandoned me to this awkward conversation and were romping with Baby Bear. Jo named the dog, by the way. Not me. I didn't name that dog after myself and when Jo did, my protests got me nowhere. It was bad enough when Baby Bear was a puppy, but at least he looked like a baby then. Baby Bear, like all Newfoundlands, got big. His weight, at five years, wavered between 180 and 185.

"I hear good things about Houston's magnet schools," I said, wondering if I could excuse myself and go do something else. Anything else.

"I'm going to the Air Force Academy after I graduate. It's in Colorado. Colorado Springs." She addressed this to the front door.

I nodded. I knew where the Air Force Academy was. I didn't think the Air Force Academy was all that big on piercings.

Jo grabbed the strap of Phoebe's backpack and pulled her toward the house. Jo can be abrupt—when she's no longer interested in a conversation, the conversation is over. Baby Bear romped alongside, leaving me and Alex alone in the front yard.

Alex shuffled his feet. "Mr. Wells? Phoebe wants to go to dance class with Jo. I could drive the girls. It's only two point eight miles from here." He grinned up at me. "I googled it."

I was shaking my head before he finished.

"No, Alex. I'll take Jo to dance. I'm going that way anyway." I was going that way because *I* was taking Jo to dance class, not Alex. I led the kid into the house and poured him some tea from the pitcher Annie keeps ready-made.

Alex leaned his butt against the kitchen counter. I sat down at the kitchen table. We were silent, listening to the girls rummaging around upstairs in the room Merrie had left behind when she started her first year at Texas Tech.

"And how are you doing, son?" You have to say something.

Alex scooped a spoonful of sodden sugar from his tea and ate it.

"Mr. Wells, I'd be a whole lot better if you'd let me take Jo out now and then."

"She's fourteen, Alex." Jo wouldn't turn fifteen until September. Not that Alex didn't know this.

"Jo says her mom was dating at fourteen."

I mulled that over. Merrie, my eldest, had a boyfriend when she was fourteen or fifteen. My memory was that they went out in groups. And her guys weren't as intense as Alex—Alex is so intense about Jo. I didn't like it.

"Then I don't know what her father was thinking."

Alex put his glass in the sink and filled it with water. "You know I'd never let anything happen to Jo. I'm not going to take her anywhere bad. She's got the cell phone."

"Son, you took her out without our permission. I'm not happy about that. I don't want to beat you over the head with it, but that wasn't right."

"I know, and I didn't . . ."

He trailed off. He wouldn't say anything bad about Jo. It hadn't been his idea for Jo to sneak out of the house; it had been Jo's.

I held my hand up. "Alex, we've been through it. It's not happening. I've got nothing against you. You're welcome here anytime it suits Jo, as long as either Mrs. Wells or I am at home." I stopped to give him a meaningful look. "But as far as Jo and the truck goes, well, it goes as far as this house here. No farther. So. How'd you meet Phoebe?"

Alex opened his mouth but closed it again when we heard the girls clattering down the stairs. Jo had her shoe bag in her hand—my mother made it a hundred years ago to hold Jo's ballet slippers. Phoebe clutched a worn pair of Merrie's cast-off black ballet slippers to her chest.

Jo saw a protesting Alex to the door and we piled into my car, girls in the backseat, me and Baby Bear in the front seat.

From: Walker Wells
To: Merrie Wells

Do you remember how old you were when you had your first real date? Was it that Chris guy?

From: Merrie Wells
To: Walker Wells

Are you giving Jo grief over Alex? He's a good kid, Dad.

———————

Jo was full of Phoebe stories that night at dinner.

Phoebe had studied dance with a Russian instructor. Gyorgy taught her some new exercise techniques she could share with Jo. On hearing that Jo had been accepted into the prestigious School of American Ballet summer program and would spend the upcoming summer in New York, Phoebe revealed that the only reason she wasn't doing the very same thing with her summer was because she wasn't interested in classical ballet, it was "too regimented" for Phoebe—a girl who aspired to the United States Air Force Academy—but she wished Jo the best. Phoebe had been to New York City a hundred times, so she could tell Jo all the cool places to go. Phoebe would probably spend the summer hitchhiking through Costa Rica, but she could access the Internet from anywhere on Earth, so she could keep in touch with Jo while poor Jo was slaving away in hot, sweaty New York City. Or Jo could follow Phoebe's blog, instead. She's been getting a lot of interest from literary agents over the blog.

Annie Laurie had begun listening with an interested smile, by the time Jo ran out of enthusiastic comments, the smile was gone and Annie had an eyebrow raised in the position referred to as "askance." I hadn't looked up from my plate once.

Annie poured herself some wine, and said, voice carefully neutral, "What did Madame Laney think of Phoebe's dancing? Is she going to let Phoebe join up?"

Jo twined the fibers of a spaghetti squash around the tines of a fork and smelled it. "Is there butter on this?" Jo is thoroughly vegetarian and leaning toward vegan. My daughter is a sixth-generation Texan and practically vegan. I think somebody snuck in some California blood somewhere along the line.

Annie said, "A little. Not enough to make a difference—maybe a tablespoon for the whole squash. What did Madame Laney say?"

Jo put the bite in her mouth and held it there for a meditative moment before chewing and swallowing. She looked a question at me before turning back to her mother.

"Didn't Dad tell you about the fall Phoebe had right outside the studio? She tripped on the curb and fell on her knee. She couldn't dance today. She's going to have to go easy on the knee for a week. Madame Laney said Phoebe could sit in on class today. If she wants to dance, Phoebe needs to bring Madame a letter from Gyorgy, saying what level she is."

Annie Laurie looked from Jo to me. I offered Baby Bear a strand of underbuttered squash and declined to meet her eyes. Baby Bear made a big deal over the single, flavorless strand.

———————

Over dishes that night Annie said, "What's up?"

There was only a dab of that squash stuff left. I shoveled it into Baby Bear's dish. Annie took the serving dish from me and told me to sit down, and I was happy to. The scar on my belly didn't look like a big deal, but I still felt achy and tired by early evening. I eased down into a kitchen chair and rubbed the wound on my belly. Sometimes it itched.

"Is her door closed?"

Annie looked at the ceiling. Muffled music reverberated. "It's closed, Bear. She's working on her algebra sheets."

I sighed. Merrie had been taking pre-AP Geometry at Jo's age.

"You haven't met Phoebe . . ."

"No," Annie Laurie agreed, "that's why I'm . . ."

"She's a little different."

"Mother Teresa different or Lady Gaga different?" She fitted a cabinet door back in its frame and bumped it with a knee to get it to stay. I've fixed it twice but the screws are stripped. Which means filling old holes, drilling new holes . . .

"Just . . . well, more Gaga than Teresa. I don't know. No, that's not true. Okay. Here's what I've heard, either from Jo or from Phoebe herself."

Annie Laurie put the last pot away, picked up her wineglass and rested a hip against the sink. "I'm listening."

"She says she's top of her class in the math and science magnet program at Torrance High School—that could be true. She could be smart."

Annie did her eyebrow thing. "Torrance? Mark Pickersley-whatever had his daughter going to Torrance?"

"That's what she says." Baby Bear insinuated himself between my thighs and I gave his ears the long, slow massage he likes.

"Hmm.

"She says she's going to the Air Force Academy."

Annie jerked her head back a little. "Hmm, again."

"Well, yeah. If it's true. You haven't met her, Annie. Remember that visit to the Academy a couple of years back? Everybody so clean-cut they squeaked when they walked? That's not Phoebe. I mean, I've never checked the requirements for the Air Force Academy, but I do know you have to have a letter of recommendation from your senator or representative, and I can't see Kay Bailey Hutchison having her picture taken shaking hands with Phoebe. Phoebe looks more like that girl with the dragon tattoo than a cadet. It's not going to happen, and I don't care if she's Richard Feynman smart. So there's that.

"Then we hear she's got a personal dance instructor, a Russian, and she could have gotten into The School of American Ballet summer program only she didn't 'choose' to, and she's hitchhiking through Costa Rica. Solo. While she writes some award-winning blog. You think her dad would let her hitchhike through Costa Rica?"

Annie tipped the last of her glass into her mouth. "Maybe. He let her go to Torrance High School."

I snorted.

"Couldn't be any more dangerous." Annie smiled at me and rinsed her glass under the faucet, swirling the stem and letting the water fountain up.

"The dancing thing . . ."

"Yes?"

"She's not a dancer."

Annie set her glass down and considered me.

"Let's move into the family room. You'll be more comfortable."

She gave me a hand up, not that I needed one; it was a friendly thing to do, that's all. We settled next to each other on the sofa. Baby Bear, after making his token attempt to join us on the sofa, settled at our feet. I put my feet on the coffee table and Annie let me. I'm getting away with a lot while I'm convalescing.

"Tell me why you don't think Phoebe could be a dancer."

I pulled Annie close to me and tucked her head under my chin.

"She's too tall . . ."

"Dancers are getting taller, Bear. The kids are getting taller."

"I think she's taller than Merrie."

"Cynthia Gregory is pretty tall."

"I don't know who Cynthia Gregory is, but if she's a ballet dancer, I'm betting she's not five feet eleven, like Phoebe."

"Okay."

"But that's not the main reason."

"Okay."

"The main reason is that the girl doesn't move like a dancer. Phoebe's ungainly and awkward." I caught Annie's look. "No, I'm not being ungenerous or too hard on her. Merrie moves like an athlete. Jo moves like a dancer. Phoebe moves like, like she's put together wrong."

Annie scooched to the edge of the sofa so she could lean her back on the sofa arm and put her feet in my lap. I slipped her sandals off and began rubbing her feet.

"Like she's not comfortable in her body," I amended. "And that 'fall' right before dance class? I saw it. I was waiting in the car for them to go inside. Jo was leading the way so she didn't see it, but Annie, that was the most contrived fall I've ever seen. It was Keystone Kops contrived. I'll tell you what. I bet Laney saw the farce through the window. That's why she wants some kind of verification from this Gyorgy guy. Get off the couch, Baby." See, what Baby Bear's attempts to get on the couch tells me is that when I'm not home, *someone is letting that dog on the couch.*

"She's only a kid, Bear."

"Annie, do you get that I don't care whether or not Phoebe can dance? You're not hearing me say I don't like her—I'm not saying I *do* like her; I'm withholding judgment."

"Sure you are," said Annie, then, "Ow!" I had accidentally popped one of her toes. She pulled her feet away from my hands and tucked them under my butt.

"I guess I'm kind of wondering what her interest in Jo is," I continued. "I mean, she's two grades ahead of Jo . . ."

"Alex is two grades ahead of Jo . . ."

"Move your feet, you've got too many bones in your feet."

Her feet were cold, too. They're always cold. "Broad-minded though I try to be, I wouldn't be thrilled if Phoebe's interest in Jo is the same as Alex's interest in Jo, and I didn't pick up anything like that."

She shoved her feet farther under me. "That's not what I was saying, Bear. How did you make that leap from what I said? So maybe it isn't Jo at all. Maybe it's Alex she's interested in."

I leaned back. All right. It could be that. And that might not be a bad thing. Annie Laurie and I had been much happier before we knew about Alex's infatuation with Jo. Ignorance really is bliss. Sometimes. Sort of. It's not like we're all paranoid about boys being around our girls—Merrie, with her blonde good looks and athletic body, had certainly gotten more than her fair share of male attention. It was the intensity of Alex's feelings, his fervor, that had us unnerved.

Alex uses the word "love." In front of us. In a challenging kind of way. As in "I am in love with Jo" and "I am in love with your daughter." Annie tells me not to dismiss Alex's feelings, and I try not to, but I do not want to hear some guy say he's in love with my fourteen-year-old daughter. I want him to sit in the family room and talk football for a respectful period of time, and then go to whatever *group* activity they have planned. I'm fine with the boy having feelings, but I don't want him sharing those feelings with me. And if he says it to Jo, I want him sitting on his hands while he does so, you get me?

So it wasn't altogether unwelcome to entertain the thought that someone else might be trying to hone in on Jo's territory.

Still. Alex is a good kid. Good grades, doesn't smoke (I'd know if he did—he wears that blond hair to his shoulders and I'd smell it on him), his pupils are always the right size (yeah, I check, this kid spends time with my *baby*). And Phoebe was a complicated person in a complicated situation, and . . .

As much as I didn't want Alex to be trouble in *Jo's* life, I didn't want any more trouble in *Alex's* life. He'd been through too much already. And Phoebe looked like trouble.

Sometimes when it looks like a duck and it sounds like a duck, it is a duck.

Three

Phoebe was a duck.

No, you know what I mean. Phoebe was trouble.

Phoebe didn't mean to be trouble. Not really. She was an angry, lost and deeply lonely child. I'm ashamed that I begrudged her the fantasies she used to clothe that past life.

She never did bring Madame Laney that letter of recommendation she had asked for. Gyorgy was always touring in Prague or Barcelona or someplace else unlikely. So Phoebe stopped going to dance class. But she spent a lot of time around our house, even when Jo wasn't there.

Phoebe would drop by right after Jo had left for dance—Jo went to dance class six days a week, and Phoebe seemed surprised each time to learn that Jo wasn't there. Phoebe would ask if she could stay and wait for Jo. If I was home alone, I wouldn't let her in. I won't let any of Jo's friends in the house if I'm home alone. There's too many ways for that kind of situation to be misunderstood.

If Annie Laurie was there, she would invite Phoebe in and Phoebe would visit with Annie Laurie, helping her with whatever job Annie Laurie was busy at. She would set the table, or help mate socks while Annie was folding clothes, or busy herself in the kitchen cooking alongside Annie. And they would talk and talk, my wife wearing something suburban like jeans and a button-up, and Phoebe in her black Emo Commando or some such outfit.

By the time Jo got home from dance, Annie would have invited Phoebe to stay for dinner and Phoebe would accept. She was at our dinner table at least three times a week, and I was okay with that. At church Mark and Liz made vague comments about how well the girls were getting along and how Phoebe needed to have Jo over, but it didn't happen. It was always our house. I never would have let Merrie or Jo spend so many nights away from home, but I'm that way, I guess. And I miss my girls when they aren't there. I miss Merrie now that she's at school.

"You know that girl is coming here to see you, not Jo, right?" I asked, interrupting Annie Laurie at her computer she has a sweet business creating home schooling programs and was working at the kitchen table while I did the dishes.

"Bear, her mom died." Annie was still writing, words coming out of her mouth and wholly different words flying off the tips of her fingers. Neat trick. "She's going to a new school and living in a new house with a stepmother who doesn't seem to be trying very hard to be a mother to the girl. She seems to find some comfort with me and we should be grateful she's coming here instead of acting out in a more negative way."

"What do you and Phoebe talk about?"

"Ahh, let's see. Whether or not Lady Gaga is a man—I'm voting no. Her costumes are too revealing to be hiding a secret like that. Whether or not Clements High School is a closed, elitist, exclusionary police state which I think it can be, sometimes. She wanted to know if you treat me nice all the time and whether or not I've ever thought about divorcing you and what would I do if you ever cheated on me." Annie wasn't looking at me but I could see her smile as she waited for the response she knew she was going to get.

I slapped the dishcloth into the sink. "What?"

"She did, too. She asked me right out."

"She asked you if I'd cheated on you?"

Annie pushed back from her computer and came over to join me. She put a finger on my chest and tapped me for emphasis. "I told her nobody is nice all the time, not even preachers and certainly not me and of course I've thought of divorcing you, every woman has that thought when she goes into the bathroom in the wee hours and sits *in* the toilet because the seat's been left up, and that you would never in a million years cheat on me because I'm all you can handle as it is and besides, my daddy keeps a gun. Phoebe tells me her granddad does, too. Generational thing."

Yeah. God gave me a houseful of women to keep me humble when I get up in the pulpit each Sunday.

"You are a bad, wicked woman, Miss Foster."

Annie put her arms around me and linked her fingers behind my back. She didn't squeeze the way she once would have. She knew I wasn't up to that yet.

"It's been a long time since I was Miss Foster, Mr. Wells."

I kissed her. "Yeah, but you've always been a little wicked." I bent my knees and put an arm around the backs of her legs so I could scoop her up and right away felt that incision protest. Instead I sat on the floor and pulled my wife down next to me. Baby Bear hurried over and pushed to be let into the middle. That dog hates to be left out. I rubbed my stomach where one bullet the size of a child's pinkie finger did me more damage than the cumulative weight of hundreds of football players did over the four years I played college ball.

"How long is it going to be before I'm me again, Annie?"

"You're you, now, sugar. You are still my Bear. It's only been a couple of months. Give your body some time to heal." She kissed the underside of my chin and I tilted my face to meet her kiss, and Jo walked into the kitchen to find her parents sitting on the floor necking, Baby Bear grumbling next to them. She got a glass, filled it with ice and water, called her dog to her, and, on the way out, suggested we get ourselves a room.

We did.

When was it that things started to go bad with Phoebe? I'm clueless about so much that goes on in my girls' hearts. The question is, when did I finally notice that Jo didn't want Phoebe coming over anymore.

Merrie and Jo have never much dealt with jealousy. There's a four-year difference between the girls, so they weren't competing with each other for friends or honors and each had their successes in very different fields. I look back at that sentence and I wonder how true it is. Were my girls ever jealous of each other? Annie and I don't play favorites, but there are other arenas. I mean, you don't really know your children, do you? You don't really know what's in their hearts. You only get the bits they choose to share with you. And when they do share something with you, ahh, be careful, careful with that treasure. Don't use it on them, don't make it a tool to teach them a lesson, don't you ever bring it up and throw it back at them. Or it may be a wearying long time before you are ever trusted with something precious again. And serve you right, too.

It could be I missed it when Jo started to show signs that she wasn't comfortable with all the time her momma was spending with Phoebe. By the time things reached a point where I couldn't miss it, it was all out there.

This is how it happened. Things with Phoebe had gone on about a month, Phoebe always coming to our house, and Jo never being invited over to Phoebe's. Not that I know of. On the few weekends when Jo's friends were over, Phoebe was there, too, sticking out among all the fourteen- and fifteen-year-olds.

But Jo and her friends weren't coming to our house anymore, the way they had for years and years. Lately, they gathered at Cara's house. They never seemed to be here. Phoebe, on the other hand, was always here.

And then the day came when Jo got a letter from The School of American Ballet telling her what supplies she should bring with her for the summer program. I put the envelope next to her dinner plate, and for the first time in weeks, my girl was full of conversation over dinner. She would need some new pointe shoes, new ballet shoes, leotards and unitards and a robe, not the one hanging in her bathroom, that was too babyish, she wanted some new wrap skirts, and a body-wrap sweater—could she have one of those? And could she and Annie go shopping this Saturday? In case they had trouble finding something. That way there would be plenty of time to find it someplace else.

Phoebe looked up from the ratatouille she and Annie had made together earlier.

"What about a new shoe bag?"

Jo said, "I've got a shoe bag."

"Ummmm, yeah, it's got dancing bears on it. Bears in tutus." Phoebe gave a snort to indicate what she thought of tutu-wearing dancing bears.

Jo's face pinched. "My nana made it."

"When you were about five. But whatever." Phoebe peeled off the melted cheese, rolled it into a tube and ate it with her fingers. "If you want, I could go with you Saturday and help you choose stuff—I know how they dress in New York."

I've been to New York. Lots of times. There is no "how they dress in New York." They dress every way in New York. There is no style that is not on exhibit in New York. Not one. Besides which, Jo would be spending six days a week in pink tights and a black leotard.

"That's okay." Jo pushed her plate away, which just thrilled me. We'd only recently gotten Jo to eat a decent dinner, now here she was pushing away food again. I raised an eyebrow at Annie and she pretended not to see me.

"It's no problem. I'm free Saturday."

Jo put her plate on the floor and Baby Bear scarfed up the eggplant, tomatoes, mushrooms and onions and left the red and green peppers on the plate.

"I *know*," Jo said. There was a paragraph of meaning weighing those two words down.

Phoebe's tone changed. "You know what?"

"I know you're free."

I made a lot of noise getting up and gathering dishes and the red-pepper grinder, the black-pepper grinder, the Italian herbs grinder, the sea salt grinder.

"Can I get anyone anything?" I asked. "Should we rummage through the freezer and see if there's any good cake left in there? I know we've got Fudgsicles. I'll have a Fudgsicle. Get anyone else one?"

Phoebe's eyes slit. "How do you know I'm free?" Which, come on, was just asking for it, though that doesn't make it okay that Jo gave it to her.

"Because you're always *here*, that's how I know." Jo used her napkin to wipe tomato sauce off Baby Bear's chops.

Annie held her wineglass up. "Bear, could you pour me half a glass and then you and I will do the dishes and let these girls get on to their homework. Don't you have a quiz tomorrow, Jo? Go on upstairs and start studying, sweetie. We'll see Phoebe out."

Phoebe leaned over the table and gave Jo a look that was meant to curl her ears and melt the rubber band holding her hair back. "And is that a problem?"

Jo is small, but she is fierce, and in her younger, unfettered days, I had pulled her off much bigger girls, and not a few boys, several times. She once attacked an umpire who made an unfavorable call during her softball game. I hurriedly cleared the rest of the china and glassware off the table and held myself ready. Just in case. Baby Bear was at the ready, too. He knew something was stirring.

But my girl has grown up a lot. She doesn't use her hands to fight anymore. She's gotten deadlier.

Very softly, but clearly, she said, "Not the first fifty times, it wasn't."

Phoebe flushed and Annie cried out, "Oh, Jo!" as Jo stomped out of the kitchen and upstairs, Baby Bear on her heels. We heard a door slam.

Annie was next to Phoebe, her hands on Phoebe's cheeks, caressing, pushing a lock of the dead black hair back. "She didn't mean it, Phoebe, honey, Jo didn't mean that the way it sounded."

Which was a lie because there wasn't any other way to take it than just the way Jo had meant it.

Phoebe stood up from the table without answering Annie Laurie or looking at her. I'd tried to busy myself at the sink but glanced up and was stricken to see a film of tears in Phoebe's huge blue eyes. Black eye makeup was puddling under those eyes. I put the dishcloth down and walked over to the awkward, discomfiting girl whom I had not really ever given a chance. I put a hand on her shoulder.

"Y'all need a cooldown period, that's all, Phoebe. Give Jo a couple of days and—"

Phoebe jerked her shoulder out from under my hand. She walked over to the back door, picked up her backpack from where she had dropped it four hours ago when she got here, today, and the day before, and the day before that, and the day before that, slung a strap over one shoulder, and opened the door.

"Oh, Phoebe." Annie was near tears herself. She tried to pull Phoebe back, holding her elbow. Phoebe shook her off. "Please stay for a bit, sugar. We'll talk."

But Phoebe shook her head and walked out into the May twilight. Annie followed after her, trailing down the driveway, offering love and comfort in the form of excuses and explanations for her daughter's behavior. I stuck my head out the kitchen door and watched the mortified Phoebe set off down the sidewalk.

From the great, deep well of my wisdom, I came up with this. "Let her go, Annie Laurie. Give them some time to cool down. It will all be okay."

What was said between Annie and Jo, I don't know. My girls and me, we talk. I take in everything they're willing to let me have. With Annie and the girls, though, there's a whole level of communication going on that I'm not privy to. So I don't know how Annie handled the blowup. My bet is she ladled on some guilt. Annie is friends with everyone. She likes everyone. Every woman is beautiful, every man is well-meaning and every kid is gifted and talented. When someone is mean to her, she comes home cross, takes two aspirin with a glass of wine, and in an hour she's telling me how the whole thing was a misunderstanding or else it was all her fault. I love that about her but I don't expect it from Merrie and Jo. You have to be born that way, and they weren't. Me, either.

A week after Jo had so conclusively ended her friendship with Phoebe, I saw Liz walking past the church offices, her arms full of workbooks. I caught up to her and took the books from her arms.

"Let me get those, Liz, I'll walk you to your car." She gave them to me. They were heavy. She should have had a cart.

"How is Phoebe settling in," I asked. Phoebe may or may

not have told Liz and Mark about the quarrel with Jo—if she hadn't, I didn't want to. But if she had, I needed to say something.

"Don't ask if you don't want me to tell you, Bear."

I said I wanted to know.

"Good. Can we find a place to sit? I need to tell someone and Mark shuts down when I try to talk to him. And I don't want to tell any of the women here. I know this situation makes me look bad."

Not surprising that Mark didn't want to hear Liz complain about Phoebe. Annie gets testy with me when she thinks I'm criticizing the girls and the girls are half mine. I stacked the books near the front door and we went to the kitchen for some coffee. Liz fetched a carton of milk from the fridge that had PICKERSLEY-SMYTHE written on it in permanent marker, which was an indication of how often she was up here at the church, working away at one project or another. She shared her milk with me, rinsed both our spoons and put them in the dishwasher. We found a bench in the great hall and sat down. That's more private than you'd think. You can be seen, but you'll notice anyone coming long before you can be heard.

Liz laid her purse across her lap. It was the size of a carry-on and had more zippers and pockets than a fighter pilot's survival vest. She blew across the surface of her coffee, tasted it and set it on the floor next to her. She put a hand on my wrist.

"Point one, thank you for asking about Phoebe. No one does. They take one look at her and they don't know what to say." She blew out a puff of air. "*Mark* doesn't know what to say and she's *his* daughter. I don't see anything of Mark in Phoebe except those eyes. I swear she's mainly Jenny's, though it's too bad Phoebe didn't get her mother's looks. Jenny didn't have a brain cell in her head but she was pretty, if you like that kind. Pretty crazy, too. I'm talking too much, aren't I?"

I told her if she needed to blow off some steam, it was okay to do it with me. I try to be a safe place for people to come to. I tasted my coffee and was relieved that it wasn't one of Rebecca's pots—her coffee is so strong it eats a hole through my stomach.

Liz touched her nose with two fingers, smoothing it from bridge to cheek. Her phone made a *brrrr.* "Just a sec." She pulled her phone out of her purse, pulled up a text message, tapped out a reply, dropped the phone in her purse and zipped it closed. She picked up her mug, blew across it again, tasted it, approved, and sipped some down.

"Point two—I have done everything imaginable to make Phoebe's transition easier. At Mark's insistence, Phoebe moved in two weeks after Jenny died. So she's been with us a month but it feels like a year. Mark stayed at Jenny's place for those two weeks because it took him that long to persuade her to come. You can imagine how excited I was about that." Another puff of air, this one with an eye roll. "What he should have done was leave her there. She would have been happier. *I* would have been happier."

"She said something about living with her grandfather—that wouldn't have worked? At least until she could have finished out the school year?" Being yanked out of your school and home so abruptly—that would make any teenager hard to deal with.

Liz's fingers flew out in exasperation. "Uh, yes, she could have if Mark would have let her. He says Jenny's father is a crazy drunk and he wouldn't leave a good hound with the man"

I thought that over. "Liz, isn't Phoebe just finishing her junior year? That's . . . yeah, I'm going to go with Mark on that one. It would be hard for me to leave one of my girls on her own that young."

Liz tilted her head down and looked up at me like I must be kidding her. "Bear, for all practical purposes, *I* was on my own at sixteen. It could have been a confidence-building experience for Phoebe. She has some money. Jenny had a life insurance policy and I don't need to tell you that Jenny didn't feel the need to pay Mark back any of the money he's been sending their way since we've been married. I want to invest it for Phoebe but so far, she won't let me. If she's going to stay with us for the next year, Phoebe should get DeWitt out and let me sell that crackerbox they lived in, too. It's really mine—I've explained that to Phoebe, but she doesn't want to hear it—"

I said, "Whoa. You lost me. You own the house Phoebe lived in?"

Liz waved away the question. "It's complicated and that's not the point here. The point is her dad doesn't have anything to give her—if she's going to college, she'll have to do it on her own."

Mark and Liz live in the most expensive neighborhood in First Colony, but Mark wasn't going to be able to help his daughter through college? Huh. Were Toby and Tanner, those golden twins, going to have to work their way through, too? If Liz had been voicing to Phoebe what she was now voicing to me, I could understand why Phoebe might be seeking out a different mother figure over at my house.

Liz worried at one of the many zippers on her purse, zipping it open and closed, open and closed. "The very first day, I sat us all down for a family meeting and I set out our family plan, and the most basic of our hard-and-fast rules."

Her purse *brrred* again. This time she reached in and silenced it.

"How did that go over with Phoebe?" My coffee had cooled but I drank it anyway.

"I believe she was grateful. Everyone's happier when they know what to expect and they know they can deliver. That's key, Bear. She wasn't happy about the no-sugar but she'll adjust."

"What's the no-sugar?"

"That's a hard-and-fast. I'm diabetic and I'm allergic to seafood. There is no sugar or seafood in our house. It's one of our hard-and-fasts. Additionally, sugar makes you fat and there's mercury in seafood which leads to retardation. I do not want to live with a bunch of fat retarded people."

My jaw dropped. Well, alrighty, then. Miss Liz had just cemented her standing for the Humanitarian of the Year Award. Liz looked perfectly normal. Above normal. On the superior side. But she was spouting the most senseless, insensitive garbage . . .

"So, Phoebe's settling in well?" I meant for Liz to hear the sarcasm in that. She missed it.

Liz stopped messing about with the zipper and half turned on the bench, looking at me full on. "Bear. Does she look like she's settling in well? Would you say Phoebe fits in in First Colony? For Clements High School? I have *begged* her to let me buy her new clothes. She can pay me back in chores. Or out of her insurance money. I've tried. And Bear . . ."

Liz put her mug back on the carpet, set her purse down next to it and slid over the bench until she was right next to me. She smelled of coffee and rubbing alcohol and . . . was it starch? Did anyone still use starch? Way back when I'd come home from school and my mother would be ironing—that smell when she lifted the steaming iron off the linens? Liz smelled like that.

She leaned into me. I could feel her breath against my cheek. "Bear, I believe that girl resents me! You have no idea what I saved them from, Mark and her, both. You don't know how they would be living if it weren't for me!"

She leaned back so she could take in my expression. I had nothing for her. *I* resented her and *I* didn't have to live under her rules, hard-and-fast or otherwise.

"Well, Liz." I knew I sounded feeble. "I don't think it's unusual for a stepdaughter to have some strong feelings about her stepmother. You might want to . . ." I pulled out my phone and notepad, clicked my contact list and wrote a number and name down. I tore the sheet off and handed it to Liz. "This is Carol Thompson's number. She's a family therapist. I think a lot of her. She's going to be a better . . . ahh . . . the whole stepdaughter thing. Carol could help you with the, the hard-and-fasts." I nodded my head, slapped my thighs and stood up. That meant we were done.

"I solve my problems analytically and objectively, Bear. I don't know what a therapist could bring to the table."

I said, "Okay . . ."

"Lately, Phoebe seems angrier that ever, Bear. She's acting out. Deliberately provoking. If she keeps up like this, that girl is headed for a fall. I see that coming. I do."

I checked the time on my phone. "Liz, consider calling Carol's number, would you? I'm going to get those books out to your car now—there's going to be someone coming to my office soon and I don't want to make them wait."

We made our way to the end of the great hall, collected the books. I stowed them in the cargo area of her Mercedes GL. Yeah. Mercedes-Benz makes an SUV. Who knew.

The person waiting in my office was Rebecca. She was on her way to Whole Foods Market to pick up lunch and did I want anything. Yeah. I asked her to bring me a tuna fish salad sandwich with sweet tea. Extra sugar, please. That's my hard-and-fast.

One week after my talk with Liz, Phoebe came by the church.

Phoebe hadn't been back to the house in the month since the quarrel with Jo, and she had avoided me on Sunday mornings. But whatever had set Phoebe on her present course, that girl was after big game. Bear, evidently.

I was trying to write my sermon and Rebecca tapped at my door, her eyebrows nearly to her hairline, and told me I had an unscheduled visitor. That's nothing new—people have problems or worries and those can't be foreseen, so I saved my document and got up to greet whoever it was.

Rebecca stepped back and Miss Phoebe made her entrance in six-inch-high platform shoes.

The shoes were the least offensive items of what she was wearing. Now, I know I'm conservative about what a young woman should wear. It didn't bother me a bit when Annie Laurie and I were dating and she wore a bikini at the pool—well, it bothered me but in a good way. But I hate it when my girls wear them. I do. But at least that's outside—at the beach or the pool, not right in my church office. Not paraded past all the other church offices to get to my church office.

Phoebe's skirt barely covered her bottom. She was wearing so much metal that a retired guy on a Galveston beach was finding his metal detector mysteriously drawn to the northwest. The tank top she had on was cut low in front and even lower in back and it was cropped short enough to expose her pierced and tattooed navel. Honestly. In suburban Texas. On a school day. At the church. It was dressing as an act of aggression.

She propped a fist on a hip, jutted the other hip forward and tilted her head down so as to look up at me through her lashes. "I wondered if we could have a talk," she said. She was trying to channel Lauren Bacall—she'd probably never heard of Lauren Bacall, but that's who she was doing.

I said, "Oh, my gosh, Phoebe, what the heck are you dressed up as?"

Okay—I know it. It wasn't a good thing to say, it wasn't what Jesus said to the woman at the well or to Mary Magdalene or to any of the other problematic women in his life, but it came straight out of my mouth without taking the usual detour through my brain.

Big surprise, I embarrassed her.

"What's wrong with what I'm wearing?" She had flushed up to her roots—newly blackened, I noticed.

Now I felt bad for embarrassing her. I said, "No, you're fine. Have a seat." I waved a hand over at the small couch and the chairs in my office. When Phoebe sat I said, "Oh my gosh," and tossed her the throw that was folded over the back of a chair.

She caught it and said, "What's this for?"

What it was for was for her to spread over her lap because the girl's panties were showing when she sat down—that's how short that skirt was. This time, my brain grabbed hold of my mouth before I could tell her just that and instead I came out with, "You look cold. It's cold in here. It's always cold in here. Rebecca, don't you think it's cold?"

Rebecca said she thought it was warming up, which was unnecessary, and she took the easy chair across from Phoebe and crossed her slim ankles. She gave Phoebe her big, friendly smile. I sat down on the arm of a chair.

Phoebe took in that Rebecca had joined us, looked all nonplussed and said, some sarcasm seeping in, "I thought we could talk in private."

I said "Oh! Absolutely," and Rebecca reseated herself at her desk outside my office as I led the way down the hall to one of our conference rooms.

It's a big room, lined with framed architectural drawings of the church building—it holds a table for twelve, notepads and pens at every chair, and nothing else. Not so much as a potted palm to hide behind. There's a couple of ficus trees, but they provide no cover at all. The conference room has a glass door, and one wall is floor to ceiling glass. Soundproof, yes, but there is not a thing that can go on in that room without it being visible to the entire church office staff and anyone else who happens to walk by. It's designed this way on purpose.

I took a seat at the table and looked expectantly at Phoebe. She gave the space a slow appraisal before curling over the chair across the table from me, her hands on the upholstered back, swiveling it gently to and fro.

"Mr. Wells, Bear." I didn't want her calling me Bear. I'm Mr. Wells at least until you're out of high school. "I wanted a *private* meeting." She swung the castered chair too far to the left, lost her footing on those mile-high heels and would have fallen to the floor if she hadn't had ahold of the chair back. She nearly brought the chair down with her. As it was, she ended up knees splayed either side of the chair, arms wrapped around its back. I pretended not to notice the mishap. It was the kindest thing to do. Her cheeks were flaming now and I felt sorry for her.

"Can you tell me what you want to meet about, because if it's this thing between you and Jo, then it's Jo you need to—"

"I can tell you in *private*."

I picked up a notepad and pen and tapped the pad of paper with the pen. "Phoebe, this is as private as it gets."

She looked around the open, glass box of a room with contempt and gave the chair a shove.

"Seriously?"

I nodded, "It's a safety measure, Phoebe."

That earned me a hard look. "I'm not afraid of you, Mr. Wells."

"It's not about *your* safety, Phoebe."

Her mouth made an *O*. "For real?"

"For real. We can talk in my nice, comfortable office, with the very discreet Mrs. Rutland to hand, or we can talk here, in the aquarium." I gave a wave to Rebecca, who could see the entirety of the room from her desk, and she waved back. Sherry, who oversees our toddler-through-third-grade program, passed by with a load of books cradled in an arm. She gave a friendly wave, too. Phoebe looked over her shoulder in time to see the wave. It ticked her off.

"With the door shut, no one can hear you," I said, "And I won't repeat what you say. Unless you're about to confess to a crime, and then I'm going to advise you to call the police, and if you don't, I'm going to do it for you, just so we have that straight. Now, what can I do for you?"

Phoebe gave an eye roll that made the full circumference of her eyeballs before she pulled the chair out and sat down. I was relieved to have that expanse of leg underneath the table. None of this had gone the way Phoebe had envisioned it. I didn't know how to rescue her.

"Why do you think I'm here?" It was a challenge.

I won't play the "guess what?" game with my own girls. It's a time waster.

"Why don't you tell me, Phoebe?"

"I want to know what you think, tell me what you think. I got dressed up and I came down here and . . ." She trailed off, shook her inky hair off her face and raised an eyebrow.

I considered, and then put the pen down and gave Phoebe my full focus.

"All right. You asked what I think. I think when you come to my house, it's not Jo you want to see, it's Annie Laurie, for which I don't blame you, because I like to spend time with her, too. Because you miss your mom. And Annie is a good mom."

Tears filled Phoebe's eyes and she gripped the arms of her chair. Her chin went up.

"But teenage girls don't usually visit other girls' moms, so you were 'visiting' Jo, and since Jo was rude to you the other night, you don't feel like you can do that anymore and you're mad and embarrassed and—"

Phoebe pushed back from the table and stood.

"—hurt and maybe you're looking to give some of that back to Jo."

Phoebe turned her back on me and walked out of the room. I heard the clatter of her heels on the stairs.

"And maybe the best way to do that was to embarrass me," I finished in the empty room. I made a big *X* on the tablet in front of me and blew out my breath. "Well done, Brother Wells. Handled like a pro," I told myself. But I didn't go after her. It wasn't likely I'd come up with anything better if I tried again, even if Phoebe would let me try again.

My belly hurt, which meant I'd been a tad tense during the encounter. I went back to my office.

When I had eased myself carefully behind my desk again, Rebecca came in with a cold can of Spicy V8 and a glass of ice chips.

She said, "That went well."

"Did you see her departure?"

"Bear, the whole building saw her departure. I'm not sure you won a soul for Jesus today."

I laughed and then groaned and held my stomach.

"Thanks for the juice." I held the glass aloft.

"You're so welcome. You want to tell me about it?" Rebecca sat down.

I shook my head no. I wanted to talk to Annie Laurie and I wanted to talk to Carol Thompson who would have been less defensive and more effective with Phoebe, but then she's a female therapist and I'm a male minister. I wanted someone else to tell me if I should go see the Pickersley-Smythes. I was out of my league. Way out. And this wasn't a league I wanted to play in.

––––––––

Phoebe's payback came the very day she made her visit to my office. I was going to tell Annie everything when I got home that night. See, any way I looked at it, it came up as entrapment. Yes, that sounds dramatic. But there was the way she was dressed, her insistence on complete privacy and the amateurish seduction moves—I do think it was meant to be seductive, even if I didn't think for a second that Phoebe had any more interest in me than she did in Big Bird. So I was going to see how Annie Laurie thought we should handle it. But Phoebe made her move first. I got a call from a jubilant Annie.

"Jo and Phoebe have made up, Bear! It's the best thing! They're going to the movies together and then spending the night at Phoebe's. It was all Phoebe's idea. Oh, it's such good news. That girl has been sitting on my heart. She seems such a lost thing."

No. Not the best thing. Not good news. What the heck was Phoebe playing at?

"I don't know, Annie. We need to talk about Phoebe. I think Phoebe has some issues."

"Oh, my gosh. Her mom died, she's living with her stepmom and Liz isn't an easy person. *I'd* have some issues. Did you tell me you didn't want Jo to go out with Phoebe?"

I hadn't had time.

"Did you tell me anything about Phoebe that should, ipso facto, mean I shouldn't let Jo go out with Phoebe?"

I was about to tell Annie Laurie about Phoebe's appearance in my office that morning, but when Annie Laurie starts borrowing her dad's lawyerspeak, it's time for me to get off the phone.

When I texted Jo, all I got back was "brb," and I don't know what that means.

Annie laughed at me when I told her about Phoebe's visit. The more I tried to explain, the harder she laughed. It was this close to being insulting. Annie made it very, very clear that she thought I was "reading too much into it," and said I shouldn't worry and could I please get ready because we were due at the Sugar Land Skeeters Grand Opening Gala in an hour. It was "cocktail attire" or "vintage jerseys." I wanted to wear my old UT jersey but Annie wouldn't let me because she didn't think a football jersey was what they were talking about since the Sugar Land Skeeters play minor league baseball. If she didn't want me to wear my old football jersey, she should have bought me an old baseball jersey. I put a suit on. I try to keep Annie happy because she keeps me happy. And it's easier than dealing with her when she's crossed.

Annie and I went to the function where I made the rounds, greeting everybody I could and making lowball bids at the silent auction because I wanted to participate but I sure as heck didn't want to win anything. I checked my phone every ten minutes or so but heard nothing from Jo. When we got back to the house at last, I made myself a cup of hot tea and went to bed.

Our house is fifteen years old and with the Gulf Coast's extreme shifts in temperature and ground moisture, a homeowner can expect their house to make some unexplained noises. There was a time when I would have slept through any nighttime noise that didn't involve running water. That would have been a time before I got shot. When I heard the noise upstairs, I went from deep asleep to wide awake.

I slipped out of bed and grabbed the first thing my hand touched as I passed the bookcase—a three-inch-thick dictionary. Maybe I could pound the interloper over the head with it. Or hold it over the place where I got shot so I didn't get shot there again. I started up the stairs.

There was a shuffling noise coming from behind Jo's closed door. She usually leaves it open—Bear likes to sleep in Jo's room even when she isn't home. A couple of months ago I discovered that Jo had been using the bedroom window that opened onto the top of the garage as her own private entrance

and exit to the house. It was possible she had shared that trick
with someone else and . . .

I flung the door open into the room.

"Dad!" Jo hissed. She was in the middle of pulling a sweaty
T-shirt off over her head. She yanked it down quickly. "Can you
knock?"

Can anyone do outrage and indignation like a teenage girl?

Baby Bear watched the scene from Jo's bed—a sure sign that
he hadn't been expecting Jo, either. He's not supposed to sleep
on Jo's bed.

I said, "Your mom said you were spending the night at
Phoebe's. And it's . . ." I checked the Hello Kitty clock over her
bed. "Jo, it's two thirty. How'd you get home? And why didn't
you use the front door instead of climbing in your window like
a cat burglar?"

"I'll tell you, but could you please bring me an ice water? I'm
dying."

"How about you tell me first?"

"Dad, please?"

I stared at my child in the dim light from her goose night-
light. She looked okay. Hot and sweaty, but okay. I put the dictionary on top of her bookcase and went downstairs and filled a
giant plastic glass with ice and water, added a cup of apple juice
to get some calories into my girl, and brought it up to her. Jo sat
cross-legged on her floor, a clean T-shirt on, her discarded
sweaty clothes in a pile on the floor.

I handed her the glass, sat down on Jo's spare bed and said,
"Start talking."

"Okay. Baby Bear, move over or get down."

"He's not supposed to be up there."

"Dad . . ." She squeezed in next to him on her bed. "Okay.
First you have to promise not to get mad."

"Honey," I said, "I'm mad already."

Big sigh and a flip of her long, dark braid over a shoulder. Jo drank some more diluted apple juice.

"So Phoebe comes up to me at school and says can we talk and I say yes even though I don't want to and no matter what you and Mom say I'm not sorry for what I said that night at dinner because it was only the truth." Jo took a drink and I nodded my head because, so far, I'm keeping up.

"Phoebe lays down this whole 'I didn't know I was crowding you' and 'if you'd only said something.' She still wanted to be friends but she would respect my space and everything and just to show how sorry she was, she'd spoken with Alex and we'd all go to the movies and then out to dinner and then back to Phoebe's house to spend the night—no, Dad, don't give me that look, not for Alex to spend the night, me and Phoebe."

Baby Bear lifted his heavy head and dropped it in Jo's lap. Jo set her glass down on top of an issue of *Pointe* and picked up a grooming comb off her nightstand to work at a matted place on Baby Bear's ear.

"First off, that didn't feel like she was respecting my space all that much, I mean, she makes all these plans with *my* boyfriend—"

I winced at the word.

"—without ever asking if it's something I'd even want to do, but I texted Alex and it seemed like he wanted to . . . just whatever. I said okay and I called Mom."

"We're talking about getting home at two thirty in the morning and crawling in the window, right?"

She gave me an impatient chin jerk. "I'm *telling* you, Dad. Mom says okay and she brings me up an overnight bag because Phoebe wanted to go straight from school, she didn't want me to come home first even though I didn't see what the big hurry was."

Phoebe didn't want Jo coming home and hearing what I had

to say about Phoebe's morning visit, that's what the big deal was. I wouldn't have told Jo. But I wouldn't have let her go if I had been home for the call.

"Phoebe drives me and Alex to the movies and somehow I'm in the backseat, Alex is in the front seat with Phoebe, and on the way over she starts with, 'Alex, what are you going to do all summer with Jo up in New York? That's going to be so hard.'" Jo put a wheedling edge in her voice while she was voicing Phoebe.

I tap my wrist where a watch would be if I still wore one. My question is still out there, getting cold.

Jo holds a finger up, telling me she'll get to it. "She wouldn't let up. The whole movie she's texting us, I mean, we're sitting right next to her, but she has to be texting the whoooole movie? Like, 'You do love Alex, don't you?' and she sends Alex this message, 'Has Jo SAID she loves you?' Like it's her business."

I wanted to know if Jo had told Alex she loved him, too, but I wasn't asking. Kids throw that word around and they start *using* it and then they start *acting* on it and . . .

"Then she wants to go get something to eat after the movie. That was the plan all along, but by the time we get out of the movie, it's nine thirty, and you know, I told Mom I'd be back at Phoebe's house at ten. She acted like having a curfew meant—"

I said, "If you went to the movie straight out of school, why did you get out at nine thirty?" I felt like I was missing pieces of the story.

Jo ducked her head and finished the last of her drink, excused herself and went to the bathroom. After a while she came back with her glass refilled with water and a wet washcloth to wipe her face.

"Messing around," she said. "Stuff."

Uh-huh. We'd get back to that.

I said, "You *are* working up to telling me how you got home at two thirty in the morning and why you used your window instead of your door, aren't you?"

"Dad. Yes. If you could be patient."

I nodded that I would try.

"Phoebe says we'll go back to her house and have something to eat there, because she and Alex need to be understanding about curfews for *younger* people. You got that? Like I'm ten or something?"

I pushed the pillow up against the headboard so I could lean back. If I wanted my answer, I was going to have to follow down the road of a story Jo was telling. We might get there in the end.

Jo sighed. "I tried to come home then. After the movie. I said I had a headache but she's all 'Oh, Jo—I didn't mean to hurt your feelings—she's very sensitive, isn't she, Alex?' And I said she hadn't hurt my feelings and Alex said no, I wasn't very sensitive, so of course then Phoebe's saying, 'Is she *in*sensitive, Alex? Is that why she's able to leave you all summer?'"

I was getting mad, the way my child had been manipulated.

"So first she stops at Kroger's to get the ingredients to her 'Grandpop DeWitt's Power Punch.' It's like her favorite beverage and this is what it is, Dad, you're not going to believe this. It's lime sherbet, three packets of grape Kool-Aid, and ginger ale. You put everything in a blender. We get to her house and she makes this famous 'power punch'—it's supposed to have vodka, too, but no we didn't, you should see your face, Dad— and it is disgusting and I don't see how vodka would make it any better—not that I'd know, Dad, so relax."

I had swung my legs off the bed. "Are you telling me Phoebe drinks?" I know teenagers drink. But the girl had my daughter in the car.

"I'm telling you that according to Phoebe, when Grandpop DeWitt makes his power punch, he puts vodka in it. That's what

Phoebe says. So maybe that's true and maybe it's a lie, how am I going to know?

"Then Phoebe's stepmom comes into the kitchen and sees the glasses of power punch, and she sees the sherbet container and the empty Kool-Aid packets on the cabinet, and she slaps her chest and staggers back like she's having a heart attack and she says, 'You have broken a hard-and-fast.' You would have thought she'd found us cooking meth in her kitchen. She goes running out screaming for Phoebe's dad and I grabbed a paper towel and I swept the whole mess into the garbage can. Phoebe said to leave it—her stepmom was always on about something, but Alex helped me and we had the countertops scrubbed and the blender rinsed and draining before her stepmom got back dragging her dad to see what we'd done, not that we'd done anything. Alex and I couldn't even drink the stuff, ours went in the sink, but Phoebe sucked it down like it was a Vanilla Frappuccino after a day in the desert. My mouth was practically black from the one swallow I took." Jo gave a shiver of distaste. I knew the shiver was for the drink but I got up and draped her quilt over her shoulders. She was still damp with sweat and the air conditioner was on.

"Her dad gets her stepmom calmed down, he says, 'We've got an audience here, Liz,' meaning me and Alex, because, yeah, embarrassing. Turns out Liz is way diabetic so she doesn't keep sweets in the house. That's what the Kool-Aid and sherbet fit was over, which, okay, I get that but then she also adds that she doesn't want obese children. She said that right out. I don't want obese children either, but I don't go around saying, 'I *don't* want *obese children!*'"

That last was done in a dead-on mimicry of Lizabeth, complete with hands on hips and head cocked.

"And then. Then Phoebe takes us up to her room, and gives

Alex the whole 'Story of Phoebe's Tragic Life,' which I've heard before, twice, and she was all serious and crying and we were holding her hands because even though I *hate* Phoebe Pickersley, I wish she were *dead*—"

I was off of that bed in a flash, "Jo!"

"You know what, Dad? Mrs. Thompson says I have a right to my feelings."

"Not those feelings, you don't. Not ever. Don't you ever let me hear that kind of hatefulness coming from one of my girls. You're working for the wrong side when you talk that way. I mean it." Jo had shocked me. There are lines we can't cross when we choose our road—Jo had crossed one.

Jo hid her face behind her hair and her hands. Baby Bear had roused himself when I raised my voice. He tried to push his nose between her fingers and when he couldn't, he snaked his tongue through and licked whatever he could reach.

"Dad," she said through her fingers.

"I mean it." My heart was thumping.

"I know. But I didn't. I only said it. It came out, is all." Her breath caught.

Okay. I needed to calm down. I can overreact sometimes. I sat on the edge of her bed and heard it groan under the combined weight of Jo, Baby Bear and me. I gave Baby Bear a shove and he dropped reluctantly to the floor. He thought he should be the one up there comforting Jo. He thought he would do the better job. He probably would have. I put a hand on her shoulder and gave her a squeeze.

"I don't care what Phoebe's done. I don't care what she has said. How we treat other people, that's about who we are, *what* we are, not who they are. You are called to be better than those words."

"I *know*, Dad. It was a figure of speech, okay? I didn't mean it."

"Words have power."

"I *said* I didn't mean it."

"Phoebe's had a hard time since moving here."

"Dad. I was about to say that Phoebe isn't totally awful because her life does stink, and if she's telling the truth, it's all her stepmom's fault because she got pregnant with Toby and Tanner when Phoebe's dad was still married to Phoebe's mom—"

"Now, now, Jo—"

"All over again, I'm feeling sorry for her—but who knows if she's telling the truth? Because, Dad, I don't want her dead, but that girl is a bald-faced liar!"

Ahh, gee. You know, in this case, I really hoped Phoebe was a liar. I did. Divorce is wrenching and complicated no matter the factors, but to have your dad start a new family before he had stepped out of the first, that's harsh.

"When did Phoebe lie to you?"

"She has, that's all! So then she starts on how classical ballet is a dead art, with nothing new to say and no new way to say it, and I was selling myself body and soul to an arcane system. What does 'arcane' mean, anyway? And why would anyone give up a boy like Alex to go practice toe points . . ."

Jo got up, quilt about her shoulders, and did a spastic parody of *en pointe*. "She did it like that. I said I *wasn't* giving up Alex and she smiles like a nutria with a can of drippings and says if I go away for the summer, maybe I *am*! And Alex smiled! But I'm *going*, Dad, I'm *going*! This has been my dream forever." And there were tears.

I held my arms out. "Come here, baby girl." I wrapped my arms about my daughter, picked her up, quilt and all, and settled in the rocking chair in her room. I'd rocked her in this very chair when she was first born. Rocked Merrie in it, too. Baby Bear roused himself to stand next to his mistress, pushing at her with his wet nose and rumbling his concern.

I said, "Jo, Phoebe is a hungry, hungry girl. I think she's

been hungry a long time, hungry for the things you have and she doesn't. I don't blame her for that. She's lost her mom—"

"I don't think Phoebe's mom was a good mom."

"Jo, most *any* mom is better than no mom." I gave her a little shake. "You *are* going to New York. You are going to take the opportunity that you have worked so hard for and God made possible for you and that your mom and I are paying out the nose for." That got me a muffled giggle. "I think Alex has better sense than to choose Phoebe over you just because she's available and you're away. But if he doesn't, then that boy doesn't deserve you, you hear me? If Alex is that dirt stupid, I don't want to know him."

Still muffled, "He's not stupid, Dad."

"I know it, baby."

"He's really, really smart. He might make valedictorian."

"I think he's a smart boy, Jo."

We rocked in silence for a while. Jo pulled the blanket over her head to shield her face from me.

"She said something else. After Alex got picked up. I should have begged a ride home but Phoebe made such a big deal."

"What did Phoebe say?"

Silence.

"Do you want to tell me about it?"

Long silence, then, "No."

I pondered on that.

"Did she tell you she came by to see me today?" I asked.

Jo lifted her head. "She said *you* saw *her.*"

"Is this the 'lie' you've been talking about? When you say Phoebe is a liar? Let me tell you about the visit." A long pause, and I could hear the *chimp, chimp* sound that meant Jo was biting off slivers of fingernails, then I felt her head nod against my chest.

I didn't go into detail, but I told her the gist of it, and I made sure my daughter knew that Phoebe Pickersley had not been alone with me for one second when Rebecca couldn't see us both clearly.

Jo sat up. Her precious face was tearstained. "I knew it, Dad. When she said you came on to her . . ."

I groaned. "Did she say that, Jo? Those words?" Those words could end a man's career if he's in the ministry.

Jo thought. "She said it without saying it."

"Implied," I said

"I slapped her face, and grabbed my bag and left."

I groaned again. I should have gotten pencil and paper and started making a list of all the apologies and explanations I was going to have to make tomorrow.

"You slapped her? Josephine Amelia—"

"The Bible *says* there is a time to throw stones. I only slapped her."

"That's 'cast away stones,' Jo. And that doesn't mean bounce them off someone's head. If I hear about you hauling off and whacking someone again, we're going to have to—"

"I'm not going to tell you stuff if I get in trouble every time I do."

Okay. That was fair. It was why, for eighteen years, I never told my mother a thing. I'm still careful what I say around my mom.

I said, "Sorry."

"It's okay."

"But you will try to keep your temper, Jo?"

"I was trying when I slapped her."

"Explain the coming in through the window part."

"I didn't have my key—"

This had to be the fifth house key Jo had lost. "Jo, *why* didn't you have your key?" I got an eloquent shrug in reply.

"—and I didn't want to wake you and Mom up, and I can get in through my window perfectly well . . ."

"Okay. Get up now, you're getting too big for this old man. Here's what we're going to do. You take a quick shower and get in bed. You'll never sleep if you go to bed with dried sweat all over you. I'm going to go have a bowl of cereal and I'll come back up when I hear the water turn off. I'll tuck you in. Okay?"

Baby Bear accompanied me downstairs and we each had a bowl of Cheerios. I gave Jo five minutes after I heard the shower stop, and then we went upstairs. We found Jo smelling like peaches and peppermint and tucked under her covers. I knelt next to her bed and put my hand on her wet head.

"Okay. How could you have handled the situation differently? In a way that wouldn't get you grounded?"

"Am I going to be grounded?"

"Yes. Tomorrow you're grounded to the house. Do you know why?"

A sigh. "Because I slapped Phoebe."

"No. I'm not happy about that, but I won't ground you for it since you told me about it yourself. Try again."

A bigger sigh. "Because I walked home by myself."

"Bingo. At two in the morning. You know better, Jo."

"Dad, I had to get out of that house."

"You could have called me on your cell and waited at the door. It would have been hard. I know it. Instead, you made what Nana would call a 'grand gesture.' But, Jo, it's not more than six or seven years since a girl only a few years older than you got murdered out here."

"Dad—"

"Bad things happen."

I got a bleak "Okay, Dad."

"You have to stay in the house or in the yard all day unless you're with me or Mom." I then relented. "But I don't mind if you have a couple of friends over."

We hugged and I said her prayers with her. We haven't done that in a hundred years, had bedtime prayers together. I hoped she still said them when I wasn't there to make sure. Baby Bear circled the rug and lay down with a "whumpf." I went downstairs to bed. I knew I would have to go see Liz and Mark tomorrow.

From: Walker Wells
To: Merrie Wells

I don't remember you losing your house key all the time. Jo has lost her house key again. Do you have a suggestion?

From: Merrie Wells
To: Walker Wells

Go to Lowe's or Home Depot. Make a dozen keys. Give Jo a new one and mail one to me, too. I lost mine at the meet last week.

Four

The next morning I filled Annie Laurie in on the night's activities—those that had gone down while she was sleeping the sleep of the just.

"I'm coming with you," she said after hearing that I thought I should go see the Pickersley-Smythes.

I told her she didn't need to. Mark and Liz were reasonable people and I wasn't expecting a problem.

Annie banged her mug down on the counter and had to wipe up the coffee that sloshed out. "You should be. If Phoebe is going around telling people you made advances to her, no one's going to be feeling very reasonable about that, Bear. If I come it will keep things calmer. I guess I'd like to think Phoebe wouldn't make any wild allegations in front of me, so there's that, too. Give them a call and see if they can see us in about an hour. I want to talk to Jo and get my own take on things and then I want a shower."

About an hour later I pulled out of the garage and Annie grabbed something from the garage freezer before slipping in next to me. She waited expectantly, and when I didn't back the car out, she looked at me.

"What?"

"What's that?" I gestured to the foil-wrapped package inside the Ziploc bag.

Annie waited a beat, her eyes on mine. "What has it been the last four hundred times I've pulled a package like this out of the freezer?"

"Pound cake."

"It's pound cake this time, too."

"Liz is diabetic," I said.

"Oh, shoot. That's right. Okay, then, Mark and the kids can eat it."

"Annie, there's no sugar in the house. It's a hard-and-fast."

"It's a wha . . . oh, forget it." She opened the car door and took the five steps to toss the cake back into the freezer. She stared into the interior for a moment and then slammed it shut. Once back in the car, she slammed that door shut, too.

"We're going empty-handed, then. I sometimes have some cheese straws frozen but there have been three showers over the last month and I'm flat out."

"It doesn't matter."

"It would have been nice," she said. "It's hard for people to get mad at you when you've handed them a homemade pound cake."

I smiled as I turned the corner. Pound cake diplomacy.

The Pickersley-Smythes don't live far from us, you can walk there in fifteen minutes if you take the greenbelts that cut across neighborhoods, or detour across the golf course. It's about ten minutes by car. But it's a different neighborhood and the homes cost more than three times what ours would sell for—and we couldn't afford our house if we had to buy it at today's prices.

Their two-and-a-half-story red brick wasn't one of the biggest homes in Sweetwater. It was an older home—by Sugar Land standards. The landscaping was mature and the oaks full grown and you would have had trouble believing that where the house stood there had once been fields of rice—when I was a kindergartener, that's all there was out here.

We sat in our car for a moment before we faced the Pickersley-Smythes.

"Do you want to say a prayer, Bear?" Annie said.

"I've been praying ever since I woke up this morning. Let's get it done."

Liz met us with a smile, which was a better start to this meeting than I'd hoped for, and showed us into a small sitting room that held a love seat piled with decorative pillows, two chairs, a low table and about four hundred pictures of Toby and Tanner being blond and photogenic. There was a white Persian cat sitting on the love seat. He slipped out of the room when we came in.

I said, "Is Mark here, Liz? Could he join us?" Because I only wanted to tell this story once.

"When we saw you drive up, he went to wake up the girls." Liz made a small adjustment to the bowl of roses on the table. "They were having so much fun last night, we let them sleep in. Teenagers." She smiled, the picture of the calm and indulgent mother.

Annie looked at me and I hesitated and we heard a tumble of steps down the stairs followed by Mark's more measured tread. Toby and Tanner burst into the room.

"There's no Jo," said one of the three-year-olds, hopping to a stop at his mother's knees. He was pleased with himself—the first to bring this unexpected news. Liz licked her thumb and wiped at something invisible on his immaculate face.

"Jo gone," said the other, confirming the news. "Phoebe is still sleepy." He put his hands together, laid his head on them and made a snoring sound. His brother gave him a push, but he ignored him, snoring louder.

Mark came into the room, smiling, but looking puzzled.

"Hey, guys—I don't know where Jo's got to. I checked the bathroom, too."

The first twin said, "Jo gone! Jo gone!"

Annie said, "She's home, we—"

Now the second twin joined in on the chant, "Jo gone! Jo gone!"

Mark said, "You picked her up early? Then—"

"Jo gone!"

"The girls had a disagreement last night," I said. "That's why Annie Laurie and I wanted to—"

Liz's smile had stretched and thinned. "This can't be over that blender mess, can it? I explained to Jo that we have a hard-and—"

"Jo gone!" They were accompanying themselves with a hop-kick dance step.

"No," I said.

Mark corralled the twins. "Go ask Phoebe to put on *Bob the Builder* for you. Tell her Daddy wants her to get dressed and come down."

The boys ran off singing or screaming the theme song, "Bob the Builder—Can we fix it? Bob the Builder—yes, we can!"

Mark sat down across from us and laced his fingers over his stomach. "What's up, Bear?"

Liz kept her smile, but you could see it was a struggle. She spread her hands on her thighs and leaned toward us. "I may have upset Jo a little bit when I found the kids messing around in the kitchen, I—"

Mark put a hand over hers. "That's not why they're here, Liz. It's not about the Kool-Aid." He didn't take his eyes off me.

I cleared my throat. Annie gave my knee an encouraging squeeze. I said, "Yesterday Phoebe came to see me at the church."

"What time was this? Before they went to the movies?" Mark wanted to know.

"It was before lunch—"

"During school hours, then?" His forehead was puckered.

"Yeah. She said she wanted to talk to me, which, of course, was fine, I was happy to, ah . . . See, church policy is that I don't meet with women, ah, girls . . ."

Annie said to Liz, all woman to woman, "Bear doesn't meet with any woman one on one—I mean, there's a couple of rooms up at the church that are soundproofed, so what you say is private, but they have a glass wall so nobody can misinterpret what's going on. Or Rebecca, you've met Rebecca, haven't you, Liz? Rebecca will stay in the room with Bear and whoever."

Mark said, "Phoebe wanted to talk to you about what?"

I said, "When Phoebe said she wanted to talk to me—"

"What did she want to talk to you about?" said Mark. "Is something wrong?" He turned to his wife who had gotten very still.

"Well, we never quite got there, because . . ." I stopped because I could hear someone on the stairs, a slow, soft *thump thump*. We all waited.

Phoebe slouched into the hall, looked in at us. Her eyes were smudgy with makeup, but I was glad to see her cheek didn't bear the mark of Jo's slap. She wore a pair of crumpled boxers and a green T-shirt that had KEEP CALM AND CARRY ON MY WAYWARD SON printed in white across the chest. After a quick scan, she turned away. She stood with her back to us, her hands on her slim hips. Phoebe gave a gusty sigh, and said, "What?" It looked like she was asking the dining room.

Mark said, "Phee. Come in." She didn't move but Mark waited and she finally turned around and made it as far as the doorjamb where she propped her lean frame. She looked at no one, her arms were crossed and her thin, white hands cupped her elbows.

"I thought Jo was going to spend the night?" her dad said.

"She changed her mind." Her eyes flickered over the pictures of her half brothers. I didn't see any pictures of Phoebe displayed.

Mark said, "Why did she change her mind? And what did you go up to the church for? What did you want to talk about? Is there something wrong? You haven't said anything to me."

Phoebe gave me a slow look. In it was a lot of anger over yesterday's humiliations and my dismissal. I was about to pay for that ineptitude—I could see it coming and I started to lift myself out the mass of cushions I was sunk in.

I opened my mouth to tell Mark and Liz what Phoebe had said to Jo, my idea being that it would be better for them to hear it from me first, for me to meet this head-on, but Annie Laurie gave my knee a restraining squeeze, and I sat back down. My course wasn't clear enough for me to override her.

Annie said, "Phoebe?" Phoebe looked at the ceiling with its ten inches of crown molding. "Jo came home with a wild story. I wonder if she misunderstood you? Jo can be so dramatic, and she doesn't always stop to think."

Phoebe looked at me again, and her eyes narrowed. I thought, *Here it comes* . . . but then her eyes met Annie's.

There was no accusation in Annie's eyes, no mockery, no dare. Annie's eyes were grave but open and loving. Phoebe met them full-on. The anger fell away and what I saw in Phoebe's face then was grief. Another loss, this substitute mother who had been put out of her reach because of my careless girl.

Phoebe's head dropped. "She could have misunderstood."

"Misunderstood what?" said Liz. I think Liz had been afraid this was going to be about her—some revelation that Phoebe could use to put her difficult stepmother in as uncomfortable a position as Phoebe had been put in, living in a home that wasn't her home, second always to the beautiful twins. If what Phoebe told Jo was true, if those boys had been on their way before Mark had ended his marriage to Jenny, then Phoebe certainly had the ammunition.

"I hope you don't feel like we've mistreated you, Phoebe, that we haven't been fair to you," Annie said.

That was a judicious word choice—if Annie had said "kind," I don't know how we would have come out of this, because neither Jo nor I had been especially kind. Only Annie had truly been that.

"What did you see Bear about?" Mark said again.

Phoebe shifted her weight and colored. She opened her mouth, but I cut in.

"Mark? Can that be private? I want Phoebe to feel like she can come see her minister"—keeping it on a professional level, there—"when she wants to. That okay?" I smiled at Phoebe. Her face stayed neutral—I was all good with neutral.

Mark glanced at Liz, but he didn't wait for her yes or no. "That's fine, Bear. I'm glad she has you to go to."

Considering how I had handled her first visit, I was certain it would also be her last. I don't know how else I could have handled what happened yesterday, but there had to have been a better way. I smiled, slapped my thighs and stood up.

As we said our good-byes, the boys streamed down the stairs and hung on Phoebe's arms. They wanted another *Bob the Builder* show and they wanted Phoebe to watch it with them. Before she could escape with them, Annie Laurie stepped over to Phoebe and put her arms around the girl, drawing her close. Phoebe was taller than Annie, but Annie held her tight and rocked from side to side for a minute. Very slowly, Phoebe put her arms up and hugged Annie back. Annie whispered something in Phoebe's ear, then pulled back and held Phoebe's shoulders so she could look the girl in the face.

"I mean it, now, you hear me?" Annie said. Phoebe's eyes shone with tears. She nodded and then climbed the stairs with Toby and Tanner.

Liz followed us out the door, her smile overbright.

"Well. A lot went on in there but I still don't have a clue what. I've got to tell you, Annie Laurie, *I've* never gotten a hug from that girl. I've poured money into her, tried to take her shopping, but she's never given me so much as a smile or a thank-you, not unless Mark drags it out of her." Liz stood in front of her beautiful home, trim and toned and dressed like a woman from a catalog. And completely clueless.

Annie laughed. "She didn't give me a hug, Liz. I took it." And then Annie put her arms around Liz and took a hug from her, too. Liz's arms hung straight at her sides until it was almost too late. Just as Annie Laurie was beginning to pull away, Liz's arms came up and she clasped Annie to her hard. Annie's face went soft.

"It's going to be okay, Liz. Everything's going to be okay," Annie said.

We didn't know it as we drove away, but Annie Laurie was wrong. Everything was not going to be okay. Everything was going to fall apart.

Five

It started falling apart the next week.

I left the Pickersley-Smythes' that Saturday feeling somewhat better about the Phoebe/Jo situation. It suited me to have Annie be my ambassador with the girl. Even if Phoebe had decided *not* to try to convince the fellowship that I was a rapacious scoundrel, I didn't want to spend a whole lot of time with her. She was too unpredictable. Sure, Annie had Phoebe feeling all soft and mushy now, but that didn't mean she'd be feeling that way tomorrow. Still. I'd give the girl a chance, I told myself. I'd try to be fair, like Annie Laurie had said.

But I was done being fair with Phoebe Pickersley when I got the call the following Saturday night from one of our summer interns, Jonathon Reece. His was only the first call of many.

The church hires six to eight interns every summer, college students who are considering the ministry as a profession. We take the selection very seriously because not only are these young people influencing our kids, but we as a church are possibly influencing their decision about whether or not to pursue the ministry. That's a responsibility, and our vetting process goes on for months before the kids come to work for us. We have our interns chosen by early February at the latest.

Interns spend the two summer months living with local families and helping our full-time youth ministers supervise the extra service and recreational activities that we plan for our middle and high school kids during the summer. Jonathon Reece was a twenty-year-old black student from Abilene Christian University, and I don't mind telling you, I'd actively courted the boy. His grades were better than good and he was a fine speaker, thoughtful and considered. He was entertaining, but he didn't play to the crowd too much, a hazard when you're in your very early twenties and you find yourself in a position of authority over kids close to your own age.

Jonathon could easily have chosen to go to one of the large, prestigious black churches—the Fifth Ward Church of Christ had invited him, and they have more than fifteen hundred members. I understood that even the famed Figueroa Church of Christ in Los Angeles had expressed an interest. But while our church is pretty diverse for a Texas Church of Christ—which means it's more diverse than "not at all"; we do have a handful of black families—I felt honored that Jonathon had chosen us. When I asked him why he'd picked our white-bread church to spend his summer at, he told me he believed the Lord had led him to our church. He'd put a hand on my shoulder and said, "I think your rich white kids need me, Brother Wells." He was smiling but his eyes were still and sure. He meant just what he'd said.

What had really won me over was Jonathon's essay. We ask our potential interns to put down on paper why they want to serve as youth ministers at our church. Many churches do the same, and most candidates write one essay and then tweak it a little for each church. The papers usually include generic stuff, like how much they enjoy kids, or how their own youth group had left an impression on them (not that any of them were long out of youth groups themselves), same old, same old.

But Jonathon's essay was a reflective meditation on the role of a youth minister. He acknowledged that one couldn't be a youth minister for long before inevitably growing out of the role—and that he saw an internship as the first step on the journey into the role of full-time pastor. He said his mother had always wanted her eldest son to be a minister, but Jonathon's elder brother had chosen a different road. He was in prison, serving out the last month of a three-year sentence for selling prescription drugs illegally. He'd be out by the time Jonathon was interning.

Jonathon wrote that he had spent time and prayer examining his heart—as much as he loved his mother, he didn't want to pursue the ministry as a way to compensate for her disappointment in his brother—and had come to the conclusion that he was genuinely called to the ministry.

The youth group retreat to New Braunfels was the first overnight trip for the summer.

It was June second, a few weeks before Jo would leave for New York, and school had been out for exactly two days. As was usual, the church high school youth group had made the three-hour trek to New Braunfels, to spend two days and nights tubing the spring-fed Guadalupe River. Jo and about two hundred kids from our youth group were there. It would be Phoebe's first overnighter with the youth group and Jo's last before heading off to New York City and ballet school. I had made the trip a hundred times myself, in junior high, high school and college. You would be hard-pressed to find a better way to spend a hot Texas summer day than to float along the icy waters between the limestone cliffs that line the river. There are times when the river is nearly tube to tube, it's so full. Parties will lash their tubes together to keep from being separated—some tie the tubes in a circle and stick a cooler of beer in the center so everyone has easy access, but of course we don't allow beer on church trips.

It was a Saturday night, Sunday morning really, and my phone buzzed. I groped for it and saw it was Jonathon Reece calling.

"Hey, Jonathon—Jo okay?" Next to me, Annie sat up in bed and pushed her hair off her face, looking a question at me.

"Yeah, she's fine." Jonathon's voice was tight and strained. "Listen. I think I'm in big trouble here."

I told Annie that Jo was fine and got out of bed and padded to the family room. Baby Bear heard me and came down to join me.

"What is it, Jonathon?" I flipped on the overhead fan in the dark room and settled into my easy chair—I've dealt with the midnight crisis of faith before.

"Man. Give me a second." There was a long pause and then Jonathon's voice came back on. "I took a second to pray," he said. "I want to tell it to you exactly the way it went down, that work for you?"

I said okay and thought that this might not be a crisis of faith. It might be a different kind of crisis altogether.

When Jonathon started speaking again, his voice was calm. "Brother Wells . . ."

"You can call me 'Bear,' Jonathon, you know that." Baby Bear rested his chin on my knee and looked at me with sleepy eyes.

"It's not *Bear* Wells I want to talk to right now. It's *Brother* Wells—the pastor of the church I was called to minister to."

I said, "All right . . ."

"Brick, Jason and I—" Brick and Jason were our two youth ministers. "—and all the rest of the interns, we had the kids in their tents, lights out at eleven thirty."

I interrupted, "We're not missing a kid, are we, Jonathon?"

"It's not like that. Everyone is safe in their tents."

"All right. Sorry. Go on." Baby Bear was falling asleep and having trouble with his balance. His eyes would close and his chin would slip from my knee, then he'd jerk awake, resettle his chin and start again. It made me smile.

"After lights out, Brick called all of us interns together and ran over the plans for tomorr . . . for today, and Jason led us in a prayer and then we all went to our own tents. Everybody is doubled up except me because Jeff couldn't come—he had to get his wisdom teeth out. I won the draw for the single." I could hear the sarcasm in his voice.

I said, "Go on." I'd lost my smile. Youth ministers and interns double up in sleeping quarters on church overnighters—that's not a cost-saving measure; it's church policy. Serves the same purpose as those glass walls in the conference room.

"I wake up thirty, forty minutes ago, and I'm not alone in the tent."

This is why it's church policy.

I said, "Go on."

"I'm in my boxers, sleeping on top of my sleeping bag, because it's hot, you know? And I wake up and someone's . . . touching me. You know what I mean?"

I didn't say anything.

"I turn over and it's Phoebe Pickersley and she is butt naked. Starkers."

I said, "Oh, dang."

"I beg your pardon?"

Baby Bear had given up the effort and was stretched over my feet, sleeping the sleep of the just. I extricated my feet and stepped over him to go to the kitchen.

"Tell me what happened, Jonathon."

"Brother Wells, even if I was going to let myself be tempted, she wouldn't be my temptation. You get what I'm saying? I yelled and got out of the tent and woke Brick up. He was in time to see a naked girl, holding my beach towel in front of her, crawl out of my tent and hurry over to the girls' side of the camp."

"So the damage is limited? You, Brick and Phoebe?" I opened the fridge and pulled out the milk.

"I'm going to say no."

The pantry offered me Alpha-Bits, Super Sugar Crisp, Grape-Nuts and Cheerios. I pulled out the Alpha-Bits.

"Because?"

"Because I wasn't the only one yelling."

I didn't say "Oh, dang" again, but I was thinking it.

"Phoebe made a scene?" I asked.

"Every tent I can see is lit up with iPhone light. Tomorrow morning—"

My phone beeped to let me know I had another call. I pressed Decline.

"—you might get some phone calls."

My phone pinged—a text from Jo: "Ya got trouble in River City."

It almost made me laugh. It's from *The Music Man*, a favorite of hers when she was about five.

"Brother Wells?"

"I'm thinking," I said. The house phone rang three times and I heard Annie answer it.

———

By six thirty Sunday morning, Annie and I had gotten twenty-four calls, and I learned that one of the callers, whom up to then I had deeply respected, was a rampant racist.

Peter Martinez and Morse Mealey, both church elders, came to the house when they couldn't get through on the phone, and, when I couldn't get off the phone right away to talk to them, had bowls of Grape-Nuts with Baby Bear who was excited at the unusual predawn activity. Baby Bear stole Morse's loafer twice. Morse was a good sport about it. Peter put on a pot of coffee, blessings on his head.

I may be the church minister, but I can't make decisions for the church—that's the elders' responsibility. Some ministers run their churches like a fiefdom—I don't think many of those churches are in the Church of Christ.

Here's what we were faced with.

Judging by the phone calls we'd had so far, a good portion of the church would walk into services that morning knowing something had happened. Shortly thereafter, the people who hadn't heard anything yet, would. Rumors would multiply like bacteria, and most of those rumors would be wrong. We wanted to nip those rumors in the butt, as my brother-in-law would say, but we couldn't. We didn't know enough.

I didn't have any doubt about Jonathon's truthfulness. I believed him absolutely.

The elders' decision was not to say or do anything until there could be a meeting between themselves, the youth ministers, Jonathon, Phoebe and the Pickersley-Smythes. Until then, our answer to any questions was to be, "Everything is in hand; we're looking into it."

Which was guaranteed to satisfy nobody.

From: Merrie Wells
To: Walker Wells

WHAT is going on in Sugar Land, Dad? I'm hearing strange things from my homeboys. LOL

From: Walker Wells
To: Merrie Wells

Not LOLing over here, I can tell you. Give me a call later tonight. I'll fill you in.

To avoid more phone calls from people asking questions I didn't have the answer to, after church Annie Laurie and I both turned off our phones and went to Houston to have lunch at our favorite barbeque restaurant, Goode Company, and stroll around the Museum of Fine Arts. It took my mind off the mess Phoebe had stirred up.

We returned to the church parking lot at three forty-five to pick up our daughter. The youth group was due at four. We had barely pulled into a parking place before a small crowd converged on our car.

Annie put her hand over mine. "Loins girded?"

I said they were and we got out of the car.

No, I said, no one had been raped, no one was hurt, yes, there had been an incident, but we didn't want to make too much of it and we didn't have all the facts in, so this was not the time to discuss it.

Then the Pickersley-Smythes pulled into the parking lot in Mark's dark-blue Range Rover.

Mark got out of the passenger seat wearing white linen slacks and an open-neck shirt, and set to releasing the twins from the backseat. Liz emerged into the heat looking cool and chic in a linen dress and toweringly high sandals. Mark and Liz looked like they were probably headed out somewhere after the pickup. Most of the other parents were dressed in shorts and tees—it was hot.

When Mark turned, a twin on each hip, I got a big smile from him and an equally friendly greeting from Liz. I thought they were taking things really well, which was encouraging.

I shook their hands, the twins' hands, too, as they'd stuck them out, and said, "Hey, Mark, hey Liz! Listen, as soon as the kids get back from the trip, the elders and I thought we'd all gather in the meeting room and talk this whole thing out and try to get an understanding about exactly what happened, would that work for you? Annie can watch the twins. She'll keep them in the playground until the heat gets too much, then she'll entertain them in the nursery. We're eager to get to the bottom of this."

Mark set the twins on their feet and grabbed their hands before they could race across the parking lot.

"Bottom of what?" He had mirrored sunglasses on so I couldn't see his eyes, but the smile was gone. Liz moved up to stand by her husband and put a hand on his arm. The stone on her wedding ring was big enough to choke a goat.

I faltered. "Didn't Phoebe call you? Were you at church this morning?" Because they would have had to have heard something.

"We took the boys to Galveston for the weekend. We didn't head back until after lunch. What's up?"

Liz let go of Mark and took a couple of steps toward me, just close enough to make me want to step back.

"Call us about what, Bear? What's Phoebe gone and done now?" She crossed her arms, creasing her dress, and I didn't need to see the eyes behind the tinted lenses of her glasses to know what her expression was.

"What makes you think Phoebe's done anything?" Mark asked his wife. The twins were using him like a maypole, running first in one direction as far as his arms would go and then in the other. Liz whirled and snapped her fingers at the boys. They both stopped instantly and stood passively next to Mark.

"You aren't seriously asking me that question, are you?" Liz said. "Shall I go into why I think Phoebe must have done something if the elders want to speak with us? Not all the parents—

us. First her teachers, then the principal—I've had a call from the *crossing guard*, Mark!"

There was a moment where a whole lot of silent communication went on between husband and wife. Without another word ever being said, something was concluded. Liz turned back to me, a big smile on her face.

"We'll see you upstairs, Bear. Not a problem." She turned to her sons and snapped her fingers again. "Toby. Tanner." They followed her like ducklings as she strode toward the other parents.

Mark called after her, "Hold their hands in the parking lot!" and without slowing, she held a hand out for each little boy.

I stood there. Mark stood there.

"Is there something I can do to help, Mark?"

He shook his head, thrust his hands into his pockets.

I nodded and we walked beside each other, back to the other parents. Standing apart from the others was a middle-aged black couple and a tall young man I hadn't met before. I thought I knew who they might be.

———

Jo tumbled off the bus hot, cranky, and impatient to wash the river out of her hair.

I pulled her aside from her friends and asked if she knew exactly what had happened.

"Dad, no. I'd be the last person Phoebe would have come running to. She made a scene. Cara said one of the guys made a pass at her and she didn't like it, that's all I know. But since I heard she was only wearing a towel, she must have let things go pretty far before she decided she didn't like it." Jo smirked. I didn't like seeing that on her face and I gave her a warning look. She looked away.

Jo wasn't happy with the idea of waiting around the church while I was at a meeting and her mother was watching the twins. I made sure she had her new house key and she caught a ride home with friends.

———————

Peter Martinez had set up a big pot of coffee and a pitcher of iced tea—the lemon-flavored instant kind, but still—on the credenza in the meeting room along with ice, cups and creamer. The meeting room is set up like a large living room, with sofas and love seats, tables and credenza, but we also brought in some folding chairs to make sure everyone could sit where they wanted to.

Seven of our twenty-four elders are assigned to shepherd the youth ministry and we had hoped all of these could be with us to meet with the Pickersley-Smythes, but two were out of town and Barrett Foley had recused himself on the grounds that his wife had been the one behind the ugly phone call Annie and I had gotten that morning. He had apologized, tears in his voice. Sally Foley was only seventy-two, but she was showing signs of dementia. Barrett didn't want to leave her home alone, and after that phone call, he sure didn't want to bring her any-where near Jonathon Reece. That left us with elders Morse Mealey, Peter Martinez, Casey Dobbins and Jack Crady—all solid. I could count on each of them.

The couple in the parking lot, the ones with the tall young man—those were, as I had guessed, Jonathon's parents and his elder brother, David, the one who had recently been released from prison. Mr. and Mrs. Reece were tall, handsome people, like their sons. Mr. Reece wore a dark, lightweight suit with a pale-gray tie and his wife had on a neat navy-blue dress and a matching hat. David, who looked like grim destiny come to claim his own, was wearing dress slacks with a button-down shirt, sleeves rolled to his elbows. Either they hadn't had time to change after church, or they had felt the gravity of the meeting called for this level of formality. I was glad I had opted for khaki slacks and a polo shirt instead of shorts and a T-shirt. Mr. and Mrs. Reece both took my hand when I held it out, David waited long enough for me to get the message, and then gripped it hard—another message. David was there to make sure we didn't mess with his baby brother.

Jonathon told me he had asked them not to come, but they had insisted, and I didn't blame them. Texas has a history with young black men, too much of it grim.

Jason and Brick, our full-time youth ministers, sat with their arms draped around Jonathon's shoulders, presenting a touching, if slightly ridiculous, united front. All three wore damp, mud-streaked T-shirts and smelled of river water and unwashed male. They greeted David with the overly friendly handshakes, smiles and slaps on the back that we dole out when we're trying to communicate, without saying it, that, hey, the past is the past, and you're all good with us, man. David took it like you'd take the attention of a pair of untrained puppies.

Liz had posed herself and Mark on the love seat, her hand on his knee. He tried to rise when Phoebe came in, but Liz's hand pressed him back down.

Ahh, Phoebe.

Phoebe had on shorts so brief I think I've seen more modest panties, and in lieu of a shirt, she wore a bikini top tiny enough to do a couple of radishes proud. She slouched against a window, her hands clasping her elbows. Her eyes looked bruised and tired and her small mouth was chapped. She was a mess, and if she'd been mine, I'd have taken my own shirt off and put it on her, or grabbed a sofa throw or tablecloth or anything and draped it around her and taken her home to her mother.

But Phoebe didn't have a mother, and Mark had let his wife

pull him back down to the love seat. I felt sorry for the girl, standing there alone. I walked over to her, intending to stand by her, even though I was mad as a hornet about how she might have jeopardized Jonathon's internship. When she saw me coming, she slipped off to the opposite corner. I didn't push it. I let her be.

Casey Dobbins opened the meeting with a prayer that God would give us discernment, compassion, and forgiving hearts and Jonathon's father audibly echoed, "Amen."

Morse Mealey asked Jason and Brick to explain the situation to the best of their understanding, and they did, not having much more to offer than that they'd seen a near-naked Phoebe leaving Jonathon's tent and "carrying on a bit" as she did.

I wanted to know why Jonathon had had a tent to himself when church policy dictated against just such an event, and Jason and Brick both manfully accepted full responsibility for the lapse, not that that was of any use to anyone right then.

"Why was it *Jonathon* who got a tent to himself? Huh? Why'd you pick him?" David hadn't sat down. He was crackling with suspicion and irritation.

"Dave." Jonathon started toward his brother.

"Dude," Brick interrupted, with a goofy grin that made me see again how young he was, just twenty-four, straight out of college. "Short straw. You know. I was jealous, man. Really. I mean, not now, but last night."

David measured Brick with his eyes until Jonathon gave his shoulder a shake. "Dave. Come on."

Jonathon, an arm around his brother, told his story. It hadn't changed from the time he told it to me last night. David interrupted once, saying, "That girl is messed up." His father covered his eyes with his hands during the telling, and wiped them down his face sharply, as if sheeting water off a newly washed face. His mother brought a manicured thumb to her mouth and nibbled her nail polish into oblivion.

Phoebe looked bored, and in the middle of Jonathon's story, slumped to the ground, her back against the wall. She pulled her feet close to her bottom, placing sole against sole, and diddled with the numerous toe rings she wore on her bare feet.

I said, "Phoebe? Do you want to tell us what happened?"

She shrugged, her attention still on the rings on her toes.

"Could you join the circle over here, Phoebe? You're a part of this."

At that I got a look from her. "A part of what?" Phoebe said, but she stood up and walked over to the circle, all eyes on her, the only young woman in the room. She sat on the arm of the love seat and her dad put his arm around her hips. I was grateful to see that—I don't care what a kid's done, they need an advocate. Not to say that what they did was okay, but to let it be known that whatever the kid's situation, they had someone on their side. Liz was not happy to see Mark embrace his daughter. She wedged herself closer to Mark and gripped his knee tighter. I know enough about stepchildren issues to have told her that for a stepparent to compete with a blood child—that's a game you're going to lose, every time. She would have been so much wiser to ally with Phoebe, not fight her.

"Did Jonathon persuade you to go to his tent, Phoebe?" asked Mark. I'd have asked the same question. It was legitimate. "Did he put pressure on you?" Even the girl's father realized you cannot strip a girl and stuff her in your tent against her will—not without waking up everyone in the fifty-plus tents surrounding you.

David made a move but yielded to Jonathon and Mrs. Reece sprang from the couch and said, "Oh, no, you don't!" before her husband said, "Evelyn. Let the man ask his questions. Jonathon has nothing to fear here." She sat down but didn't lean back against the cushions. Her husband cradled her hand in his, either to comfort her or to contain her. See, that's what I mean about an advocate—no matter what, Jonathon knew he had people on his side, people who were assuming from the beginning that he was in the right.

Phoebe's eyes wandered over the faces in the room, some mad, some concerned, and settled on mine.

She wasn't feeling ashamed or guilty or embarrassed. She didn't seem to feel the weight of David's angry stare. None of that was in her face. "You said I'm a part of this—well, what *is* this? The Inquisition? I like Jonathon, I wanted to make him happy but he squealed like a little girl. I don't know why. Maybe he's gay."

David drew breath in between his teeth but didn't say anything. Phoebe set one bare foot nonchalantly on the coffee table, admiring her toe rings.

Jack Crady, a good and grave man who has four adult daughters, said gently, "Phoebe, you say you like Jonathon. Didn't you know that your actions could have cost Jonathon his job? More than that, if Jonathon had been weak enough to accept your offer, do you know he could have been arrested? Jonathon is twenty and you're a minor, and—"

Phoebe snorted.

Liz stared fixedly at the foot Phoebe had propped on the table. She suddenly leaned forward and pointed.

"Is that my class ring? Are you wearing my class ring on your *toe*? Mark, that's my class ring! How did she get my class ring to fit her toe? How did she *get* my class ring? Have you been going through my drawers?"

Phoebe gave the first smile I'd seen that day. It was a wide, genuine smile. She had been waiting for Liz to notice.

"I cut the back of it with wire cutters. Because it's real gold, it cuts easy. Bends easy, too. You never wear it. I didn't think you'd mind. And you go through my drawers *all the time*. I figured it was like a house rule, a hard-and-fast."

Liz moved so quick none of us could react. She reached across Mark and slapped Phoebe across the face. Hard. Mark, too late, snatched Liz's wrist and yanked her back. There were cries and gasps but not from Phoebe who had reeled from the strike, but now stood up straight, shoulders back, eyes burning, the white imprint of a hand across one cheek.

Phoebe said, "If I tell my grandfather you slapped me, he'll kill you dead." She said it like she meant it. You could hear dry ice in that voice.

Liz was up, pushing against Mark and leaning toward the girl; her face was a fist, tight and clenched.

"That house is mine. You get that? Everything in that house is *mine*. Every stick of furniture, every fork, every spoon—the *light*bulbs are mine. The clothes on your slutty back are mine—"

We were all on our feet now. Mark caught Liz by the shoulders and swung her around to face him. He dragged her into him until their noses were nearly touching. "Can you get it together or do we need to—"

She jerked free from him. It took her long seconds to calm herself, her breath ragged in front of all the horrified onlookers.

Phoebe surveyed her audience. It couldn't have been better. She had a good portion of the church's hierarchy—some of whom numbered among the community's movers and shakers—here in the room with her. She was incandescent with triumph. This was her moment and she was going to enjoy it.

Her words came as deliberate and measured as an assassin's bullet. "I'm sorry, did you call *me* a slut? Is that what you said? My 'slutty back'? At least *I* never slept with another woman's husband. At least *I* never got pregnant to trap another woman's husband into—"

Liz's hand was up again but Mark caught her wrist and held it firm.

Mr. Reece stepped forward decisively and held his hand out to his wife.

"Evelyn." He looked at his son. "Jonathon." He addressed me and the other men in the room, never looking at Liz or Phoebe. "We'll say good-bye. Jonathon will be coming with us. He won't be back here. He won't be working for this church. No."

Jonathon said, "Dad—" but Mr. Reece held a hand out to quiet him. Morse, who'd been busy at the credenza, slipped back to the circle and handed Phoebe a clean handkerchief filled with ice and gestured for her to put it on her face. She looked up at him, her eyebrows high, and put the cold pack to her cheek. He patted her arm and gave it a squeeze and then pulled her down on the couch next to him, an arm around her bony bare shoulders.

"I'm sorry," Mr. Reece told me. "Our prayers are with you. If Jonathon were a grown man, it would be different. I might encourage him to stay and fight the Lord's fight here. God in Heaven knows you need all the help you can get. But his mother and I will not allow our son to work in this poisonous environment. He's still young. He's growing. We're not ready for our son to be tested by fire. No, sir. No, sir." Jonathon's mother nodded her vigorous agreement. There were big tears in her shocked eyes.

There was a rumble of protests at this, with Jonathon's imploring "Dad!" loudest of all.

I didn't say a word. I didn't blame the Reeces. I thought they had made the right decision. For Jonathon, not for us. But we weren't their responsibility.

Mrs. Reece put her hand in the middle of Jonathon's back and pushed her son gently toward the door. She said, "Not another word, Jonathon. You will obey your father."

And he did. One of the most gifted interns this church had ever had the pleasure to employ walked out the door and down another road, to another place and another ministry. His brother lingered long enough to stare each of us down—he saved his most venomous examination for Phoebe. Before he walked out the door, he pointed his finger at her—an Old Testament prophet calling down judgment. She never even noticed.

There was silence in the room after the Reeces walked out. Then Casey Dobbins said to the Pickersley-Smythes, "The elders will have to meet privately to discuss this situation, but until you hear from us, Phoebe may not attend any youth group activities without the presence of one of her parents. That includes classes." He turned to Phoebe. "I'm afraid, Phoebe, that you may not go on any more overnighters. Period. This isn't about punishing you, Phoebe. That's between you and your parents. It's for your protection as a minor child—"

An elaborate eye roll from Phoebe, who stood cross-armed and sullen, the angry mark from Liz's hand livid on her cheek. She squeezed Morse's handkerchief, letting the water drizzle onto the carpet, and then put the ice-filled handkerchief back to her face.

"—and for the protection of the other minor children under our care and supervision." Casey reached out and took Phoebe's unwilling hand and held it in both of his. "Your God loves you, Phoebe. We do, too." He took a breath. "Now, Phoebe, I'm going to ask you a question, and I ask you to answer truthfully." He paused, watching her face. She blinked.

"Has your stepmother hit you before this? Was this the first time?"

There was a long silence. Phoebe shook her head. Casey said, "Use words, Phoebe. She hasn't hit you before, or this wasn't the first time?"

Phoebe said, "This was the first time."

Casey nodded. He held on to Phoebe's hand. Now Casey addressed himself directly to Liz and Mark, and his voice was hard. "Let me be very clear, Lizabeth. If I ever, *ever*, see or hear of you striking your stepdaughter in such a vicious and violent manner, if you *ever* lay a hand in anger upon the child that God has given into your care, I will report you to the authorities, so help me God, I will. That goes for every man in this room." He looked at us in turn. We all nodded.

"This is *not* church business," Liz said, spitting the words. "This is *family* business." All the carefully applied makeup, the elegant, simple dress, the expensive leather sandals—it looked like camouflage to me now. It looked like a disguise. Liz stood before us exposed, and she knew it. The face she directed at Phoebe was so full of hate that I stepped forward. But she didn't go for the girl. It was costing her a lot, but she was holding herself back.

"Oh, yes, this *is* church business, Lizabeth," Casey said. His voice was firm and his face severe. "This is everybody's business. The protection of children? That's *everybody's* business. And, Mark? We understand that this is a difficult time of adjustment for your family, and we want to be of assistance to you in every way we can. You can call on any of us day or night. But you look to the care of your household, young man. This is *your* responsibility."

Mark bowed his head. He took Phoebe's hand, and reached for Liz's, but she snatched her hand away and shouldered her way out of the room. She would have slammed the door, but it's got those fancy hinges that slow it down. You can't slam it. So, no dramatic exit for Liz.

After Mark and Phoebe followed Liz out, and the door had sighed to a close, Brick dropped onto the couch and covered his eyes with an arm.

"I feel like I've been through it. I know exactly how sausage feels right now."

Jason said, "That Mrs. Pickersley-Smythe—do you believe what Phoebe said? About her getting pre—"

"We're not going there," I said. "Phoebe was mad and embarrassed. She was trying to hurt Liz." I pulled up the seat of a folding chair and closed it with a snap. "What Phoebe said? That doesn't leave this room. Whatever the truth is, it's in the past."

———————

That had been four months ago. I didn't realize it at the time, but that would be the last time I'd see Phoebe Pickersley alive.

Six

It was now October, and more than four months had passed since that meeting with the Pickersley-Smythes. Four months filled with the excitement of Jo's stay at the School of American Ballet, her crushing disappointment when she was not invited to join the program during the school year, and her first weeks as a sophomore at Clements High School. Merrie came down from Texas Tech a handful of times over the summer but never stayed more than a weekend except for Jo's fifteenth birthday, when she stayed four days—that's what Jo had asked for from her sister. The girls spent every minute together. Merrie even slept in Jo's room. The girls hadn't slept in the same room together since they were in elementary school. Merrie must have worked some magic, because when she left to go back to Tech, Jo seemed easier about not getting the opportunity to train full time at the School of American Ballet. She didn't discuss it with us, but we could tell.

Four months since I had last seen Phoebe, and this time when I saw her, her rosy cheeks were pale, her blue eyes staring, and the last page of her life had finished like the final chapter of a short story that should have been a novel.

Detective James Wanderley, not yet thirty but carrying the authority of a man his father's age, arrived on the heels of the

EMS guys. Wanderley investigates homicides with the Sugar Land Police Department; he isn't called out for suicides or accidental deaths. But we had some history and he had answered my text. But he wasn't happy to see me. He wasn't happy that I'd moved Phoebe's body. He wasn't happy that Jo wouldn't say a word to him, only kept shaking her head, her eyes hot and dry and her trembling fingers kneading Baby Bear's coat.

Wanderley isn't all that easy to deal with when he *is* happy.

Phoebe's death was an accident. We all knew it was an accident, it had to be. Except Wanderley said he didn't know that. Wanderley said it would be best to do a full investigation.

We sat in the family room. Annie lit a fire, even though it wasn't cold enough for one. Sugar Land is just outside of Houston, and on the Gulf Coast, we feel lucky if we can wear a sweater in October. But I was glad for the bright, dancing flame.

Wanderley was dressed in running clothes—it was the first time I'd seen him without the blazer and fancy cowboy boots he usually wore, clothes that made him look older than his twenty-eight years. In running clothes he looked smaller and less intimidating. Not that *I've* ever been intimidated by Wanderley.

Wanderley pushed his dark hair aside and furrowed the brows that nearly met over his nose. He tried again to talk to Jo.

"What time did Phoebe come over, Jo?" He leaned forward, his elbows on his knees and his hands loosely clasped. He waited. Finally Jo shrugged.

"You don't know what time it was when she got here?" Very patient. Very relaxed.

Jo shook her head and Baby Bear licked her chin and stuck his nose in her ear and sniffed. She pushed his great big head away. Annie came in with four water bottles. Wanderley twisted his open and drank. Jo held hers without looking at it. After a minute Annie got up and took the bottle from Jo and set it on the coffee table.

"Was it full dark when she got here?"

Another shrug.

"Jo, you don't remember if it was dark?"

No response. Wanderley finished his bottle of water, screwed the lid back on and set it on the side table next to him.

I said, "Listen, honey, if you could only tell—"

Wanderley slewed his eyes my way and I shut up. He waited a long time, watching Jo.

Finally she said, "I wasn't here."

Wanderley took this in. A blue guitar pick appeared in his fingers and he popped it in his mouth, an odd tic of his.

"How'd she get in? You left the door unlocked for her?"

Another long pause and then a head shake. Jo snaked her hands in Baby Bear's coat and he grunted and pushed against her. He wasn't supposed to be on the couch.

"You didn't leave the door unlocked for her? So . . . how'd she get in?"

"She had a key."

Annie and I both sat up. I said, "You gave Phoebe a key to the house, Jo?"

Wanderley said, "Bear? Could you please—"

Jo lifted her brown eyes to mine then tilted her head in a futile attempt to keep the tears from spilling out. In a second they were rolling down the sides of her face.

"I didn't mean to."

"What didn't you mean, Jo?" Wanderley said.

"I didn't mean to give her a key."

"That's not so awful, Jo. To give a friend a key."

"She's not my friend."

Annie got up and sat down next to Jo, her arm around Jo's shoulders, leaving Jo sandwiched between dog and mother, daring us to make a move on her.

"So why did you give her a key?" Wanderley took the pick out and danced it over and under his fingers, magician-like, then put it back in his mouth.

Long, long silence while Jo watched the propane flames leap in the fireplace.

"Because I'm an idiot."

Annie crooked her arm and drew Jo's head over to be kissed. "You're not an idiot," she murmured. Wanderley didn't tell *Annie* to be quiet.

"The time I went over there, to Phoebe's house? She made a big deal over how her house was my house, friends forever, all garbage. But she gave me a key to her house. So I gave her mine." My girl looked at me and I nodded. I remembered the night she was referring to; Jo had left Phoebe's home in the middle of the night. We'd had some words about that.

"I laid Phoebe's key on the foyer table when I left," Jo said. "When I saw her at school, I asked for my key back. She said she threw it in the water hazard in back of her house." Like many homes in the master-planned First Colony, the Pickersley-Smythes' home backed up to the golf course. Jo shrugged.

I said, "You could have told us."

Annie covered her eyes with a hand. She said, "Oh, Bear. Oh dear, Bear. Phoebe is our house fairy."

―――――――

The "house fairy" activity had started after we took Jo to New York in late June for the School of American Ballet summer program. It was a quick trip, only the three of us since Merrie was working as a camp counselor in Colorado.

We planned to spend a long weekend in New York helping Jo get settled, and before we left—between making sure that Jo had everything she needed, and getting Baby Bear packed off to the kennel, Annie Laurie turning in her latest project before deadline, and me . . . well, I can't remember what it was I had to do, but it was important—we left the house a mess when we drove off to the airport. Not the end of the world.

Once there, we got Jo settled into the barracks-style housing that The School of American Ballet offers the kids in their summer program. I thought the place looked like reform school accommodations. Annie took on the job of explaining to Jo's snippy roommate from Ontario that just because she had moved into the room first didn't mean she could take *all* the drawers in the dresser, to which the nasty little peanut said yes, it did, too, and stood her ground. So Annie and I went out and bought some Rubbermaid containers for Jo's clothes and Jo stowed them under her narrow bed.

Even though Jo is a vegetarian and a picky eater to boot, we had planned to take her to some of New York's famous eateries, like the Carnegie Deli—they have lots of salad choices and it's the kind of place you don't find in the Houston area. We waited for a table for twenty-six minutes and then Jo ate a pickle. That's all. She said she wasn't hungry. Right. Or maybe she wasn't hungry because after Jo had introduced herself to some of her new classmates, one stick-thin redhead said, "Texas? That explains it. They grow them big in Texas." Jo is five feet two inches and if she's not wearing her Doc Martens, she weighs in at less than a hundred pounds. Thanks, Red.

Jo was jittery with nerves and close to tears when we left her in New York. She was putting too much on this opportunity. We knew that. It was a big deal to get into the summer program—the few spots they make available are competed for, and the competition is tough. Jo believed that at the end of the program, she would be offered a position in the year-round school. The school often made one or two offers. One or two out of all the hopefuls who attended the summer program. Jo believed that if she wished it hard enough, it would happen. We believed she was setting herself up for a heartbreak.

We worried over her the whole flight home and hadn't stopped worrying when we dragged our luggage into the house we had left in a mess the Thursday before.

The house looked perfect. Like a hotel service had come through.

The beds had clean sheets on them and a turndown service presentation. The dirty dishes in the sink had been washed and put away, the dishwasher unloaded. There were new rolls of toilet paper on all the holders and the paper had been folded into points—not part of our regular regimen. There were lines in the upstairs carpet from the vacuum cleaner. The towels that had been left in the dryer were folded and stacked on the kitchen counter. The houseplants had been watered; a little too much, but still. In our bathroom was a vase of yellow roses next to the sink Annie used.

"What on earth?" said Annie.

"Your sister?" I asked. Stacy lived a few minutes away from us and has a key to the house.

"You think?" said Annie, dropping her luggage and walking through the house, noticing the stacks of squared-off magazines, the dust-free piano, the straightened throw rugs.

Uh, no. I didn't. I have a good imagination, but I couldn't imagine my sister-in-law coming over and cleaning the house for us. Stacy is . . . not the greatest homemaker in the world. I'm not blaming her—she's got three boys, six, eight and ten, and her husband Chester is never there to help her. But even with paid housekeepers coming in once a week, Stacy's level of disorganization, and her penchant for acquiring stuff that has to be stored, means that her house maintains a constant level of barely controlled chaos. The state our house had been in when we'd left was better than Stacy's is on a day-to-day basis.

We called Stacy but after she listened breathlessly to our questions, over the sounds of her three sons trying to take each other apart, she asked us if we had lost our minds. "You find that house fairy"—the first time we'd heard the expression—"and send it to *my* house. I swear, Annie, you always do have all the luck, I don't know why, I work ten times as hard as you and— Wynn, you pour that pitcher over your brother's head and so help me—"

We heard a splash.

"Gotta go." Stacy hung up. Annie Laurie and I agreed it was unlikely that Stacy had produced the wonder we had come home to.

While Annie made a few more inquiring calls, I unpacked our luggage, left the stuff for Annie to put away and stored the bags under Merrie's bed. After a shower and a bowl of cereal for dinner, I sat down to read my Bible, finding my place by the frayed silk ribbon attached to the binding.

There was a loose knot tied in the ribbon. Huh.

———

That first visit, the big visit, we chalked up to some über-friendly neighbor whom we had accidentally left a key with, or to the Ladies' Bible Class, or to . . . you know what? We didn't know. But it's not like it was a threatening gesture, so we ultimately let it go.

After that? The small things? The mended vase and the organized pantry and all the other little kindnesses? Secretly, I thought Annie Laurie was doing it to please me. Turns out Annie Laurie secretly thought I was doing it to please her.

———————

Wanderley looked at me from under that unibrow.

"House fairy, Bear? Really?"

I shrugged.

"So when did the house fairy visits stop?"

"They stopped tonight, James," Annie Laurie said.

Seven

Detective Wanderley gave a grunt and stood up.

"I've got to get to the Pickersley-Smythes. As their pastor, Bear, do you want to come?"

Of course I didn't want to go. But of course I did.

I slipped on a sweatshirt and picked up my Bible. I fingered the new knot in the ribbon marker. There were eight now in the ribbon. If Phoebe had been trying to tell me something, I wasn't getting it.

Wanderley drove. His car was an immaculate black late-'90s BMW 325i. There were no fast-food wrappers, cigarette ashes, or empty water bottles. No dust or dirt, either. The floor mats were clean and the car smelled of Windex or something like it. There was a princess-pink car seat strapped in the backseat, with a black satchel next to it, evidence of Molly, Wanderley's two-year-old daughter, whose mother had declined to marry Wanderley. I understood there was some friction between them over that.

We pulled out of my driveway, past the emergency vehicles parked in the street. Even at this late hour, some of my neighbors were standing in their yards, watching.

Wanderley said, "What isn't she telling us?"

My mind was still on the knots in my ribbon, on what that was supposed to mean. "Who, Phoebe?" I was looking out the window. Mrs. Hsu mouthed, "What's going on?" as we passed. I waved.

"Uh, Jo. She's holding something back."

"She's not holding anything back. What makes you think she's holding something back? What's that supposed to mean?" I said.

Wanderley glanced over at me, then back to the road. "I'm a cop, Bear. Jo feels guilty about something. You don't see that? I want to know what she feels guilty about." Wanderley drove around the golf course and changed topics entirely. "Where do you think the girl got the drugs?"

"Phoebe? I don't know. What makes you think it was drugs? Maybe she had a heart attack. That can happen to kids," I said though I thought it was probably drugs.

"I've seen people dead from heart attacks and I've seen people dead from drugs and my money is on drugs. Where do you think she got them from?"

"How would *I* know? She's got money, and she goes to Clements. Does it need to be harder than that?"

Clements High School, Jo's high school, is an award-winning, fiercely competitive public high school, and too many of the kids have too much money. Some of them have an entrepreneurial streak—the results are predictable.

Wanderley nodded. "It would be from someone she knows, though. Kids don't buy from strangers."

There was a long pause. "It was your house she came to. Jo's room she died in."

Now he had my attention.

"Okay, pull over. Stop the car. I mean it, Wanderley. Stop the dang car."

Wanderley pulled to the curb and put the car in park. He put his emergency lights on.

"Are you saying you think Phoebe overdosed on drugs *Jo* gave her? Is that what you're saying? Because that's crazy. Annie Laurie and I aren't stupid. We'd know if Jo was using drugs. You think she could have competed in that summer program if she was a drug user? There's no way. You're out of line, James."

Wanderley's hands flexed on the steering wheel. He turned to give me one of his really irritating looks of pity. "Bear, of *course* she could have competed at that ballet school if she was a drug user—she might have felt she *had* to use if she was going to be competitive. I guarantee you, no doubt about it, lots of those dancers use. They're athletes, Bear. You don't think athletes use drugs? Don't you read the paper? Listen to the news?"

"Jo does not use drugs." My heart was doing that hard thump-thump that hurts your chest.

"Can I drive on, Bear? Or you want me to take you home? I can handle this on my own."

"No. I'm coming."

Wanderley considered me for a while and then pulled back onto the road. We were in the Sweetwater neighborhood now. The homes were all four to nine thousand square feet, with garages that held fleets of cars.

"Don't get all defensive on me," Wanderley began, then looked over like I was supposed to say, *Okay, I won't get all defensive when you attack the integrity of my fifteen-year-old daughter. Go right on ahead.* I gave him back a look that said, *Be happy I'm not tearing your head off.*

Wanderley sighed and went on. "From what I saw, I'm guessing Phoebe took some kind of opioid. Or a barbiturate. Nothing she could have gotten over the counter would have done this to her. Right now, back at your house, the team is going to be taking Jo's room apart, looking for a stash—"

My fist hit the passenger window. "They won't find anything."

Wanderley said, all slow and calm the way people do when they're talking to someone they consider irrational, which just makes the irrational person feel more irrational—and murderous, if my own experience is anything to go off from—"And even if they don't find anything, they aren't going to see that as conclusive. No one knows how long Jo was there before she called you."

I exploded. "You're saying you think Jo would have been scrambling to save her own fanny if she came home and found Phoebe in that state? You don't think she would have called nine-one-one right away?"

Again, very measured. "Bear, she *didn't* call nine-one-one right away. She didn't call them at all. *You* called."

The hamster wheels in my head started spinning.

Wanderley continued. "She could have had plenty of time to hide or dispose of something—that would have been the smart thing to do, and Jo is a smart girl. She could have had a friend come by and pick it up for her. These are all possibilities the investigative team is going to look into. Because everyone is going to want to know why Phoebe came to your house, took a lethal dose of drugs, and died there. You get me? You see where they're going to be coming from? This isn't personal, Bear. It's not between you and me."

Yeah. Not personal. Here's the thing: if one of my daughters is involved, then, yeah. It's personal, bub.

"It's hard for me to imagine you could seriously think a fifteen-year-old girl could be mixed up in selling drugs," I said.

Wanderley said, "Hah!" and shot me a look. "For a tough guy, Bear, you are such an innocent. You think you're living in *Pleasantville*? Sure, I'd be surprised if a fifteen-year-old girl was selling drugs on her own—surprised but not shocked. More likely she'd be delivering for someone else, like a boyfriend. What do you think? Does Jo know anyone like that?"

Wanderley gave me another sidelong look. See, I'm glad I'm not a cop. It's Wanderley's *job* to assume the worst about everybody. It's *my* job to assume the best. I look at Jo and her friends and I see great kids. And my Jo is not the kind of fawning female who would let someone use her. She's more secure than that. At least, she was before The School of American Ballet program. Before she learned they would not be offering her a year-round position. Jo has had some hard months. It's not easy to give up a dream. But drugs? No. Not Jo.

"What do you know about the Pickersley-Smythes?" Wanderley asked.

I told him what I knew, the basics. Pretty much repeated the speech Liz had given at the church's new member's class— about turning a packaging company around straight out of school with her newly earned MBA. Told him about Phoebe's mom dying, and how she'd had to change high schools and come live with her dad about six months ago. I didn't tell him about her fight with Jo, or the incident with Jonathan Reese.

In two minutes, we would be at the Pickersley-Smythes. I had to get my head in a different place if I was going to be any use to them. I said a silent prayer and then forced a conversation change.

"How's Molly?" I asked.

Wanderley didn't take his eyes off the road.

"She's got to be close to three now?" I said.

"In about two weeks. October twenty-fifth. The party is the twenty-seventh."

We drove in silence past the dark homes, some lit up, some clearly down for the night.

"You want to come?" Wanderley said.

"What?"

"Would you and Annie Laurie want to come to the party?"

No, I didn't want to go to his daughter's birthday party. He had just insulted *my* daughter. I'm not big on parties for three-year-olds, anyway. The food stinks and I'm no good at the games. I didn't know why on earth he would want us there.

"Sure," I said. There was no enthusiasm in my voice, but we didn't have anything going on that weekend and I don't like to lie—not even those little social "white lies." And I don't know how to tell a man that I didn't want to go to his little girl's birthday party.

Wanderley didn't say anything. He nodded and pulled into the ring road that circled in front of the Pickersley-Smythes' home, pulled his car to a stop, and turned it off. We sat there together listening to the engine tick. Two fathers of daughters, coming to tell a father the worst news there is, that his daughter was dead.

There have been times when I have been on hand when a parent learned of a child's death. Usually, it was an expected death. Four times it's been after a long struggle with cancer. When I was growing up, I don't recall ever hearing of a child dying of cancer. Fifty years later, I've known several children who spent most of their short lives fighting a foe who would not let loose. But when a child dies from cancer, the pain is mingled with relief and resignation—the suffering has been so great and has gone on so long, and if the parents are believers, they take comfort in knowing they will someday see their child again. I'm not saying that makes the pain go away; from what I understand, the pain becomes a part of the family. They are forever changed. They go on, have joys and happiness. But there is never a day, not an hour, when the precious lost one is not remembered. Grief becomes a sixth sense. They tell me that when they meet someone new, they know, within minutes, if that person has also lost a child.

There have been times of unexpected death, too, typically car crashes. Three instances came to mind—all young men, and all driving gorgeous sports cars their parents had bought them. There was no resignation from the parents there, just fury, and horror, and a well of guilt and blame so deep that two of the couples I knew were never able to climb out from it. The third couple still vibrate with the pain even twelve years after the accident, but they have held on to each other and to God. A younger daughter has given them grandchildren. I'm sure that helps.

But never have I had to tell a parent that his child may have committed suicide. Because that's what Phoebe had to have done. I didn't really think this was an accident. There was too much deliberation for it to have been anything else. Never have I had to tell a father that his daughter, his baby, his love and his heart, had felt such despair that she'd chosen dying over living. I couldn't help thinking of my own girls. What if it had been Merrie or Jo? Oh, God, please take the very thought from me.

"Give me a second?" I asked Wanderley and at his nod, I stepped out of the car and called Merrie. The phone rang twice and she picked up. Tears pricked my eyes when I heard her voice, bright and happy, party noises behind her.

"Hey, Dad! Late call. What's up?"

I cleared my throat. "Wanted to hear your voice, is all."

Now there was concern in her voice. "What's up, Dad? Everyone okay?"

I paced the drive, the gravel scrunching under my feet. "We're all okay. We got some bad news tonight. You don't know the people. I'll tell you about it tomorrow. I just needed to hear your voice."

"Okay."

"And make sure you know how much I love you, baby girl."

She was subdued now. "I know it, Dad. I love you, too."

"And if there's ever anything wrong, you'll let me know. You won't try to solve it on your own. There's nothing so bad we can't fix it together, right?"

"Dad. You're scaring me. You swear everyone's all right?"

I nodded, my throat too full to speak. In the background, a boy was urging Merrie back to the party.

"Dad?"

"Yes, baby. Your world is safe."

Long, listening pause.

"Okay then. You going to be all right, Dad?"

"I'm good."

"Do you want to talk some more?"

Wanderley was out of his car, waiting for me.

"No. Gotta go. Go with God, Merrie Elizabeth." I shut my phone off, powered it all the way down. During the next hour or so, I wouldn't be taking any calls.

Wanderley said, "You ready?" As if anyone ever could be.

"Yeah."

The yard was lit up with landscaping lights, but the house itself was dark. It was close to midnight. We'd be waking the family up with this news.

When we walked up to the beveled-glass door, a motion sensor turned the front porch light on, startling us both. We could see the huge, white, Persian tomcat sitting on the carpeted stairs, blinking at us through the glass. Wanderley rang the doorbell. I prayed that God would give me the words to help this family endure the unendurable. *Let the words of my mouth and the meditation of my heart be acceptable in Your sight, O Lord, my rock and my redeemer.*

There was no response, and Wanderley rang again. One of the three-year-old twins appeared at the head of the stairs looking down at us. He was wearing Spider-Man pajamas, the kind with the feet sewn in. My throat tightened and I coughed. Wanderley touched me with his elbow.

"Cowboy up, old man," he said.

I nodded.

Mark appeared beside the child, touched his face and said something. The boy shook his head and clung to his father's leg. Mark lifted the child to his hip and came down the stairs. He looked through the glass door, recognized me, and set the boy down to turn the dead bolt. Mark wore black, silky sleep pants and a long, elaborately embroidered kimono. His feet were bare.

The heavy door swung open and Mark said, "Bear? What is it?"

Wanderley held his ID out to Mark and asked if we could come in.

Mark stepped back reluctantly and we went in. He switched on one of the lamps that sat on a dark wood chest.

His son said, "Chocolate milk."

"You go get in bed, Tanner, and Daddy will bring it to you as soon as I can." The boy protested but Mark was firm, and with a whimper, the boy climbed the stairs. A door shut.

Mark led us into a study. There was a mahogany table that served as a desk and a wall of beautifully bound books. This room, too, was a shrine to the twins. A picture of Lizabeth cradling her bare, bulging belly, a picture of the sleeping newborns curled together on a black velvet throw, the ubiquitous Texas shot of the children in a field of bluebonnets. There were none of Phoebe.

The Persian drifted in, circled the room and leaped to the back of a chair. He watched with interest, his tail swishing.

Mark gestured to chairs and a love seat and we sat down. He knew it was bad.

Wanderley said, "It's about Phoebe. Do you want to get your wife?"

Mark shook his head, not smiling. "No, I'll deal with it. Me and Phoebe. Do you want me to go get her or do you want to talk to me first?"

Wanderley opened his mouth, shut it again.

Mark said, "Is it that bad? Has she done something that bad?"

I took a breath to speak but Wanderley stopped me.

"Mr. Pickersley-Smythe, an hour and a half ago, Jo Wells discovered your daughter's body in her bedroom. In Jo's bedroom. It looks like a drug overdose." Wanderley dropped his eyes. Cracked a knuckle. "I'm sorry for your loss."

Mark's brow puckered. "Phoebe's in her room. I could hear her music when I went to bed." He looked at me, took in my face, and sprang to his feet. He took the stairs three at a time and we heard a door thrown back. And then he screamed.

Eight

Mark was still screaming when we reached the room. He had torn the bedclothes off the bed, Phoebe's backpack lay next to a wall where he'd thrown it, textbooks splayed. He was on his hands and knees, pounding the floor with his fists and his head, screaming in hoarse roars. His sons ran into the room and to his side, adding their screams of terror to his. Finally, Lizabeth hurried into the bedroom, peach silk billowing, matching slippers on her feet.

She handed a struggling twin each to me and Wanderley and dropped to her knees next to Mark. Lizabeth pulled Mark to his knees and wrapped her arms around him, crooning, "My love, my love, I'm here. I'm here, Mark. You've got me." Liz lifted her face from his neck and waved us off. Wanderley handed me the twin he was holding and sat down on the stripped mattress.

I stood there, two hysterical three-year-olds in my arms and then carefully navigated the stairs down to the kitchen. I used my toe to swing the door shut behind me, shutting out some of the frightening noises their father was making. I leaned a twin over to the wall and said, "Can you get the light for me, Tanner?"

The child stopped crying and stared at me, bleary-eyed. "Toby."

"You're Toby?" A solemn nod. I held him out from my body

and checked his pj's. The Incredible Hulk. Spider-Man was Tanner, The Incredible Hulk was Toby.

Tanner stopped crying, too, and leaned across from his brother to flip the light switch, which earned a flailing fist from Toby and more tears from both. I sat them down on the kitchen island and clapped my hands once, sharply. They startled and stopped crying. Two pairs of round blue eyes looked at me. If they'd been my babies, they'd have to wear dog tags or ID bracelets or something—I couldn't tell one from another, not without the pajamas, and they don't wear pajamas in the bathtub.

"Chocolate milk?" I asked. Vigorous nods. "Where's the sippy cups?" Blank eyes. I opened cabinet doors onto collections of china and stemware that would have had Martha Stewart doing the happy dance. Nothing I would hand to a three-year-old. Checked the built-in drawers in the island and found one full of sippy cups and lidded bowls and dishes for toddlers. I held two of the cups up for the boys to see.

"Sippy cups," I said.

"Nuby," they responded in unison.

Whatever. I got out the milk and bottle of sugarless chocolate syrup, filled the cups, screwed the lids back on, put a finger over the spouts and shook. Toby and Tanner reached out and I handed them their cups. They drummed their superhero heels against the cupboard doors while they drank. I opened a drawer that looked like it might hold kitchen towels. It did, so I took one, wet it and wrung it out, and wiped down the boys' faces. They didn't fuss.

When they had finished a second round of chocolate milk, I took them to the downstairs powder room to pee. Afterward, The Incredible Hulk burped and Spider-Man giggled and produced one of his own. Together, they yawned, their mouths opening as wide as a cat's.

It was quiet now, only a soft murmuring coming from behind the shut door to Phoebe's room, so I chanced returning upstairs. We climbed the stairs, a small hand grasped in each of mine, and the boys pulled me to their room. A little-boy paradise. Or a rich momma's idea of a little-boy paradise. The boys ran to their beds, helpfully labeled TOBY and TANNER with big, red, wooden letters attached to the wall above the headboards. It was necessary that I admire the stuffed partners they slept with—a penguin for Toby and a Clifford the Big Red Dog for Tanner—and then Tanner handed me a book and said, "Read."

From below, I heard the front door open, and the sound of feet on the stairs.

The book was a scuffed and worn copy of Margaret Wise Brown's *Goodnight Moon*. It had been a favorite of my girls' long ago. Before I could start, Tanner patted the book and said, "Phoebe read."

"What?" I said.

Toby nodded agreement.

"Did Phoebe read this book to you?"

Two heads nodded. Toby said, "All night."

"Every night," corrected Tanner.

I opened the front cover:

> *For our Phoebe Peapie,*
> *From Daddy and Mommy*
> *On her second Christmas*

"'In the great green room there was a telephone and a red balloon and a picture of—'" I stopped and cleared my throat.

A drowsy Tanner said, "Read."

By the light of a teddy bear lamp, in a room where there were stacks of books and puzzles and toys, a chalkboard, two small rocking chairs, a table with crayons and manila paper, I read Phoebe's *Goodnight Moon* to Phoebe's baby brothers, a book she read to them every night.

"'Goodnight stars—goodnight air—goodnight noises everywhere...'"

I closed the book. They were asleep, superheroes in toddler beds, so healthy and beautiful they looked as if they'd been genetically engineered.

I turned off the lamp and shut the boys' bedroom door behind me, then walked to Phoebe's room. Wanderley had been joined by two officers in uniform.

"No. No," Mark was saying as I came in. "Why do you want to? What do you think you'll find?" His face was swollen and puffy and his shoulders sagged. He sat on the side of Phoebe's bed, the covers and sheets heaped in one corner. Mark held one of her pillows over his stomach, clutching it like he was keeping his insides on the inside. I understood. Phoebe wasn't my child and I still felt ripped open.

His wife sat behind him, a bent knee on either side, pressed up against his back with her arms tight around his shoulders. She was trying to pour her comfort, her strength, into the man. I had my issues with Lizabeth—I'd seen her maybe at her worst. But right now, I admired her compassion.

"Mark," she said, "we have nothing to hide. You were a wonderful father to Phoebe—"

Mark cried, "Oh, God!"—such despair in the cry—and buried his face in the pillow. I didn't stop to think, I just knelt by Mark's feet and put a hand on his knee.

"Let's go see her, Mark, let's go see your girl." It's what I would have wanted. Mark nodded, face still in the pillow.

Liz looked up. Her tone had changed completely. "That's not a good idea, Bear."

"That okay, Wanderley?"

"We can do that." Wanderley had been leaning against Phoebe's dresser, arms crossed, but he straightened.

Liz's hands flew out and she caught hold of Mark's silk robe. "Oh, no, Mark, let's don't do that. You don't want to do that." She turned him to face her—he looked away but she laid a palm against his cheek and drew him back. Her hands moved from his face to his shoulders, smoothing the silk, caressing the muscles beneath. It was an intimate, possessive touch. "You've had enough for tonight. There's nothing you can do for Phoebe now. The boys and I—we're your family. Stay here. Stay with us." You would have thought the man was leaving for good. She tightened her hold on Mark's shoulders.

What? I thought. His child, his baby, is in the morgue, lying somewhere cold and hard and scary and she is all alone. Why *wouldn't* he go to her? My admiration for Liz dimmed. For her to make it sound like Mark had to choose between his daughter or his wife and sons—well, to me that showed a profound inability to imagine what her husband was going through.

Mark pulled his wife's hands off him and stood up. Liz continued to remonstrate but he ignored her. He put the pillow at the head of the bed and made an effort to spread the nubby tapestry coverlet over the bare mattress, but he gave it up. He asked us to give him a minute, and disappeared into the master bedroom, Liz following and becoming increasingly strident.

When Mark came back out less than five minutes later, he wore jeans and a dress shirt both so wrinkled I knew he had to have pulled them from the dirty clothes hamper and now that's what Liz was on about, the way the man was dressed. She followed after him, a pair of slacks and a clean shirt hanging off her arm. Couldn't he at least put on clean clothes? She had them right here, it would only take him a second . . . I caught her eye and put a finger to my lips. Liz froze. She stopped midsentence and pressed her lips tightly together. I watched the effort it took her to pull herself in, but slowly, she nodded.

"Let me come too, then. Can I come, Mark? I can get Mrs. Holsapple to come stay with the twins. I should be with you. You need me. Let me come with you."

Mark shook his head, but he did turn back and press his lips to her cheek. She reached up and took his face in her hands and moved his lips to hers. She held him there a moment and then released him.

"Before you go, Mark, come with me." She led him to the door of Toby and Tanner's room and pushed it open. That sweet baby-boy smell, and the night-light and the dear, dear sound of sleeping children breathing, steady and true and so alive. Mark stood in the door and took it in and then squatted between the two absurdly ornate toddler beds and laid a hand on each golden head. Liz stood behind him, her fingers resting on his shoulder. His hand drifted and he took Tanner's small, plump hand in his own, before he stood and headed to the stairs, to go out the door and get into the car to see his daughter one last time.

I'd never been to a morgue. And I didn't have a clue, when I made the suggestion, that going to see Phoebe meant driving all the way out to Galveston, more than a hour's drive away. Sugar Land doesn't have a morgue of its own, so it sends all questionable deaths to Galveston to be autopsied. And one hour is like ten when you are driving through the night with a grieving father come to see his dead child.

A morgue is not a people-friendly kind of place. I had a sweatshirt on and I was cold. Mark had come out in his dress shirt, so of course I had to give him my sweatshirt. It seemed like the only tangible way I could minister to the man, though after I did, *I* was freezing.

I'm not afraid of being dead. I am step-out-into-the-dark confident that when I leave this world, I'm going to a better one. I will know the way I'm known.

I *am* afraid of *dying*. I'm afraid of the pain and the loss of control and the myriad humiliations that go with old age and sickness. I'm afraid that I won't die well. Mainly I try not to think about it.

You can't do that in a morgue. Death is everywhere. I'm telling you, when they wheeled Phoebe out and uncovered her face, I knew I had made a mistake suggesting this trip. She just looked so much more dead than she had in Jo's room. Premises vacated. Lights out.

Gone.

———

It was the wee hours when I let myself into our home. Baby Bear padded out of my room to meet me and we each had a bowl of cereal. After Baby Bear had chased down his last Cheerio, he took a potty break in the backyard and clicked his way to my room, me on his heels.

Annie Laurie had heard me come in and was awake in our bed, curled around a sleeping Jo. Baby Bear settled down on Jo's bathrobe on the floor. Annie gestured me over, and when I bent down, she kissed my ear and breathed, "She couldn't be upstairs by herself, not even with Baby Bear. Could you sleep in Merrie's room?"

Yes, I could. I went to Merrie's room, looking at the portraits of my girls as I climbed the stairs. I want those pictures to keep going on forever. No stopping at eighteen. I want the pictures to go up and up and someday include nice young men who won't possibly be good enough, and then some kiddos to make up for the nice young men's deficiencies. I want my girls to live forever, or at least long, long after I'm gone and composting the garden.

Jo's door was shut tight. I leaned my head against the door, listening, and then jerked back. Exactly what was I listening for?

After dropping Mark back at home, Wanderley had taken a call. Once he'd hung up, Wanderley told me the team had found nothing suspicious in Jo's room. Like I needed him to tell me that. Like I didn't know my own daughter.

Okay, there may be some things about Jo I was willing to admit I might not know. But drugs? I'd know if my girl was involved with drugs. Shoot, Jo didn't even smoke. I know that for sure because when Merrie had tried smoking, it didn't matter how much mouthwash she used, you could smell it in her hair. Jo's hair falls to her waist. So I'd know if she was doing drugs.

So I told myself, anyway.

Merrie's room had the cool, foreign feel of a room that isn't being used regularly. There was a copy of Joe Hill's *Heart-Shaped Box* on the bedside table. I thought a mindless moment with a romance might soothe me to sleep.

Heart-Shaped Box is *not* a romance.

From: Walker Wells
To: Merrie Wells

Sorry about the phone call last night. I didn't mean to scare you. Call me when you get a chance. We had a bad time here last night.
I read your *Heart-Shaped Box*. I'll bet Stephen King is proud of his son. Pretty grim.

Nine

———

Annie Laurie let me sleep late. I could have slept even longer, since it was a Saturday, but Baby Bear pushed Merrie's
door open with his nose, breathed heavily into my face, and
communicated psychically that it was time we both got out on
the levee and chased some squirrels. I groaned and turned over,
but Baby Bear walked to the other side of the bed, put his front
paws on the bed so he could get right in my face and said it all
over again. I could have argued, but what was the point? Baby
Bear only understands me when I'm saying what he wants to
hear. You know, it's hard not to notice that even though *I'm* the
one who takes Baby Bear for all the gruesomely long walks and
runs a dog that size requires, it's still *Jo* who is his favorite.

Annie had left a note on the kitchen island—next to the bag
of Gina Redman's rolls, so she could be sure I would find it—
telling me that she'd taken Jo and some of her friends to the
mall for the afternoon. That meant Annie was trying to distract
Jo. It also meant that Jo had decided not to go to Saturday ballet
class, something that was happening more and more since she
hadn't made the cut at the ballet program.

I'd wanted to talk to Jo. About the drug thing. Not that I
doubted her. But because I figured she might know someone
who did that sort of thing. I could see that, that she could know
someone who sold drugs and not tell me and Annie Laurie. I'm

not sure I would have told my parents, at her age. As a matter of fact, I *know* I wouldn't have. Because I didn't.

I needed to go see the Pickersley-Smythes. As their minister. I hated that I hadn't yet touched base to see what I could do for them.

I called. The phone rang until the answering service picked up. I left my message.

Baby Bear looked at me and I looked back.

"Give me ten minutes, Baby Bear," I said. I figured I'd take care of two tasks at once, and walk Baby Bear over to the Pickersley-Smythe house.

I needed to e-mail the news about Phoebe's death to a number of people at the church so they could rally around the family. The youth ministers needed to know, and the elders; whoever was heading up the prayer committee; the Ladies' Bible Class coordinator, who would put together a food committee to provide the eternal casseroles. With Baby Bear pulling at my sneaker, and a roll in my hand, I typed a message and sent it off and then took Baby Bear out the side door to the street. He hesitated. He preferred the levee to the street, but decided not to quibble and we set off toward the Pickersley-Smythes.

It would have been a shorter walk if we had crossed through the golf course, but on a gorgeous October Saturday, it would have meant interrupting a dozen games, and golfers have killed for lesser offenses. I used the greenbelts and that cut down the walk.

Baby Bear stopped and said hello to every child and every tree we passed. The greetings were different, but they both took time, as did the kids' questions.

"What kind of dog is that?" "Does he bite?" "Can I touch him?" "Will he bite me if I touch him?" "Can I sit on him?"

"Will he bite me if I sit on him?" I always answer "yes" to the last question.

I got a new question that day: "How much did he cost?" That was a swatting offense when I was a kid, asking how much something cost. As it happened, Baby Bear was a gift, so I told the precocious mogul that Newfoundlands were free if you knew the right person. Let his folks deal with that.

There were several cars parked in front of the Pickersley-Smythes' house, and three in the circle driveway. There was a bashed and battered pickup that had been navy-blue once and was now faded to Confederate gray, and a pair of mint-condition Ford Fiestas, one lime-green and one egg-yolk yellow.

I tapped on the door.

An old woman in a pale-blue polyester pantsuit answered the door. I didn't know her but I recognized those eyes, in spite of them being swollen with unshed tears—she was the one who gave those blue eyes to Mark. And his children—all of his children.

I introduced myself and asked for Liz.

She said, "Oh," uncertainly, looking from me to Baby Bear who grinned up at her like a benign Hound of the Baskervilles. Her breeding insisted that she invite the preacher in, but most preachers weren't accompanied by huge hounds.

I said, "If you don't mind, I'll wait for Liz out here. The weather is so nice."

She didn't mind at all. I took Baby Bear off his leash so he could anoint the Pickersley-Smythe bushes.

A minute later, Liz was at the door, the Persian doing that ankle thing cats do. She put a hand out and said, "Please come in, Bear, we need you." Baby Bear romped up to see if Liz might need him, too.

"Is your yard fenced in, Liz? He's not a digger."

"It's fenced. I'll meet you around back."

Annie and I garden together; we enjoy it. Even in the worst of the summer heat, we spend several hours at it every week. But when Baby Bear and I stepped into Liz's backyard, I quickly learned that money trumps labor.

The yard was full of gorgeous magnolias, tons of the ubiquitous crape myrtles, two orange trees and a fourteen- or fifteen-foot tall mature Meyer lemon tree. I will never be able to have a Meyer lemon tree. We don't get enough sun in our yard for fruit trees. All around the pool (of course they had a pool, this is Texas—*I* don't have a pool, but . . .) were huge terracotta urns with trailing pansies, yellow and blue and white and deep maroon and those near-inky purple ones. Pansies are annuals. You have to replant them every year. They can't survive the Texas summer.

There were also banks of Knock Out roses, red and pink and coral, and pink with yellow centers. October, and they're blooming their heads off, and they'll keep blooming until we have a frost, which here on the Texas Gulf Coast isn't always a given. The Knock Out roses hardly ever even get black spot. They're so hardy, Texas has started planting them on the sides of highways.

I turned in the yard taking in the colors, the sounds of the water falling into a mini grotto, and the sweet, green fragrances and the . . . stale cigarette smoke.

There on the patio floor was a pile of butts. Someone couldn't find an old flower pot saucer? Or a jar lid? Or *something*?

Liz's voice called me back, wanting to know if I was coming in. I'd been delaying.

I made sure the gate was securely latched, told Baby Bear not to drink too much of the pool water and not, under any circumstances, to get in to the pool. I pulled out my handkerchief and gathered as much as I could of the disgusting butt pile, and went to the back door.

The Pickersley-Smythes have a huge kitchen, a good thing as it was currently full of people, sitting at the kitchen table, hovering over the range top and rinsing out coffee cups at the sink. The twins were upstairs in the playroom with Mrs. Holsapple, the woman who came in to help with the boys, Liz told me, and Mark had locked himself into his study.

Everyone went all expectant when they saw me, and I greeted the people I knew—several women from the church were laying out casseroles that had been waiting in their freezers—evidently my e-mail had gotten a fast response—and there were some pound cakes out, too—it looked like the hard-and-fast had been relaxed for this day. There were several people there I didn't know. Liz made introductions.

"This is my mother, Susan, and my sister, Sue Ellen. Mom, our minister, Walker Wells."

Susan and Sue Ellen could have been sisters instead of mother and daughter. But that was less of a compliment to the mother; in this case it meant Sue Ellen looked about as old as her mom did.

Both were big, broad women with strong features and big noses. Susan had dyed hair the color of a ripe banana. She wore a straight, navy dress that looked expensive, and she looked about as comfortable wearing it as I would have if I'd had to wear an expensive navy dress.

Sue Ellen was defiantly not dressed up, wearing a Texans jersey over jeans that fit her like panty hose. She wasn't being kind to those jeans and the jeans were getting their own back. As her mother struggled from her chair, Sue Ellen stuck her hand out for me to shake.

"Sue Ellen *Smith*," she said, rhyming the last name with "myth." She was making a point. It wasn't "Smythe" like Liz pronounced it.

"Don't get up, Mom, the preacher understands about bad feet. Don't you figure, Lizzy?"

Liz gave her sister a cool look and a cooler smile, and slipped out of the room with an excuse about checking on the boys.

I glanced down at Susan's feet. It wasn't that her feet were bad. It was that they were crammed into a pair of low-heeled black pumps—nun shoes, Merrie would have called them—that didn't fit.

After I had shaken hands and made the appropriate comments and ascertained that these were at least two of the smokers, to judge by their breath and teeth, I was led to the other end of the table where the old woman who had opened the door for me sat with two men. She was Mark's grandmother and the older man was Mark's grandfather. The other man was Jenny's father, Mitch DeWitt.

I'd guess the Pickersleys to be in their early eighties, but they hadn't been easy years. I've got eighty-year-olds in my church who travel to Estes Park, Colorado, every year and hike up to Flattop. If you've spent most of your long life working long, hard hours for small pay and fewer benefits, you won't be in the hiking crowd at eighty.

Mr. Pickersley had once been tall. He'd curled in as he aged and he was very thin now. His wisps of gray hair had been slicked straight back, and he wore a suit that had fit him when his shoulders were broader and he had stood straighter. His shirt wasn't new, and his tie was circa 1960. He had his handkerchief out and he mopped the tears from his face before gravely thanking me for taking the time to drop by.

Mitch DeWitt was a much younger man—he didn't look much over sixty. He'd lived some hard years, too. His shoulders were rangy with the kind of muscles that come from hard work in the sun, not from lifting weights at the gym. His tight, white shirt was sheer enough so that you could see the V-neck undershirt he wore beneath it and the pack of Marlboros tucked in his breast pocket. He stuck an unlit cigarette back in the pack and put a hand out to shake.

"You're the preacher, right? Phoebe died at your house, that right? You weren't even home—that's what I heard. Opened your house up to our little girl and then left her there to die all alone. I heard your daughter couldn't even be bothered to call nine-one-one like you see three-year-olds do all the time on the news, rescuing their mamas." He held on to my hand while he said this. I caught a whiff of bourbon along with the smoke and it wasn't even noon.

I got my hand back. It had gotten quiet in the kitchen. People were listening.

I said, "Phoebe did die at our house. My daughter found her and called for help." She had—she had called me. "We weren't expecting Phoebe and we didn't have any idea what kind of . . . what distress Phoebe . . ." I didn't know exactly what had happened. I let the sentence trail off, but I met DeWitt's eyes.

"I'm only saying, is all. Keeping it straight."

Keeping what straight?

"Did you know Phoebe well, Mr. Wells?" This was Mrs. Pickersley. Her unadorned face was bleak with grief, but she offered up a tremulous smile, all the same. She put her cool, bony hand upon mine and clasped my fingers. Her wrinkled skin was as soft as an old dollar bill.

I told them I hadn't known her for long.

"She was our snowdrop, Mr. Wells," said old Mr. Pickersley. "When she was a mite of a girl, her hair was as fair as dandelion fluff, her eyebrows so light you couldn't see them at all."

His wife shook her head hard and she blew her nose into a crushed tissue. "All that black hair and the holes all over her dear face—that was a disguise, Mr. Wells. That wasn't

Phoebe. She never did a thing like that 'til after her momma got sick."

"We don't want you to think that was the real Phoebe," said Mr. Pickersley. "She was grieving. You know how a long time ago, Hawaiians would knock out their teeth when someone died? Saw it in a movie. That's like what Phoebe did. Same idea. But she was still a snowdrop underneath." He picked up his mug of coffee and brought it to his mouth but set it down without tasting it. "We'd like to know who gave her those drugs, is what. Our girl had to move all the way across Houston to your fancy neighborhood here to get mixed up in drugs. Someone is not raising their kids right." He looked at me from under lowered eyebrow shrubs, not accusing, exactly, but looking for an accounting. "She was at your house and Mark tells us Phoebe and your girl had had a falling out, so—" He turned his hands palm up. "—I have to ask you, why, Mr. Wells? What drew her to your house? I don't want to think unkind thoughts, but I want to know why."

I sat down at the kitchen table and gratefully clasped the mug of coffee someone set in front of me. "Mr. Pickersley, I don't know why she came to our house. She wasn't finding drugs there. We've never had that kind of problem with either of our girls. I'm kind of wondering if she wasn't looking for my wife, Annie Laurie. The girls didn't get on too well but Annie and Phoebe did. It's been more than four months since I've seen Phoebe over at our house. The girls did have a disagreement, and, you know, there were two years between them. Jo turned fifteen in September. That makes a difference when they're this young."

Mrs. Pickersley murmured, "Three years, then."

"What?"

She said, "Phoebe turned eighteen last January. She missed so many school days, nursing her poor sick momma, that she lost a year—they made her repeat it and that was a shame because her test grades were always real good. But that didn't matter. You miss so many days of school and you got to do the year over.

"Chet, here," she patted the back of her husband's wrist, "he went on up to the school to talk to the principal but he said it was district policy and there wasn't a thing he could do about it. Said they'd sent home about twenty notices, but there wasn't anyone there except Jenny and Phoebe and Jenny was too sick to be bothered and Phoebe was determined to be there for her momma.

"We were afraid the holdback would put paid to her dreams of going to the Air Force Academy, but it turns out that should have been the very least of our worries." Phoebe had told me about the Air Force Academy, and I hadn't believed her.

Tears fell. "I wish we'd taken her in ourselves—we only have the one bedroom and Mark has this big old house and we thought it was best for her to be with her daddy—there had been some hard feelings when . . . but there never would have been drugs if she'd been living with us!"

Mr. Pickersley said, "We don't believe it, you know. That she committed suicide. That's what they're hinting around, asking those questions like was she depressed and all. But Phoebe would never have done away with herself. She was so strong. She stayed at her momma's side nearly a whole year, and she must have known it might mean they wouldn't take her at the Air Force."

"She was such a good girl," Mrs. Pickersley said. "We will never believe our snowdrop killed herself."

DeWitt had lowered himself into the chair next to me. "Not one thing went right for Phoebe after your Mark left my Jenny. Mark has brought this all down on hisself. I lost my daughter and now he's lost his, too."

Chet Pickersley gathered himself and with great dignity he said, "Mitch, you have had three wives that I know of and two of those were common-law. Constance and I won't argue with you that Mark has made some mistakes, but it won't be up to you and me to be pointing them out. We are sinners, all."

Mitch pinched the tip of his cigarette out and stuck it back in the pack he kept in his shirt pocket. Without a word, he got up and left the room.

Mr. Pickersley trumpeted his nose and wadded the hand-kerchief. "Give Mitch his due, it was hard on Phoebe when her daddy took up with Liz. But if things had been that bad, she would have come to us. She knew we would always be here for her. She knew she could count on us if things weren't working out for her here."

Mrs. Pickersley shook her head, determined to be fair. "Now, Chet, I'm not sure she would have, either. There had been a rift, you know there was. When Mark left Jenny . . . Phoebe wanted us to take a hard stand. She wanted us to cut our boy off—bring him to his senses." To me she said, "Now, we didn't approve of what all Mark and Liz got up to, but I told Phoebe, I said, 'Phoebe, in our family we don't cut people off because they don't behave the way we want them to.' It's not Christian. But I don't appreciate Mitch DeWitt coming over all holier than thou.

"He's living in that practically new trailer, too! It's a very nice trailer and Mark is still paying for the space it sits on even though he gave it to Jenny after the divorce."

A *trailer*? Another surprise. If I had it right, that meant Phoebe Pickersley had been living in a *trailer park* while her dad was living among the multi-million dollar homes of Sweetwater. See, it's not that a trailer park is such a terrible place to live—I wouldn't want to be in one during a Houston hurricane or one of our rare tornados—but you can be happy most places if you put your mind to it. It's the contrast that got to me. I had been thinking Phoebe and Jenny were living middle class; now it sounded more like borderline poverty.

"Are Mark's parents here?" I asked.

"On their way," said Mr. Pickersley. "Jimmy is working construction over in New Orleans. There's work there and he and Lou like it. Jimmy said he had to take care of some loose ends and then they'll pack up and head this way.

"They wanted Mark and Jenny to join them out there, you know. After Hurricane Katrina? There was so much construction work available, and even though Mark had been working machines for several years, he still knew his way around a construction site. Jimmy said with Mark's looks and brains, he would have made foreman in no time. Mark and Jenny and Phoebe could have hitched the old trailer to the truck and made a new start in New Orleans. Jimmy said there was plenty of work." He was silent, thinking about this lost possibility. Then he said what I knew he was thinking. "Wish he had. Might none of this happened." He shook his head in regret.

A hand topped up the still-full cup of coffee on the table in front of me, and then filled the Pickersleys' cups. Lizabeth wore a tight smile

"We sure are proud of those two little boys!" Mrs. Pickersley added hurriedly.

"We sure are!" Mr. Pickersley said.

Liz put a hand on my shoulder. "Could I have a word, Bear?"

I stood up with my cup of coffee. Susan and Sue Ellen were looking daggers at the old couple sharing the farmhouse table with them.

Liz led me to the empty study where Wanderley and I had torn Mark's life apart the night before. She gestured to a chair and after I'd sat, balancing my cup on my knee, she sat down across from me.

It had been a rough night for Liz, too. Her face looked puffy and her color wasn't good. Dark circles ringed her eyes. Her clothes were perfect, though. Tailored slacks and a neat, fitted blouse.

"You have to help us, Bear."

Before I could respond, there was a shriek from upstairs and then an avalanche of small sneakers hurrying down the stairs. The fast clip of a woman's shoes followed after.

"Doggy! Doggy!"

"Boys, stop! No! That's a strange doggy, we don't—Mrs. Pickersley-Smythe!" That had to be Mrs. Holsapple, the boys', what? Nanny?

I set my cup down and caught up to the twins right at the kitchen door.

"Hey, there, fellas, hold on and I'll introduce you." I grabbed their hands. Mrs. Holsapple appeared at my side, an attractive woman of fifty or so. I said, "Mrs. Holsapple? Sorry. I'm Walker Wells. That's Baby Bear. He's a Newfoundland and they're great with kids. He wouldn't hurt them, but come outside and I'll introduce you all."

I opened up the door and the boys screamed again, beside themselves with delight. Baby Bear saw me and lumbered out of the pool where he'd been taking a refreshing dip. Like I said, that dog only listens to me when he wants to.

The boys dragged me forward and I opened my mouth to yell "No shaking!" just as Baby Bear shook himself, liberally sprinkling us with pool water. The boys laughed their heads off.

Mrs. Holsapple didn't laugh. I made the introductions and left her to it. I hoped Liz paid her well.

I patted myself down with a dish towel and rejoined Liz in the study, making my apologies as I passed through the kitchen again.

Liz took up where she'd left off. "Mark won't come out of his study, Bear."

"What's this room?" I asked, confused.

"Why, this is the library. Mark's study is upstairs."

They had to be running out of names to call their living spaces. "He probably needs some time to himself, Liz, after last night—"

"Excuse me, Bear. What about me?" she asked, putting a hand on her collarbone. "I have all these people here and he won't even come out and say hello and listen to them tell him they're sorry for our loss!"

"Liz," I said, finally understanding her concern, "don't give it another thought. Nobody is expecting Mark to play the host. He's in pieces. No one here is going to think badly about—"

"He's in pieces? *He's* in pieces? What about *me*? This is *my* loss, too. I, I'm *very* upset that Phoebe is dead. How do you think this looks to everyone? And the boys," she added them as a second thought, "the boys are just *devastated.*"

They hadn't seemed devastated two minutes ago.

"Mark should be out here with his *family. We're* his family— me and the boys! We *need* Mark. After all I've done for him, wouldn't you think he'd have some consideration for *us*?"

I sat there, looking at her. Was Liz trying to tell me that Mark should get out of that room and come take care of *her*? She couldn't be. No one could be *that* self-centered. I must have misunderstood.

I tried again. "Liz, Mark's daughter, his sixteen . . . eighteen-year-old daughter is dead"—I found myself speaking unnaturally slowly and clearly—"and Mark has a hole in his heart that he can never fill—"

"That's nonsense," she said.

I kept going. "—that he can't ever fill and it's going to be a long time—"

"*No!*"

I said, "No what?"

Liz's eyes were filled not just with tears, but with near panic. Her reaction baffled me. She got up to sit next to me on the sofa and took my hand in both of hers. Her hands were trembling.

"We don't *have* a long time, Bear. It took me twenty-four years . . ." She closed her eyes and tears slid down her cheeks. She took a breath, wiped her eyes with her cuff and went on. "It took me twenty-four years to get Mark to notice me. Those weren't easy years. Everything you see here?" She made a head-to-toe gesture, taking in her body, her clothes. "I created all this." Her arm swept around the room. "I created all *this*. My work. My money."

I nodded. It was an accomplishment. Her mom and sister weren't anything like Liz. It was hard to believe they were related. If that was where she had come from, then Liz had traveled a long way up.

"I was . . . who I used to be . . . that was someone Mark couldn't see. It wasn't that he didn't like me—he couldn't *see* me. I have *always* loved Mark. We were *always* meant for each other—but I was invisible to him. Do you understand? I waited *so long* . . ."

There were twenty-four years of aching loneliness in those two words.

". . . to have Mark to myself and I only had him four years before that girl moved in and did everything in her power to take him away from me. And now she's dead, and even *dead*, she's taking him away from me. I won't allow it, Bear. I can't wait another *long time* for him to come around." She shook her head. She sniffed, blinked, and with an effort, brought back her CEO persona, the one I was used to.

"Now, I know he's sad and all that, but he has two *perfect* boys to make up for that disturbed girl who didn't have a grateful bone in her body."

I tried to stop her. "Liz—"

"No. That sounds harsh, but that girl was hell-bent on destroying what I . . . what Mark and I had created here. You know she did, Bear."

Liz waited for me to acknowledge what she had said.

What Liz said was true. Phoebe *had* wanted to destroy what Liz had with Mark.

Ten

I stared at the woman who sat across from me. Yes. Phoebe had wanted to tear down Liz's world. Because the way Phoebe saw it, Liz had torn down Phoebe's.

"You know I'm right, Bear. Now, Mark needs to be a man, and come down here—"

"Liz—"

"—and thank my mother and sister for making the drive, and tell his grand—"

"*Liz*—" I put the untasted coffee down.

"—parents that if they don't stop insulting me in my own house—my house that I bought with my money and no help *ever* from *anyone*—" The tears were back and Liz didn't wipe them away this time. "—then Hell will freeze rock solid right down to the ninth circle before they see Toby and Tanner again. I want you to go get Mark out of there—his grandfather is useless. I've asked him five times and he won't do a *thing*."

I slapped my hands on my thighs and stood up. "All right."

"You'll go get him out of there?"

"I'll go talk to him." I started for the hall.

"Good. I'm going to go get a hammer and chisel in case you need to take the door off its hinges." She headed toward the garage. Was she for real?

"I don't need a hammer and chisel," I said.

"I don't think you can get the door off its hinges without a hammer and chisel," she called over her shoulder.

"I'm not taking the door off its hinges, Liz!"

"I'll put them at the foot of the stairs just in case you change your mind."

Halfway up the stairs I stopped and went back down to the kitchen. "Mr. Pickersley, will you come with me?" I asked Mark's grandfather.

"I am not taking that door off its hinges, Mr. Wells."

"Me, either."

"No?"

"No."

"I will!" said Sue Ellen, holding a highball of ice and something golden that I would have bet was not apple juice. Clearly, we had moved on from coffee.

"Sit down!" said Mr. Pickersley and her mother. And me.

Mr. Pickersley scooted his chair back and got to his feet. He kissed his wife's forehead and she patted the hand on her shoulder. "Tell him his grammy loves him," she whispered.

"I will, Constance, and he knows it."

We climbed the stairs together. I said, "Are you praying people, Mr. Pickersley?"

"We are."

"This is a good time to start praying, then."

"Do you think we've stopped since hearing this news?"

Good. I felt fortified.

The boys' door was open. The master bedroom door was open. I tried a handle and it opened onto a closet filled with out-of-season clothes, including a full-length fur. Mr. Pickersley looked at me.

"Down here," he said, and followed the hall down to a spiral staircase.

We climbed the twisty metal staircase to a small landing.

"He's got a bathroom in there. A small fridge, too. I figure he can stay there awhile."

"Good," I said.

"You want to pray out loud?" he asked me.

"You say it," I said. Liz was a terribly unhappy woman, and I felt for her. She'd had a hard time getting to where she was and I admired the work she had put into it. Nevertheless, I was having un-Christian thoughts about Lizabeth Pickersley-Smythe. It might be better if the prayer came from Mr. Pickersley.

Mr. Pickersley got down on his knees. There was hardly any room on the tiny landing, but I got on mine, too. My knees cracked but not Mr. Pickersley's, who had to be thirty years older than I am. Part of the price I paid for playing college ball. He blew his nose in his handkerchief before beginning.

"Our Holy Father, You know the pain my grandson is in. You know he's made some mistakes, but that's no reason to forget the boy. I know You've got our girl there with You. I know she's fine in Your care, but we're all broken up down here. Now, Mark is in a fix, and I'll tell You straight, Lord, I don't see how he can make the way clear. He's going to need You with him every step of the way. I'm counting on You. You and me, we've always been good together, right? So I'm calling You on that Psalm one-oh-three. 'Their children's children.' That means Mark, Lord. Don't let me down. In Jesus' name, amen."

Psalm 103 is where God promises His love is with those who fear Him, and his righteousness with their children's children.

I said, "Amen."

From inside the study we heard a faint, "Amen."

Mr. Pickersley used the banister to get back on his feet.

I leaned against the door and said, "How ya doin', Mark?"

A raspy chuckle. "Not so good, Bear. My daughter is . . . Phoebe is gone. And I'm married to a hellhound from Mars."

"Umm, I think that's Venus, Mark."

"No, Bear, this one is from Mars."

"Ahh."

"Yeah."

"Well, she's certainly not at her best right now."

Another laugh.

Neither of us said anything for a minute.

"Granddad?"

"Yes, son."

"I didn't do a very good job, Granddad." Mark's voice caught.

Mr. Pickersley mopped his eyes. "We know it, son. We love you anyway. Grammy said to make sure you know she loves you."

More silence.

"Bear, did Liz send you up here to make me get out?"

"She's pretty exercised about it."

"Do you think I should come down?"

"Heck, no. I'd stay in there as long as I could, if I were you. Best place for you. The twins are fine. I don't think they understand what has happened. Can I bring you anything?"

"No. If I need something, Granddad will get it for me."

"Yes, I will," Mr. Pickersley said.

"Is there anything I can do, Mark?" I asked.

"That Detective Wanderley is a friend of yours, isn't he?"

"Well . . . sort of. We have a relationship."

"Do you know why my daughter died, Bear?"

"I think it will be Monday or Tuesday before we hear anything, Mark, and I know Wanderley will call you first. He won't call me."

"Not how. I meant do you know *why* she died?"

Ahh. "No, Mark."

Long silence.

"Thanks for coming, Bear. I'll call you if I need you. Would you go now and let me have a minute with Granddad?"

"I'm on my way. God be with you, Mark. You're in my prayers."

I was nearly to the bottom of the stairs when I heard the doorknob turn and the door open.

"Granddad?"

If Mark wasn't in the arms of his Lord, he was at least in the arms of God's emissary.

————————

After nearly tripping over the hammer and chisel that had been left smack-dab in the middle of the bottom stair, I walked into the kitchen to hear, "Why can't I have that trailer, now? It's not like you or Mark would be caught dead in a trailer, and *Phoebe* has obviously decided she won't need it for *her* plans anymore—"

That was Sue Ellen haranguing Lizabeth. They saw me standing there. I'm hard to miss at six three. But they didn't seem embarrassed to have me in on this argument.

Constance Pickersley had gone off somewhere and the rest of the crowd was gathered around the sink or scattered about the house. Liz's mother Susan had backed a kitchen chair into a corner and had it tilted back onto two legs. Her own legs were splayed, an ankle twisted around the chair rung. Susan had joined Sue Ellen in the pre-lunch tipple but was not engaging in the conversation. The too-tight pumps had been abandoned under the kitchen table.

"Did you just hear me say Phoebe's grandfather is living in that trailer?" said Liz. "Can't you at least wait until after the funeral? And I guess you know you're asking me to make you a gift of thirty-four thousand dollars, because that's what that

trailer cost me—that's what it cost me to get Jenny to quit dragging her feet about the divorce. I should be glad that's all it cost
me. There are a couple of trailers in that park that would sell
for more than seventy. What if one of those had come up for
sale?"

"Sure, it's all about you and your needs, 'What's it gonna look
like? What'll people say?'" Sue Ellen mocked. "It's not enough
you live the 'lifestyle of the rich and famous,' you got to hang on
to every measly nickel you ever—"

"Earned. That's the word you were looking for, Sue Ellen. I
earned every nickel I have and God knows no one lifted a finger
to help me—"

"I don't need your help. I don't even want your filthy money.
I don't want a penny of it. I only want that old trashy trailer you
don't have any use at all for, and then a little help getting it
outfitted so I can start grooming dogs professionally, but you
can't bear the idea of someone else being successful, so—"

"You don't want, you don't want—who is making the pay-
ments on that brand-new Ford Fiesta? That wouldn't be me and
my filthy money?" Liz swung around on her mother. "And what
about yours?"

Susan belched loudly and with as little self-consciousness as
a child, caught her youngest daughter's eyes on her and struggled to get all four legs of the chair back on the floor. She belat-
edly covered her mouth and said, "Beg pardon," as she refilled
her glass from the bottle of Johnnie Walker Black that sat on the
kitchen table (neat, no ice). Susan put one hand up but kept
the other securely clasped around her full glass. "You girls settle your squabbles on your own—don't drag me into it."

Mitch slouched in. He had a chicken-eating-hound look on
his face—one part guilty, two parts satisfied. I didn't know what
was coming but I didn't want to share the moment with Liz and
her family.

"Liz? I'm going to—"

"Heard you talking about that trailer," said Mitch DeWitt. "What're you going to be doing with it? Well, you don't need to bother about that. It's mine, now. Phoebe left it to me." He picked up a glass, walked to the table and poured himself three fingers of scotch. He took a long drink.

Liz stared at him. Sue Ellen put her scotch on the table with a thump, thrust her shoulders back and her chin forward and got close enough to Mitch's face that if she'd been a man, he would have been obliged to knock her down.

"How do you work that out?"

I said, "Liz—"

"You heard what your sister said. She gave it to Jenny as some sort of measly compensation for breaking up a happy home—"

Liz said, "Happy home?"

"—and Jenny left it to Phoebe and Phoebe left it to me."

Sue Ellen turned an outraged face to her sister. "Can she do that?"

Liz ignored her sister, walked over to the window overlooking the backyard and stood there, watching Baby Bear romp with her sons, with Mrs. Canning and Constance Pickersley watching on. DeWitt shifted his weight but didn't budge. Liz said, her back to us, "You're telling me Phoebe made a will?"

DeWitt said, "She did." Levelly.

Still facing the window Liz said, "And she left what she had to you? Not her dad? Not her little brothers? I guess you get the insurance money, too?"

"You'd be guessing right." You could practically see the feathers around his mouth.

"Hah!" It was a bark of laughter. Liz spun around and her mouth was as thin-lipped as a cat's. "I knew it. That girl had no more feeling for him than her mother did. You know what? I'm not sorry for any of it. You can have that trailer, Mitch DeWitt. And you can get your butt out of my kitchen and out of my house. I don't want to see you ever again. Don't come to the funeral, not unless you want to pay for it yourself. You won't be welcome."

DeWitt tossed back the rest of his drink, set the glass down hard on the countertop. He paused at the door.

"I'll be at my granddaughter's funeral. You see if I won't." And exit stage right.

"You're busy," I said to Liz. "We'll talk later. I'm just going to slip out so y'all can—"

Liz swiveled around to me like a gunner in a turret. "So where is he?"

I said, "Liz, Mark needs some more time alone. He'll—"

She put her hands on her hips and advanced on me. "You go back up there and tell Mark—"

She was two inches from my nose, which was about a foot and a half too close. I *know* what I *should* have done. I *should* have backed down. What I *did* do was to put my index finger on her nose and push, the tiniest little bit.

I said, "Back off, Lizabeth. You aren't my mother and I'm not five years old. If you'll take the time to notice, you'll find that Mark isn't five years old, either. He'll come out when he's ready to. Right now it's all about what Mark needs, Liz. It's not about you."

Liz's mouth fell open.

I hesitated. "Liz, I know you're hurting. I know you need Mark, and if you'll be patient, he'll be there for you. But give him some time, okay?"

I gave her shoulders a squeeze and stepped around her. "It was a pleasure to meet you, Mrs. Smythe, Miss Smythe," I lied.

"It's 'Smith,'" hissed Sue Ellen.

Whatever.

I was halfway out the back door when Lizabeth said, "I hope you don't think *you'll* be doing the funeral, *Mr. Wells*." She said my name like she was spitting a curse.

Outside, Mrs. Pickersley was sitting next to Mrs. Holsapple, watching the twins play with Baby Bear.

"He's very good with children, Mr. Wells," said Mrs. Holsapple. I agreed that he was. Newfoundlands are famously agreeable with both people and other animals. They were bred as rescue dogs, not hunting dogs.

"We'll see you at the funeral, Mr. Wells," said an exhausted-looking Mrs. Pickersley, and I agreed that she would—even if I wouldn't be handling the funeral, I'd certainly be attending it.

The twins howled when I whistled for Baby Bear but he was glad for the reprieve. I rewarded him for the babysitting as soon as I could by getting us on to the levee where he could romp without cutting through the golf course.

Eleven

We got in a good walk, Baby Bear going twice as far as I did, what with his squirrel-chasing diversions. Houston is beautiful in October. The heat is over and you can expect most days to be clear and relatively humidity-free. We arrived home both feeling better, me for the fresh air blowing all that Pickersley-Smythe unhappiness away, and Baby Bear for having put the fear of the Newfoundland into the fuzzy-tailed scourge.

Rebecca Rutland, my secretary, called my cell as I was wiping down Baby Bear's paws and asked if there was any way we could watch her two beloved pug dogs, just for the night. She was meeting a friend in Galveston. The trip was an unexpected one, and Rebecca hadn't been able to find a hotel room where the pugs were welcome.

I interrupted her to tell her about Phoebe, and after Rebecca had said all the sad things you say in a situation like this, she said to never mind, the friend would understand and—but I interrupted again. That woman does favors for me every day of the week. She has transported Baby Bear to and from the kennel for us a number of times. And both those pugs together don't weigh half what Baby Bear does. How much trouble could they be?

Besides, I thought, pugs are naturally clownish, funny and

unpredictable and they would be great for taking Jo's mind off last night. I said I'd check with Annie and get right back to her.

I met Rebecca at her house for the pug handoff. The pugs were four-year-old Tommy (short for Tommy Lee Jones because the actor is "so ugly he's good-looking"—"I mean, Bear, that man would be a nice place to visit, but you wouldn't want to have his babies, would you?" Seeing as I did not want to have Tommy Lee Jones's babies, I agreed and tried not to examine too closely exactly what the statement said about my secretary), and eight-year-old Mr. Wiggles (there was a long, involved story about why he's named Mr. Wiggles, but I stopped listening). Tommy and Mr. Wiggles were sitting on Rebecca's front porch swing, wearing identical green harnesses and French-print bandanas around their fat necks.

Rebecca handed me a ream of printed papers with a cover sheet titled, "How To Take Care Of Tommy and Mr. Wiggles," and a big, plastic cat-litter carton that was full of their special dog food. After I stored those items in the backseat, Rebecca also gave me a shopping bag filled with dog toys, chicken jerky, very special feeding and water bowls (a total of six because I "might want to put a set in several rooms—the boys feel more secure when they don't have to walk too far for their food") and two paw-printed fleece blankets, along with a miscellany of other things I didn't discover until I got home. Last were four dog beds, two large denim pillows and two nice-sized beanbags covered in creamy-colored faux fur. The denim pillows, according to Rebecca, were for the kitchen so the pugs could watch me and Annie cook ("They're very interested in food preparation, Bear, it's a pug trait") and the furry beanbags were for our bedroom. I paused mid-stow and drew myself out of the backseat to look at Rebecca.

"Rebecca, they'll sleep in the kitchen, okay?"

Rebecca hesitated and then said, "Whatever works for y'all," and smiled at me.

I stared at her for a moment, but gave up trying to interpret that smile.

In spite of the cool October weather, the pugs had gotten themselves worked up. They were panting like steam engines, so I got the air conditioner cranked while Rebecca fussed over her bug-eyed porkers. She finally shut the passenger door and made her way around the car to my side, motioning me to un-roll my window.

Rebecca stooped to lean her elbows on my window and look at me searchingly.

"Bear?"

"Yes, Rebecca."

"I know you don't take my boys all that seriously."

"Oh, now, Rebecca, I do too . . ."

"But you know how you feel about that horse you call Baby Bear?"

I said I did.

"And you know how you said Baby Bear maybe saved Jo's life when all that mess happened and you got yourself shot?"

I did not get myself shot, someone shot me, but I nodded yes.

"Mr. Wiggles, the old one? I got him as just a five-pound puppy when Craig divorced me. I don't know if Mr. Wiggles saved my life, but he made me feel like I had a reason to live again. Mr. Wiggles always thinks I'm beautiful and he's always glad to see me. So maybe he did save my life. And Tommy? I got Tommy when Craig married that girl half his age and had the baby he'd never given me. These two boys are all the family I have to come home to after work, and when I'm sad or lonely, they . . ." She started to tear up. "Oh, Bear, I didn't mean to cry."

I said, "I'm going to take good care of your dogs for you, Rebecca."

"Okay then, that's fine." She patted the roof of my car.

The pugs looked at me with their pop-eyes and I again promised Rebecca very sincerely that I would take very good care of her boys. As I pulled away from the curb, I quickly real ized that the pug breed is not the Einstein of the dog world, because even though those two dogs had watched me pack all their worldly belongings into the back of the car, even though they had suffered themselves to be put into the front seat of my car, and even though Rebecca had kissed and hugged them, wept over them and told them good-bye for a wearying amount of time, it wasn't until I pulled away from the curb that they realized they were going away, and Rebecca wasn't coming with them.

Oh. My. Gosh.

Both pugs catapulted their top-heavy frames at the passenger window, screaming—I'm not lying, the noise they were emitting could only be described as a scream—screaming at a note that really should be too high for human ears, and pawing frantically at the window until one of the little wretches must have stepped on the window control because the window silently unrolled and had I not glanced over to discover why cool air was pouring into the car, had I not retained the lightning-fast reflexes that made me a starter on the University of Texas football team some years ago, had I not managed to grab the harnesses of those two insane lapdogs, I would have been responsible for the demise of Rebecca's entire doggy family two minutes after I'd picked them up.

I hadn't even had time to get off her block.

With a knee on the steering wheel, a hand searching my armrest for the window control and the child-lock feature and another hand grappling with Rebecca's insane doggy progeny, I turned the corner and was out of sight before the still-waving Rebecca could realize the near miss.

Based on the last three minutes, there was every indication that this was going to be a looooong, long two days.

———

After ten minutes of that awful noise, the pugs stopped screeching at the same moment, like they had come to a unanimous decision that it was time to stop. They stood looking out the window another forlorn minute and then turned their bodies to face me. I assured them that Rebecca would be back soon and that we would have fun this weekend. Evidently, that was an invitation to get better acquainted. Tommy stepped over the console and settled himself on my left thigh. I tried to ward him off but he persisted and I gave up. Mr. Wiggles then picked his way over and settled on my right thigh, adding a good twenty-five pounds of pressure to the gas pedal. I didn't protest.

My cell buzzed to let me know I had a text. Knowing very well that I shouldn't—texting and driving is a dumb thing to do, even if you're just reading not texting—I glanced at my phone. It was from Michael Edwin, a church member who acts as general contractor any time the church is having a general contractor-like need. Michael was hoping I'd meet him at the church to take a look at some carpet he'd picked out for the youth room. I couldn't have cared less what carpet was chosen to replace the tattered and stained carpet we had, but Michael gives his time free to the church in spite of having a demanding job that requires him to fly all over the country to oversee the building of sports stadiums and multiplexes, and I feel it's only right to act like I know a thing or two about whatever it is he brings to my attention.

It didn't make sense to keep Michael waiting while I drove the dogs to the house and got them settled, so I went straight on to the church. I had the sense to rummage around in their luggage until I found their leashes, and I had them firmly in check before I opened the car door.

The pugs came along all cheerful and friendly and as if they had never known a Rebecca Rutland, much less mourned for her not twenty minutes ago. They were excited about the new sights and smells, and they took time to anoint each and every shrub we passed, which delayed us some, but since I was taking them inside the building I was glad to have them divest themselves of any extra liquid they were carrying around.

Michael was waiting for me in the youth room and had to hide a smile when he saw me with the two dandies. They do have kind of a fancy-lad walk. "Bear! New companions! Love the matching bandanas—we need to get one for you, too."

"They're Rebecca's. We're watching them for the weekend but I didn't want to keep you waiting while I—"

"Don't explain! A man has a right to his softer side. Listen, take a look at this."

Michael unfurled a four-by-four-foot sample of carpet on the floor. The label in the corner informed me that it was greige, a beige/gray mixture that looks like wet cement.

"You like the color?" I asked Michael.

He glanced up from stroking the carpet like it was the pelt of a dead animal.

"What I like, Bear, is the hardiness of this high-traffic carpet. This carpet can take anything without staining—you drop a Dr Pepper on this carpet? Blot it up and nothing, not a sign of a stain. Ditto coffee and tea, and those two, those are problem liquids, carpet-wise . . ."

Tommy and Mr. Wiggles were inspecting the sample, sniffing up the faintly chemical smell like a couple of glue addicts. Tommy tested the ply with his paws, first just one, then all four, walking gingerly on the spongy stuff.

"In the showroom," Michael continued, "they take a full can of Coke and have you pour it over the carpet—then they take a wad of paper towel and . . ."

Tommy delicately lifted a hind leg and urinated gushingly on the carpet sample. I don't know where he came up with the liquid—he really had paid attention to every shrub in the churchyard.

Michael and I looked at the rotund beast who was now smelling his own discharge.

I said, "How's it do with pug pee?"

Michael stood hands on hips looking at the puddle that was, credit to the carpet manufacturer, beading on top of the carpet and not being discernibly absorbed.

"I don't know, Preacher. Go get us a roll of paper towels and let's find out."

———————

Neither pug was the least bit chagrined by the episode at the church. They sashayed back to my car and waited on the passenger seat for me to buckle up, then insinuated themselves back on my lap.

When I pulled into the garage, I could hear Baby Bear's joyous greeting through the kitchen door, but I didn't make immediate introductions. I put both pugs on their leashes and led them to the front yard where they squirted everything in sight except my legs. Baby Bear had followed our progress from the inside of the house and was now watching us narrowly from the dining room window. He didn't look happy.

After I was as sure as I could be that every last drop had been squeezed out, and I could safely introduce a distraction, I unlocked the front door and let Baby Bear out.

Baby Bear was on the lawn with one bound. Then he stood stock-still. The pugs looked at the Newfie. The Newfie looked at the pugs. There was a cautious advance on both sides, accompanied by a great deal of the sniffing of hindquarters. That done, Mr. Wiggles walked off and sat down on some purple and gold pansies Annie had recently planted. He yawned. Tommy placed himself right in front of Baby Bear and dropped his forequarters to the ground, leaving his bottom and ridiculous curled tail up in the air in what was clearly meant as an invitation to play.

Baby Bear still has a lot of puppy in him—he adopted the same stance, and the game was on. It was sad to watch. Baby Bear is fast. He is. For a big dog, he can make tracks. I guarantee you that on a long run, Baby Bear would leave Tommy snorting in the dust. But for maneuverability—well, Tommy weighed 25 pounds to Baby Bear's 180. It was like pitting a Mini Cooper against a Mack truck: the Mini Cooper has go-kart handling, and so does Tommy. Tommy literally ran circles around Baby Bear, and then expanded the circles into figure eights so that I was included in the game, too. Baby Bear couldn't even track Tommy with his eyes, Tommy was that fast.

It was a good workout for both dogs. When I opened the front door, Mr. Wiggles rose from the crushed pansies and entered just behind Baby Bear and Tommy. All three followed me to the kitchen and while I unloaded all the pug stuff from my car, they fought over Baby Bear's water bowl. Baby Bear lost again, but I filled a mixing bowl with water and set it up on the window seat where only Baby Bear could reach it. He sucked down half of it before he raised his dripping muzzle. He sank to his haunches and watched the two pugs, their front feet planted inside Baby Bear's regular water dish, drain it to the bottom. He looked happy. It must have been like having cousins come for a stay.

I took a shower with an audience, Baby Bear and the pugs sitting outside the stall watching in interest, and had toweled my head dry when I heard the doorbell. I grabbed a robe and went to the door. I opened the door to Detective James Wanderley, and Baby Bear gave the detective his best doggy greeting—it's too enthusiastic for most people. Tommy and Mr. Wiggles added their noise, too.

"Can I come in?" Wanderley asked.

I stepped back, thinking that's what the little girl vampire had said in *Let the Right One In*, and that hadn't turned out well for anyone involved.

"There's coffee in the kitchen," I told him. "Help yourself while I finish getting dressed."

When I got back, Wanderley was sitting in my chair sipping from a giant mug that said BIG BOSS that was clearly mine, but I didn't make a fuss. I poured myself a cup, which was still good even though it had been in a thermos since Annie Laurie and Jo had left, and added real half and half. None of that powdered awfulness.

I removed the pugs from the couch and sat down. Baby Bear was attempting to mouth one of Wanderley's immaculate cowboy-booted feet.

"What is your dog doing?"

"He's inviting you to play Steal the Sneaker but he can't find a shoelace or an edge to get ahold of." Baby Bear had given up looking for a handle and had gently clamped his teeth around Wanderley's ankle. Wanderley said, "No!" so loudly and emphatically that Baby Bear released him at once and scurried over to my side looking frightened and wounded. In league with Baby Bear, Tommy ran over to Wanderley and tried a stare down. Wanderley didn't notice.

"I don't mind the dog slobber so much, Bear, but I don't want my boots scratched." Wanderley pulled out a handkerchief and polished the offended boot. One of his grandfather's, I surmised, knowing that Wanderley had a whole collection of vintage cowboy boots left to him by his grandfather. They're all beautiful and he takes good care of them.

He said, "You're keeping Rebecca's pugs?"

"How'd you know they were Rebecca's?"

"We keep in touch. Talk books sometimes. I like her."

"I understand." I sipped my coffee. "So, do you know how Phoebe died yet?"

"No. We're pretty sure, but there hasn't been an autopsy yet."

"Do you think it was drugs?"

"We know she didn't get shot or bashed over the head or stabbed."

"So you've narrowed things down quite a bit," I said. I got a sour look.

"Is Jo here?"

I put my coffee cup down. I didn't slam it down. There's glass over the wood so it makes a lot of noise, that's all. "Wanderley, you can't really think Jo had anything to do with this."

His eyes didn't waver. "Bear, your daughter was the first person here when Phoebe Pickersley was dead or dying. I want to talk to her. If you feel like there's something to protect Jo from, if you're afraid she might incriminate herself, call a lawyer. He'll sit in on the interview and listen to me ask my very reasonable questions and then he'll send you a bill for five to seven hundred dollars." He gave a shrug to let me know how he didn't care one way or another—he was going to talk to Jo.

"She's out with her mom," I said. "You could have called and I'd have told you."

"I was in the area."

Okay. We drank our coffee for a while.

"Pretty tough last night, huh?"

I agreed that it had been, but told him this morning had not been any more fun. I gave him a rundown of the morning's events. Wanderley listened carefully and grunted when I finished.

"One big happy family over there, huh? I feel for the girl, though it would have been smarter and braver to strike out on her own instead of offing herself, if that's what she did."

Wanderley finished his coffee and set it down. He took out a guitar pick and popped it in his mouth the way another man would have a breath mint. He folded a leg over a knee and clasped the shank of his boot with one hand. "I don't like this. Last night felt wrong. Phoebe Pickersley won't be my first teen suicide by a long shot. It happens. But last night felt . . ." He struggled for the word. ". . . off. Something is off about this one." He pulled the pick out of his mouth and fiddled with it.

Baby Bear jumped up on the couch. Like I was going to miss a 180-pound beast making himself comfortable. I shoved him back down and he nosed the pugs away to make room for himself at my feet.

"Did you notice the stepmom last night?" Wanderley said. He was quiet for a while. "Does Annie wear makeup to bed?"

"Why do you want to know what Annie wears to bed?"

Wanderley grimaced. "Don't be a perv. Does she?"

"No she doesn't wear makeup to bed. We sleep in the dark, so what would be the point?"

"The point is that Lizabeth Pickersley-Smythe was made-up last night. Her hair was brushed and she had makeup on and it wasn't smudged as though she'd left some of it on a pillow-case."

"Okay . . ."

"But the big thing for me is, she never asked what had happened."

"What?"

"Mark went straight to Phoebe's room, he's screaming his head off, and there's an appreciable passage of time before Lizabeth joined him. The kids were there. You and I were there. And then Lizabeth appears, all tidy and hair brushed and makeup on, and her husband and kids are screaming, and she never says, 'What the hell happened?' Did you hear her ask?"

No, reviewing the evening, I didn't remember Liz asking what had happened.

"Yeah, but Wanderley, Mark was screaming Phoebe's name. She knew it had to be Phoebe."

"Phoebe what? Phoebe had a car accident? Phoebe's in the hospital, or in jail, or joined the army, or got pregnant by a biker? The stepmom didn't ask. I don't like it. And we couldn't find Phoebe's phone. It wasn't with her clothes in Jo's room, or in her purse, it wasn't in her car—"

"Phoebe has her own car?" She hadn't, the last time I'd seen her.

"Of course she has her own car. She's over sixteen and she lives in First Colony. Everybody there over sixteen has a car. And if you live in Sweetwater, your *dog* has a car."

Baby Bear's ears pricked up but I told him to forget it.

"There's no phone in her room. We'd very much like to have that phone. And there's no letter. No last words. No message. Teenage girls *always* leave a message. They leave long, dramatic, romantic messages. They like to imagine the letters being read out loud, all their loved ones sobbing. But not Phoebe. No letter. Except for a cryptic message on Facebook, there was nothing."

"What was the post?"

"Around eight last night, Phoebe Pickersley wrote 'A mercy.'"

"Is that all?"

Wanderley nodded.

"What's that supposed to mean?"

Wanderley looked like his patience was being tried. "Bear? You know what 'cryptic' means?"

I ignored the taunt. "You checked everywhere?"

"What? Yes, we checked everywhere, Bear, we're detectives. We detect. What do you think? Did we look everywhere—hah. Except for those two words on Facebook, she didn't tweet, no mystery e-mails."

"Okay. It was a stupid question."

"Yes, it was a stupid question."

"Okay, then. Settle down. Climb off your high horse, cowboy. I get why you don't like the situation. But Phoebe didn't look like she'd been attacked. There was no overturned furniture, nothing like that when we got home. We didn't touch anything except for Phoebe."

"Oh, yeah, and can we talk about that for a minute?" Wanderley got up, still talking. He went into the kitchen and got himself some ice water. It's interesting how at home he makes himself in my house. Not that it's a problem. "What were you *thinking* moving that girl? Don't you watch television? Your *dog* knows better than to move a dead body. The sandwich you had for *lunch* yesterday knows better than to move a dead body. The nutrias in the *levee*—"

"You want to rein that in, cowboy?"

"And what the hell is with all the 'cowboy' talk? It's getting on my nerves."

He'd started it the night before, telling me to "cowboy up," but I told him okay. "Annie Laurie and I got a text from Jo telling us to come home and we come home to find our daughter on the floor, holding a girl who is clearly dead. What did you want us to say, 'Don't move a muscle, Jo, we don't want to corrupt the scene'? Maybe that's what you would do if it had been a fifteen-year-old Molly."

"Watch it, Bear."

"It's a legitimate point."

"I took it, Bear. I don't want to talk about Molly in this context."

"No? Well I don't want to talk about *Jo* in this context. I don't want her a part of this. I want this to never have happened. How is she ever going to sleep in her room again? *I* don't want to sleep in that room!"

Wanderley nodded. "I hear you. I'm sorry." He crunched on his ice, the sound of which had the pugs lined up at his feet, looking at him expectantly.

"I'll tell you what I know," I said, "about the Pickersley-Smythes. Do you want only what I know firsthand, or do you want what I've heard, too?"

"Everything, Bear. Every rumor, every bit of gossip, the hearsay, the scuttlebutt, and what the pot told the pan. Start with Liz and Phoebe. Not that I'm on about the wicked stepmother—stepfathers are the lethal ones. But tell me how the two of them got on. Did Liz welcome the addition of a new stepdaughter?"

"That's going to be a no. Liz tries hard at the happy family picture—Phoebe didn't fit in that picture and she didn't have any interest in trying to."

I went on and told Wanderley about Liz's frustration with Phoebe—the conversation we'd had months ago in the church hall. I told him about how shortly after that conversation, Phoebe had made a visit to my office, wanting a "private" consultation. And how, when she learned that the consultation could be no more private than what could be managed either with Rebecca present or in an all-glass conference room, she left in a huff. I added the story of the New Braunfels overnighter and the subsequent scene with the elders. I told him about Phoebe accusing Liz of trapping her dad into marriage. I told him about Liz slapping Phoebe. Everything I could think of, I told him.

He listened carefully, even after Mr. Wiggles began a loud, cement-grinding snore.

"After that scene with the elders—you're telling me the Pickersley-Smythes kept coming to your church?"

"Yep. Not Phoebe but Liz and Mark and the boys did."

Wanderley whistled. I'd been surprised, too. *I* had been humiliated by the scene and no one had called *me* a slut.

"That Lizabeth Pickersley-Smythe is one ballsy woman, Bear."

I agreed that she was. I would never have told Wanderley if it hadn't been for Phoebe's death and the questions he was asking. Neither the elders nor the youth ministers would have dreamed of discussing the particulars with anyone who hadn't been at the meeting. So if Liz was assuming we wouldn't have spread the story around, she was assuming correctly. But it would have been nearly impossible for Liz to come to church and not bump into at least one of us who had been there. I don't know what went down with the others, but when she next met me, she acted as if nothing untoward had ever passed between us. I, on the other hand, blushed so deeply I could feel it in my hair follicles though I kept my preacher smile on and shook hands with Mark and Liz and asked about Phoebe who, they told me, was home with a cold.

Wanderley asked, "What happened between Jo and Phoebe?"

"They had a fight, is all. They're girls. Girls fight."

Wanderley let the silence go on long enough to make me uncomfortable. I knew what he was doing. I wasn't going to fall for it.

Tommy added his own whiffling snore to Mr. Wiggles's. Baby Bear paddled in his sleep.

"What?" I said. "You want me to tell you the whole fight?"

"Please."

I told him. "The last time Phoebe was our guest, Jo was not her most welcoming. Phoebe left on bad terms and Annie Laurie and I couldn't get Jo to apologize."

Wanderley gave a snort through his nose. "Why not?"

"We said surely she was sorry that she had hurt Phoebe's feelings, and she said she wasn't. But a little while after that, Phoebe asked Jo to go to the movies and spend the night. Jo felt manipulated into accepting but she did anyway. Turned out it was payback."

"Can I have one of those rolls in the kitchen?" Wanderley indicated the bag with Gina Redman's homemade rolls.

I said he could, and he found the butter, got himself a plate and made himself a pile of butter and roll sandwiches. He poured himself a glass of milk and settled back into my chair. At the sight of food, the pugs were instantly awake and on full alert.

"Go on," he said.

"That's it. That's why they weren't friends anymore."

"The payback. That part. How did Phoebe pay Jo back?"

"You're making too big a deal out of it, Wanderley. Sometimes girls fall out with each other."

Wanderley sat up straight, briefly losing control of his plate and tipping one roll to the ground. The pugs were on it like red-bellied piranha. Before Baby Bear could so much as raise his head, that roll was a memory. "Listen. Here's what I can't get around, Bear. You tell me, and Jo tells me, that Jo and Phoebe weren't friends, hadn't been friends for months—that's a long time when you're a kid. But last night Phoebe was in your house. This is where she died. And Jo was with her, either right before or right after she died. I'm trying to understand that. That's why you're getting the questions." Tommy stood on his hind legs to see if Wanderley had any more rolls that could be persuaded onto the floor. The detective held his plate up higher.

"So could you tell me how Phoebe worked her 'payback'?"

I told him all about Jo's terrible night—about Phoebe humiliating Jo and implying that I had hit on her, and the blender drink and making her look young in front of Alex . . . I gave him the whole blow-by-blow. Took about half an hour.

Wanderley heard me out, fingers steepled between his thighs.

"Let me tell you how I would have told that story," he said when I was finished. "I'd've said, 'Phoebe claimed I hit on her and Jo gave Phoebe a smack in the face and that was the end of the friendship.'"

I thought on that. "I gave you more than you needed?"

Wanderley stood up and held his thumb and forefinger out, an inch apart. "A leetle bit more."

"Okay."

We shook hands and I got the door for him. As he stepped out he handed me a baby-blue envelope with a princess sticker keeping the flap closed.

"Party invitation," he said, and he was off.

I'd forgotten about Molly's third birthday party. I slid my thumb under the flap and pulled the invitation out. Next to a pretty princess in a green-and-white dress were the words, "Come be a princess for a day!" Inside were the details. It would be held at the Heights Playground in Donovan Park, from ten in the morning until twelve thirty on Saturday, October twenty-seventh. There was a number to call "Chloe" to RSVP. The specifics were written in a beautiful script. That would be Chloe's handwriting, I guessed. Underneath, in a different hand, was written, "Thanks for coming, Bear and Annie."

Aughhh. I didn't want to go to that kiddie party. It was all the way across town, and Annie and I wouldn't know anyone there except for Wanderley, and we'd be nearly as old as Molly's grandparents. Why did Wanderley want us there? I like Wanderley, but we don't have a social relationship. It took Phoebe dying to get us together this time. I sighed.

Twelve

———

The dogs and I had some lunch. There was a container of homemade chili and beans in the fridge, enough for all of us so I shared it out. We were finishing as Annie Laurie and Jo walked in from the garage. Annie Laurie looked whipped and Jo had dark circles under her eyes.

Having the pugs over had been a good call. Jo dropped her purse and a bright-yellow Forever 21 bag on the island and got on her knees to receive the frenzied greeting the pugs were offering. She let them kiss her face all over and Baby Bear stood for this misappropriation of attention as long as he could before he used his bulk to push the pugs aside and get his fair share of attention. Jo nuzzled and stroked Baby Bear until his eyes rolled up into his head and he about wagged his tail right off.

"What's this?" Annie asked, picking up the three dog bowls. "You didn't feed those dogs chili and beans, did you?"

"There wasn't that much left—did you want some?"

"I can't think it's a good idea to feed dogs chili and beans, Bear."

"Oh, they loved it." I pulled Jo to her feet and gave her a hug. "How's my girl?"

That brought it back to Jo and she shook her head and her eyes filled.

"I know, baby. Not a good night. I'm so sorry."

Another head shake. Annie tried to communicate something to me with her eyes, but I didn't get the message.

I said, "Detective Wanderley was here earlier. He wants to talk to you. Is that going to be okay?"

Jo pulled away and went to the cabinet for a glass. She filled it with ice and water and drank standing over the sink.

"I guess," she said after drinking.

"Could you tell me and Mom about last night?"

She shook her head.

"Come here, Jo." I took a reluctant hand in mine and drew Jo over to the couch. Annie sat on the coffee table across from us and put her hand on Jo's knee.

"Tell us, Jo."

And the story stumbled out. Jo had been at her friend Cara's with another girl, Ashley—we knew that part of the story. Alex and some other boys had also apparently been over—we hadn't known about that, but it was okay. We know Cara's parents and they're good people. Jo came home and—

Annie Laurie asked, "Why did you come home, Jo? Didn't you and Ashley plan to spend the night?"

A slow nod.

"So what made you decide to come home, then?"

"I just did, that's all." The tears were gone and that last came out a little grit-toothed. I couldn't decipher what was behind it. Annie Laurie touched Jo's arm to get her back on track. "All right, Jo, you decided to walk home. Then what?"

There had been a tiny shift in Jo's eyes. I didn't think Jo had *walked* home. I let it pass. For now.

"I came inside and Baby Bear didn't come meet me. I heard him whimpering, so I called him, and he ran to the head of the stairs and barked and then he ran back to my room. I . . . I didn't want to go upstairs. The house was dark . . ."

That kind of thing had never bothered Jo before. My girls are gutsy. They've never been squealy.

"I went upstairs. Baby Bear was crying for me but I was still really slow and I felt it more every step I took."

"Felt what, Jo?" Annie kept her voice low. She took Jo's hand in her own.

"I don't know! Only, my heart was beating faster and faster and I felt like I couldn't breathe."

"You were frightened." Annie bent her head and kissed Jo's knuckles.

"Yes."

I squeezed my girl up close to me.

"When I walked into my room, my heart was thumping so hard I thought I'd pass out and Baby Bear came to me and then I saw Phoebe just sitting there."

I said, "Phoebe was alive?"

"I thought so. I mean, she was sitting there, cross-legged, bent way forward with her arms loose in front of her and her hair covering her face and I said, 'Phoebe?' and she didn't *answer* me, I was standing two feet away from her and I said her name and she didn't even *move* and then I touched her arm and she fell over and her eyes were *wide open* and I think I screamed!"

I didn't blame her. I think I would have screamed, too.

"I called you to come home——" That would have been the text. "And then you finally came home." There was rebuke in her tone, but we had gotten there as soon as we could.

"Why didn't you call nine-one-one?" asked Annie, which amazed me. *I'm* usually the one who says the wrong thing.

Jo's mouth dropped open and she said, an ocean of horror opening up in front of her, "Could she have *lived*?"

"No," I said quickly. "She could not have. Phoebe was gone before you got here."

But it was too late. Annie had released the evil djinn of

doubt and guilt and now we couldn't get him back in the bottle. "I don't know *why* I didn't call nine-one-one! I don't know! Why *didn't* I?" Jo sobbed and stormed and paced and questioned herself and refused to be consoled.

The pugs picked up on her distress and trumped her with their shrieking. Baby Bear followed at her heels, whining his anxiety. I gave up trying to reason with Jo and appealed to her instead. I said, "Jo! You're scaring Baby Bear. And the pugs are going to wee in the house if you can't get them calmed down. Make sure the gates are closed and take them in the backyard. They need a break. They're picking up all this tension and Rebecca told me that when Mr. Wiggles gets upset, he barfs."

Jo stopped the noise. She blew her nose on the tissue Annie handed her and went into the backyard to check the gates. When she came back to the door, three muzzles were pressed up against the glass. It made her laugh, thank you, God.

After Jo took the dogs outside, Annie touched my arm. "Oh, goodness, Bear! What was I thinking?"

Heaven knows I've been there, saying the wrong thing, so I didn't have anything to offer her. I put the kettle on for tea, because the English have that right. A cup of sweet, milky tea is better than Prozac. I mean, I haven't had Prozac, but tea is a good, calming, soothing alternative.

Jo had herself back under control when the four of them came back in. There was even some color in her cheeks from the cool October weather. All the clouds had been swept from the dogs' eyes, leaving sparkling, sunny, happyhappy, joyjoy. One of the nice things about having almost no short-term memory.

Jo's mug was waiting for her on the kitchen table. I'd added extra sugar and even heated the milk before pouring it in and I could tell she felt better when she sipped it and that made us feel better, too. I picked up her shopping bag.

"Let's see what you got, Jo," I said. It was a shopping ritual. After you go shopping, you come home and show Dad what you bought. My girls, including Annie, like to show me, and, at least where Merrie and Jo are concerned, it gives me an opportunity to register a complaint if the article is too suggestive. Annie Laurie is more liberal about how the girls dress than I am. She says that's because I've never been a girl. I say that's because she's never been a *boy*.

Jo got to her feet and dumped out a bag of black lace and chains and two huge, clunky black shoes. The stuff didn't look like anything Jo usually wore. It looked like stuff *Phoebe* wore.

She held up the fall of black lace. It looked like a skirt with a wide waistband, but of course, it couldn't be. You could see right through it.

"What is it?"

Jo looked at me. "It's a skirt."

I said, "How can it be a skirt? You can see through it."

"No you can't, Dad. It's got an underskirt."

That wide waistband? Yeah. *That* was the underskirt. I kept my mouth shut.

The jangle of chains, it turned out, was a bracelet. It consisted of a ring to be worn on the middle finger attached to a multichain bracelet. Looked exactly like the slave bracelets girls used to wear when I was a kid.

I said, "Jo, that's a slave bracelet. Why would you want to wear a slave bracelet?"

Now she really gave me a look.

"Dad, it's not a *slave* bracelet. It's a warrior *queen* bracelet."

Okaaay. But I believe in the power of the word, so, okay. I'm good with a warrior queen bracelet. Warrior queen daughters aren't nearly as worrying as slave daughters.

"Let's see the shoes."

Jo picked up the hideous monstrosities. They were black

fake-suede platform oxfords, according to the tag pasted inside. Overall, the heel height had to be five inches. Five and a half, Jo corrected me.

I took one from her. It felt like a block of balsa wood. "Can you walk in these?"

"Dad. Yes. I can walk in them."

"How far?"

"Dad!" A pause and then she admitted, "They're form over function." Uh-huh. Everything in the bag looked like form over function to me. Baby Bear sniffed the shoes, decided he had the same idea about plastic shoes as I did.

"You could break an ankle in those shoes. No more ballet."

Jo's eyes widened. "Keep the receipt, Mom."

I asked Annie, "How much did all this cost?"

Annie was feeding Cheerios to the pugs and Baby Bear. She shrugged her shoulders. "Jo used her own money. What did it come to, Jo?"

Her own money? What money? Jo doesn't have any money. She's never had a job—ballet takes up too much time—and we only give her twenty dollars a week. How the heck could she have used her own money? Unless my child was running drugs for some greedy . . .

"Where'd you get this kind of money, Jo?" It came out harsher than I'd meant it to. My heart was thumping like I'd run a mile with a rottweiler on my tail. I sat down.

"You bought a skirt, shoes, jewelry—what did all that come to? I want to know where you got the money."

She flushed. My heart beat sped up. Annie said, "What's up, Bear?"

"Dad, it was my money, and I . . . I earned it and anyway, everything together was less than forty dollars and—"

"You're trying to tell me you got all that for less than forty dollars?"

Jo took the skirt thing and held the tag out to me. Eleven ninety-nine. You can buy a skirt for eleven dollars and ninety-nine cents? I spread my hands. "Jo, you say you earned the money—I want to know how. As far as I know, you don't baby-sit, you don't do lawns, you're at ballet class every afternoon—"

Jo flinched. Her color deepened. Her eyes were filling with tears and I thought my heart was going to break like a dropped china plate.

"You are at ballet class every day, aren't you, Jo?" I didn't want her to answer. I didn't want to know that my girl had taken a turn down a dark, dark road.

"Dad, I . . ." She stood in front of me trembling, the tears spilling over.

If Jo had sold drugs—if she had been a part of what killed Phoebe Pickersley, a girl younger that Jo's own sister, there would be nothing I could do to fix this. All the money in the world wasn't going to be able to fix this.

Annie clutched the length of black lace to her chest, her eyes going from me to Jo and back. "Tell me what's going on, Bear. What's this about?"

"It was *my* money. They were *mine* to sell," said Jo.

Oh, dear God.

"And I was never going to read them again and I got a hundred and seventy-five dollars for all of them together and postage cost me around twenty—"

What? "What are you talking about?" I asked her.

"My Marguerite Henry horse books. I sold them on eBay."

Annie said, "You got a hundred and seventy-five dollars for those old books?"

I didn't give a dang about the books. She could do what she wanted with them. But that wasn't all of it. I could tell Jo was holding something back. I'd seen her flinch.

"Your afternoons, Jo. Are you spending them with Madame Laney?"

She closed her eyes and held on to the kitchen island. "Most of them, Dad."

The kitchen filled with silence. Baby Bear, unhappy with the tension in the room, came to me and barked. Tommy sat down and barked at everyone. Wiggles snored in the family room.

"What have you been doing in the afternoons, Josephine Amelia? All those afternoons when Mom and I thought you were at ballet class—where have you been?" My voice was calm. My mind was spinning, my heart about to quit on me, but my voice was calm.

She kept her trembling lids closed, the tears leaking out from under her lashes. She shook her head.

"I need to know, Josephine." My child had done something so shameful, she couldn't bear to look me in the eyes.

At last she whispered, "Going to RCIA classes, Dad."

What? "What's RCIA?"

Jo turned her back to me and tore off a sheet of paper towel and blew her nose. Annie watched us both like she was seeing a Kurosawa movie without subtitles. Jo kept her back to me and answered, "Rite of Christian Initiation of Adults."

Rite of Christian Initiation of Adults—what the heck was that? I'd never heard of any rite of Christian whatever. I didn't know of any program like that going on up at the church. "What is that? Some kind of Bible study? You're going to some kind of Bible study?" I was still missing something. What were the tears about? What was all the drama for?

She drew in a quavery breath. "I'm studying to become a Catholic, Dad."

"Oh."

Oh.

Ohhh.

Jo's hands were cupped over her face and her shoulders shook. The thing to do would be to go over there and put my arms around her.

She wasn't a drug dealer. She had sold her own books. And she was spending her afternoons studying to become a Catholic. I should have felt enormous relief. I did. My heart had slowed way down. I was relieved.

But I was also devastated.

Jo turned around at last, but now I was the one who couldn't look at her. I sat down at the table and rubbed my fingers together. Mr. Wiggles came to me. I picked him up and stroked his fat back. He felt like a seal pup. His coat was short and silky. He grunted with pleasure.

"Dad?"

"Yes, Jo."

"Are you mad at me? I was afraid you'd be mad at me."

"I'm not mad at you."

"And I was afraid it would hurt your feelings."

I opened my mouth to tell her my feelings weren't hurt. I closed it again. I was hurting. Something was hurting.

"Ahh, Jo. We're talking about a matter of conscience here. How other people feel about the decisions we make . . . that has to come second. I . . . I mean . . . I'd like it if we could talk this over together. If you could tell me why you . . ."

I stood up. I needed some air.

"I'm going to take the dogs to the levee. They need a walk."

When I passed Annie to gather the leashes from the back-door hook, she squeezed my arm and briefly leaned her cheek on my shoulder. I patted her back but didn't pause. All three dogs pressed against my legs, having seen the leashes and knowing it meant a walk.

"Dad?" Jo's voice was small and tremulous.

"It's all right, baby. I just want some time. It's a lot to think about." I opened the back door.

"Do you still love me, Dad?"

I went back in the kitchen and bent down to hug her.

"With all my heart," I said into her hair. "Always and forever."

———

Our house backs up to the levee, so we can go straight out the back gate and onto the levee without going near a street. The pugs looooved the levee and Baby Bear acted like landed gentry showing his properties off to the local dirt-scratchers. The levee was raised ten or fifteen feet to keep flood waters out of our neighborhood (there's another neighborhood on the other side of the levee—don't know what happens to them in a flood—maybe the same guys who told *us* the levee would protect *us* told *them* the levee would protect *them*); and is flanked by residential backyards. We had it pretty much to ourselves this afternoon. I let the dogs off their leashes. Mr. Wiggles lagged behind with me, never speeding up past an amble, but Tommy was off like a rocket the second he was free of his leash. He ran circles around Baby Bear and then raced down the levee, making a *huh, huh* breathing sound that I think was supposed to make it sound like he was going faster than he was. That pug was supplying his own sound effects.

On this long stretch, Baby Bear caught up with Tommy easily. In one stride Baby Bear could cover four times the distance Tommy could. As soon as Baby Bear caught up to Tommy, Tommy would turn on a dime and race back, tongue and ears streaming back, as joyous a creature as God has ever created. Baby Bear was still trying to figure out the rules to the game, but he was a player.

Late October is a good time to live on the Gulf Coast. It was cool and sunny. I lifted my face up to the sun and took in a big breath.

Okay. So Jo was studying to become a Catholic.

Out here in the cool air, watching the dogs play, my throat started to loosen up. My mind stilled enough for some rational thought to get into it.

I wasn't raised to believe that everybody who didn't understand God exactly like me was going to Hell. Father Nat Fontana, the priest at Saint Lawrence, is a friend of mine, a good man and a devout Christian and . . .

Why was this so painful? Twenty minutes ago, I'd been on tenterhooks thinking my own girl might actually be selling drugs. Might have contributed to the death of another man's daughter. Well, she wasn't selling drugs. She was becoming a Catholic. That's good news, right? Right?

Right?

So why was my heart sore when everything in my head told me I should be rejoicing? In this day and age, when our children are turning away from the faith of their fathers by the *droves*, in our own overmoneyed, overindulged, self-invested suburb of Houston, Texas, I had a child who was so serious about her faith that she was undergoing the very taxing process of becoming a Catholic as an adult.

What I should have been doing right then was giving praise, on my *knees*, that my daughter was alive, healthy, and in a committed relationship with her Lord.

I mean, as far as I knew.

As far as you can know another person's heart.

This was no small undertaking Jo had started.

In the Church of Christ, if you are willing to proclaim your Lord's name and take on His spirit in baptism, you're in. No tests. No classes. No creeds to memorize. Your authenticity of spirit—that's between you and God.

Not so in the Catholic Church. They require that you understand Catholic doctrine and be familiar with the liturgy. You'll be expected to participate in an intensive study of the Bible. There are a number of ceremonies to go through and services to offer. If you decide to become a Catholic as an adult, you need to be serious about it. I have a lot of respect for the process. That Jo had stuck it out, that was a real accomplishment. Especially since Jo has a reading disability—anything on the printed page—that's real work for her.

That was dedication.

I don't believe in churches keeping score—it's not about adding bodies to your roster, it's about bringing people into a relationship with Christ, the Lord God on high.

So why did I feel . . . what? What was I feeling?

Rejected. Something like that, anyway. Bigger than that.

My stomach was hurting. I had let us get farther down the levee than I'd planned. When it was time to turn back, Mr. Wiggles made it about halfway and stopped. I called to him and he sat down. I hollered and he lay down. He wouldn't budge. The old boy had had his walk and he was done. He didn't have any more walk left in him.

I went over and hefted him up. He was one solid dog. Those pugs look little, especially when contrasted with Baby Bear, but I don't ever carry Baby Bear. At 180 pounds, I *couldn't* carry Baby Bear. Mr. Wiggles was maybe 25 pounds—not all that much. But he got heavier each step I took. I had his back against my stomach, one arm under his haunches and another crossed in front of him to hold him close.

Soon we got to our back gate.

That's when Tommy stopped. I opened the gate with my

elbow, my arms being full of fat, lazy pug, and Baby Bear obediently passed through. Tommy declined. He wasn't done playing. He didn't want to leave the levee. He wanted more romping and racing. And he was off the leash.

I tried to scoot Tommy in with the side of my sneaker, but he evaded the move and hunkered down, forequarters on the ground, butt in the air and that curly tail waving in a way meant to entice me to chase him. I tucked Mr. Wiggles under my arm like a football and made a grab at Tommy. I got nothing but air.

I'd had those dogs out for more than an hour. I'd given the spoiled furball a very generous walk and I was carrying his fat comrade and I was ready to go in. Not too much to ask.

Tommy did a sizzly figure eight and took up his play position again. I wasn't in the mood, and decided to just wedge the gate open and go into the house without him, figuring the porker would be crying to be let in within two minutes.

Annie Laurie was sitting in the family room all cool and comfy with her long, tan legs folded under her, reading Rebecca's theses on the care of pugs. She had a sheaf of already read pages in her left hand and a tree's worth in her right, her reading glasses perched on the end of her lovely nose. She put the papers down and came into my arms.

"Where's Jo?" I asked.

She said, "She's upstairs. I told her to have a lie-down. She didn't sleep all that well last night."

"Is she all right?"

"She will be. Are you all right?" Annie Laurie had been raised in the Episcopalian church and had tried out several denominations before she met me. I knew she couldn't understand my anguish over Jo's decision to leave the Church of Christ, but she didn't call me a fool for feeling the way I did, she didn't try to reason me out of my feelings, and I was grateful for that.

"I will be. I don't want to talk about it right now. Let me have some time, okay?"

She pulled my head down and rolled her forehead against mine before she released me. "You were getting at something else, weren't you? You didn't know Jo was taking these classes. What was it you were worried about?"

That's when I finally got the chance to tell Annie about how Wanderley was investigating the possibility that Jo might have supplied the drugs that had killed Phoebe Pickersley—that Jo might have supplied them for a price.

It made her mad. She snatched up the pug papers and then slapped the papers down on the coffee table. "I can't believe you let him get away with spouting that garbage, Walker Wells. What's his number? I'm going to call that boy. Is he telling other people that bull? Because if he is, I'll call Daddy." Annie Laurie's dad is a lawyer.

I pushed her back in her chair. "Do me a favor. Could you let me handle it? Calling in lawyers will only make it look like we have something to hide. And we don't. It threw me when Jo turned up with all that stuff, is all. It didn't help that she started acting like she'd been caught out in a Ponzi scheme. But I never believed Jo could be into something like that."

"You let James say it." Annie can be very old-school Texas about the honor of her family.

I said, "I did not. I punched him out and stuffed him in the trunk of his car."

She tried to kick my leg but I stepped out of reach. She pointed to the sheaf of papers on the table. "We're going to be sorry you let those pugs eat chili beans."

"You think so?" I filled the water bowls and Baby Bear and Mr. Wiggles lapped gratefully.

"Rebecca specifically warns against beans of any kind. I think we have sown the wind and we will reap the whirlwind."

I laughed.

Annie took her glasses off and nodded. "You should read this thing. These two pugs have some peculiarities we need to keep in mind. Who was Rebecca meeting in Galveston?"

"I dunno. It came up suddenly. She really wanted to go." I drank some ice water and wiped my face on my sleeve. Annie looked past me, frowning.

"Where's the other one?"

"The other what?"

Annie unfolded her legs and came into the kitchen, searching the floor. "The other *pug*, Bear, where's Tommy?"

Oh.

"He's right outside the door," I said, opening the back door to an empty doormat. I stuck my head outside the door. "Tommy?"

Annie pushed past me. "Tommy boy, come here, baby! Bear, why on earth did you leave that dog outside?"

I said, "He wouldn't come in—I tried to get him to come in and he got all coy with me."

Annie was searching the bushes. "And you didn't have him on the leash?"

"We were on the levee! Where was he going to go?" I'd made it to the back gate, where I'd last seen the little stinker. He was nowhere in sight. "Tommy!" I called. You know what? I didn't need this right now. I didn't.

"In the instructions Rebecca left you, she specifically says not to take Tommy off the leash unless he's in a fenced yard. She says he gets wild with freedom and it's hard to get him to obey. Just so you know."

Annie went back into the kitchen, calling over her shoulder that she'd get something. I kept yelling Tommy's name, worrying about the pug. We have owls in Sugar Land. Big ones. I think an owl could . . .

Annie came out holding a cocktail sauce cup full of peanut

butter. This is one of Baby Bear's favorite treats. She got on her knees on the lawn, facing the back gate and crooned. "Oh, Tommy boy, come see what I have for you!" To me she said, "Move, Bear, don't block the gate. He may not want to have anything to do with you after you locked him out."

"I didn't lock him out. He wouldn't come in. I left the gate open. I was just teaching him a lesson." I moved out onto the levee and called for him. Man. It didn't look good. Oh, please, God, help me find that dog, Rebecca will die if anything happens to that dog . . .

Annie yelled, "I've got him!"

And I said thank you.

Tommy, with enormous self-restraint—or a pathological determination to make a point—ignored the cup of peanut butter and walked into the kitchen. I think he was trying to do dignified, but when you're twenty-five pounds of curly-tailed, bug-eyed corpulence, dignified ain't going to happen. I told him so and Tommy suddenly stopped in his tracks and started to choke to death.

It was the worst asthma attack I'd ever heard in my life. His eyes bulged nearly out of his skull and he struggled desperately for breath. I yelled for Annie to call 911 and dropped to my knees, already feeling guilty and now ready to make the ultimate sacrifice for Rebecca's baby and give the chinless wonder CPR. I was trying to get a finger on his tongue to hold it down when Annie stopped me.

That woman laughed out loud, put a hand out before (thank you very much) my lips touched pug lips, and stroked Tommy's throat. Within seconds, Tommy's breathing eased, his eyeballs returned to their sockets, and he let Annie know that he'd give that peanut butter a try now. She was still laughing her head off while she made more servings of peanut butter for Mr. Wiggles and Baby Bear.

"You want to tell me what the heck that was?" I asked.

Another giggle. "Tommy just had a pharyngeal gag reflex."

I grunted. "And what's that when it's at home?" I was still on the floor, watching for signs of relapse.

Annie set the three cups of peanut butter down in front of two very impatient dogs and one grateful one. The well-behaved dog was Baby Bear. *We* don't spoil our dog.

Annie poured a glass of wine—it being Saturday, she gave herself permission—and walked over to plant a kiss on the top of my head. "You really should read Rebecca's instructions, Bear. Pugs are prone to the pharyngeal gag reflex, also known, descriptively, as a reverse sneeze. It's something to do with their short noses and anything at all can set it off. Excitement, for instance. Dust. Tommy has had plenty of both today. It's absolutely not dangerous and if we did nothing at all, that pug would have been fine. But if you stroke their throats, it helps to calm and relax them and that helps them through the attack. It's all in your info pack, Bear."

Uh-huh. I don't expect to be studying *info packs* when I have grandkids; I'm *sure* not doing it for pugs.

The doorbell rang, sending the pugs into atonal howls and Jo tearing down the stairs to answer the door. She walked into the kitchen with Alex in tow, holding a ridiculously extravagant bouquet of two dozen roses (yes, I counted them—I wanted to know) ranging from a creamy white to pink, deep rose to burgundy. Jo handed them to her mom to admire and said, "Alex, those are my favorites. How did you know?"

I happen to know that yellow roses are actually Jo's favorites. She was acting shy with me, not sure about her reception. I made sure to give her a squeeze.

While Annie Laurie arranged Jo's roses in a crystal vase, Jo and Alex went to the television room to watch a movie.

"Keep the door open!" I yelled up after her and got snorts in return. Baby Bear is a lousy chaperone. He would never let any-one hurt Jo, but smooching doesn't bother him. It bothers *me*.

Annie Laurie made a tray with a plate of crackers, a block of Monterey Pepper Jack cheese, and two apple juice bottles and took it up to the kids. I told her I wanted to know if that door wasn't full open and Annie Laurie snorted at me, too. The pugs, who had been watching this food preparation with interest, scrambled up after her so they could commence begging.

Thirteen

Detective Wanderley called around five. He wanted to come over and speak to Jo. I trudged up to the television room, making as much noise as possible, to tell Jo to expect Wanderley in half an hour. Jo and Alex were sitting in front of that ridiculous cartoon with a milk shake and a meatball as main characters. The pugs seemed avidly interested in the cartoon, but Alex and Jo weren't actually watching it; they were engaged in an intense conversation. I didn't like that, but I liked it much better than an intense anything else. Jo jumped up, looking unnecessarily alarmed, but Alex tugged her down and said something soothing, and she relaxed against his shoulder.

"'Kay. Be down soon."

Annie Laurie put a pitcher of ice water and an assortment of glasses on the family room coffee table, and then made up a tray of tuna salad sandwiches. The pugs, sensing the possibility of another meal, raced down the stairs in a panic that they might miss a morsel. They were lucky not to upend themselves—with those big, heavy heads and those disproportionately small butts, it's a hazard.

I told Annie it wasn't necessary to feed Wanderley, and that I was surprised she would think to, what with Wanderley practically accusing our child of being a member of the Medellin cartel, but Annie murmured, "Coals of fire, Bear, coals of fire," and added a bowl of potato chips and paper plates and napkins.

That made me think we wouldn't be having dinner, we'd be having interrogation tuna, instead. The pugs indicated that tuna was fine with them, and they waited at the coffee table with increasing impatience, Tommy going so far as to stand on his hind legs to scan the table and presumably report his finds back to Mr. Wiggles.

Once Wanderley arrived, he said he wanted to visit with Jo alone, but Annie and I agreed that we weren't having that. First of all, Jo is a minor, and secondly, didn't he see the coffee table spread out with drinks and sandwiches? Maybe he thought that was all for him?

Alex shook hands with Wanderley and then left, his hands buried in his jacket pockets. Wanderley helped himself to sandwich halves like a man who thinks good homemade tuna sandwiches are a dinnertime treat. Tommy and Mr. Wiggles gathered at his ankles and looked at him expectantly. Wanderley, who is clearly made of stern stuff, pretended they weren't there. After swallowing the half a sandwich he had fit into his mouth, Wanderley said to me and Annie Laurie, "What I want tonight are Jo's thoughts and Jo's words. You're going to want to help her out. I'm asking you not to. If you feel like I've asked something inappropriate, you can stop me. But please don't answer for Jo, and please don't interrupt her. Are you both good with that?"

Why Wanderley thought it was necessary to spell that out for us, I don't know. We agreed that Jo could answer for herself, and I broke a sandwich half into two pieces for the pugs in order to purchase thirty seconds of peace. Jo indignantly gave Baby Bear a whole half sandwich for himself and an exasperated Annie removed the sandwich plate to the kitchen. After that, the pugs settled down for a nap, and Wanderley's entire attention was on Jo.

Jo picked up two walnuts from the bowl on the coffee table and rolled them back and forth in her hands. They made a loud, gritty noise and I wished she would stop, it made her look nervous, but I had my instructions from Wanderley so I didn't say a word.

Wanderley got right down to business. "We can't find Phoebe's phone, Jo, we didn't find it here, it's not in her car, or her room. Do you have any idea where it is?"

Jo shook her head.

Wanderley made a *tsch* sound. "I don't like that. I really don't. We'll subpoena the phone company but that's always a battle." He sighed. "Well, then."

He took his paper plate to the kitchen to load up on more sandwiches. From the kitchen he said, "It looks like Phoebe died from a drug overdose. Some kind of barbiturate, maybe. We won't know for sure until after the autopsy, but that's what we're guessing." He came back, his plate piled high. "Any idea where she could have gotten the drugs?" He looked all casual, but he watched Jo carefully.

Jo had no reaction other than to frown. No flush, no trembling, no tears. My girl might be "guilty" of converting to Catholicism, but she wasn't feeling guilty over drugs. My insides relaxed.

"You mean like names? You want me to give you names? Because I don't know," she said. "I hear things—I might have an idea, but nothing I'm sure enough of to tell you. I don't run with that crowd, and it's not like they put ads in the school newspaper, you know."

Wanderley nodded and took a bite. "It's just—well, Phoebe hasn't been at Clements long—only a few months, and you're one of her only friends, and—"

"I wasn't her friend." Jo's frown deepened and then she looked up at Wanderley, eyes wide with surprise, half smiling. "You think she got them from *me!*" She turned to me and her mom to make sure we'd gotten the joke.

Wanderley said nothing. He stood there, studying her. The silence grew. Jo looked around again. Three serious faces looked back at her.

"You really do. You think she got them from me." She shook her head hard. "I don't do that stuff. I know some dancers do, but not me. It messes with your timing. The girls at the ballet school? The ones who use, they don't use downers, they use uppers—helps them keep the weight off. But it makes them twitchy. Know what I mean?" She mimed a quick spasm.

Wanderley said, "Had you ever seen Phoebe do drugs before last night?"

Another emphatic head shake. "I *didn't* see her doing them last night. And, no. I've never seen her take anything, other than a drink now and then. And she did more talking about drinking than drinking. She didn't smoke. Her mom smoked and she got cancer."

Wanderley nodded. "Did she talk about drugs?"

"No. Not with me."

"But with someone else?" He was quick to pounce on the limitations of her answer.

"How would I know if she talked about drugs with someone else? If I was there when she talked about it, then she would have been talking about it with me. Right?" Jo was using her You Big Dummyhead tone of voice, but Wanderley didn't want me to step in so I let him handle the inflection issue.

"So you don't know anything about drugs."

Jo's eyes got slitty. She paused in the middle of gathering her hair up. "For real? You're asking me that? I go to school at Clements. So yeah, I know something about drugs. But I don't do drugs. I don't sell drugs and I don't know where Phoebe got her drugs. *If* she got her drugs. *If.*" Jo twisted her hair up in a band and bent to pick up a sleeping Mr. Wiggles. She draped the pug over her lap. He didn't wake up.

Wanderley had Jo go through her evening again—she didn't say anything she hadn't said last night. He nodded and acted like he was checking his notes. He wasn't. Then he sprang this:

"Do you know why Phoebe would want to kill herself, Jo?"

"I don't know why *anyone* would want to kill themselves. If you don't want to live, why don't you go to Darfur and try to get some good done before someone else does the job for you? That's suicide by proxy but the good kind."

That made some sense to me. I made a note to run it by Carol Thompson; she might want to use it with her next suicidal client.

"Really?" Wanderley's unibrow did that up and down thing. "What about a terminal patient, could you understand someone like that killing themselves?"

Jo shook her head hard enough to shake strands of hair loose from the knot on top of her head. "It's not the same. That's not killing yourself. That's, like, speeding death up. If you're going to die anyway, it doesn't count."

"Hmmmm. Well, everyone's going to die sometime, but people *do* kill themselves. Why do you think they do that?"

Her answer had the relentless simplicity of the young. "Because they're quitters."

"Really? So you think Phoebe was a quitter?"

"No."

"No?"

Jo, who had answered the question already, stared back at him.

He said, "You don't think Phoebe was a quitter?"

Jo said nothing at first. I heard one of the walnuts crack. She said, "She wasn't a quitter. She was a fighter."

"Tell me about that," said Wanderley.

"You know. All the things that happened to her."

Wanderley was patient. "No, I don't know. I know her

mother died and she went to live in a nice house in a nice neighborhood with her dad and stepmom and two stepbrothers. It's hard to lose your mom, but it sounds like Phoebe landed on her feet. You see it differently?"

Jo held up a finger. "First she had to deal with her mom and dad divorcing. Then"—she held up another finger—"her dad got married like half a second later to that awful stepmother."

Annie and I both said, "Jo!" and we both got a look from Wanderley. It was Annie's first time having one of Wanderley's glowers aimed at her—*I* get them all the time.

Jo ignored us and held up a third finger. "Three. The awful Liz was pregnant with twins even before she walked down the aisle in a poofy white dress that was designed for the child bride of a shah." She took in our expressions. "That's how Phoebe described the dress. I mean, she wouldn't have been showing, but that's how I see it."

Jo coughed and Annie poured ice water into the glass she held out.

"And that's not cool, the being pregnant part. Especially because Phoebe said her dad had like started this whole new life and this whole new family, and he was all like you are so nearly grown up and, oh, you'll understand the new babies neeeeed me so I can't take you to practice or come shopping with you or give you a birthday party or whatever. Only she wasn't completely done being a kid, she still needed her dad, you know? And you can be the prettiest girl on earth, which Phoebe wasn't, and you still aren't going to be as cute as a new puppy and that's pretty much what you're competing with. Phoebe was only . . . give me a sec." She furtively counted on her fingers. "She would have been like, thirteen, right?"

Wanderley said, "Fourteen. Phoebe was eighteen, Jo. She was going to turn nineteen this coming January."

"Are you sure? She was just starting her senior year—"

I said, "She missed a lot of school, taking care of her mother. She had to repeat a year."

"Yeah?" Jo gave that some thought. "Then that was Liz's fault, too. So all of a sudden, she hardly ever sees her dad, and he's all rich now, and about to be a dad all over again, only the whole subtext here is this time he's going to do it right, like that being Phoebe, he really screwed it up with Phoebe, which makes her feel all fine and great, right? She loved her little brothers because she couldn't help herself, but it was kind of hard, seeing the way they were growing up and remembering the way she grew up."

I said, "Subtext?" and Jo colored and said, "That's what Phoebe called it. I looked it up. I'm using it right, right?" I told her she was, thinking that in a short period of time, Phoebe had left her impression on Jo.

Jo had trouble regaining her story and Wanderley cleared his throat and asked me if I didn't need to go work on my sermon for tomorrow or something. I said I'd be quiet.

Jo tried again. "Well, anyway, so after her dad left, Phoebe and her mom are living in this tatty little trailer in a tatty little trailer park—"

Wanderley frowned, "Really? Your dad told me Liz had bought Phoebe and her mom a new mobile home."

"She did. It was better than the first one, but it's still a trailer and it's still in a trailer park."

Waverly said, "Have you been there?"

I don't know how he knew to ask—it hadn't occurred to me.

"Yeah, Green Vista. I went there with her once. It's near Hobby Airport." Her eyes widened as soon as it was out of her mouth. Jo isn't allowed to take off like that. She can't leave First Colony, our little part of Sugar Land, without permission. Hobby Airport was forty minutes away.

Annie said, "When did you go there, Jo?" Wanderley tried the look again, but Annie ignored him.

Jo pulled free a strand of hair and got very busy checking the tip for split ends. "That time she took us to the movies, me and Alex. That's why we went to the later movie, because she took us the long way. That's how she said it, 'We'll go the loooong way to the theater.' And it was, too—it took us two hours to get there and back—Phoebe said it was because of the Friday afternoon traffic."

Annie said, "Why didn't you ask us, Jo?"

It was a dumb question—I agreed with Jo. "Because you would have said no, that's why. And when I told her I couldn't go, Phoebe acted like I thought I was too good to go to a trailer park. She called it 'slumming.'" Jo looked up at Wanderley. He was closer to her age than he was to mine. Her eyes looked heavy. "I'm sorry she's dead and all that. I wish she were alive and she could get a job and save up and move to New York and have a *life*. But she wasn't a nice person, you know. She did mean things."

Wanderley had crushed a handful of potato chips in his hand and was feeding broken pieces to the pugs. Baby Bear had tried one and decided that the effort was too much for the tiny reward.

"What kind of mean things?"

She shook her head. "Stuff."

"Can you tell me about the 'stuff'?"

No, she couldn't or wouldn't. Jo kept her eyes on the tip of hair she was worrying.

"Go on," said Wanderley. "Tell me about Green Vista." He gave me and Annie a look that meant, "No more interruptions!"

"It's not that bad a trailer park. Not that I'd ever been to a trailer park before, but it wasn't what I imagined. It has trees. It's like an itty-bitty town. There's streets and some of the trailers"—she gave a shudder—"you can't believe people live there, but some people build porches on to the trailer and put up bamboo fences so they have some privacy when they're sitting outside and they have outdoor grills and flowers planted and the sides of their yards are picked out with bricks or tires that they painted white. You can tell they've made a real home there. But honestly, her dad is living in this completely posh house that's probably three times as big as ours is and he's driving a sweet car and Phoebe and her mom are living in a trailer that looks like one of Nana's vintage flour canisters. Does that sound right to you?"

It didn't.

"And each time Phoebe sees her dad with his new wife, her mom would cry and carry on about how when she was young she could have married a rich guy, she could have had any man because she was that good-looking but she chose Phoebe's dad because it was true love and then this rich . . . witch comes and steals him and did Phoebe have any idea what an ugly, fat, tub Lizabeth was in high school, so that's real fun, right?"

"Jo!"

Wanderley had put up a hand to stop me but the hand didn't do it. He swiveled in his seat. "Bear, could you save your moralizing until I'm done here? Would that be okay with you? Would you rather I take Jo into another room and talk to her in private?"

Annie got up. "You can't talk to Jo at all without one of us present, not without our permission, and we aren't giving it." She started gathering plates and napkins. "I know very well that you know that and I'm offended that you would try to intimidate us. We want to help you and we want Jo to help you but from now on out, Bear and I are both going to say anything we feel we need to. What you call 'moralizing' is what Bear and I call 'parenting' and we won't be stopping that anytime soon. Get your boots off my coffee table."

Jo said, "Dude." It was a rare event for Annie Laurie to have a temper flare. Jo was feeling for the young detective.

Wanderley had whipped his feet down almost before Annie finished her sentence. Annie Laurie disappeared into the kitchen and was making a big racket out of loading the dishwasher.

"Can she still hear me?" he mouthed.

"Oh, yeah," I said.

"You put *your* feet on the coffee table," he said, sotto voce.

"She's not mad at me."

"Huh."

"Yeah."

"Is it going to be okay if I go ahead with my questions or do I need to wait for her to come back in?"

I was feeling expansive. I don't mind Annie Laurie's temper when it isn't aimed at me. "You go on," I said. "I'm here for Jo."

Wanderley listened to the clattering going on in the kitchen. Over his shoulder he called, "They're off the table, Annie Laurie."

"They better be," came back.

He said, "I won't do it again, Annie Laurie."

Annie Laurie moved to the opening over the kitchen sink so she could see Wanderley. She said, "You better not. I'm not really talking about the boots. You can put your boots on the table if you want to but don't tell me or Bear to be quiet again."

"I'll try not to. I'm sorry."

"When you use words like 'moralizing,' you undermine us." Her arms were crossed.

"I'm telling you I'm sorry, Annie." They held gazes.

Annie relented and nodded.

"Will you come back in then and sit down?"

She nodded, dried her hands and resettled herself on the

couch. When she was comfortable, Wanderley picked up his questioning.

"Phoebe's dad and stepmom knew each other in high school?"

Jo smiled grimly. "I saw Mrs. Pickersley-Smythe's yearbook picture. You can hardly recognize her. She was fat and ugly."

"Jo," I said, "that may be the unkindest thing I've ever heard you say."

Jo's mouth turned down. But her color was raised.

I ignored Wanderley's look—he wasn't stupid, he didn't say anything this time—and continued, "You are slim and pretty, Jo, and ninety-nine percent of that is because you got lucky with your genes. You got what you got and Lizabeth got what she got and I guarantee you, your life has been easier than Liz's. So have some compassion."

Jo's face was flaming now, but I wasn't backing down. There is enough misery in the world without us adding vitriol. I won't have it in my house.

Jo took a breath. "Do you honestly think I would ever say something like that to someone? Or talk behind their back that way? This"—she gestured around the circle where we were sitting—"it's different. You want information—I'm giving you information. I didn't say she looked like a baboon. I said she was fat and ugly. If you showed Liz's senior picture to any guy on earth, the guy would say, 'fat and ugly.' She needed to see an orthodontist and I promise you she's had a nose job and she was carrying around thirty or forty pounds more than she is now. I don't know how many pounds. Enough so you would say 'fat' not 'heavy.'

"In a way, I'm complimenting her, you know that? Because she isn't fat and ugly now and I think she must have worked really hard to look the way she does. I don't think she's pretty but she looks fine and no one is going to walk past Liz today and think 'fat and ugly,' okay?" She turned from me to Wanderley.

"Do you want me to be all PC about what I tell you or do you want to hear what I know whether it's nice or not?"

Wanderley closed his eyes for a second. "As much as possible, I'd like your impressions. Is that okay, Annie? Bear?"

We nodded.

Jo looked to Wanderley for permission to go on, because she was on a roll now. "Like three months after her dad moves out, Phoebe's mom gets cancer of the throat." She put her hand up and touched her own smooth, lovely neck. "It's esophagus cancer."

"Esophageal," corrected Wanderley.

She ignored him. "It is a totally stink cancer to get. So, for a long time before she knows what she has, Phoebe's mom can hardly swallow, and she quits smoking, and she's losing weight and that part she likes. Phoebe's mom—her name was Jenny— she was a cheerleader and everything in high school. Phoebe showed me her picture and she was naturally blonde blonde— like Barbie-doll blonde. And she was built like a Barbie doll, too. And her dad played football and they looked like Barbie and Ken in high school, these two totally good-looking people. Back then when they were young. But he's still good-looking for an old guy and she wasn't and that was even before she got sick and, you know what? Instead of all the cancer warnings they put on cigarettes, they should put a picture of what you look like at forty if you do smoke and what you look like at forty if you don't, because Phoebe's mom looked all scabby and old. And she smoked like a haystack—"

"Like a chimney stack," I said before I could get a handle on my tongue. Everybody ignored me.

"But Phoebe's mom said she lost her looks because Phoebe's dad didn't make enough money and he was always fighting with her and then he walked out and she told Phoebe, 'Who wouldn't be sick after all that?' so she didn't go to the doctor for a long time but it wouldn't have mattered anyway, because this kind of cancer, it's almost always too late when you find out."

Jo took a breath and Wanderley and I did, too. Jo and the Apostle Paul are like *this* about run-on sentences. Annie refilled Jo's glass a third time from the pitcher she'd set on the table.

Jo drank and picked her tale back up.

It was Saturday and after five, so I went to the garage fridge and got Wanderley and me bottles of Shiner Bock and I poured a glass of pinot grigio for Annie.

Jo said, all casual as though it were apropos of nothing, "Did you know Phoebe drank wine with her folks even though she was barely two years older than me?"

I said, "Nope."

Jo said, "They did."

I said, "The 'nope' was for you having wine."

Wanderley, who was here on his own time, drank from the dark, frosted bottle and sighed.

"Phoebe told me and Alex what it was like when her mom was sick. It was the worst thing in the whole wide world. I could never have done it."

She could have. We can do so much we don't think we can.

"She had to do everything. Phoebe did the shopping and the cleaning and the cooking and she would try to cook things her mom liked and that she could swallow. But it got so her mom couldn't swallow anything." Tommy jumped onto the couch and clambered into Jo's lap. Jo hugged him to her. "Her mom got sicker and sicker. And every minute of every day Jenny was in pain." Jo looked at Wanderley. "Remember when my dad got shot?" she said, avoiding my eye.

Wanderley nodded.

"That was the worst time ever, watching Dad in the hospital pretend he was okay when really he was hurting a lot."

Ahhh, my girl. When we're really suffering, it's hard to re-member that the people who love us are suffering, too.

"And the thing is, I knew he was going to get better. He wasn't going to be hurting like that for the rest of his life—he wasn't going to die. But what Phoebe was dealing with was knowing that as bad as it was, it was only going to get worse. The doctors told her lots of times because they thought her mom should be in a hospice place. Only her mom made Phoebe prom-ise to let her die at home." Tommy turned circles on Jo's lap like a cat before settling down to sleep.

"Phoebe said her grandfather, her mom's dad, would come around, but he didn't help any. He'd just rant and rave about how Phoebe should get her dad to 'do the right thing' and Phoebe said it's not like her dad had any more money to send them because he kept telling Phoebe that *he* wasn't rich, *Liz* was rich and he was already doing everything he could. Her grand-father didn't believe a word and kept saying this was all her father's fault and that Phoebe's mom would never have gotten sick if her dad hadn't left.

"But it got worse and worse and Phoebe said how she could hear her mom crying at night because the pain was so bad and in the end, Phoebe even had to help her mom shower and use the toilet. Phoebe was afraid that her mom would slip and fall and she was lonely and she was afraid she would hurt her mom. Phoebe's grandfather wanted to move in and take care of his daughter—he said Phoebe could go back to school that way but Phoebe would never in a million years leave her mom alone, even with her grandfather who, like I said, wasn't any help. And he drinks." Jo pulled at Baby Bear until he rested his head and front paws on her lap, dislodging Tommy who grumbled.

"You know what? If you were the kind of person who would commit suicide, that would have been the time to do it, right?

A handful of pills for mom, a handful for you. But she didn't, did she? Phoebe made it through that. So that's why I know she wasn't a quitter."

Gently, gently, Wanderley said, "Then why do you think she killed herself, Jo?"

"I don't," Jo said, her face buried in Baby Bear's coat. "I think someone else killed her."

Annie reached over and stroked Jo's cheek. The idea that Phoebe was killed, not a suicide, well that might be easier for Jo to take than thinking that anything Jo had done, or not done, had contributed to this sad girl's death.

Wanderley scooted to the edge of his seat and said, "Work that out for me, Jo."

Jo said nothing.

Wanderley said, "Phoebe was in the house when you got home, do I have that right?"

Jo nodded.

"And you found her in your bedroom?"

Jo nodded.

"She didn't say anything?"

Jo bowed her head. "I don't think she was breathing. Her eyes were open. She didn't move her eyes. They were like doll eyes."

Wanderley said, "That's what I thought, Jo. We haven't gotten the lab results yet, but I don't believe there was anything you could have done for her. I think Phoebe must have taken something very strong, and once a substance is thoroughly in your system, there's not a whole lot that can be done. But she was the only one in the house when you got home?"

Jo said she was.

"Yet you think Phoebe was murdered."

Here Jo faltered. "She must have been. She wouldn't have killed herself."

Wanderley shook his head. I was confused, too. "I'm not sure what you're saying, Jo. What do you think happened?"

Here Jo lifted her brown eyes. They were fearless and frank and matter-of-fact.

"I don't know. I'm going to find out."

———————

That brought a storm down on her head. On mine, too, since I seem to be the go-to guy when something goes wrong.

"Oh, that's great," said Wanderley, putting his beer bottle down too hard, considering the wooden coffee table was covered in a sheet of glass. "You know how well that kind of thing worked out for your dad, right? He got a bullet in his stomach. That was a treat, wasn't it, Bear?"

Completely unfair, blaming that on me. Not my fault. But I was with Wanderley on not wanting Jo to go trying to "find out" anything. Baby Bear, meanwhile, had picked up on Wanderley's tone of voice, and he'd gotten to his feet in front of Jo and barked in a firm and authoritative manner at the detective—not threatening, mind you. Baby Bear was just laying down some boundaries for Wanderley. *I'm* not allowed to yell at Jo; Baby Bear wasn't going to tolerate it from a near stranger. The barking woke up Tommy, who didn't know what the upset was about, but he was on Baby Bear's side, whatever it was. He hopped off the sofa and barked at everybody indiscriminately. Mr. Wiggles opened his sleepy eyes, scanned the group, then dropped his head back onto his paws and picked up his snoring again.

Annie Laurie went over and took Jo's face in her hands and made Jo look her in the eyes.

"Josephine Amelia, we've given you a lot of privileges in the last year or so, haven't we? You got the phone you asked for, and we aren't monitoring your computer use anymore. We let you spend the whole summer alone in New York, and that was a scary thing for us. You would hate to lose those privileges, am I right?"

Jo's gaze didn't waver. "Yes. I would."

Annie Laurie nodded her head. "Then we understand each other?"

"Yes."

Baby Bear gave a final "woof" as if to make certain that Wanderley understood, too, and then subsided at Jo's feet. Tommy did a business of staring everyone down so we knew how tough he was, not any easy thing to carry off when your tail curls over your back and leaves your anus out in the open for all the world to see. Then he noticed that Wanderley had left a crust of sandwich on his plate, so he ran over to see if Wanderley would consider giving it to him.

Wanderley went over everything again. And again, and again.

I finally got him to the door. He was halfway out when he said, "Hey, Annie Laurie, thanks for coming to Molly's party. I look forward to seeing you there." Annie said it was her pleasure and after the door closed she turned to me with her eyebrows arched and said, "What party?"

Saturday night, we were all ready for bed early. We made up a bed on the family room couch for Jo. She wouldn't go upstairs by herself. She wouldn't go in her room at all. We kept our bedroom door open so we could hear her if she needed us.

Three big Rubbermaid boxes of books blocked the pugs in the kitchen. Baby Bear stepped right over them, but they were the Great Wall of China for the pugs. That didn't matter, though. They had no plans to stay in the kitchen. The pugs ignored their denim pillows and the fuzzy beanbags we'd laid out in the kitchen and cried piteously to be let into our room. Piteously and relentlessly and pugs don't cry like dogs. They ululate. I looked it up. Skip the first definition, which pretty much says to howl like a dog—strike the whole dog-noise thing right out of your mind, because that's not what pugs do. They hang their proficiency on the second definition: "to utter howling sounds, as in shrill, wordless lamentation; wail." Their cry is piercing and high-pitched and unendurable.

I could have held out, but Annie Laurie gave in pretty quickly. I fetched their furry beanbags and put them on the floor next to Annie's side of the bed because she has more floor room and because Tommy was treating me like a child molester. The pugs gave me injured looks and curled up without another protest. Baby Bear slept on the floor next to Jo—Annie Laurie and I fell asleep in each other's arms.

I'd completely forgotten the snoring, and when the appalling sound began and Annie sprang up, I started laughing. Annie whacked me with her pillow, and Tommy added his tremolo to Mr. Wiggle's gravel-grinding exhalations and then Annie got the giggles, too. I got her my Bose headphones and found some swim plugs for my ears and we went back to sleep. I'd have slept until morning had it not been for the pug farts.

I woke up gasping in a miasma of gas. Choking, I stumbled to the window, yanking on it twice before giving up and opening the French door in our bedroom that leads to the backyard. I rushed out and stood there sucking in the fresh air before I even had a thought about Annie Laurie. I stuck my head back in the door—Annie Laurie lay still and quiet, breathing regularly. I decided not to wake her up. Mr. Wiggles and Tommy stirred and stretched and got out of their beds and strolled outside to pollute the sweet air of Sugar Land with the noxious emissions from their backsides. Mr. Wiggles had a self-conscious air about him, but not Tommy. I lit a balsam and cedar Yankee Candle and turned on the ceiling fan. Note to self: no beans for the pugs. None. Not one. Ever, ever, ever.

From: Walker Wells
To: Merrie Wells

Hey, sweetheart. What's up? Listen, are you still going to the Broadway Church of Christ? Because if you aren't happy there, if you haven't made a connection, there are some others you might want to visit. Maybe I could fly up and we could visit one together. If you aren't happy at Broadway, I know some people at Sunset.
I want you to find your church, Merrie Elizabeth. It's important to be in a community of believers.

From: Merrie Wells
To: Walker Wells

Uh, Dad? What's up?

Fourteen

Sunday morning, Lizabeth Pickersley-Smythe and Toby and Tanner came to church, second service. She looked all noble and suffering, but—and I *know* this is cynical and I *know* cynicism is an unattractive quality, especially in a minister—I felt like it was all show. Liz was dressed perfectly in a dark-gray tailored skirt and sweater, her hair just so, and those twins in matching navy wool shorts with jackets. It was all very president's-grieving-widow, if you know what I mean. She was thronged with sympathizers, and she couldn't have been more gracious. It felt . . . staged.

I tried to put a positive spin on Liz being at church. I thought to myself, *Well, this means that Mark can have some fresh air, and a shower and change, and he can restock his fridge and still be safely bolted back in before Liz gets home.* And then I thought what it must be like for a man to have to hide away in his own home. And then I thought that it *wasn't* his home. And that was so depressing.

From: Walker Wells
To: Merrie Wells
Subject: Baby Bear and pugs

Hey, sweet Merrie—I attached a picture of Baby Bear with Rebecca's pugs. We're watching them this weekend. Rebecca picks them up at two. I don't know if Baby Bear will be glad or sad when they're gone.

From: Merrie Wells
To: Walker Wells
Subject: Re: Baby Bear and pugs

Ohhhhhh! I want a pug for my birthday!!!
How's Jo? Back in her room yet? You're going to have to sell the house, Dad.

––––––––––

There was a knock on the door at eight thirty Sunday evening.

Our house was winding down. Rebecca had come to collect her dogs, the kitchen was clean, and Jo was doing homework.

The knock was unexpected, and with that awful weekend behind us, alarming. But it was Salihah Fincher at the door, and unless you are the Devil himself, she is not an alarming sight. What Salihah is, is a tiny warrior of God. I don't know what else to call her. She's my mom's age, and about five feet nothing, not including the three inches for the luxuriant bouffant of rich, black hair that crowns her head, and another two inches for the kitten heels she wears. Her features are distinctively Egyptian, her birthland—straight off an Egyptian scroll. And her voice, still accented after a half century in the United States, is high and sweet and girlish.

Salihah had met her American husband, Blake Fincher, some fifty-five years ago, when she was a nursing student in Cairo and he was a young engineer working for one of the oil companies. That wasn't a happy time in Egypt—Wikipedia can tell you about the Sinai crisis better than I can. At one point, the nursing college was being peppered with sniper fire. That meant no one could safely leave the hospital wing, a real problem since the morgue was in the building next door, and the Egyptians had a particular horror of being under the same roof as a dead body. And there *was* a dead body, causing everyone in the hospital very real distress. But no one would budge to remove the body, not the administrators or the orderlies, their distaste for being shot at outweighing their phobias about the dead body. If I'd been there, I don't think I'd have been volunteering, either. It was twenty-year-old Salihah who eventually girded her loins and wheeled the body-bearing gurney across the expanse of open parking lot to the morgue, and then came back to take up her responsibilities again. She didn't get shot. She thinks it was a miracle, and maybe it was. Maybe it was a miracle, maybe the sniper didn't want to be the man who cut down that lovely, brave young woman. I don't know. All I know is that the beautiful Salihah fell in love with Blake and he married her and brought his bride back to the States.

I said, "Hey, Salihah," and stepped back to let her in. She allowed me to kiss her on the cheek.

"I need to see Josephine." Her high voice was determined. Salihah had been Jo's favorite Sunday school teacher all through her elementary years.

"She's doing homework . . ."

Annie Laurie had come to see who was at the door and took Salihah's hand and led her to the family room.

Jo was doing her homework in our bedroom. I poked my head in the room. Jo was stretched out on our bed on her tummy, working linear algebra equations without any enthusiasm. Baby Bear was drowsing on the floor near her.

"Mrs. Fincher is here to see you, Jo."

"Miss Salihah?"

Jo rolled off the bed and followed me into the living room, where she gave Salihah a hug and sat down on the couch next to her. Salihah stirred what seemed to be a quarter cup of sugar into the mug of tea Annie had given her.

Salihah said, "Josephine, God told me to come over tonight."

Whoa. Jo's eyebrows lifted.

"Becky tells me you are not sleeping in your room anymore. That is right?"

Jo nodded, her mouth tight. I wouldn't want to be Becky when Jo saw her at school tomorrow.

"Because that poor girl died there Friday?"

Another nod, her mouth even tighter.

"What was her name?

"Phoebe."

"Phoebe. That is right." Salihah nodded and sipped her tea. "That is Greek, you know, Josephine. It means ray of light. Was that a good name for her, Josephine, do you think?"

Jo was silent, looking for a way out of this dilemma, but she answered truthfully. "Not so much."

"Yes. That is what I have heard. That is where the tragedy lies. It is not terrible to die, Josephine. It is not even terrible to die young—much pain may be avoided if you die young. The tragedy is that Phoebe died before she could grow into her name."

God help me, Salihah was right. I'd come to think of Phoebe as a young woman who was destined to give and be dealt unhappiness. But that's absurd, and wrongheaded to boot. I have a lot of friends who started out life on the rocky side of the shore, but they changed, or something changed them, and they have good lives now. But Phoebe never got her chance to break away from everything that had gone wrong with her life. She didn't get her chance to change. We will never know how God might have used her to work His will.

Salihah said, "Is it that Phoebe is haunting the room, Josephine?"

Jo said. "I don't believe in ghosts."

Now Salihah shook her head in dismissal. "You believe, you do not believe. The Witch of Endor called forth the ghost of Samuel for Saul. Read your Bible."

Jo gave me an alarmed look and I made a mental note to discuss Second Samuel 28 with her sometime soon.

"You do not believe Phoebe is haunting your room. Yet you do not want to sleep in your room. Why should that be, Josephine?"

Jo dipped her head so that her hair veiled her eyes. "I don't know."

Salihah smiled and snapped her fingers. "Good. You come with me. We're going to use God's power to clean that room."

Oh my. I trust Salihah. I know she is a woman of God. God doesn't operate that way with me, but I'm prepared to accept that He does give Salihah direct messages, only, Jo is fifteen and she's very suggestible and—

Jo got up like a reluctant puppy and followed Salihah.

Annie Laurie said, "Is it okay if we come, too, Salihah?" for which I mentally thanked my wife.

Salihah gestured for us to come along. Baby Bear wasn't waiting for permission. If Jo was going, he was going, too. He was torn between wanting to lead the procession and the problem of not knowing where the procession was off to. Baby Bear forced his way to the front of the line and then kept stopping, trying to anticipate the direction. The result was that Baby Bear was tripping people up until Jo took him by his collar and kept him next to her.

We continued up until we all, Salihah, Jo, Baby Bear, Annie Laurie and I, stood outside Jo's bedroom door. I didn't feel any fear, but a heaviness of heart filled me. Sadness, I think. Grief for Phoebe and great sadness that my daughter's happy room had been stained by a young girl's death.

"Josephine, you have lived in this house all of your life. I remember your mommy and daddy"—it sounded like "Tati"—"moving to this house when he came to be our new minister. Your sister was a baby then. Has this been a happy house for your family?"

"Yes," Jo said.

"There have been many, many happy times in this house? There have been celebrations and books to read and family dinners and friends gathering?"

"Yes," Jo said.

I heard Annie Laurie sniff. I wasn't a crybaby, but I knew what Annie was feeling. Nights rocking our girls, the two of them splashing in the bathtub, their first attempts at cooking—if we were going to count "firsts," almost all of Jo's happened right here in this house. Her first solid food, her first steps, first tooth . . .

"Josephine, before we go into your room, will you share with me one happy memory you have of this room?"

She thought, her fingers rubbing Baby Bear's ear. "Once I got Baby Bear housetrained, Mom said he could sleep in my room."

"The dog makes you happy?"

Jo's eyes gleamed with tears and she nodded.

"How many nights has Baby Bear shared your bedroom with you, Josephine?"

She shook her head. "I don't know. He's like, five, so a lot."

Salihah nodded in satisfaction. "Yes. That is what I thought. Josephine, I ask you. Is it possible, my child, for one bad thing, one tragedy, to erase all the good that has happened in this house?"

Jo said, "Nooooo . . ." But her voice trembled.

Salihah said, very gently, "If one bad thing could make all

the good go away, Josephine, that would mean that darkness is stronger than light. Could that be true, Josephine?"

Jo couldn't speak. She shook her head, her face unhappy and fearful. But I looked at Annie Laurie, and her face was calm and confident.

Salihah said, "We're going to hold hands now."

Oh, my gosh, I thought, if Salihah started a *séance* here I was going to have to—

"Dear Father in Heaven," Salihah started. "This is Your daughter Salihah. I am asking You to give Josephine Wells comfort and courage and the peace that passes understanding. In Your Son's holy name, amen." She pushed the door open and we shuffled inside.

The wooden shutters were open and moonlight pooled on the floor. The big plastic goose lamp in the corner glowed. I reached for the light switch but Salihah stopped me. She turned and looked at the room. Usually it would be untidy—Jo is not Obesessive/Compulsive about anything but ballet—but after church earlier, while Jo was out with her friends, Annie and I had cleaned this room from top to bottom. Jo's room smelled of Lemon Pledge and vinegar. We had changed the sheets on both beds, washed her quilts and stuffed the pillow-cases with new pillows we'd bought at Marshalls on the way home from church. The carpet had been vacuumed twice, and before we'd vacuumed we had sprinkled and brushed it with those carpet granules that are supposed to clean ground-in dirt. We wanted to be thorough, is all. We had washed her windows inside and out, me standing on the roof of the garage to do one of them, and on a ladder to do the two others.

"Josephine." Salihah was smiling her wide, warm smile. She turned, taking everything in, her arms spread wide. "Josephine. This is a happy room. If Phoebe had to die, I am so grateful that she had this happy room to die in. That was a last gift you gave your friend."

A last gift to a lonely girl. Jo tried to keep it together but tears spilled from her eyes and she brought a hand to her mouth.

"She wasn't my friend, Miss Salihah. We hadn't been friends for a long time but she wanted me to be her friend and I wouldn't, I wouldn't even talk to her. I can't do anything about it now. It's over and there's nothing I can do—I can't tell her how sorry I am." She started sobbing.

I'm supposed to be smart. I made good grades. Great grades if you keep in mind I was playing ball. I did well in my master's program and my Ph.D. thesis was published. Nobody read it all the way through, except my dad, but the Rice University Press had accepted it.

And it still hadn't occurred to me that what was eating up my girl was guilt.

Salihah sat down on Jo's bed and patted the cover next to her. Jo sat down. Salihah said, "Yes, Josephine. Phoebe *was* your friend. You were angry and you were hurt by her, and you were not yet ready to forgive her. Phoebe must have hurt you very badly for you to refuse to speak to her. I know you, Josephine. You are not unkind. Before you can ask Phoebe to forgive you, you must forgive Phoebe."

"I do, but I—"

"No. Before you forgive Phoebe, you must acknowledge what you are forgiving her for. You must take in completely how she injured you. Only then can you completely forgive her. It is no good if you pretend you have nothing to forgive her for. Do you understand?"

Jo sat there, snuffling and wiping her eyes on the hem of her T-shirt until Annie handed her my handkerchief. Finally she nodded.

Salihah said, "Now I want you to tell Phoebe that you forgive her. Tell Phoebe that you take that hurt she gave you, and you bury it deep in the ground. It is no more. It is dead. Let Phoebe know that you restore to her your friendship. You give her your love, freely."

Jo cried and cried and Salihah held her in her arms and Jo got the words out. They weren't Salihah's words. They were less eloquent, but they were the words of a fifteen-year-old, and they were powerful.

Afterward, Salihah said, "Josephine, now, ask Phoebe to forgive you."

"But she's dead!"

It was a wail.

"Josephine! Do you not believe that Phoebe is with our Lord Jesus?"

Jo sniffled and said, "Even though I forgive her, Miss Salihah, she wasn't a very good person. She told lies and she said mean things and—"

Salihah lifted shocked and reproachful eyes to mine. I was shocked, too. "If you think you are going to Heaven because you are a good person, Josephine, then your daddy and I are going to have a talk."

"No, but—"

"There is no 'but.' It is grace that saves us, Josephine." She thought for a second, her forehead crumpled. "This is what my daddy told me. He said, 'Salihah, you are a good person. Your friend Layla, she flirts all the time with boys, she answers back to her daddy. But, Salihah, please see it this way: You and Layla, you stand on the shore of Alexandria. Heaven is Cyprus. Layla, she swims less than a mile. She can swim no more, and if the lifeboat of grace does not come and save her, Layla drowns. My Salihah, she swims for miles and miles and miles, so strong, so swift. But even my Salihah, she cannot swim to Cyprus. If the lifeboat of grace does not come and save her, my Salihah will also drown. She will not get to Cyprus either.'

"Phoebe could not swim to Cyprus. But Josephine, neither can you. We can't be good enough to get into Heaven. If you think your Lord closes the door on us because we are sinners, then we are none of us getting in. It's about relationship, Josephine. It's about knowing who you belong to."

Fresh tears. I wondered if Salihah would mind if I used her father's analogy in a sermon.

"Now, Josephine, ask Phoebe to forgive you."

Jo did. I felt wrung out, but Salihah wasn't done. She had us each lay a hand on a wall of Jo's room (I'd heard "Josephine" so often in the last half hour that I'd almost started to think of Jo as Josephine—I mean, it is her name, but we only use it in extremis, like when she's going to get grounded for the next seventeen years). Then she had us ask for God to bless the walls of the room, to bless all who entered the room and all who left its door (I mentally added window, knowing that Jo has, on occasion, used it as an exit or entrance). Salihah asked that all unhappiness and despair be driven from the room and that God give Jo sweet and peaceful sleep in this room. And then we all said, "Amen."

———

Annie Laurie and I sat in the family room, listening to the sound of the upstairs shower running. I brought Annie a glass of wine, and poured myself half a glass. We both needed it. I took Baby Bear out to do his business and when we came back in, Annie was on her way upstairs.

"Problem?"

She shook her head, a film of tears over her eyes, but with

a smile. She held her phone up for me to see a text from Jo:
Come tuck me in?

Five hundred years.

That's how long it's been since our baby had asked to be
tucked in. I felt jealous. In a good way. I watched Annie and
Baby Bear climb the stairs to tuck Jo into bed in her own, safe,
room.

I thought about Salihah's words. About forgiveness. I spent
some time on my knees. I spent a long time on my knees. Then
I made a call.

"Hey, Mom. It's me. Is it too late to call?"

Fifteen

Monday afternoon, Detective Wanderley called and told me that Phoebe Pickersley, it turned out, had died from a massive overdose of Dilaudid, a morphine substitute. There were no signs of violence on Phoebe's body except for those terrible piercings, and she'd done that to herself; and Wanderley said, no, he didn't consider a nipple piercing an act of violence and maybe I ought to go ahead and reserve my room at the old folk's home. Wanderley and his team were no longer considering Jo a suspect in Phoebe's death, as it wasn't likely Jo would have had access to Dilaudid. I said thank you very much. Dilaudid, it turns out, is not a street drug, not a drug commonly abused for recreational purposes. It's a palliative opiate most commonly used in oncology practices. That means it's a painkiller for cancer patients.

Phoebe had taken the Dilaudid in a concentrated flavored syrup—it is commonly prescribed as a liquid if the patient is having trouble swallowing. If, say, the patient has throat cancer, the way Phoebe's mom did.

It had indeed been prescribed, Wanderley told me, to Jennifer DeWitt Pickersley. Wanderley said it's not uncommon for terminal patients to hoard their pain medicines, in case they decide to make an early exit. He said that, very likely, Jenny Pickersley had hoarded her Dilaudid and either died before she got desperate or had been too far gone by the time she was ready to use it.

That means Phoebe hadn't been looking for the highs and lows an addled teen might seek with a drug cocktail.

That means she'd been looking for an exit.

That means that in Jo's parlance, Phoebe *was* a quitter.

I was with Jo. She should have gone to Darfur.

———————

There was still no sign of Phoebe's phone, and, since there was some indication that Phoebe had deliberately killed herself, the case had been closed and the subpoena to the phone company would not be requested, so if Phoebe had written her last message on her phone, or if she had called or texted anyone in her last moments, those words would stay a secret. Unless the phone turned up or whoever she had contacted came forward.

At dinner I told Jo and Annie Laurie the news that Phoebe's death had been ruled a suicide, and Jo's face turned into rock and she put her plate on the floor for Baby Bear, dropped her silverware in the sink and walked out of the house without a word. Baby Bear abandoned his plate and scratched at the door to be let out. Annie took his leash off the hook, wound it and put it in his mouth.

"Stay with her," Annie said, and opened the door. He took off.

"Next time," Annie said to me, "would you wait until after dinner? I don't know if you've noticed, but Jo's weight is down to half of nothing."

I said I hoped there wasn't going to be a next time.

———————

Mark Pickersley-Smythe called me on Tuesday and asked if I could meet him for lunch. I asked if we would be eating in his study and he said, no, he would meet me at Perry's Steakhouse and he'd take care of the check. Perry's Steakhouse is about burnished woods and comfortable leather seats and two-dollar-a-stalk asparagus and slabs of succulent, decadent, please-don't-let-it-be-a-sin-to-eat-meat steaks. I was glad I'd worn nice slacks to the office that day.

Mark had already secured a corner table and an icy-looking martini with three jalapeño-stuffed olives on a pick.

He stood as I approached the table and held his hand out to shake.

"Hi," he said and shook my hand firmly. "Let me *re*introduce myself. My name is Mark Pickersley. That's 'Pickersley' without a 'Smythe.' Have a seat and let me get you a drink." He held a finger up for the waiter. "I want to recommend the martinis. I ordered dry with two olives, but my fine waiter"—he nodded to the man now standing at his side—"informs me that you can't drink a martini with an even number of olives because it's unlucky." The waiter bowed and confirmed this information. Mark slapped himself on his forehead. "*That* explains *so much*! It's been the olives all along!"

The waiter asked what he could get me and I asked for iced tea and some water. He wanted to know did I want still or sparkling and I said I wanted tap, with lots of ice. The waiter was very nice about it and didn't get snooty.

I opened my mouth but Mark shook his head and handed me a menu. "Decide what you want and let's get it ordered. Then we'll talk."

I asked for the New York strip, rare, which at Perry's meant it would have a cool, bloody center. Mark ordered the same thing, with sides of creamed spinach, au gratin potatoes, and roasted sherried mushrooms for the table. On a second thought he also added the iced seafood tower to start, and the beefsteak tomato salads for us both.

"Do you think we ordered enough?" I said.

Mark's mouth fell open, but he raised his finger.

I said, "It was a joke, Mark," and he apologized to the waiter and sent him away.

"Tell me how you're doing, Mr. Pickersley," I said.

Mark drew a deep breath in through his nose. He took a sip of his martini and blew his cheeks out to let me know his drink was cold and strong and delicious. I drank some ice water.

"Detective Wanderley told you about the lab results?" he asked.

I said yes, I hoped that was okay.

"I asked him to tell you. So, the good news is my daughter wasn't a druggie, the bad news is, she wanted to die. I'll have that to live with." Mark lifted up from his seat and pulled his wallet out, flipped it open and showed me a school photo of a much younger Phoebe. I took it from him.

She would have been twelve or thirteen here. I recognized her—there were those huge, blue eyes, and the slightly weak chin. But here her hair was as blonde and straight as corn silk and it fell past her shoulders. Her eyelashes and eyebrows were so fair they were nearly invisible against her pale skin. She had tiny pearl earrings in her ears, no other piercings that you could see, and was dressed in a blue button-down shirt that matched her eyes. She wasn't a beauty, but she might have become one. In an exotic, bird-like way, she might have grown into beauty.

I gave him the photo back.

"You know why it's an actual photo? Why I'm not showing it to you on my iPhone?"

I put sugar and lemon in my tea and stirred. "It's a school photo, isn't it?"

"I'm not showing you a picture of Phoebe on my iPhone, because by the time I could afford an iPhone, *any* kind of cell phone that could take a picture, she didn't look like Phoebe anymore. She'd done the whole"—he waved his hands over his face and his hair—"and I hated it. She embarrassed me. I was embarrassed of my daughter. That's the truth. I'm going with the truth from now on." He pulled the silvery pick from his martini and bit off an olive. "That's why I'm dropping the Smythe. The people I come from don't do hyphenated names. Incidentally, Liz started as plain Liz Smith. No 'Smythe' to rhyme with 'blithe.' But that's her business. She can spell it and pronounce it any way she wants to because I ain't going to be carrying it around anymore. There's something else I want you to know." He took another sip from the icy glass. "No, there's a lot I want you to know. You got time?"

I told Mark my time was his.

"Thanks. You'll get a good lunch out of it. You should have a drink."

I assured Mark I was good with my tea.

"You know how Liz tells everyone that we met at work? Like I was a hotshot executive or something? We did meet at work, but she was the hotshot executive—I was working a machine. You know, name embroidered on my Dickies' pocket? I graduated from high school with a C average and that's only because I was their starting quarterback and got helped a lot. I injured my knee my senior year and that was the end of my college dreams. No one in my family has ever been to college. I would have been the first.

"Jenny and I thought Phoebe would make it for sure. Phoebe was smart. Not like me. Not like her mom. She was never popular, the way we were, but our daughter was *smart*." He took a piece of bread from the basket, buttered the whole piece and took a bite. "I know I'm supposed to break a piece off, butter it and so on—Liz had me in hard-core charm school for the first year of our marriage. Phew." He rolled his eyes to the ceiling.

"That was a kick. Every bite I put in my mouth, she had something to say about it. That's over, too. I'll eat the way I want to eat—if Liz can't stand to watch, I'll go eat in front of the TV." He took another bite and chewed with enjoyment.

Ahh. This was going to be a confessional lunch. I was okay with that. I said, "Did you find a letter? Did Phoebe leave some kind of explanation? Did something happen right before . . . right before?" I wanted to know why that girl had killed herself. What had been going on in her life for the months we hadn't seen her? I wanted to know it wasn't anything our family had been a part of. I'd never seen anything like that in Phoebe— anger, grief, yes—but that black despair? That hopelessness? No—if anything, I'd seen Phoebe as a fighter. She was mad at Jo, well, she got back at Jo. She felt hard done by Liz—she sure as shoot made Liz pay. Those are the acts of a *fighter*.

Mark put his fork down and shook his head. "Nah. There was nothing. And no note. I could tell Detective Wanderley didn't like that. I think he thinks we found something that makes us look bad, but we really didn't find anything. And I look plenty bad even without a letter."

"So you don't have any clue?"

"I know Phoebe was unhappy and mad but I'd have expected her to kill *Liz*, not herself." He paused. "I didn't mean that. She wouldn't have killed Liz. I only mean that she seemed angry, not depressed. That's all I mean. The last time I saw her, she and Liz had a knock-down-drag-out in the kitchen and Phoebe went flying up to her room. I was going up to talk to her but Liz stopped me and said to let her go, that this couldn't go on and she'd handle it. Liz went up to Phoebe's room for a half an hour or so, and when she came out, she said they'd reached an understanding and that Phoebe wanted to be alone for a while and I should respect that. So Liz thought everything was going to be okay from now on." He smiled. "Liz doesn't always read people that well." The smile slipped and Mark closed his eyes. "But I have no clue why Phoebe would . . . you know."

The waiter came over with the iced seafood tower, and set two plates down in front of us. You should have seen it. This thing was sex as food. I'm not lying. Crab, shrimp, scallops, calamari, lobster—be still my heart. I tried not to attack it too eagerly.

Mark paused, his fork in the air. "Know how many times I ate in a restaurant like this before Liz? Not one single time. Are you kidding me? Did you see these prices?" He loaded his plate. "Before I go any further, will you speak at Phoebe's memorial service? Thursday. Six thirty. It's going to be at that funeral home on the Southwest Freeway, right up here. It's called . . ." He snapped his fingers in frustration.

"Settegast-Koph."

"Yeah. Cremation. Phoebe hated the idea of . . ." Mark stopped, struggled. He picked up his martini glass, didn't drink from it, put it back down. "Give me a minute," he said and left the restaurant.

Cremation? Well, the case *was* closed. And there had been an autopsy. Still . . .

The waiter drifted over looking concerned but I waved him off. Drank some tea. Broke a bread roll into pieces.

Five minutes and Mark was back.

I said, "Liz doesn't want me to do the funeral, Mark. She wasn't too happy with the way I handled things at your house Saturday."

Mark picked a shrimp up by the tail, dunked it in rémoulade and popped it, tail and all, into his mouth. "Ahh. Because you wouldn't pry me out of my study? Yeah. She's cooled down about that, but she's still mad at you. Doesn't matter. Phoebe wasn't her daughter. Liz told me that a thousand times. That means I'll make the funeral arrangements, and I don't have anyone else to ask. You're it."

"I'd be happy to speak at Phoebe's memorial service." Not a compliment that I was only being asked because he didn't have anyone else, but *I* wouldn't ask me if there had been anyone else.

Mark asked the waiter to box up the rest of the cold seafood. "You'll take that home, Bear."

I refused but he reminded me that Liz was allergic to seafood and wouldn't allow it in the house. The waiter said he would keep it chilled until I was ready to leave.

I said, "So what's with the name change?"

Another waiter appeared with the beefsteak tomatoes.

"Like I said, I'm not living the lie anymore. Who does that hyphenated name thing, anyway? Not East Texas machinists—I'll tell you that. I'll wear the clothes. If I'd had money back then, I would have dressed this way. I like nice clothes." He considered. "Except those white linen slacks are going to have to go—I didn't pick those out." Mark ate a bite of bright red tomato. "But I'm done being Liz's poodle."

You know, the polite thing would have been to protest, but it would have been false, so I didn't. He had been playing the lapdog. I mean, God help the man who has to *lock himself away* from his wife.

"Did you know that Liz and I went to high school together? I didn't *know* her, but I knew who she was. She was the smart, fat, ugly chick. That's actually sort of a compliment to Liz; when we talked about her—which was almost never, she wasn't even a blip on our radar screen, but still— 'smart' always came before 'fat' and 'ugly.' I know how that makes me sound, but I'm telling you how it was. I was a high school god." He saw my expression and laughed out loud. "I was, Bear—you played ball. You have to know."

"I was a lineman," I said.

"Oh, then you were only a demigod. Me, I was the quarterback and I was the best my school had had in years. I played serious ball and I was good at every sport I'd tried. I was good-looking and I didn't crap on people. That's all it takes in high school. If I hadn't taken that one bad hit, I'd be selling toothpaste and doing color for ESPN today."

I gave an embarrassed laugh.

"Bear." He still had his smile, but he was serious now. "I was that good. Jenny had every right to expect the big bucks."

Mark focused on his salad. He was eating with gusto.

You know what was weird? It was like Phoebe's death had somehow freed him from Liz's control. Like he had thrown off the pretension and all the kowtowing to Liz, and I was glad he had. It's only that I hated that it taken the death of his child to make him be a man.

What if he could have stood up to Liz earlier? What if he could have said, "Look, she's my daughter and she's sad and mad right now, but we're going to stick with her through this—we're going to see her through to the other side and if you can't get with the program, then go sit down with a therapist and *find out how*"? Maybe Phoebe would have come around. Maybe she and Jo would have made up, and Phoebe would come over, say, once or twice a week instead of five or six times, and . . .

". . . that I was on top of the mountain and Liz—Liz never made the foothills."

I started listening again.

Mark lifted his water glass and our glasses were refilled.

"I dated the prettiest girl in school, Jenny DeWitt. Phoebe's mom. And everyone knew we were together. And then Liz, who was *wallpaper* in high school, she was *invisible*, decides she's *in love* with me. This is in high school, like, our junior year. Everybody has their role and there is no budging. Not in high school. Not unless you're starring in a teen flick.

"But it's like Liz didn't know that. Like she didn't know that the quarterback never ends up with the fat girl at the end of the movie." He shook his head, remembering the audacity of the plain, brainy girl who had aspired to the high school football star. I thought it had taken a lot of guts. "And she would *call* me." Mark fished an olive out of his drink, poked the sliver of jalapeño out with his little finger, ate the pepper.

"Once—and this still makes me cringe—Liz called and kept me on the phone because I had no clue how to get off the phone, because I was a nice guy. I was. And I finally said, 'Let me get something to eat,' so I set the phone down and I go in the kitchen and get something and a friend comes to the back door and I go off with him. Not on purpose. I forgot Liz was on the phone. I get home, I don't know, had to be a couple of hours later, and I notice the phone off the hook, and I hear, 'Mark? Mark?' She had *waited* for me.

"Liz tells that story to show how romantic she is but, Bear, it was *pathetic*. I stopped answering the phone. When I stopped answering the phone, she started coming up to me at school. I'm with my friends and she comes up and she asks me to a cotillion! I don't know how she got invited. The rich kids gave them. The popular kids got invited. I got invited, but I couldn't afford it. Liz wasn't rich or popular, so I don't know how she got an invite. Maybe she did a rich kid's term paper or something. I said I had plans. There was no way I could go with her. But, damn, I could not shake her."

All the while he's talking, I'm seeing a sixteen-year-old girl, overweight, not pretty, who found the courage to call her high school's brightest sports star. I'm seeing her, sweaty-palmed, her heart thumping, dialing his number, and then hearing him pick up. And he lets her talk, says a few words back, and I can see her face change and glow because she's thinking maybe this could really happen, everybody says what a nice guy he is, maybe he can see the real Liz, the Liz under the pounds and the lousy clothes, and I can see her face when he says he's going to get a bite to eat—still happy, maybe glad for the chance to catch her breath, because she's the one doing all the talking, you know she is, and then I can see her, holding a phone to her ear, waiting. Waiting. Waiting for a sixteen-year-old boy, who went out his back door with never a thought of her, the nice guy, and she's still holding on. Waiting. Every once in a while saying, "Mark? Mark?" And I want to leave this restaurant, and drive to Liz's house, because it is *her* house, and I want to wrap her in a bear hug and say, "Liz, put the phone down. Put the phone down, sweetheart. Don't you wait for a boy who is careless with your heart. You let him go. Find yourself a man who feels *honored* to have you on his arm. Don't you settle for less. Let him go, Liz."

And I am more than twenty years too late to tell her those things, and if her no-show daddy was before me now, I would wring his neck and I'd do it for Liz, because he wasn't there to say the words that might have made all the difference in the whole wide world, and she never let go. And I know now, Liz is still waiting.

Our steaks and sides arrived and Mark busied himself over the food, which looked delicious, but I couldn't touch it. I had a sixteen-year-old girl sitting heavy on my heart and she was giving me heartburn. And Mark didn't look that golden anymore.

Mark said, "I'm telling you all this because . . . I don't know why I'm telling you." He slid the two remaining olives into his mouth. Still chewing he said, "Yeah, I do." He drank off the last of his martini but he shook his head when the waiter offered to bring him another. "I'm telling you because this is why Phoebe died. It's my fault. It's mainly my fault, but it's Liz's fault, too.

"Jenny and I got married right out of high school. She was pregnant, no surprise there, and my dad said I had to do the right thing. Whether he would have felt that way if I'd been playing college ball, I don't know, but my knee was busted and I wasn't and I married her. We lost that first baby, but Jenny stayed married to me, mainly, I think, because she didn't know what else to do with her life. She didn't want to move back with her dad, and her mom was living with a guy who had eyes for Jenny—that wasn't an option. Jenny lost two more pregnancies after that. I was ready to walk, and Jenny was, too, and she'd tell me so when she'd had too much to drink, and then we got pregnant with Phoebe.

"Do you remember, Bear? The first time you held your baby in your arms? I wanted to be there for that baby. I wanted to be the dad she needed. We both loved Phoebe. She's what kept us together for a long time." Mark spooned some mushrooms onto my plate. "My parents helped us with the down payment on a trailer. What does your dad do?" he asked.

I told him my dad taught calculus at Houston Community College.

"So you never lived in a trailer?"

I said, "No." My dad never made much money when I was a kid, but we did have a house.

"Where I'm from, the people I'm from, a trailer isn't anything to be ashamed of. A house was better, yeah, but when you're starting out, a trailer was a step up from an apartment. You 'owned property.' Jenny was happy in the trailer for, ummmm, maybe fifteen minutes. She was a beautiful woman and she could have had any man she wanted. I know that because she told me so five times a day. She should have used that beauty and married a rich man, because beauty is a commodity and it has a sell-by date." He shook his head. "I didn't know I was poor growing up. I thought I was middle class. Here in Sugar Land, I'd have been poor. No trailer parks in Sugar Land."

"There is one." I sawed off a bite of steak but I didn't put it in my mouth.

"A trailer park?"

"Off of 59. Near Grand Parkway. It's close to the paintball place."

"Hunh!" Mark worked on a bite of steak. "What about at Clements High School? Do you think there was a whole crew of other trailer park kids there along with Phoebe?"

"Probably not. But when I met her, Phoebe wasn't a trailer park kid—Phoebe lived in the most expensive neighborhood in First Colony, and that was all the kids at Clements would know unless Phoebe told them differently."

"And that would count with them, right?"

Was there a place in the world so pure that money didn't count? If there was, then it wasn't in Sugar Land, Texas.

My plate was still full but I stopped pretending to eat.

"So about a dozen years go by, and then, ahh, four and a half years ago, I'm working at a fourdrinier machine, that's . . . never mind what it is, it's a machine that makes paperboard. I've been at the job three, four months and it pays some better than the job before that, but not a lot. One day a salesman is walking clients through the work area, and who's with them? Liz Smith. Turns out Liz *owns* the damn company." Mark gave a bark of laughter. "I didn't know. How would I know? I knew the company was owned by someone named L. L. Smythe; I'd known Liz as plain Liz Smith. I'd never have put two and two together. And when I saw her that day, I *didn't recognize* her. The nose is gone, for one thing. She's had her teeth fixed and she has lost a ton of weight. She's like, I don't know—all put together. She's a blonde now and—I never would have recognized her. But she recognized me, Bear, oh, yes. Liz recognized me. I'm working, not paying any attention to the management and clients walking through—what do they have to do with me? We're in different worlds. All I know is, some executive woman stops dead in front of me, staring like I'm the Second Coming and she knows for sure she's got a place in Heaven. She is lit up like a Christmas angel." Mark gave a snort of laughter. "I look over my left shoulder, look over my right—it'd been a while since a woman had looked at me like that. Besides, there's something about having your name embroidered on the breast pocket of your coveralls that doesn't usually work for women in blazers."

He put his fork down. He'd been playing with his food, too.

Mark said, "I know what this is going to make me sound like, but I'm going to tell you anyway. Yep. I was promoted *that day*. I'll tell you—those clients? They walked away thinking they'd seen the beginning of one of those old Meg Ryan movies. She tells my foreman she wants me in her office and those coveralls were *gone*. The very next day, Liz had me training to be a salesman. The deals are falling in my lap, since Liz was doing the real selling—it was my name on the contract, but she was doing the hard stuff. Not that anything is hard for Liz. And, 'Oh, Mark, now that you're in sales, you need a new wardrobe'— she chooses everything. 'It'll come out of my commissions,' she says.

"I'm having lunch with Liz three times a week so she can go over my 'career objectives.' And then I'm having dinners with her. And then I'm in her bed."

It's not a surprise. I'd been expecting this part of the story.

"I told Jenny about Liz. Not about the bed part. But the

promotions and all and she knew how Liz felt about me in high school. Jenny's all, 'Don't blow this chance, too—you better make good on this one.'"

Mark pressed the tines of his fork into his thumb. "It was just Jenny pimping me out. It felt good to be someone's ideal again. Liz made me feel like none of it was my fault—that it was Jenny who held me back." Mark made a disgusted face. "I knew it was bull. Even then, I knew it was bull. But I was milking it. An expense account. Me! I got Phoebe new clothes—not from Walmart, either and she was, ahh, she felt pretty in them.

"Now, I'm not smart, but I'm not stupid, not anymore, and I'm being careful but Liz says I don't need to worry. Liz tells me she's on the Pill, and, anyway, we're both a sneeze away from forty.

"Only, turns out the pill she was on wasn't birth control, it was fertility treatments. Less than a week after she saw me, she started *trying* to have a baby."

I was glad I hadn't eaten that steak. This story had started out Oprah and gone to Springer. Mark nodded at my expression. "Yep. Liz is goal-oriented. She even told me—this is after she was pregnant, she knew enough to realize these would not be words of seduction—she says that with her brains and my looks and athletic skills, our baby will be C-level across the board. Know what that means? *C* is for CEO. I was a sperm donor, Bear!"

A well-paid one, I thought.

The waiter did his discreet hovering act and Mark got him to pack up the rest of the meal and add it to the seafood box in the back.

"My life was out of control. I had a daughter who was going to need money for college and a wife living in a trailer park who thought someone owed her a house on River Oaks Boulevard. The extra money I'd started making was just enough to give

Jenny an appetite for more. I'm sleeping with the woman who writes my paychecks, and that woman tells me, *a month and a half* into the affair, that she's having my babies. Two babies. Two. You get that?"

I got it. I didn't *want* it . . .

"Here's what Liz communicates, not as bluntly as I'm putting it, but she ain't mincing words, either: She wants to get married. She's always loved me, on and on." Mark gives a tight smile. "If I decide not to marry her—keep in mind I'd never told the woman I loved her, because I didn't—if I decide not to marry her, she's sure I would understand that she wouldn't be able to work 'alongside' me anymore. So I'd be out of work, although she *would* expect me to pay child support on the two babies."

I think *Fatal Attraction* should be required viewing for all men between the ages of thirteen and eighty-five. You think you can eat the cake and the icing and someone else will pay the tab? Watch that movie.

"And when I sit Jenny down to talk to her, what I get back is not, 'Oh, I love you, don't leave me.' Jenny thinks this could be *her* ticket out. Right? You got that? I'd be married to a rich lady and I could make a nice settlement on her. Jenny is *excited*. Our marriage was clearly over—at least that part I know I didn't ruin.

"But Bear, rich people don't get to be rich people by throwing their money away. Liz's lawyer has me move out of the trailer and into an apartment while he handles the whole mediation—I'm not even there except for the end when he calls me in and says 'Sign here' and I do."

I had started this lunch feeling sorry for Mark. I wanted to help him be a stand-up man—the more I heard, the less I liked him.

"The divorce is finalized three months and one week after

Liz promised Jenny the new trailer and the lawyer tells her she'll get thirty percent of my salary. I'm getting married to my *second* pregnant wife. Then Jenny finds out that she is going to get thirty percent of nothing. Liz has structured my salary so that I'm not making much more than I was when I was working the fourdrinier machine. *And* Liz wants me to pay 'my fair share' of the household expenses. Bear, when I'm done paying those two women, I got *nothing* in my pocket. I had to go hat in hand to Liz to ask for money to pay for Phoebe's *school pictures*!" He's smiling as if this is all a funny story and not his own messed-up life.

"I'm going to have a beer," he said. "You want a beer?"

I shook my head. I wanted to go home and take a long walk with Baby Bear and then tuck Jo in bed if she'd let me and then pull Annie into the shower with me and scrub her back and hold my good woman in my arms and tell her I would never stray because even if I didn't think it was wrong, it is way too complicated for this old guy.

You know that play, *No Exit*? One of those French existentialist guys wrote it. It's about personalized Hell. That's what Mark was describing to me—my version of Hell. The man could have his house and his garden. You know what? The price was too damn high.

The waiter brought Mark a frosted glass. It looked good but it was early afternoon and I was going back to the office. If the story was ever over.

"Then, because that's not enough, right? God hasn't punished me enough already. The boys come early and they have to be in the incubator and however I felt about Liz, I loved those boys the second I got ahold of them. What little fighters."

Mark threw his hands up, "And then Jenny gets sick. Look. I didn't love her anymore. But I didn't *hate* the woman, and I wouldn't wish throat cancer on Kim Jong Il—or his son. Phoebe is there and I can't get her to come live with us, not that Liz is encouraging her to. And, oh my God, when I go over there to get Phoebe? If Mitch, Jenny's dad, was there, he'd get on me like pitch, he never stopped, what a lowlife I was, that it was my fault his daughter was sick. On and on he went. That old man was a loon. How was it my fault Jenny got cancer? She smoked two packs a day! *That's* why she got cancer!" Mark pointed his fork at me. "Do you know Mitch had a life insurance policy on Jenny? With *himself* as the beneficiary? I could see it if the money had been for Phoebe, for her college fund, say. But for himself? Do you have policies on your daughters?"

Okay, this was awkward. I had to admit I did.

"The girls have whole-life policies. If they cash them in when they're fifty, I think, they'll be worth a little money. My agent convinced me."

Mark looked surprised but he didn't comment. Instead he continued, "Jenny had a life insurance policy on herself. I think some good-looking salesman talked her into it. That one goes to Phoebe—went to Phoebe. Mitch will get that one, too. The way he lives, he won't have to work again." Mark propped his elbows on the table and leaned over to me. "One thing Mitch DeWitt had right. I did have to help out some, you know? Only where's the money coming from? Not Liz! I barely brought the subject up and Liz crawled right down my throat, grabbed a handful of my testicles and pulled them up to my sternum before she let go. Damn me." He shook his head at the memory.

"I pawned my Rolex. *I* didn't know how much Liz had paid for it. I didn't know a watch *could* cost that much. I gave the money I got to Jenny and right away, I mean, a *day* after the watch was gone, Liz noticed it was missing. I told her I lost it. I go to sleep and she wakes me up in the middle of the night holding the pawn ticket. She went through my wallet." Mark drank deeply and then laughed mid-sip, spraying foam across the table. "Oh, geez, Bear, I'm sorry." He handed me a linen napkin. "Only, Bear, you should have seen her. She's holding the ticket in my face and she is shaking, she's so mad. You remember those old cartoons, there'd be a bull, ripping up the sod with his hooves and smoke coming out his nose and the bull is making a sound like a steam engine? That was Liz." His laugh died down. He pulled a cuff up to show me a blue-faced Rolex surrounded with diamonds. "See that?" he said, "I'm not supposed to take it off. Not even to swim—it's waterproof to some depth I don't plan on going to. I wear it when I sleep. She wants that damn watch on, and if I want any peace, I've got to wear it."

"What's next, Mark?" I didn't want to hurry him . . . no, I did want to hurry him. I didn't want to *look* like I was hurrying him.

"This is my plan." He knew I was getting impatient and he got to business. "First, the memorial service. Next, I'm taking Toby and Tanner to the Hermann Park Zoo, and we're going to ride the train. I'm going to get the last car in the train, and I'm going to scatter Phoebe's ashes on the train tracks."

"What?"

"I didn't have any money when Phoebe was little, but I had enough for the zoo and the train. We went to the zoo almost every weekend. Jenny would pack us a lunch and she'd go have a day with her friends while Phoebe and I went to the zoo. And we always rode the train, even if it rained. She loved it. It made her happy." He finished his beer and put a platinum card on the table. It was whisked away almost before it settled. "It's not like she's going to be in that box anyway, Bear."

I knew he was right. I hoped the conductor didn't catch him.

"Once that's done I'm getting a job."

"I thought you were working?"

His mouth twisted. "Not after she sold the company. I follow her around while she looks for investment property. But I'm through with that. I think I can get a job as a golf pro at Bridge-water. I won't make that much, but it will be my own money."

"How's all this going to go down with Liz? The name change, the job?"

He gave a shrug. "Guess I'll find out." He gave me his perfect-toothed grin. "My granddad says Liz will thank me if I start acting like a man. We'll see. Liz may be a different breed of woman than what Granddad's familiar with."

"What if she tells you it's her way or the highway?"

"She won't." A quick, tight smile, no teeth. "As long as I don't push her too hard, as long as she can spin it, 'Mark is such an independent spirit,' something like that. She's not going to want her picture broken up even more."

I thought Mark was probably right about that.

Sixteen

The Pickersleys got a huge turnout for Thursday's seven o'clock memorial service. There's nothing like dying to make a teenager appreciated. Kids love a tragedy. Something to do with hormones.

Liz was surrounded by women from the church and I'm glad to report that she was composed and dignified and if she wasn't warm when she greeted me, neither did she dance around me on her toes, hissing like a lizard. So that was good. I wondered if she would give as composed a greeting to DeWitt when he showed up. After all, she hadn't told me I couldn't come. She had said I couldn't do the service—it was DeWitt she had told not to come. I wasn't expecting Mitch DeWitt to ignore his granddaughter's service.

Liz's mom, Susan, was there, again wearing beautiful clothes and looking uncomfortable in them. Sue Ellen stood outside the funeral home door and smoked cigarette after cigarette before dusting the ash off a black jacket and stalking inside. Mark's grandfather introduced me to his son Jimmy, Mark's father, who looked mad, and Mark's mother Lou who looked weepy. Annie Laurie sought them out and told them stories about her times with Phoebe. Dan's eyes filled and he looked madder than ever.

Alex arrived and scanned the building. He saw me and headed my way.

"Where's Jo?"

"I thought she was coming with you."

"Yeah, well, she changed her mind, but she should be here by now, shouldn't she? The service starts in fifteen minutes."

I interrupted him to greet a newcomer.

Jonathon Reece had come with his brother David. Jonathon had kept in touch with Brick and Jason, our youth ministers, and had learned about Phoebe's death from them.

I shook David's hand, but it was withdrawn too quickly for me to be able to read the letters tattooed across the knuckles.

I asked Jonathon where he had ended up interning after leaving us.

"Mr. Wells, I think God has turned me in a different direction. All the churches I had applied to had already filled their rosters, but by a happy chance, a pastor I know told me his brother's law firm was looking for an intern. I spent the summer at Cobble and Shelby in Dallas and I loved it. I'll be taking the LSAT in January."

Ahh. That was a disappointment. I really did think this young man was cut out for the ministry. I know many fine lawyers, good and godly men and women. But that's the thing—I know a ton of them. There are so few gifted young people who feel drawn to the ministry.

With an effort, I kept my smile on. "That's fine, Jonathon. I know you'll be a success." The idea that our church had played a part in his decision to turn away from the ministry just made me sick. "How does your mother feel about the career change?"

Jonathon checked out the tips of his shoes. "Fine. Mom's fine about it."

David spoke up, his voice a low purr. "Our mom is getting on her knees every night praying Jonathon will see things true again. It's a shame your church didn't protect your interns as well as you protected your own kids."

I flushed and Jonathon grabbed his brother's elbow to pull him away, but David stood his ground.

Alex touched my back. "Mr. Wells—"

I said, "Wait a minute, Alex. David, you're right, we should have done a better job and we have put some changes in place—"

"Too late for Jonathon, you hear what I'm saying?"

"David, would you please—" began Jonathon.

"Jonathon could have gone to any church he wanted to. My parents never wanted him to come out here to your rich white—"

Jonathon swung his brother around. "This is not—"

Alex stepped in between us and said, "Mr. Wells, I have to talk to you *now* and no, I can't wait a minute. I'm trying to do the right thing here but if you don't come with me right this second, I'm doing it on my own."

The three of us stared at Alex, who stared back and then strode off.

I said, "Excuse me, please." The boy had his car keys in hand and was out the door before I caught up to him. "Alex, what the heck?"

"Jo isn't here. She's on her way to that trailer park."

"What?"

He didn't slow down. "Jo's headed to Phoebe's trailer."

"*What?*"

"I'm going to go get her." He unlocked the huge, red Ford F-150 truck his grandfather had bought him for his sixteenth birthday. It was a big truck made bigger to accommodate the thirty-five-inch Toyo all-terrain tires beneath it.

"Wait a minute, Alex—"

"She's got at least fifteen minutes on me and I'm not waiting. You want to go, get in the truck."

"I'll drive," I said.

"You don't know how to get there," he said, and swung himself up into the cab.

I held my keys up and jingled them. "You could give me directions, Alex. I can take directions."

He shut his door in my face and powered down his window. He looked down at me from the ridiculous height that truck was jacked up to. "Can you?" he asked. "Then get into the truck."

I didn't know where the trailer park was. I couldn't even remember the name of the place. Out by Hobby was all I knew. I climbed into Alex's jacked-up truck and buckled my seat belt. I was mad but he had me. There was no way I was going to let this boy take care of a situation that called for a man.

The truck had a new addition: a gun rack in the back window, complete with a glossy Remington 1100, an automatic shotgun

"You allowed to carry that thing?"

"I am. This is Texas."

I sighed. Cold dead fingers and all that.

"I've got to make a call," I said and punched in Brick's number.

He answered right away. "Bear?"

"You're going to have to do the eulogy, Brick, I've got an emergency." I checked my seat. Alex was not driving to impress his girlfriend's dad tonight. He was driving to get from point A to point B in the shortest time possible.

"What?"

"You heard me, Brick."

"Wait. Me? Oh, no. Ask Jason. I can't do it."

"I didn't ask Jason, I asked you. And I'm not asking you, I'm telling you. This is a job, Brick. Sometimes that job means you fill in for someone else. Today you're filling in for me. You're going to have about twenty minutes, so go someplace quiet, collect yourself, say a prayer and jot down a few notes. Talk from the heart. You'll do fine."

"What's wrong? Why can't you do it? Didn't they ask you? I've never done a eulogy. I don't know any dead people."

Alex didn't bother with the driveway. His monster tires bounced off the curb and onto the frontage road.

"You knew Phoebe. Do your best. That's all I was going to do."

"Oh, Bear, I can't do this, I—"

"Cowboy up, Brick." I closed the phone call. "What the heck is going on?" I said to Alex.

He didn't let up on the gas pedal. "I'm going to be dead for telling you this," he said, "but if anything happens to my Jo, I die anyway."

See, this was the kind of talk Annie Laurie and I object to. *His* Jo. I tried Jo's phone. No answer. "She's not *your* Jo, Alex. She's mine. I know my daughter better than you ever will."

Alex cut in front of an eighteen-wheeler and entered the freeway a quarter inch ahead of its bumper. The driver gave us a taste of his air horn. I used a word I haven't used since college.

"Really? Know about the tattoo?"

I didn't reply. There was no tattoo. The girls know how I feel about tattoos.

"Don't crack up over it, Mr. Wells. It's the size of my thumbnail. A gray-and-white bird. A phoebe."

"Oh yeah? Where is it?" There was no tattoo.

"On the nape of her neck. She got it Monday. After school. You know that place across the block from her dance class?"

I had noticed the small storefront when it moved in and thought it didn't have a chance of surviving in the suburbs.

Alex glanced over when I didn't say anything. "Don't worry

about it. Her hair covers it. She's going to tell you. I made her promise she would."

Alex had made my daughter promise to tell me. To let me in on the news. To allow me to be a part of her life. My daughter. *My* Jo.

"All right, fine. I don't know anything. You want to tell me what's going on?" *Or do you want to keep on lording it over me?* I added silently.

"You told Jo that Phoebe killed herself by overdosing on Dilaudid."

"So? Oh, my gosh, look out for that Mini!" I saw a white-faced passenger stare out at us as Alex whipped to the side of the slow-moving toy car.

"*So*, Jo doesn't think Phoebe killed herself. Either she can't, or she won't, believe it. She wanted to go to that trailer to look for . . . to see if she can find out anything and she asked me to take her. I said we didn't want to miss the service. Jo said there was more than one way to honor a person's death and she was honoring Phoebe in her own way. I said I'd take her tomorrow, it wasn't safe at night. We had a fight and she stomped off."

"Well, dang it, Alex, she's not at the trailer then, she doesn't have any way to get there." I didn't add "Duh," but I thought it. It's not like the greater Houston area is known for its public transportation system. Every Texan over sixteen has a car. It's practically the law.

"Cara took her."

"Cara didn't take her—whoa!" Alex took the entrance ramp to the Sam Houston Tollway at a speed the engineers had not planned for. I began again. "Cara can't drive, either."

"Yes, she can. Better than—"

"Cara's fifteen, too!"

Alex squeezed between a van and a tow truck and I swallowed my teeth.

"She can't drive *legally*, but her dad started teaching her when she was five, out at their ranch. She can drive." He threw me a look. "Cara's parents are at the memorial service for Phoebe. She took her dad's Jeep." Alex blew through the first EZ TAG station.

"The one with no top or doors?"

"That's the only one he has."

See, that's not a vehicle, that's a grown-man's toy. That's not the car you stick a newbie driver in. Annie Laurie and I had given Merrie a 1993 Volvo sedan. It won't go very fast and it's armored like a tank. That's a good car. I felt sick. I sent Annie a text so she could feel sick, too.

"Where is this place?"

"Telephone Road between Almeda-Genoa and Hobby Airport."

That would be a half-hour drive, easy, if you never hit a red light and everybody else in the city was driving somewhere else, leaving the roads wide open for you.

Telephone Road is a broad, flat ribbon of a road lined with strip centers with check-cashing stores, liquor and convenience stores and the kind of resale shop that stacks worn and battered baby furniture on the sidewalk outside its doors. There are a number of charmless apartment complexes promising the first's month's rent free. Telephone Road is the kind of place where men congregate in parking lots and on corners to do their drinking and talking and fighting. It's not a place you want your fifteen-year-old daughter and her fifteen-year-old friend to be out after dark in an open-top, doorless Jeep that can't be locked.

I had a vision of the girls stopped at a red light. Oh my gosh.

"Let me drive," I said.

"No."

"Well, can you go any faster?"

Alex pressed his foot down and the red monster roared. Up ahead, cars were parting for us.

"Jo isn't answering her phone," I said after trying for the twentieth time to call her.

"I know it." He didn't add, "Duh," but it was clear he thought it.

"So how do you know what she's doing?"

"Because Cara posted it on Facebook."

Well, sure she did. Because if you're fifteen years old, it doesn't occur to you to go or do anything without letting the whole world know it—just on the outside chance that someone might be interested.

I shut up. We were making too big a deal of this, me and Alex. It couldn't be that bad. I was overreacting. Lots of girls live on Telephone Road . . . lots of girls who know where it's safe to be and where it isn't; lots of girls who aren't driving their daddy's forty-thousand-dollar modified Jeep Wrangler, sans top and doors, in a glossy burnt orange, Go Texas!

"How do I get on Facebook?"

"Aw, Mr. Wells, don't go there, okay?"

Alex took the Telephone Road exit. He didn't even slow when he turned left and pulled between crumbling brick columns that held up a sign reading VAN MANOR.

I yelled, "Alex!" and he slammed on his brakes before he hit a scruffy puppy blinded by his lights. The puppy wobbled off the road and Alex crept forward through the narrow, unlit alleys, trailer homes and RVs on either side. Alex slowed to a stop.

I saw the orange Jeep parked next to a green-and-white mobile home. The Jeep was empty. I had my hand on the door handle when a girl's face slapped up against my window. I yelled.

It was Cara, her eyes saucer-big. She fumbled at the door

handle and in spite of her, I got the door open. Cara fell into my arms and grabbed my head. She put her mouth to my ear.

"Mr. Wells, Jo's inside but someone's there and he was yelling and he's got a gun and I called nine-one-one and I didn't know what to do and Jo was crying!" The last three words were a soft wail in my ear.

"Cara, get in the truck with Alex and lock the doors. Stay there. Lie down on the floor. Don't either of you dare move until the police tell you it's okay."

Wanderley would have told me to wait for the police, too. I set Cara aside and moved toward the trailer. There were no lights on. Behind me, I heard the squeak of a screen door opening. I turned and saw the large form of a woman. A soft voice said, "That's Mr. DeWitt's trailer."

My blood was roaring in my ears. I didn't see a doorbell. I knocked on the trailer door. Nothing.

I knocked again and said, "Hello? This is Walker Wells, I'm going to come in and get my daughter and then we'll leave, okay?" I tried the handle. Locked.

The soft voice said, "He's gonna be drunk."

The trailer had an open window next to the front door. From inside I heard a whimper. It was Jo's whimper. I put my shoulder against the door and shoved until I heard the latch pop and the door fell open. I stepped inside. As I did, from behind me I heard the slap of a Remington 1100's bolt slamming home. That, I knew, would be Alex's Remington. Alex, who had not stayed on the truck floor with the doors locked. I didn't have time to think about Alex, except to say a quick prayer that he wouldn't go all Texas Ranger on me.

The trailer was dark and stank of cheap liquor and un-washed body.

My daughter was sitting in front of a small kitchen table,

her back to me. Leaning against the kitchen sink was the dark shape of a man pointing a rifle at her.

Might have been a shotgun. It was dark. I didn't care. I didn't want it pointed at my kid.

I stepped forward and Mitch DeWitt said, "You stop right there."

I did. I was close enough to put my hand on Jo's neck. Her warm fingers reached up and twined around my thumb. Mitch gestured toward Jo with the rifle.

"That girl, right there"—the muzzle of the gun wavered between Jo's forehead and her breastbone—"broke into my house." He spoke carefully, overenunciating each word. "To rob me."

"She shouldn't have done that, sir. I apologize for her behavior. You'll get a written note of apology." I got a good grip on the neck of her jacket.

Jo said, "No, he—" I put some pressure on her and she shut up.

I put my other hand under her arm, her bones small and fine under my big hand, even through her jacket, and pulled her up. "I'm going to take her home and ground her. I promise you, she'll be punished, okay?" In one move, I yanked Jo the rest of the way out of the booth and over its back. She stumbled to her feet. I grabbed the back of her jacket and thrust her behind me, but held on because Jo does not obey and she did not yet understand, as I did, that she could die. We could both die.

From a distance there was the howl of a siren.

Mitch was slow, but not that slow. He lifted his rifle to my face.

"I will just tell you what. You broke into my house, too," Mitch said. And behind him the window exploded.

Jo screamed and I threw myself at the gun. I had to wrestle him for the gun. He was a drunk old man and he stank of body odor and decayed teeth and alcohol. But he was strong and desperate and he didn't fight fair. I had to have at least twenty pounds on the guy, but I wasn't making them count. I wasn't trying to hurt Mitch—all I was trying to do was get that gun away from him. But Mitch, now, he was trying to do me serious bodily damage.

I heard the snap of teeth near my ear—the guy had tried to Tysonize me. DeWitt was sitting on my belly with his arms stretched out over my head, trying to free the stock of the rifle from underneath a kitchen drawer that had come open, trapping it. I got an arm free, drew it back and punched him in the stomach, hard. There was a gasp of fetid air near my face and he grabbed his stomach. I rocked forward enough to tumble him over backward but before I could get my legs out from under him, he twisted over and reached into the drawer. He drew out a kitchen knife, the kind you can get for a dollar at the discount stores. Maybe you can't make radish roses with a knife like that but it would work just fine for the job he had in mind. My right hand was patting the floor behind me, trying to lay hold of that gun. With my left hand, I grabbed for his wrist and got the blade. I felt a searing pain and then suddenly Mitch DeWitt was off me.

Alex had the stock of his shotgun in both hands—he'd put it under Mitch's chin and pulled him clear. Thank God in Heaven I had managed to keep hold of the knife, or Alex might have fared worse than I did. I pulled DeWitt's gun out from under the drawer, scraping the skin off my knuckles on the metal runners that supported the drawer bottom. DeWitt finally struck home with a kick and Alex loosed his grip. De-Witt twisted free, elbowed Alex in the face, and ran out the door, screaming for help, into the twirling red and blue lights of a police car.

At least the way it all played out this time, I didn't get shot.

Not by the drunk guy and not by the cops, either, who were pointing their guns indiscriminately until they could figure out what was going on, which took some time.

I staggered out of the trailer after Alex, holding Mitch DeWitt's gun. The cops didn't like that. They ordered me to the ground and cuffed my hands behind my back. I lifted my head and saw Alex, also belly down and handcuffed, but before I could say anything to him a hand the size of a catcher's mitt pushed my face into the gravel drive.

"Jo!" I hollered. "You okay?"

"She won't let me go!" Jo's voice.

"Honey, do not struggle with the police, that's a bad idea, okay? Don't do it. You hear me? Listen, tell Cara to call your mom and Uncle Chester, okay?"

Someone standing over me said, "No talking."

"She's not a cop, Dad!" Jo wailed.

"This is Lacey Corinda, sir," said the same soft voice that had spoken to me earlier from next door, "and I was keeping your child from running right back into that trailer full of guns and badness. But I'm going to turn her loose now."

I turned my head toward Lacey, trying to get a look. "No! Listen, don't let her go. Could you call my wife—"

A broad face bent down to me and said, "Sir, don't talk any more. I'm asking you nicely this time. This time, hear?"

A crowd had gathered. This was a better show than anything Thursday night television had to offer. I heard the distinctive click of cell phone cameras. I put my face back in the ground, visions of YouTube dancing behind my eyes.

Mitch DeWitt was helped into a squad car, protesting all the while that he was the victim here, of home invasion and assault.

He didn't get cuffed and if he hadn't been as drunk as a grackle in mulberry season, I'm not sure he would even have been put in a squad car.

I *was* arrested.

What was I being arrested *for*? I wanted to know.

Had I broken in the trailer's front door? Uh-hunh? That would do to start, the officer told me. He'd get around to the gun and the assault and battery later. He pushed my head down and shoved me into a black-and-white.

Jo and Cara were not being arrested, thank you God for that, but they would be taken to the station for questioning and safekeeping.

Alex was arrested, too. I was going to be in a lot of trouble with Annie Laurie.

———————

Now, I've seen the inside of a police station before, and not only as a visitor. Back when I was in college, I'd been in a fracas or two. And I'd been hauled off to the station where my buds and I had been invited to cool our heels and our tempers, but they hadn't officially arrested us—they hadn't processed us. We played ball for the University of Texas and back then that meant special treatment. I'm betting it still does though an amazing number of college athletes find themselves on the wrong side of the law nowadays.

This time I was sent to an empty white room with a bank teller's window. There I was invited to slide all my personal belongings through the tray beneath the glass. The unsmiling lady behind the glass printed out an inventory and passed it back to me to sign and date.

1. One black leather bifold wallet.
2. One hundred and seventeen dollars and thirty-five cents.

3. A MasterCard debit card, a Visa card, a Lowe's cash card (I had returned a tool set without the receipt), my health insurance card, and my proof of insurance. A picture of Merrie and Jo at the beach, circa 2005. A picture of Annie Laurie circa 1987. Four business cards with my name and title (Senior Minister), as well as the church name, address and phone number.

4. An iPhone.

5. A SONIC Drive-In mint.

6. A completely useless pearl-handled pocketknife Annie gave me for our first wedding anniversary.

7. My car and house and mailbox keys, a key to the church, all on a silver James Avery key chain in the shape of a shield, FEAR NOT, FOR I AM WITH YOU engraved on the back.

8. A black leather belt, size thirty-eight.

9. A pair of black shoelaces.

10. My jacket.

11. My wedding band.

When I left bloody handprints on the forms I had to sign, the officer sighed, asked to see my hand, told me to wash it—I did—and handed me a bandage the size of a nickel. I stuck the bandage in my shirt pocket and clasped a wad of paper towel. That did the job.

Then I was escorted to a holding cell. The sign over the cell said, MAXIMUM CAPACITY: FOUR. I joined six other men already inside. Five minutes later, Alex made us eight. His cheek was scraped and an eye was swelling.

"You okay?" I asked Alex.

From the floor, a large black guy who clearly worked out on a regular basis said, "Don't bother the kid, old man." He said it like he meant it.

Alex told the guy, "It's okay, I know him."

The guy shook his head in disgust. "Dude."

"His daughter is my girlfriend."

"She's your friend," I said before I could stop myself.

"No, she's my girlfriend, Mr. Wells. Cara is my friend. Ashley is my friend. Jo is my girlfriend."

"Truth," said a voice from the back.

I saw a tattoo on the protector's biceps—the number seventy-five and the U of H cougar. "You go to U of H?"

A grunt of affirmation. I took in his size. "Play ball?"

"Offense."

"Hey!" I stuck my hand out. "Offensive line, UT, 1985."

The guy's huge hand engulfed mine. "Dude." He nodded sagely.

I looked for a place for Alex to sit, but there was nothing beyond the open metal rim of the toilet in the corner, and I didn't suggest that. The floor space was taken up by five of the six other guys already sitting down.

"What's with the eye?" I asked Alex. "The cops didn't rough you up, did they?"

From the back, "Testify!"

Alex touched the puffy flesh around his eye. "No. That was Mr. DeWitt. I pulled him off when he was trying to knife you. Used my gun to put him in a headlock. He caught me in the face with his elbow. "

There was a soft chorus of "Dude!"

A skinny white guy stood. "Sit your ass down, son. That was some stand-up action." Alex said no, but hands reached out and pulled him to the open floor and he sat.

"What the gun for, dude?" someone asked.

"This old man had a gun on my girl."

Everybody in the cell looked at me.

"This one here?" asked a voice that made James Earl Jones sound like Tinkerbell.

"No, man, I told you, that's her dad."

There was a general shuffle as the men settled back down.

"Tell the tale, bro."

Alex told the story. He told a good story. Of course, he was the hero of this story, but I'm usually the hero of my stories, too.

Fist bumps all around.

"Righteous!"

"You fight for your lady, bro."

"You get out, you take your girl on the town. Gotta celebrate."

Alex, warmed by the approval, and wearing his black eye like a war wound, said, "Can't." He gave a head toss in my direction. "He won't let me take her out."

Seven pairs of eyes fastened on me.

"She's barely fifteen," I explained.

Alex said, "She's been fifteen for a month."

I made my appeal, "Anyone here have daughters? How am I supposed to keep her safe?"

The offensive lineman rose to his feet and draped an arm over my shoulders. He looked down at me. I'm six foot three. I don't think anyone has looked down on me since I was a child before this night.

"I have a baby sister," the guy said. "She's four years younger than me and since our dad died, I'm all the daddy she's got. I hear your pain, man. But you can't. You can't keep the girl safe. Because you can't tie her up, and the more you try to, all the more the girl is going to run. You dig? You teach her right, you lay the truth out there for her to see, tell her where wrong acts take a girl. Dig? And you pray, man. I got calluses on my knees praying for my sister."

I had calluses of my own.

A round man who was dressed like a Mormon missionary in a short-sleeved white business shirt said, "What you have in the boyfriend, here, is an ally."

The chorus said, "Amen!"

He continued, "This young man earned his stripes today. He didn't tackle the problem on his own. He recognized your rights and your interests. He told you about the situation even though he knew he'd pay a price with the lady in question. And he put his life on the line. A man who will lay down his life for your daughter—"

I leaned my back on the cold bars, and it's different leaning your back on the bars when you're a forty-plus preacher than it was when I was a twenty-year-old lineman with my buds around me singing "Jack and Diane" and Bobby Bee, our running back, doing a nice, but not called for, falsetto. I said, "The old guy was too drunk to hit a wall."

U of H gave me a gentle squeeze that sent my breath rushing out.

"Is that what you thought when his gun was on your daughter?" My heart got hot and heavy remembering DeWitt's gun pointed at my baby girl.

The short-sleeved business shirt said, "Do you think Alex laid it on the line for your daughter?"

I nodded. Swallowed.

"Sounds like he saved your butt, too. That about right?" It was U of H talking.

The piping voice said, "Alex, that's the glory part, rushing in and saving the chick. But you gotta do right by her, understand? No playing fast and loose, got it?"

A voice cried out, "Or the old man bust your butt!"

U of H released me and sat down so he was on eye level with Alex. "*I'll* bust your butt, dig?"

"This mean you let the kid take her out?" asked a new voice.

"I have to talk to her mom," I said.

Alex said, "You *know* Mrs. Wells thinks it's okay for me to take Jo out."

"Dude," said U of H.

I didn't say anything.

"*Dude,*" said U of H.

"All right," I caved.

Alex sprang to his feet and held his hand out to shake. Unnecessarily dramatic, but I shook. The cell applauded and a guard came in wanting to know what the noise was about. No one told him. He told a Peter Cartwright that he was being released and a guy dressed in scrubs gave us a wave and left. The skinny white guy sat down in Cartwright's space.

After that, Alex insisted I take his floor space and I said no and he insisted and I said no and U of H grabbed me by the pants leg and pulled me down until I was sitting.

The dinner hour arrived, none of us knowing what hour that was, as watches and phones had been confiscated. Dinner was served on school lunch trays without cutlery of any kind. It consisted of chicken-fried meat patties with cream gravy, canned corn, little cubes of carrots, and month-old rolls. It looked like a school lunch that had been sitting uncovered in a warehouse for nine months.

The short-sleeved business shirt said, "Look." He picked up his cutlet of ground meat and a neat circle of congealed gravy rose from the tray with it. He gave the cutlet a shake and the gravy flapped like stingray wings.

I said, "Dang," and the James Earl Jones guy rumbled with laughter.

"Wait until you see breakfast," he said.

U of H put his tray on the floor and slid it out of the cell. Alex and I followed suit.

Business shirt propped his stingray cutlet over the roll and built a carrot square rampart around it. He flicked corn kernels at the stingray, making bomb noises. You have to appreciate a man who can create his own entertainment.

A guard came to the cell. "Seventy-five? Your coach is here. He bailed you out."

U of H groaned. "Coach is going to run me until I drop. I hope you let him know this is all about an overdue registration sticker," he said to the guard.

"You got arrested over an overdue registration sticker?" I said incredulously.

We exchanged names and numbers that we couldn't write down and probably wouldn't remember. But I would remember his jersey number.

———————

The cell thinned and filled, thinned and filled. I made Alex sit down. Sleep was impossible, but some slept.

At last, a guard called our names and Alex and I went through the interminable business of recovering our belongings, relacing shoes, threading belts through belt loops, slipping my wedding ring back on my finger.

As we were escorted into the receiving room, Jo launched herself at me—uh, no. It was Alex she was aiming at. Alex, her white knight.

Annie sat in a molded plastic chair, smiling at me. I walked over to her and she stood and put her arms around my waist.

Her mouth touched my ear. "Bear," she said, "I've always had a thing for bad boys, you know that?"

I laughed.

"Come on. Let's go to The Breakfast Klub," Annie said.

Seventeen

W e piled into the car and went to The Breakfast Klub, a Houston institution. Any morning of the week, you'll find the power elite drinking coffee and talking politics, hipsters and musicians who haven't been to bed yet, construction workers and businessmen, standing in line for their turn at one of the dozen tables.

Alex and I were starving, and between us we placed orders for plates of fried catfish, grits and eggs, for waffles and fried chicken wings, for pork chops and eggs and biscuits. Jo wanted only coffee but Alex insisted she drink a glass of Breakfast Klub Choco-Milk with him and she did. She wouldn't have done it for me.

Over the roar of the gospel music being blasted from the sound system, Jo and Annie Laurie filled us in on what Alex and I had missed.

Jo and Cara had arrived at the trailer park full of bravado. Jo knew where the extra key was hidden—Phoebe had shared this knowledge with Jo and Alex in case they ever needed a place to "be alone." Uh-hunh. What Jo didn't know was that there was someone living in the trailer—Phoebe's grandfather. Mr. DeWitt had moved there a few months after Phoebe had moved in with her father. But Jo and Phoebe were no longer friends by then—Phoebe hadn't given Jo that update.

All the lights were out, so Jo wasn't alerted to the fact that there was a new tenant. She let herself in and was patting down the walls, looking for a light switch, when she stumbled upon Mitch DeWitt, who had been sleeping on the floor. He rose up and scared Jo half to death. Evidently they both screamed and DeWitt grabbed his gun.

To my mind, a gun is a tad excessive when you're facing down a five-foot-two-inch mite of a girl. About the worst you could have coming to you would be a heavy dose of sarcasm—teenage girls are masters of sarcasm. I mean, what was she going to do? Flail him to death with her itty-bitty hands?

It turns out Mitch DeWitt was on solid legal ground, though. In Texas, a "person is presumed justified in using deadly force to protect themselves against an unlawful, forceful intrusion into their dwelling." I asked if it could be considered a forceful intrusion when Jo had used a key to get in? A key that had been offered for her use by the then-owner of the trailer? Annie put one of her biscuits on my plate and told me she had asked her sister Stacy's husband Chester, a lawyer, exactly that question. His response was, did we really want to go to court to find out?

Annie said that Chester had called Mark Pickersley, who called Mitch DeWitt, and told him that if he wanted to continue to live in the trailer, he needed to drop the charges. Mark said he was the one paying for the space the trailer took up. DeWitt dropped the charges. Annie told Mark we would pay for having a new front door installed, since I had damaged the bolt, lock and the framing around the door in my eagerness to get in.

"How did Brick do with the eulogy?" I asked Annie.

She put two of her fried chicken wings on my plate and I ate them, too. I hadn't had anything to eat since lunch the day before.

"You would have been proud, Bear. I can't describe it to you. It will have been recorded. You need to listen to it. It was comforting. Reassuring."

"How was Mark about the last-minute change?"

"He was confused, but it all happened too quickly for him to react, and then Brick did such a lovely job."

I nodded. I crooked my hand at Jo to come over, and she put down the biscuit she had been nibbling on and came to me. I sat her on my knee, her back to her mom, put my hand beneath the weight of her hair, and I lifted it up. High on her nape, right below the first tendrils of dark hair, was a tiny bird. It looked red and sore and there was a sheen of salve on it. I tapped beneath it with a finger. Annie's mouth made an *O*.

"It's a phoebe. That's a bird." Annie's eyes got watery and she sniffed.

"Did it hurt?" I asked Jo.

Jo's eyes were level on mine, unflinching. "Yes. It was supposed to."

Okay. My child was atoning. I got that. I would have preferred a less permanent mea culpa, but if it had to be a tattoo, well, this was a small and discreet tattoo. I could live with it. Just as well, since I was going to have to.

Alex had watched the exchange carefully. He said now, "Jo, your dad says it's okay if we date."

Annie added eyebrows to her *O*.

Jo looked at me for confirmation and I nodded. "You're grounded now, but when that's over, yes. You can go out with Alex. There's going to be restrictions, but yes."

Annie said, "How did that come about?"

I explained that our entire jail cell had voted and Alex had won. Jo slipped off my lap and went back to Alex. "How long am I grounded for?"

"Five hundred years."

"Dad!"

"Four-fifty."

"Dad!"

"Your mom and I will talk about it, Jo. It's going to be a long time. You could have been killed. This is a big deal. But I don't want to talk about it right now. Where is Cara, by the way?"

"Home and grounded," said Annie Laurie.

"Good," I said.

Jo had guts, I'll give her that. I like a woman with guts. I like them to stay alive, is all I'm saying.

From: Merrie Wells
To: Walker Wells

Jo says you spent the night in jail. I bet her $50 you were there to bail someone out. Do I owe her or does she owe me?

—————

After my shower, I had to go over to the Pickersley-Smythes... wait. Scratch that. I had to go over to the Pickersleys', as I would now be calling them, and apologize for letting them down at the memorial and for Jo's prying. I called ahead.

Mark met me at the door and took me back to the kitchen where Liz was constructing an elaborate sugar-free dessert tray to drop off for her Bunco group. She gave me a crimped smile and asked me why my daughter thought it was okay to break into other people's homes and had we had this problem with her before.

"Sit down, Bear. She doesn't mean it that way." Mark poured

me some iced tea and pushed a bowl filled with sweetener packets my way. He leaned against the kitchen island and watched his wife's preparations. I drank the tea unsweetened. I hate sweeteners. I know lots of diabetics, all of whom keep sugar on hand for the thousands of people in the world who aren't diabetic. But not Liz.

You know, I was there to do the groveling bit, but I thought it was a little harsh to call Jo a housebreaker. Especially since Phoebe had entered our house without permission more times than we could know. I said, "Liz, Phoebe showed Jo where the extra key was hidden, and—"

"It's not Phoebe's trailer, anymore."

"And she didn't know anyone else was living there—"

"Does she break into the model homes here in the neighborhood? Since no one lives in them?" Liz set a pastry down on the tray with enough force to crumble it. "She likes to use other people's property as if it's her own, is that it?"

Mark choked on his tea. "Liz, could you stop busting his balls? What do you care, anyway? It's a lousy trailer—you've barely even set foot in it."

"Excuse me, Mark, but I'm the one who cleaned that trailer from end to end when Jenny died and you moved Phoebe here. I thought the idea was we'd sell it to give you some much-needed personal funds. In case you wanted to contribute. To the household." She gave him a poisonous smile and he smiled right back.

So it wasn't just *my* balls she was after.

"I didn't know then," she went on, "that all my labor was going into making that trailer more comfortable for a drunk." Another tart met its demise under Liz's hand. She gave me a sharp look as she picked the broken tart up and dropped it down the disposal, like it was my fault the tart had broken.

I said, "I want to apologize for not being there for the memorial service—"

"It's okay, Bear, Chester explained," Mark said. "Brick did a fine job. He did a good job."

"What I'd like to know, Bear, is *why* Jo broke into the house," Liz harped on.

God tells me I have to love everyone, and I do try. But he doesn't say anything about liking them. I didn't like Lizabeth Pickersley-Smythe. I guessed she was still using the "Smythe." "Jo feels guilty about what happened to Phoebe and—"

"What *happened* to her?" Liz wrapped the dessert tray around and around with Press'n Seal so tightly, it looked like a scene out of *Dexter*. "Nothing *happened* to her. She *killed* herself. She never gave a thought for anyone else, and poor Mark has—" She froze when Mark reached across the island and put two fingers on her lips.

"That's enough, Liz."

I stood up and put my iced tea glass in the sink. "So, anyway, Annie and I wanted to tell you how sorry we are for everything, and to please send us the bill." I headed for the door. The woman whacked the tray down on the counter, probably breaking all her carefully wrapped tarts, and followed me. Mark came along, no enthusiasm for the task.

"I still don't understand what Jo thought she was doing in that trailer. If you could explain it, I could—"

My hand on the door handle, I turned to face her. "Lizabeth, I don't *know* why Jo let herself in to Phoebe's trailer—"

"It was never really Phoebe's trailer—"

"I know Jo is feeling haunted by Phoebe's death—"

Liz put her hands on her hips. "So now Phoebe is a ghost? Is that right? She's *haunting* Jo?"

I closed my eyes and took a breath. Opened my eyes. She

was still there. Hard to believe I once thought she was a hand-some woman. If Mark Pickersley was paying for his sins, then God preserve me from the sin of adultery—that is a price too high.

"I'm going to say good-bye." I opened the front door and stepped out. Liz stepped out, too. If she started down the street after me, I might just break into a run.

"Send Jo over," said Liz. "How about that? Let her explain for herself. I'd like to have a word with her. Maybe she can explain to me why she thinks she's entitled to go breaking into other people's—" Mark had her by the upper arm and was pulling her back into the house.

I walked to my car and got in, Liz still talking. I shut the door and started my engine. I could still hear her, so I turned the radio on really loud.

———

I took a personal day from work for the rest of Friday and went home to sleep. Of course, it left me an insomniac later that evening, so around one A.M., I gave up trying to sleep and went into my office and found Brick's eulogy on the church's web-site. I played it. Annie Laurie was right. Brick had done a good job.

Jo's bedroom door opened and I heard the heavy pad of Baby Bear's feet and Jo's lighter tread. They came into the office and Jo curled up on the easy chair and listened to Brick try to sum up a young girl's unhappy life. At one point she stiffened, got up and took the mouse from me. She drew the cursor back and played a segment again. Then she stopped the recording.

"Is that true?"

"What, honey?"

"Was she really going to go to the Air Force Academy?"

"Before everything went wrong for her, yeah. It looked like she had a shot."

Jo gave me a long, considering pause. "Can I see something?" She unplugged my laptop and carried it to the easy chair. She did some typing and some scrolling and then closed the page she'd been looking at. She handed me back the laptop and then rubbed her fingers together, calling Baby Bear to her. "Night, Dad," she said, and they went back up to bed. I listened to the rest of the eulogy. Afterward, I looked at the History button, which showed me that Jo had gone first to Wikipedia, then to the United States Air Force Academy, then to the United States Air Force page.

I thought I heard Jo crying in her room.

From: Walker Wells
To: Merrie Wells
Subject: Updates

Hey, Sugarpie—Remember when I was in the hospital and I said I missed you and you said you would keep in touch more often?

From: Merrie Wells
To: Walker Wells
Subject: Re: Updates

Hey, Dad—Sorry. Meant to. Everything is fine here. Same stuff over and over. I'm working hard at track. Really hard. *Really* hard. It's not like high school. No games, no songs at practice. And Dad, I'm not tall here. 5'10"—that's not tall in college. You know what they call me? Midge. As in Midget. I'm Midge Wells out here. I'm thinking of dropping.

From: Walker Wells
To: Merrie Wells
Subject: Re: Updates

What you lack in inches, you have in smarts. You run smart, girl. Try harder. You'll be fine. Don't be a quitter, Midge. The Wellses aren't quitters.

From: Merrie Wells
To: Walker Wells
Subject: Re: Updates

Don't call me Midge, Dad.

From: Walker Wells
To: Merrie Wells
Subject: Re: Updates

Coming home when, babyheart? I need to see my girl.

Eighteen

Saturday was Molly's birthday party. Neither Annie Laurie or I had ever met James Wanderley's child, or her mother, and we weren't all that excited about going to the party. Because Jo was grounded, she would normally have had the choice of coming with us or spending those hours over at her aunt Stacy's house. But Jo woke up looking like death on stale bread.

"Come here," I said when she walked into the kitchen Saturday morning. "Let me feel your face." I didn't feel any fever.

"Do you feel okay, sweetie?" Annie Laurie asked, after also feeling no fever. "Will you be okay here alone? Dad and I have to go to a birthday party for James Wanderley's little girl."

"Wanderley the detective?"

"You know another one?" I said.

Jo shook her slump off. "I want to come."

"Really?" Annie said. "It's all the way across town—it's in the Heights."

"I'm coming," said Jo. "I'll go get a shower."

"We have to leave by nine fifteen," I hollered after her.

"What's up with her?" asked Annie once Jo had left the room.

"Beats me." I was stoking myself with coffee. Caffeine is my drug of choice.

"Do you think she might have a crush on Wanderley?"

I said I thought Alex was the man of the hour, and I took Baby Bear on the levee to do his business.

Nine fifteen and both my women were in the kitchen, gift bags in their arms, ready for the party. Jo had wrapped up one of her many tiaras—if you take ballet as long as Jo has, you're going to collect a lot of tiaras. I almost never have to wait on Annie or my girls; Chester, on the other hand, tells me he regularly gives Stacy an event time that's an hour earlier than the invitation, just so as to have any hope at all of arriving on time.

I whistled for Baby Bear and he came running.

"Nuh-uh," said Annie Laurie. She put a foot out to block Baby Bear's way. He sat down in front of her and offered her a paw. That worked every time when he was a puppy.

"Why not?"

"Baby Bear isn't coming to a three-year-old's party, Bear."

"Why not? Baby Bear loves parties and it's outside at a park—why can't he come?" Baby Bear put down his right paw and offered Annie Laurie his left.

"He can't come because half the toddlers and all the parents will go into hysterics."

"Baby Bear loves kids."

"There's no argument here, Bear. He can't come. Baby Bear is the size of a pony and he's covered in black hair and he looks like he can fit a child's head in his mouth. That makes parents nervous. *You* know he would never hurt a child, *I* know he would never hurt a child, but no one else knows that and you are not going to be able to reassure twenty or more strangers that our huge dog isn't going to start hunting babies like hamsters. So make your apologies to Baby Bear and get in the car. We're going to be late, and if we're going to do this thing, we're going to do it right."

Baby Bear could hear the bad news in her voice and he gave

a yowl of disappointment and slunk into the family room to sulk. He would be on the couch the second the car pulled down the drive.

"I'll bring you some birthday cake!" I yelled and got in the car feeling a little sulky myself. Jo didn't say a word to back me up and she is *still* Baby Bear's favorite.

Jo was quiet during the forty-minute drive, but she said she felt fine. I told Annie Laurie to stop fussing.

———————

The Heights is a hundred-year-old neighborhood that has undergone gentle gentrification over the past twenty years. Instead of tearing down the old Victorians, buyers have by and large refurbished and added on to them, maintaining the wide wraparound porches and gingerbread trim. And Heaven help a new homeowner if he takes out one of the massive oaks on his property.

In Houston, the Heights are so called because they're high ground—but that's a relative thing. That means instead of being on really low ground, if you live in the Heights, you live on not-so-low ground.

Donovan Park was typical of the Heights: huge spreading oaks and inventive playground equipment and an eclectic mix of people gathered to enjoy the cool October weather.

Molly wasn't the only one celebrating a birthday that Saturday, but there was a big pink banner declaring MOLLY IS THREE! so we didn't have any trouble finding the right group. A troop of toddlers had occupied a nearby castle-like structure.

Wanderley had shown me photos of Molly, but that was a while ago and I couldn't pick her out from among the fast-moving group. Luckily, Wanderley saw us and came over to greet us. This was a different Wanderley than I had ever met before. He wore a loose polo shirt over frayed jeans and sneakers instead of his usual cowboy boots. He looked excited and flatteringly happy to see us all there. He called to the cluster inhabiting the castle, but Molly did not appear. He held a finger up for us and ran over and plucked a child from the slide. He returned with the girl on his hip, rubbing his chin in her curls.

Molly was a sugarplum. Her white dad and black mom had each contributed the best of their genes. Molly had big brown eyes, loose black curls and coffee-and-cream skin. She had an elegant, rather adult nose that needed growing into, but it gave her a quirky, intelligent air. Annie Laurie and Jo said, "Awwww," winning smiles from baby and dad alike.

Wanderley made introductions, and with some prompting, Molly put out her hand and shook. Then she scrambled down and was away before he could do any more showing off.

"Come meet Chloe and her parents." He led the way through the crowd, introducing us to friends and to a brother so briefly that I couldn't catch any of the names, and stopped when he came to a couple in their early sixties.

"Dr. Hensler, Mrs. Hensler, these are my friends, Walker and Annie Laurie Wells, and their daughter, Jo. Bear and Annie and Jo, meet Molly's grandparents on her mom's side. Dr. Hensler, this is the minister I told you about."

Everybody shook hands and said the right things. Dr. Hensler kept my hand after shaking and said, "I was pleased to hear that Molly's father has finally taken an interest in the church, Mr. Wells. Is he attending regularly?"

Before I could catch a fly in my open mouth, Annie answered for me.

"Why, we often see James at the church, don't we Bear? And, you know, Bear and James have had some very deep conversations in Bear's office. Isn't that right, Bear?" See, God sent me Annie Laurie for a reason. I'm slow, and she's fast. I get caught on quibbles, and Annie Laurie doesn't.

I nodded, pumping Dr. Hensler's hand gamely.

Strictly speaking, Annie had spoken the truth. Wanderley had been up to the church several times and we had had some deep conversations. Now, as far as I know, Wanderley had never been to a service or class at the church, and those deep conversations we'd had had been about murder; but talking like a Pharisee, Annie had saved the day.

Don't think I hadn't noticed that not only had I not been invited to call Dr. Hensler by his first name, but the father of Dr. Hensler's grandchild was still calling him by his title. Hmmmm!

At last we met Chloe, Molly's mother. When Wanderley spoke of her, I'd never gotten the feeling that he had asked her to marry him (she'd declined) because he wanted to "do the right thing." If I was guessing, I'd say Wanderley had been very much in love with Chloe Hensler. From the way the man looked at her, I'd say he still was.

Chloe stood as tall as Merrie, at least five ten. Her skin was dark brown like her father's and she was long-legged, slim-hipped and full-bosomed. She had that high-cheeked beauty that Ethiopian women often do. Kind of regal and disdainful. I'm talking about her looks here. She was perfectly friendly and shook my hand with a firm cattle-rancher's grip.

Rebecca arrived, which meant Wanderley wasn't joking when he'd said they gotten along, and she came with those two pugs (nobody told Rebecca she couldn't bring *her* dogs) and the introductions were made all over again.

At least five toddlers descended on the pugs and let those dogs lick their faces, and the parents stood by and took pictures as if that were the cutest thing they'd ever seen. I've babysat those dogs. I don't want their tongues anywhere near my face. Baby Bear is much cleaner in his habits than Rebecca's pugs but the pugs got to come to the party and he didn't. Newfoundlands are hero dogs. They save people all the time. There are people saving *contests* for Newfoundlands. Yeah. People jump in a lake, pretend they're drowning, and Newfies go save them. You can watch it on YouTube.

You know what pugs are famous for? Eating. Next time somebody needs to fish a kid out of a pond, try calling a pug. See where it gets you. I'm just saying.

Rebecca dropped her car keys in my hand and asked me if I could go get Molly's birthday present out of her car because she hadn't been able to manage the gift and the pugs together.

Halfway to Rebecca's car, I was stopped by a couple asking if I knew where Molly's party was. I pointed the way and introduced myself and met Ben Wanderley and his wife Fifi. Ben was Wanderley's dad but I would have laid down a hundred dollars that Fifi (no, her name wasn't really Fifi, it was Kiki or Gigi or some other poodle name) was not James's mom. Not unless she'd given birth when she was ten.

On the way back to the party, as I struggled back with Rebecca's present—it wasn't heavy but it was so big I had trouble getting my arms around it—I met Clarice Crawford, a fiftyish woman with a big smile and shoulder-length, shiny gray hair. Clarice, it turned out, was James's mother.

There was the usual drama when a three-year-old opens presents in front of other three-year-olds. The pugs made a total nuisance of themselves chasing after ribbons and balls of gift wrap. Of course, everyone else thought that was too cute.

Our presents were a hit. Annie had given Molly a set of wooden tools, a hammer and saw and screwdriver, a whole set with a matching carpenter's belt with loops to hang the tools from. Molly loved it. She tried to disassemble the picnic table.

Molly immediately set the tiara from Jo in her curls. It was crooked and the rakish angle added to the charm. Cameras and cell phones clicked. The tiara was the favorite gift of all until Molly opened Rebecca's present: a pink Hot Wheels tricycle. That became so fought over that Dr. Hensler took it away from the squabblers and locked it in the trunk of his car.

For a party where we hardly knew anyone, and where the lunch was a choice of chicken salad sandwiches with the crusts cut off or pimiento cheese sandwiches with the crusts cut off, it was a nice party.

I made sure that Baby Bear got his piece of cake. I asked for a piece with a rose on it and wrapped my serving up in a napkin. Annie was visiting with a young dad with a baby in an African print sling and a toddler leaning against his leg—Jo was nowhere to be seen. We had stayed for two hours and I was ready to get home.

I checked the car but Jo wasn't there. I wandered around the community center, and finally saw her at Wanderley's car. I stopped and watched them. He was stowing presents in the car and Jo was talking. I was too far away to hear what was being said, but whatever it was, Jo was intent upon it.

Wanderley shook his head no, listened, said no again and threw up his hands. Then he nodded. I saw him cross his heart. He listened. And then he grew intent, too.

Jo showed him something on her phone. Whatever Jo was saying, she had Wanderley's attention. He listened for a long time, then went and slammed the trunk of his car closed. He stood there, both hands on the trunk like he was trying to keep something from escaping. Then he faced Jo again and started talking; now Jo was shaking her head no. There was lots of head shaking. They weren't coming to an agreement and they weren't happy with each other.

I didn't feel guilty about watching. Jo is my daughter, and strange things have been going on.

Phoebe had died barely a week ago. In that space of time, Jo had broken into a mobile home and had gotten me arrested and now she had commandeered a detective at his child's birthday party. I wanted to know what was going on.

Wanderley looked up and saw me. Jo turned and wiped her face but I could see she had been crying.

"What's up?" I said as I drew near.

Wanderley was grim. "Ask Jo. I have to get back to the party." He walked off and didn't look back.

"What's up, Jo?" I asked.

"Nothing." Jo snapped a hair band off her wrist and pulled her long hair into a messy knot.

"It's something, Jo."

"Dad, 'nothing' doesn't mean 'nothing.' It means 'nothing I want to share with you right now,' okay? You don't have to know everything in my life." She shoved her hands in her jacket pockets and stalked off to rejoin what remained of the party.

I caught up to Wanderley and helped him gather folding chairs.

"Jo's not talking. Is there something I should know?" I asked him.

Wanderley slammed a metal chair closed and added it to a stack. "It isn't anything I can tell you, Bear." He hesitated, started to say something, closed his mouth and picked up another chair.

"Has she done anything wrong?" I asked. "Is she going to do something dangerous?"

Wanderley stopped, three folding chairs under each arm, "All the time, and almost certainly."

I put down my stack of chairs with a crash.

Wanderley said, "Calm down. I'm not telling you anything you don't already know. She's a terrific kid, she really is—she's going to make some man miserable when she grows up, but you should be proud of her. 'Blessed are those who hunger and thirst for righteousness,' right? As far as I know, she doesn't have anything dangerous planned for today or tomorrow. Or at all. But she's wired that way, Bear. Jo is someone who is always going to be out on the tip-most end of the limb."

"Wanderley, what are you on about?" I picked the chairs back up, and we dumped them in his brother's pickup bed.

"She made me promise not to tell anyone about it. She made it a condition before she told me anything."

This was rich. Wanderley had given me a forty-minute lecture on my stupidity in making that same promise once, and now here he was . . .

He ducked his head, acknowledging the unspoken accusation. "I've told you all I can. She'll calm down. Jo brought me a . . . a problem I can't fix. I don't have the power. She's mad at me, but I can't help her."

———

The drive home was almost as quiet as the drive there had been. Annie Laurie was the only one who wanted to talk.

"You do realize now why we were invited to the party, don't you, Bear?"

"No."

"We were there to make James look respectable."

I snorted. "Did you tell everyone I spent Thursday night in jail? That I got arrested in a trailer park?"

"No. It would have been fun, but James wouldn't have thanked me for it. He'll be at church tomorrow."

I took my eyes off the road to see if she was joking.

"He owes me," said Annie Laurie. "From what Dr. Hensler

said, you can tell James has made it sound like the church visits have been more than business. I backed him up so he has to make it true. He owes me a month's worth of visits."

"Essentially, you fibbed to Dr. Hensler and then you black-mailed Wanderley into coming to church."

"Oh no, that's so ugly, Bear. It's a tit-for-tat thing. I did something for him and he has to do something for me. It's not like I asked him to fix speeding tickets for me, Bear."

Annie Laurie is a lawyer's daughter, you know. That's going to come out in the blood, one way or another.

I studied Jo in my rearview mirror. Her eyes were teary but her face was set. Annie caught me and turned around in her seat.

"What *is* it, Jo? Are you feeling bad, sugar?" She twisted in her seat belt and put a hand on Jo's cheek. "Still no fever. Tell us what's wrong, Jo."

Jo didn't say a word, but big tears slid down her white cheeks.

———————

Jo was grounded, but we did allow her to have friends over, and that night, eleven showed up. Eleven! There was Alex (of course) and a mixture of school and church friends, all of whom disappeared into the television room. I noticed Jo's friend Nolan was among them and wondered if I could get the kid to take a look at my laptop—it was slowing down. Nolan is a computer psycho-genius, and whatever that kid develops someday, I'm investing in it.

I was rewriting my sermon in the study. Annie Laurie brought me a cup of hot kava and sat in the easy chair, her own mug warming her hands. She had a book open in front of her, but she wasn't reading. She was listening.

"What?" I said, looking up from my text.

She put her fingers to her lips. "Listen."

I did. I didn't hear anything.

"*Why* don't we hear anything? No music, no television, no laughing. What are they doing?" she said.

I put my papers down. "Let's go see."

Annie untucked her legs and put her mug on my desk. "No. You stay here. I'll go bring them soft drinks or something." She rummaged in the kitchen and put a tray together and went upstairs.

I heard her tap on the door and open it without waiting for an answer. There was a murmur of voices thanking her. The door shut and she padded downstairs to our office.

"What's going on?"

Her forehead creased. "I don't know. It looked like a counsel of war. Very serious faces. They all had their phones in their hands—bad news, maybe? If so, they weren't interested in sharing it with me. At least everybody has their clothes on." She shrugged and picked up her book.

I went back to going over the sermon that a third of the congregation would not hear a word of.

The storm was gathering, but we didn't know it.

Nineteen

—————

S unday morning at church, the natives were restless.
        The youth group usually occupies a block of six or so
pews. This Sunday, something was up.

I'm used to the discreet use of phones during service. If
I caught one of my girls doing it, I'd have confiscated their
phones for a week, but when the user is seventy-five-year-old
Mr. Yu, I'm going to pretend I didn't see it and go on with my
sermon. The phone keeps Mr. Yu awake, and since he used to
sleep through my sermons, it's a silver lining.

However, this Sunday, I couldn't ignore it. The youth group
pews were boiling. Hands passing phones over and under pews,
muffled exclamations, earbuds being shared like everybody was
a blood relative. And their faces! I thought I had a good message, but girls were breaking down in tears, getting up and leaving the sanctuary. I saw an irate father come down and insert
himself between his daughter and her friends, and that quarter
grew still, but, my gosh—I'd never seen anything like it.

Jo, I couldn't complain about. She was as still and stone-
faced as an Easter Island monolith, the turmoil washing up
against her but not drawing her in. I was proud of her compo-
sure. Mark and Lizabeth sat toward the back but they must have
slipped out right after services. I didn't see them in the foyer.

Wanderley was there as promised, but I don't think he got
much from the service, either. He seemed worried and preoc-

cupied. Annie asked if he wanted to come to lunch with us, but he said he had plans. Jo passed us with a covey of teary-eyed friends.

Wanderley caught her by her sleeve. "Jo, could you give me a minute?" he said.

She pulled away from him. "Sorry," she called over her shoulder, "can't help you. I don't have the power."

———————

Monday, a week and two days after Phoebe died, the storm broke.

The elders were meeting to discuss the possibility of adding a Spanish-language service on Sundays. It would mean cutting our three English-language services down to two, and hiring a Spanish-speaking pastor. I was all for the addition but I got pulled out of the meeting when Rebecca cracked open the door and said she needed me.

I didn't ask if it could wait. Rebecca is as sound a person as God ever made. Besides that, her eyes were red. She'd been crying.

I trailed her back to my office and sat at my desk as she shut, and locked, the door. Rebecca has never locked my door.

"Boot your laptop, Bear."

I did. When she told me to pull up YouTube, I did that, too. She walked over and typed something in the search bar, hit Enter.

A line of screens popped up. Rebecca scrolled until she came to one titled, "For Phoebe," posted by someone calling themselves "vngnzizmn." Rebecca clicked the full-screen box, unfolded a tissue clenched in her hand and blew her nose.

The screen filled with jumbled images—the corner of a bed, a hanging light fixture, a blurred view of trim ankles in dark shoes. The impression was of a cell phone video, a video

made by someone who didn't want to be seen filming. At times
the scene went black and muffled as though the phone had been
hidden in a pocket or the folds of a shirt. The one time the
camera caught a face, it was blurred, too. You could tell it was a
woman, that's all. But I already knew it was a woman. I recognized her voice. It was Lizabeth Pickersley-Smythe.

The voice was low and controlled but white-hot with fury.

". . . -vry thing you touch, you've been a bag of snakes
from day one. You were a waste before you ever came here so
I'm not taking the blame. You—" The word was bleeped out.
"—this family was happy before you came and *ruined* everything we worked for."

Phoebe's voice now: "We were happy before *you*—"

"You think he was happy? You think your dad was *happy*?
Working in a nowhere job? Growing old at forty? You think
he was *happy* with your drunk mother and his chinless daughter? Happy living in that crackerbox because your mother was
too stupid to get a job and thought that playing the lottery was
a viable path to security? You were a millstone around your
father's neck, you both were, holding him back from what he
should have been. Your father is *ashamed* of you, he *hates* the way
you look. You know that, don't you? You've noticed he won't
look you in the eyes? You weren't a beauty to start with but what
you've done to—" A portion was muffled out. ". . . without a
conscience. Every time he answers the door, picks up the phone
at night, he knows you've done something else to humiliate
him, and he's *praying* that one of these nights that call will be to
tell him you're dead—"

The other voice, Phoebe, cried out at this.

". . . before you totally disgrace him and you—" Again,
muffled. "—and it would be a relief to him if you did, a mercy,
the kindest thing you could do."

"Liar! Liar!"

"You're calling me a liar? Are you so stupid you can't see it for yourself? Look at this—he texted me, he texted that he wished you were *dead*!"

"Liar!"

"Read it, then, if you think I'm lying—"

"Get away from me—"

"Read it for yourself—you don't believe me—read it! No? I'll read it for you then. '. . . if she would only disappear, and never come back . . .' What do you think that means? Look! It's right here! Two days ago, check the date, read it if you don't believe me." A terrible silence followed and then a hoarse cry. Phoebe must have dropped her phone, all that showed on the screen was a blank ceiling.

"Liar." The conviction was gone.

"All that medication I cleaned out of the sty you were living in—maybe your mother wasn't saving it for herself. Maybe it was for you all along. I brought some of it home, you know. I never waste anything. It's under your sink where I keep what I need to clean filth out of my house. You should check it. Just in case. Maybe it was meant for you." The blur of a body moving and then the sound of a door shutting.

I could hear soft sobs. A hand reached out for the phone and the screen closed. The video ended.

I sat there. The last words Phoebe had posted on her Facebook page—"a mercy." After hearing the recording, those words sounded like the suicide note we'd all been looking for.

Rebecca's hands covered her nose and mouth. Her eyes were streaming. I looked at the video box. It had been posted two days ago. It had 18,541 hits.

"How did you find this?"

"It was on the church website."

"No."

"It's off now. I called Derek. He's trying to figure out how someone got in to post it. What are we going to do?"

I called Wanderley.

"James," I said.

His voice tensed. "What is it?"

"You in the office? Near a computer?"

"Yeah."

I told him what to look for. I waited. It was torture listening to that conversation again, muffled as it was over the phone line. Wanderley cut it short.

Wanderley said, "Pull her out of school, Bear. Pull her out of school and meet me at your house. You do it or I'm going to and if I have to, I'm going to make it official."

I didn't think he could do that. "Has she broken any—" He hung up on me.

It's less than a mile to Clements High School from the church. I had my picture taken, signed a badge and a ledger and was escorted to an office where I filled out a request to withdraw Josephine Wells from school for the rest of the day. Under "Reason for Withdrawal" I wrote "family emergency." That was the truth.

I texted Annie even though I knew she was teaching a seminar today and wouldn't check her phone until she was on her way home.

Jo walked toward me down the long tiled hall like the Lady Jane Grey on her very last walk. I didn't say anything to her and she didn't speak to me the five minutes it took to drive home. She knew what this was about.

Wanderley was on our front porch and Baby Bear was looking at him through the glass door, trying to tell him that no one was home.

I pulled into the garage and pushed the remote to close the

door behind us. I turned the car off, unbuckled my seat belt and took Jo's hand.

I said, "I love you, Jo. I believe in you. Whatever happens, don't tell a lie. If you're certain what you did is right, if you prayed about it, then I'll back you up. Hear me?"

Her chin trembled.

"What happened to Phoebe? I'm mad, too, Jo."

She flung her arms around my neck.

Baby Bear was standing inside the kitchen door telling us over and over again that someone was at the door and he didn't have any thumbs. We got out of the car.

I left Jo in the kitchen to put water on for tea. Baby Bear rubbed and pressed against her until she had trouble keeping her balance.

I showed Wanderley into the dining room we hardly ever use. I didn't want this conversation in our family room where we read together and play Scrabble and set up our Christmas tree.

Wanderley pulled a chair out from the table but didn't sit down. "Where is she?"

"She's making us some tea."

"I don't want any tea."

"Don't drink it, then. I want some and I told Jo to make it." The kettle whistled and we sat together listening to Jo pour the hot water into the teapot, clap the lid on, and gather spoons from the flatware drawer, then the rattle of cups on saucers. She used her hip to open the swinging doors between the kitchen and the dining room. She set the wooden tray in the center of the table and poured out three cups of tea. She put two full spoons of sugar and a dollop of milk in my cup and handed it to me with a napkin and a spoon. She poured a cup for Wanderley and held the sugar spoon in her hand, waiting expectantly.

Wanderley looked at her. I know what he saw. Five feet two

inches of lithe dancer, long wavy brown hair hanging to her butt. Jeans and T-shirt and a Texas Tech sweatshirt Merrie had forgotten to take with her. She looked like Joan of Arc. And I was proud of her. I was troubled by what she had done, by what she had taken on herself, but I was proud of her.

Wanderley waved off the sugar and took the cup. "When you showed me the app, you told me your questions were hypothetical."

"What app?" I said.

Wanderley sipped at the tea, scalded his tongue and put it down. "At Molly's party. She showed me a recording app. She wanted to know what I could do if she had proof on a recording app. But the situation she gave me, the *hypothetical* situation she gave me, wouldn't have constituted proof of anything."

Jo kept her eyes down as she stirred milk into her tea. "You told me there wouldn't be anything you could do, if a situation like that came up. When you told me you couldn't help me, then the problem *stayed* hypothetical for you. It wasn't your problem, then. It was mine."

Through the dining room window I saw a big red truck screech around the corner and come to a stop half an inch from Wanderley's bumper. I heard Wanderley suck his breath in. Alex bounded from the truck and raced to the front door, banging on it even though he could see us through the window. Baby Bear made a big deal about letting us know there was someone at the door, all of ten feet from the dining room table. Jo got up and opened the door for Alex.

"Becky said you got pulled out of class—" Alex began.

Jo asked him to have a seat and went to the kitchen to get him a cup and saucer. While Jo fixed Alex's tea for him, not needing to ask him how he liked it, Alex surveyed the chairs, took one from the end of the table and dragged it around. I sat on Jo's left, Alex sat on Jo's right.

Across the table from us Wanderley said, "Give me a break." He sipped from his cup, grunted and put a spoonful of sugar in his cup. "What it comes down to is this: you lied to me, Jo."

"No, I didn't."

"At Molly's party, when you brought this up, I asked you if you had Phoebe's phone and you said you didn't."

"You asked me if I knew where it was, and I said I didn't."

"I had Phoebe's phone," Alex said, "If you want to throw someone in jail, then it's me you want."

"Tone that down a little, would you, Alex?" Wanderley said. "Did you hear me say anything about jail?" He shook his head and drank from his cup. "So you had Phoebe's phone," he said to Alex. "How did you come to have Phoebe's phone?"

"Jo gave it to me."

Wanderley refocused on Jo. "How did my officers miss it—when they searched your room?"

Wanderley's men were going to be getting a crash course on searches when he got back to the office.

"When they were all over my room, Mom told me to get what I needed out of it so I could sleep downstairs with her that night. I got my pajamas and my toothbrush and my retainer, which I keep in a red bag that says 'retainer.' I picked it up and I took it downstairs with me."

"They didn't ask to see what you were taking with you?"

"They did. I held the stuff out and they said I could go down with Mom."

Wanderley's eyes narrowed when he heard that. Someone would be going back to How to Search a Room 101.

Wanderley put his elbows on the table and leaned over. "And you couldn't tell there was something else in that retainer bag? It wasn't heavier? Shaped wrong?"

"I knew." She sounded small.

"But you didn't tell anyone."

"I wanted to see what it was first. If I told, you would have taken it away."

"Yes. I would have." He stared at her. She didn't look away. "Tell me the rest."

"Alex came over Saturday. Dad said you wanted to talk to me and Alex said he would hide the phone and not tell me where it was so I wouldn't know where it was so if you asked me, I could answer truthfully that I didn't know."

Wanderley stared at the two teenagers and said, "You've got yourself a couple of lawyers, Bear."

Jo said, "Uncle Chester says that precision in speech is critical to the smooth functioning of commerce and legislation."

"That right? What's your position, Bear?"

I sighed and put an extra spoonful of sugar in my tea. "I think that the intent to deceive is a lie."

Wanderley nodded, his eyes still on Jo and Alex.

Alex slapped the table and I winced. His class ring made a ding in the smooth wood, but he didn't notice.

"Let's talk about intent," said Alex. "*Our* intent has been to find out why Phoebe was dead. *You* closed the case."

Alex was the son of an attorney.

"I didn't have any choice," said Wanderley.

Jo said, "I talked to Uncle Chester. He says you're right," she said to Wanderley. "There's nothing you can do. He says what happened to Phoebe is outside of the law. He says you can't positively identify who is in the video unless you did some kind of expensive voice recognition program and that even if you had proof that that was Lizabeth Pickersley-Smythe speaking, it wouldn't make any difference as far as the law is concerned. He said he's not a criminal attorney, but he doesn't see a case here."

Chester takes client confidentiality seriously. He hadn't said anything to me and Annie Laurie.

Wanderley said, "What did he think about you posting a video of someone else's private moment?"

Alex said, "Have you ever *been* on YouTube? You know half the stuff on YouTube is private moments going public, right?"

Jo said, "Technically, I didn't post it."

"But you know who did."

"Uncle Chester says he doesn't think anyone in their right mind would want the video associated with them so they aren't going to make any kind of protest. What are they going to do? Contact YouTube and say, 'That's me telling my stepdaughter she should go kill herself, and that was a special moment between the two of us—could you please take it down?' I don't think so."

Wanderley pushed his chair away from the table. Baby Bear came to him, started to mouth Wanderley's boot, remembered Wanderley's policy regarding boots and dog teeth, and flopped under the table with a groan.

"Jo, you didn't feel like you were withholding evidence? By not giving me the phone?"

Jo hesitated. Alex said, "We thought that if—"

Jo touched his arm. "Wait. Let me answer." Jo took her time, getting her words in order. She held her cup tightly in her hands. "I was at Cara's. I get this text from Phoebe who I haven't talked to in like forty years. Phoebe told me she was leaving me something in my room. That's why I went home that night, the night she died. I knew she still had my key, I knew she could get in and I didn't want her in my room. I wanted my key back." Jo shivered and zipped the sweatshirt closed. She drew the sleeves down over her fingers.

Alex put his arm around her shoulders. I'd been about to do that same thing.

"Alex brought me home. He didn't come in with me because Mom and Dad get bent out of shape about that even though

Nana says a gentleman should go in and make sure everything is safe before he leaves a girl home alone. I'm only telling you what she says, Dad."

It wasn't the time to argue the point.

"I found Phoebe upstairs just like I told you. I honestly forgot what she said about leaving me something because . . . it was a bad night, okay? So I didn't think about it until I picked up the bag I keep my retainer in. I loop it over the post on my bed, and she knew that. Her doing it that way—I knew that phone was meant for me." Jo waited for Wanderley to agree with her. He didn't respond, and she gave up. "She could have sent that video to me. She could have sent it out to anyone. She didn't, I don't know why. She came over here and she went up to my room and she put it someplace only I would find it.

"But then I couldn't get *into* the phone because she had it password locked and I didn't know her password. She forgot to send it. If you're on drugs, you're not going to remember everything, right? I looked up Dilaudid. You can have hallucinations, you get light-headed.

"I went to her trailer because Phoebe said she kept things there, anything that was important to her, that she didn't want Liz to get her hands on, that's where she kept it, at the trailer. Liz has no respect for privacy. She would even go through Phoebe's purse and backpack. Phoebe said the trailer belonged to her and back when she told me all this, her grandfather wasn't living there. It was important to her that she have someplace to go in case she couldn't take it anymore being at Liz's and she said there was no way she could live *with* her grandfather at the trailer because even though she loved him, he was pretty messed-up.

"So that's why I went to the trailer, to see if she had left stuff there or something that would give me her password because I *knew* there had to be a message for me on the phone. I'd tried every password I could think of and I couldn't get into the phone. I thought maybe she had a pet name when she was a baby, maybe she'd had a dog or something and she'd used the dog's name—I could maybe find a clue in the trailer. Because that's what she left me—" She looked at Alex and he squeezed her. "That's what I thought, and Cara thought so, too." He nodded.

Wanderley crossed a leg and clasped his boot shank. "If you had given me the phone, I could have petitioned the phone company—"

Jo interrupted, "No, you couldn't have, right? Because it was a suicide and case closed. So if I'd given you the phone, you would have given it to her dad or her stepmom and that would have been the end of it. And then what could I have done? Phoebe left that message for *me*." She pressed her hand, still covered with the sweatshirt sleeve, against her heart, leaning in toward the detective. "Because I *owed* her. Because even though Phoebe was awful to me, I should have cut her slack and I didn't. Instead, I cut her off." Jo wiped her nose on the sleeve cuff.

"So that's why me and Cara went to the trailer. I'd tried every password I could think of and I couldn't get into the phone. I thought maybe she had a pet name when she was a baby, maybe she'd had a dog or something and she'd used the dog's name—I could maybe find a clue in the trailer. But then Mr. DeWitt pulled a gun on me and I never got a chance to look around—"

Wanderley yanked his chair back to the table. He bumped the edge and sloshed tea from his cup onto the fine wood. Jo and I both instinctively snatched up napkins. Annie had trained us well.

Wanderley said, "Stop. What is this about a guy pulling a gun on you?"

Jo said, "Didn't Dad tell you? I thought you guys were friends!"

Not being part of the generation who thinks it's cool to spend a night in jail, I hadn't told *anyone*. Certainly not my friends. I had taken a personal day on Friday

I piled the sodden napkins on the tea tray. I said, "See, on Thursday night—"

Wanderley interrupted, "Is that why you weren't at the memorial service? I thought Annie was suspiciously vague when I asked her about it."

Jo and Alex told Wanderley the story. I interjected occasionally to clear up some misconceptions (for instance I did *not* just present myself as a great big target and Alex did *not* save me from sure death). Wanderley surveyed us like he was sitting across the table from the three big sillies who had tried to sieve the moon from the pond. "What are you people putting in the communion wine over there? Are you all completely crackers, or what?"

I couldn't think of a response that was going to raise Wanderley's opinion of me so I didn't say anything. Alex said, "It's juice."

"What's juice?"

"The communion wine is juice," said Alex. "Church of Christ. No wine."

Wanderley stared at us. We stared back at him.

"How'd you get the password?" Wanderley said at last.

"I'm not giving you the phone."

He said, "Hah! It's a little late for that. I just want to know how you figured it out. Will you tell me?"

Alex and Jo shared a look. Alex said, "We tried everything we could think of—nothing worked."

Jo took up the tale. "Then at the memorial service— I watched it online with Dad—when Brick said how Phoebe really *had* had a chance to go to the Air Force Academy? Then I knew it was really, really important to her because it's a big freaking deal to get in there. You have to work super hard to get admitted. Like, they only take the few and the proud."

"That's the Marines," said Alex. Jo shrugged his arm off her shoulders.

"I googled the Air Force Academy and tried a ton of stuff and then I googled the Air Force. Do you know what the Air Force motto is? It's 'Aim High.' That was her password. Phoebe wasn't always messed up. 'Aim High.' Yeah." Jo nodded. She could admire someone setting high goals for herself.

"All that business Sunday at church—that was your doing?" Wanderley said. "You thought during church would be a good time to paint someone black?"

Jo went red, but she stuck her chin out. "The video went on YouTube Saturday night. Some people didn't hear about it until they got to church."

"You know how many people have seen that bit of work?"

Alex said, "Forty-seven thousand, two hundred and sixteen, last time I checked."

Wanderley pulled his phone out of his holster. He clicked and scrolled then peered at the tiny screen. "Congratulations. You broke a hundred thousand. You are at . . . let's see, one hundred twenty-two thousand, seven hundred and fifteen."

Alex and Jo exchanged raised eyebrows.

Wanderley said, "If it keeps up, you'll make some money on the video—would you like that? Get your revenge and get rich doing it?"

Jo started to answer but Alex cut her off. "He's trying to get a rise out of you, Jo. Don't play the game." To Wanderley he said, "Yeah, that's a moral quandary we're going to need to wrestle with—I'll bet soft drink companies are lining up to have their names associated with *that* particular video," he scoffed. "You know that's not what this is about. And anyway, we didn't post the video. Jo told you that. If there is money, it's not going to us. And the guy who . . . the person who posted, he's stand-up—he's not going to be taking blood money." Alex gave it a moment's thought. "He might use it for college. I don't have an issue with that." He looked to Jo for confirmation but she looked uncertain.

"Have you read the comments?" Wanderley asked.

Jo crinkled her nose, "A few. There's some nasty—"

Wanderley interrupted. "Then you wouldn't know there's been some death threats. Veiled, but death threats all the same. Did it occur to you that you could be setting some psycho vigilante on Lizabeth Pickersley-Smythe's trail?"

Jo rolled her eyes. "That kind of stuff is always up there. You should see what they say about the Kardashian sisters. Nobody ever does anything."

Alex added, "Besides, only a handful of people know the background. Nobody is using names in their comments. Nobody wants to get sued."

Wanderley produced the guitar pick, passing it over and under his knuckles the way he does sometimes. "What about Mark? What do you think this is going to do to their marriage?"

Because I was sitting on the same side of the table, I could see Alex's quick movement, snatching Jo's hand and holding it between his own hands.

Alex said, "You don't think we've thought this—"

Jo pulled her hand free and laid her hands on the table. Her nails were short, with chips of worn polish on them. They had been bitten to the quick. She said, "Alex? Could you let me answer? Could you let me own this? I'm not ashamed of what I've done, and I'm not afraid, either." She took a breath and looked straight on at Wanderley.

"I don't know what this is going to do to their marriage.

That's not something you worry about when you arrest someone, is it? You're not thinking, 'Wow, his poor wife, what's going to happen to her,' right?"

She was speaking rhetorically, but Wanderley answered her, leaning way over the table, his fingers laced and the guitar pick still.

"Yes, Jo, I am thinking about that. Lots of times, I'm thinking just exactly that. About the kids involved, the companies that could fail and put people out of work, the marriages that could be destroyed. It is no small thing to interfere in people's lives. I try to never do it lightly. But I have a job to do and I do it."

She nodded. "You arrest them anyway. If they've done something wrong. Because it's not okay to go tromping all over other people, stealing and cheating and killing. And that's your job."

"That's right. It's my job. But it's *not your* job, Jo."

She hid the bitten nubs of nails in her palms. "Most of the time, it's not my job. But this time, this one time, Phoebe *made* it my job. And there's not anything I can do about it, do you get that? If she were still alive . . . if she'd come to me and been all mysterious, 'If anything suspicious happens to me, I want you to find out the truth . . .'" Jo used a quavery ghost voice for the departed Phoebe. ". . . then I could have said, 'No way. Find someone else. We're not even friends anymore,' and then she would have to lay all this on someone else. But the way it is, it's me or nobody. I tried to put it on you. It's not like I *want* to be all mixed up in this—I *hate* this—I *hate* that I heard that video—I don't want to know that people can be like that. But Detective Wanderley, if I didn't do something, it's like the whole world looked the other way and pretended nothing happened. That's not okay." Her eyes were glassy with tears. "And if her dad really texted that to Liz? He's the same as her, then. Even if he thought Phoebe would never see it."

Wanderley stood up. "Are you done, then? Is this enough or do you have more punishment planned? I'm not sure what you could do to top this, but I'd like to know ahead of time."

A set of brown eyes and a set of blue eyes stared back at Wanderley, unblinking, resolved. From beneath the table came an exhausted, yowling yawn—Baby Bear letting us know how boring this conversation was.

Alex said, "Nothing illegal."

"You sure about that?"

"Yeah. I'm sure."

Wanderley left. He wasn't happy with us.

————————

Annie Laurie, who is, in most ways, a restrained and reasonable woman, wanted to go over to the Pickersley house and burn it down after she saw the video.

I told her not to watch the video. I told her I could summarize it for her perfectly well. I tried some "head of the family" business on her. You can imagine where that got me.

Annie watched the video. She watched the video three times and then she went to the kitchen and started slamming cabinet doors shut and banging pots down on the stove and pulling out a celery bunch and whacking it to bits with a cleaver without bothering to wash it or strip the strings from it. I was afraid she would hack through a finger, the way she was going, and I took the cleaver away from her and made her come sit down in the family room and when I let go of her arms, she punched me in the shoulder. And covered her face and cried and cried.

"What should I do?" I asked her. She punched my arm again so I held her hands.

"You should go to the house and get the twins for me and then burn it to the ground and sow the ground with salt."

"They also have a cat."

She wrested a hand from me and blew her nose on a paper towel. "You can bring me the cat, too."

"Annie Laurie, I'm asking you. What do I do? Do I go over there and talk to them?"

Annie punched the couch.

"Oh, Bear. She came to us. That poor girl needed us and we sent her away."

"Jo sent her away, not us."

"We let it happen."

"We put Jo first. We're her parents. That's our job."

"No, Bear, you're wrong. Jo has everything she needs and most of what she wants."

"You can't force a friendship, Annie. Phoebe was nearer Merrie's age than Jo's."

"*I* could have stayed friends with her. *I* could have been there for her."

"Honey, you tried."

There was a cold bottle of white wine in the garage fridge. I brought Annie a glass of ice water, a glass of wine and two aspirins. She crunched the aspirins before swallowing. She always does that and it sets my teeth on edge.

Annie drank the water and sipped the wine, and leaned her head back on the cushion. I stroked her hair off her face. She took a long, quivery breath and let it out. I knew my girl was her reasonable self again.

"Okay," she said. "Do you want to cook dinner and I'll go over and burn their house down or shall I cook dinner and you go burn their house down?"

———

I checked YouTube late that evening. The video had had 177,024 hits. I glanced at the comments, but I couldn't read them. The creative spelling, the you're/your, their/they're confusion and the indiscriminate use of the F-word give me a headache. But I was with Jo. From my quick look, these were not people to be worried about. These were not the best and brightest to have come through our public school systems.

———————

I couldn't go over there. There was no way I could call. What, exactly, could I say?

Twenty

J o was grounded for three weeks. She asked for an exception for Halloween, Wednesday night, but we said no, she would have to miss it. That was going to be hard on her. In Sugar Land, the teens trick-or-treat through high school. Nobody minds. Only a few grumblebums complain. I'll gladly buy an extra bag of candy and let the teens be kids a year longer. Most of us feel it's better to have the teens on their feet trick-or-treating than to have teen drivers cruising when little ones are apt to be darting across the streets.

Usually Annie Laurie and I put a table up on the front porch with battery-powered lanterns and our cauldron of candy. Annie sets up a portable CD player so she can play spooky music, and she always puts a costume on Baby Bear. Last year Annie had gone to Target the day after Halloween and gotten a child's costume at seventy-five percent off. She had made some alterations, and now Baby Bear, tethered to a porch column, was dressed as a big pink-and-white rabbit. He looked ridiculous but he didn't care. Baby Bear isn't a self-conscious dog.

Annie tried to get Jo to come out of her room and join us, but Jo said no thanks, she was going to study and go to bed early and she would appreciate it if we didn't disturb her again. We said we wouldn't and took up our posts outside.

There weren't that many trick-or-treaters this year. Most of the kids who came by were driven in beat-up cars from neighborhoods that can't afford to hand out "good candy." That doesn't bother me any more than handing out candy to teens does. One night a year we give candy to poor kids—what's wrong with that? Everybody I know dumps the extra candy in the End Hunger red barrels at the grocery store anyway.

By nine o'clock we decided to pack it in and moved our paraphernalia from the front porch to our foyer. That's when my phone buzzed. It was Mark Pickersley.

"Bear," he said. "Could you get over here?"

"What's up?"

He gave me a long silence. "Could you come?"

I said I would, and stripped the costume off Baby Bear and took him with me. This would be the first time I'd seen or spoken to Mark and Liz since the video had been posted on You-Tube. That had to be what the visit was about—someone had let them know that Jo was responsible for the posting. I was not looking forward to this sit-down.

Baby Bear and I walked over—I don't like to be driving Halloween night, either. All those tiny bodies in dark costumes running excitedly to and fro. We cut across the golf course and came out on the street that intersects with the Pickersleys'. I saw the red and blue lights well before we got there. For a quarter second I thought about what Annie Laurie had said about burning down the Pickersleys' house, but the lights weren't from fire trucks. There were cop cars at both ends of the block, flashers swirling. Neighbors stood on their porches and steps looking worried or interested. Lots of them were filming or taking pictures. Three officers patrolled the street and kept it clear.

The sidewalks were impassable. Dark-clad bodies stood five and six deep along the sidewalk in front of the Pickersley house and across the street. Each body wore a black hooded robe or sweatshirt. And every one wore the mask from the movie *Scream*.

Shoulder to shoulder they stood, gaping eye sockets turned toward the Pickersleys' dark home, the white rubber mouths stretched wide in horror. There had to have been more than a hundred, and more were coming on foot. They were utterly silent—no whispers, no coughs. It was eerie.

Baby Bear growled and jerked at his leash. I wrapped the extra length around my hand and drew him close to my side. There wasn't any getting to the Pickersley house if we stayed on the sidewalk. We stepped into the road and walked the gauntlet of those hooded, staring eyes. It was so quiet that I could hear the pad of my sneakers and the click of Baby Bear's claws on the street. An officer signaled for me to stop and I waited for him to reach us.

"Out of the road, please."

I said, "I know the home owners." I pointed to the dark house that was the focus of the rubber-masked gathering. "Mark Pickersley asked me to come. I'm his minister."

"Hold on," he said and moved away from me. He spoke into his handheld, listened and gestured me forward. I got a two-officer escort to the front door. When it was clear where we were headed, a hissing started up. Baby Bear jerked and lunged on his leash, trying to get at the menace he sensed behind the white rubber.

Up and down the street, those white faces hissed at us. My skin was crawling.

Before I could knock or ring, Mark opened the door and I stepped in, pulling Baby Bear inside with me.

"Sorry," I said, apologizing for the dog's presence. "I didn't know what was going on—I planned to tie him to a rail or something, but I won't leave him out there. Is it okay if he comes in?"

Mark urged us both in and shut the door behind us. He turned the dead bolt.

"Let's sit here, okay?" There were no lights on, inside or out. Mark sat down on the carpeted stairs in front of the door. Baby Bear and I took a stair below him. Through the beveled-glass doors and the matching side windows, we could see the crowd growing larger. Baby Bear whined and pushed me with his head. I told him everything was fine and rubbed his head and ears.

"Where are the twins?" I asked.

"Asleep, thank God, before any of this started about an hour ago. I first noticed the people outside after I put the boys to bed and glanced out their bedroom window. There were six of them then, all wearing those slasher-movie masks—standing on the sidewalk across the street, looking up at the house."

"How is Liz taking it?"

"I don't know. I didn't tell her. She's having some trouble with her blood sugar levels and she went to bed with a headache before I put the boys down for the night. She spent most of the day trying to find a replacement for Mrs. Holsapple and she's not finding what she wants. I think the stress threw her off."

"What happened to Mrs. Holsapple?"

"She quit. Called up Monday and quit without giving any notice. She didn't give a reason. She called, said she wouldn't be in that day, that she was quitting. She asked us to mail her what we owed her."

"Ahh."

"Anyway, I came downstairs, and by the time I looked out the front door, there had to be twenty people outside. I've been sitting here on the stairs, watching the crowd grow. One of the neighbors must have called the cops. It wasn't me."

"What do the cops say?"

"They say it's a Halloween prank. A flash mob. It's harmless and not personal. They aren't worried. As long as the group doesn't block the road, or drop garbage or make a lot of noise, the police aren't going to bust it up."

"Do you think it's harmless and impersonal?"

He breathed out. "Oh, it's personal." He stared out into the night. The street was well-lit, lights shining down on the masked crowd at regular intervals.

Ostensibly, what we had here was a costumed group on Halloween night—nothing sinister, not really.

But it felt sinister. And it felt very, very personal.

"Thanks for coming," he said. "Sitting alone here . . . I needed some company, you know?"

I said I was glad to be there. I was. I wouldn't want him to do this on his own. At our lunch, I'd gotten down on Mark—that story about leaving Liz on the phone. Pretty judgmental of me. Mark had been sixteen then. There have been lots of times when I've done things I'm not proud of, and I was older than sixteen.

The masked group had grown so large they were having trouble staying on the sidewalk. I went over to the study window. The crowd stretched from end to end of the long block. In their midst was a television film truck. I could see a tan-suited reporter smiling big and gesturing back to the scene behind her.

Mark and I sat on the stairs in the dark and watched, neither of us saying a word.

The white cat made its stealthy way down the stairs and parked itself four stairs out of Baby Bear's reach. The cat pretended not to see Baby Bear and began an elaborate tongue bath. Baby Bear wanted to know if I was aware we were being insulted.

The television crew eventually left when it was clear nothing more exciting was going to happen. The crowd continued to grow until eleven o'clock, the people on the sidewalk becoming more and more packed. Then, as quickly as it had come together, it melted away. Within fifteen minutes, there wasn't a *Scream* mask in sight. The cops got in their cars and drove away.

The event was over.

"That's not Liz and Phoebe in the video, Bear." Mark finally spoke into the darkness. "I don't know how it ever got around that that was Liz and Phoebe. There aren't any names used on the video, you notice that? It doesn't even sound like Liz."

I didn't say anything, I just listened.

"It doesn't, Bear."

"Okay."

"Another way I know it wasn't Liz and Phoebe—I didn't send a text like that to Liz. I would never. I didn't feel that way about Phoebe. I love my daughter. Loved her. Love her."

At lunch Mark had told me he was ashamed of the way Phoebe looked now. Liz had also said that to Phoebe on the video.

There was the snick of a door opening somewhere upstairs.

"For another, I don't text. If there's something I want to say, I call. I *get* texts from Liz, telling me to pick up the cleaning, stop for milk. But I don't text. Nothing more than a *K* to let Liz know I got her message. Usually not even that.

"That's how I *know* that the video isn't Liz and Phoebe. For Liz to have shown Phoebe a text that came from me, Liz would have had to write it herself. She would have had to borrow my phone, text the message to her phone, and then delete the message from my phone. So I wouldn't see it the next time I got a text to pick up milk."

I couldn't tell if Mark was trying to convince me or himself.

"And if Liz had done that, I wouldn't be able to see this as . . . it would mean she hadn't lost her temper. The way she did at the church when she slapped Phoebe. This would be different. This would have been . . . planned. So I know the video isn't of Lizabeth and Phoebe." He mulled this over, taking his time.

"Because if it was, I'd have to kill her."

At that, I found some words. They tumbled out—"in God's hands" and "knowing all the facts" and "forgiveness" and "divine justice."

Mark stood when I petered out of words, my cue to leave. "But it wasn't Lizabeth and Phoebe. Didn't you hear me?"

A door clicked shut upstairs. Mark smiled and shook my hand.

Outside, Baby Bear took the opportunity to water the Pickersleys' lush landscaping. I looked up at the expensive home, filled with every good thing money could buy. A woman was framed in the top right window, blonde hair pulled back from a pale face. Our eyes met and held. She didn't look away. Baby Bear nudged my leg to let me know he was ready to go home. I tipped my head to Liz and turned and walked away.

———

Once home, I remembered to drag the garbage and recycling bins to the curb. Thursday is garbage day. I don't know what made me lift the lid to the garbage can, what I thought I was going to find there besides garbage.

Inside there was a wadded hooded robe and on top of the mass of cheap black fabric was a white face, its mouth open in silent horror, staring up at me. A *Scream* mask. I shut the lid.

———

Mark and Liz didn't come back to church after that—not our church, at least. Maybe they were going someplace else. Lizabeth sent me an invoice for the damage I had done to the trailer when I'd broken down the front door, and I mailed her a

check with another note of apology. I called several times to
ask Mark to lunch, but he always had other plans.

From: Walker Wells
To: Merrie Wells

How was the meet?

From: Merrie Wells
To: Walker Wells

I didn't finish last.

One morning in early November, I left Baby Bear home and
went to the Clements High School track to run instead of running on the levee the way I usually do. I'd timed it on purpose.
Father Nat Fontana was getting in his four miles. We ran in
easy companionship and when he stopped, I stopped with him.
We caught up on news and he turned to leave, hesitated, and
walked back to where I stood waiting.

He clapped me on the back.

"This is about Jo, isn't it?"

It was.

"Ahh, Bear. As soon as I learned who she was, I urged her to
tell you. I told her it was the right thing to do—you needed
to know."

"Why didn't you tell me?" Nat and I were friends. We've
probably seen each other nine or ten times since Jo had apparently started her RCIA training.

He wrapped an old gym towel around his neck, shook his head. "It wasn't mine to tell. It had to come from Jo." He studied me. "It hit you hard, didn't it?"

I guess it had. I had deliberately waylaid a Catholic priest, trying to get some information out of him.

"That's why Jo wouldn't tell you. That's why she *couldn't* tell you. She knew it was going to hurt you. Let's go get some coffee. What's the closest place?"

"My house," I told him.

"Can you make a Vanilla Frappuccino? That's what I want."

"That's not coffee. That's a coffee-flavored milk shake."

"You're so legalistic, Bear. Get in the car. We'll go to that Starbucks across from Kroger's. I'll drop you off when we're finished."

At Starbucks, Nat ordered a tall Vanilla Frappuccino and I had a cup of coffee. We sat outside under a red-and-white-striped umbrella.

"Have you talked to Jo?" Nat asked.

"It came out. We haven't really discussed it."

"Why not?"

I stirred my coffee, tasted it, stirred it again.

Nat said, "Is it that bad, Bear? You can't even talk to her about it?"

"It's like . . ." I shook my head.

Nat threw his head back and laughed. Then he put a hand on my wrist and gave me a serious, concerned look. "Use your words, Bear—help me help you."

I laughed, too. I had to, otherwise I was going to punch him. "Okay, Nat. Let me try this out on you. That nephew you're so proud of, what's his name again?"

"Nicolas. Nicolas Francis Braulio Tomas Nathaniel Fontana."

"That's a lot of name to live up to."

"He goes by 'Nick.'"

"Well he might. Okay, say Nick marries a girl—"

"He's Catholic, Bear—that's the only kind of marriage we do."

"And instead of spending Christmas at your sister's every year, or even every other year, he spends every Christmas at his in-laws. He spends every major holiday at his in-laws. How would you feel?" That didn't cover it. I tried again. "I mean . . . this is how it feels to me—it's as if Jo chose your traditions over mine. Your *family* over mine. As if she said, 'I don't want to be a Wells anymore—I want to be a Fontana.' Only it goes way, way deeper than that."

"I'd get over it."

The door to Starbucks opened and a barista came out with two cookie-sized cherry pies. She put them in front of us.

"For Father Nat and his friend." She included me in the beaming smile she had given Nat, asked us if we wanted free refills and went back to her job.

"It's *good* to be the priest," I said, paraphrasing Mel Brooks.

"Yes. It is. It is when it isn't." He ate his pie in two bites. I wrapped mine up to take home to Baby Bear. He loves pie.

"I can do you better than that, Bear. Nicolas doesn't attend the Catholic Church. His wife of fifteen years is Lutheran. He hasn't renounced the Catholic Church, but he goes to the Lutheran church and his kids are being raised Lutheran. Now, the Church of Christ doesn't have a policy on members switching denominations, does it?"

"The Church of Christ is nondenominational."

"No it isn't, Bear. Don't be ridiculous. Answer the question."

"I don't know of a Church of Christ that has a policy on members leaving for another denomination."

"That's what I thought. The Catholic Church *does* have a policy covering that. It's not okay. It's a serious matter in the Catholic Church. It is a very serious matter for a Catholic not to raise his children Catholic. Ecumenism only goes so far in the Catholic Church."

"So how did you handle it?"

Nat used a plastic spoon to scrape chocolate powder off the sides of his cup. "I didn't. I'm letting God handle it. I love Nick like the son I never had. He is a good man. From what I can see, he's not just going through the motions, he believes in the Christ."

I threw my empty cup into the Starbucks waste can. "You're telling me not to do anything."

"What *can* you do?"

———

That night after dinner, I asked Jo to walk Baby Bear with me. It was a cold, crisp night. November on the Gulf Coast is dry and cool and if we don't get the gorgeous foliage color, well, we don't often have to rake leaves, either. The sickle moon hung above us, clean-edged, crisp. Jo held Baby Bear's leash. We went down the sidewalk to the greenbelt. Baby Bear romped like a puppy, delighted with the cold weather and the novelty of having Jo with him on a nighttime walk. Houses back up to the shared greenbelt. Even so, it's private and wooded and a good place to have a conversation on a cool November night. Baby Bear lives in hope of catching one of the chittering squirrels.

I had prayed beforehand. I didn't want to put her on the defensive—I wanted to know, is all. Had I failed her in some way? Had my faith failed to satisfy, to answer her questions? Why had my child chosen a church that would cut her off from me? I wasn't being narrow-minded. It's a fact. The Catholic Church practices closed communion. If Jo became a Catholic, I could no longer share the Lord's Supper with her . . . no. *She* could no longer share it with *me*.

"Jo, can you tell me what you find in the Catholic Church that you don't find in the Church of Christ?"

Her head tilted up. "Yes." Just that.

"Will you tell me?"

"I don't want you to be sad." The dried grass and leaves crunched underfoot.

"It's not about how I feel. I need to understand."

"If I tell you, you're going to try to talk me out of it. You're a better talker than I am and I'm not going to be able to answer all your doctorate of theology kinds of questions."

I thought on this. I thought Jo was a very good communicator. She'd done a good job with that last sentence.

"What if I don't ask any questions at all? What if I don't answer back, and only listen?"

She blew out a long, gusty breath. "You aren't allowed to make me feel stupid."

"I've never thought you were stupid, Jo."

"Sometimes you make me feel stupid."

We walked half a block before I could respond to that. "That's not okay. No one should ever make you feel stupid. I want you to tell me when I do that, and I won't get mad."

She nodded. "I'll try to tell you about Catholicism, but if you say anything, I'm going to stop. Okay?"

"Yes."

"The Catholic Church feels holy to me. Quiet and ... I don't know the word I want. Like, awe. Like, more than that moon up there." She pointed and then let her hand fall flatly to her side. "I'm not getting it right. Okay. I like that the Catholic Church goes back all the way to the beginning."

I didn't say anything. I wanted to tell her that the Church of Christ has tried to restore the first church, the church of the apostles.

"I like it that the Catholic Church has saints."

"All believers are saints, Jo." It was out before I could stop myself. Luckily, it didn't keep her from talking.

"I don't *want* everybody to be only as good as I am. I *want* some people to be so good that they can make miracles happen. If everybody is the same, then . . . see, that's scary to me." She remembered my promise. "Hey, you said you wouldn't answer back."

"I'm sorry. Don't stop, Jo. I'm listening."

"Don't listen just so you can work up arguments to change my mind."

"All right."

"Hold the leash, okay? Baby Bear's pulling me."

I took the leash from her.

"I like it that everything is set out. Everything I need to know is out there, simple and clear. They don't chew the scripture to bits, everyone having a different opinion about what a verse means. It's all decided already. I like that it's settled."

I nodded.

"I like it that we kneel in church. Why doesn't the Church of Christ do that?" I opened my mouth. "Wait! Don't answer. You can tell me another time. I'm just telling you that I like that—it feels holy to me. It feels right."

I had not missed that Jo said "*we* kneel in church," as though she were already apart from me.

"When everybody says the same thing at the same time, it makes me feel part of something really big." To my surprise, she began to recite, "I believe in one God, the Father almighty, maker of Heaven and Earth, of all things visible and invisible. I believe in one Lord Jesus Christ, the only begotten Son of God . . ."

Jo continued through the Nicene Creed. She had it pin perfect—an accomplishment for my dyslexic child. When she

got to "the forgiveness of sins," I joined in with her and we finished together, ". . . the resurrection of the dead, and the life of
the world to come. Amen."

Now she was surprised. "You know that?"

I nodded.

"Do you know the whole thing?"

I nodded.

"Do you believe all that?"

Again, I nodded.

"Huh."

We had walked through the greenbelt and back out to the
sidewalk and now we were nearly home.

"There's more but that's all I can think of for now." She
sounded exhausted. She probably was.

I moved the leash to my left hand and held my right out to
Jo. She took it and we walked home that way. Hand in hand,
together.

Together and apart.

———————

That night I woke up sweating from a nightmare.

In the dream, Jo and I were walking in the greenbelt when
the greenbelt lights went out and we were left in total darkness. I let go of her hand and told her to stay right there—I was
going to feel around for one of the light poles, and I would get
the light back on. I did get the light on, but I couldn't find Jo.
She wasn't where I'd left her. She hadn't stayed. I called and
called until my throat was raw, but she didn't answer. I couldn't
find Jo.

No need for me to call a shrink and have that dream explained.

Twenty-one

After that first successful weekend, we found ourselves called upon to babysit the pugs so often that Rebecca made us up a pug kit, including beds, food, special dishes and treats, and left it at the house. When they arrived, they walked around like they owned the place. Baby Bear almost never challenged this sense of entitlement except when it involved Jo. Jo could pay only so much attention to the porcine visitors before Baby Bear would push his way between her and the interlopers.

And where was Rebecca going all this time?

Rebecca had met someone. She wouldn't tell us much except that she had met him online, he met her criteria which was taller, stronger, smarter and better than she was (the first two maybe—I would not agree that he could be smarter and better), and she wasn't ready for him to meet the "boys" yet. That was wisdom—Rebecca had doubtless posted as a single/no kids. Not entirely honest when you take into account the relationship she has with those dogs. She wasn't ready for us to meet him, either. I liked that. It meant she was taking things slowly. It's a statement when you introduce someone to your friends.

Wanderley appeared at services on Sundays for exactly the number of weeks he had promised Annie Laurie, but no more.

Finally, Merrie came home for Thanksgiving. We hadn't seen her much since July—she'd had to go back to Tech early for track practice. All the scholarship athletes did. Then, between her away track meets, and our obligations here at home, there hadn't been one weekend when she thought she could get away, except for Jo's birthday.

We were lucky we got her at Thanksgiving. Merrie's boyfriend's family had invited her to go to their Hill Country home for Thanksgiving, and she wanted to. Annie Laurie said we should let her. Not me. I wanted to see my girl. Annie Laurie made me promise not to put a load of guilt on her so I didn't. I was glad when Jo called her sister and asked her to come home for the holidays. That's all it took. Jo asking. I paid for Merrie to fly. I didn't want her wasting the nine hours there, nine hours back drive time. I missed her.

Annie Laurie was working like a stevedore in the kitchen so I got to pick Merrie up Tuesday night at Hobby Airport. I was in the luggage area half an hour early. Ten minutes before her plane was due to land, I had stationed myself at the foot of the escalators.

I saw her before she saw me. My oldest is five feet ten inches of healthy, blonde American girl. A natural athlete and beautiful without being flashy. Don't laugh at me, but my eyes pricked when I caught sight of her. Then she saw me and gave a big wave. I hugged her so hard I lifted her off her feet.

"Merrie!" I said when I set her down. "You've lost weight!" She hadn't needed to lose weight.

She smiled and nodded. "A little bit."

I stepped back and gave her a once-over. "More than a little bit. Are you okay? You look tired." She looked tired. It was ten thirty now, but that's not late when you're nineteen.

She gave me a push. "Dad, you don't tell women they look tired—that's like saying they don't look good. You should say, 'Merrie!'"—she did her Bear voice—"'you look great!'"

I took her carry-on from her and put an arm around her shoulders. "Merrie!" I said. "You look great!"

She laughed and told me that was better. She hadn't answered my question, but we had all the long Thanksgiving holiday.

It was good to have my girl all to myself. I took her home by way of Telephone Road even though it wasn't the quickest way back. Merrie wanted to see Green Vista—she said hearing all our stories from a five-hundred-mile distance made it feel like a movie. She wanted to see the setting.

I asked if Jo had shared anything with Merrie that she hadn't shared with us. Like about skipping dance classes and going to RCIA and that flash mob—was that Jo's doing? Merrie told me she wasn't worried about Jo. Jo had her head together.

When we turned onto Telephone Road, Merrie got quiet. Green Vista and the green-and-white trailer Mitch DeWitt called home made her whistle softly between her teeth.

"Dad, I can't imagine doing what Jo did at fifteen. I don't think I could do it now. It's . . . Dad, it was a brave thing to do. You get that, right?"

"I think it was foolhardy." I got a good look at Lacey Corinda's trailer for the first time It had an outside conversation nook with nylon-webbed folding chairs and a white plastic table, and a raised four foot section of garden, full of wildly blooming plastic flowers and a densely planted clan of garden gnomes. If there had been lights on, I might have stopped to thank her for taking care of Jo, but it was almost eleven and the mobile home park was quiet and dark except for a few bright windows.

———————

The morning after she got home, Merrie grabbed a well-mouthed tennis ball and joined me and Baby Bear for a jog on the levee the way she used to when she was in high school. Baby Bear was ecstatic and stayed underfoot for the first fifteen minutes, nearly tripping Merrie up. Merrie took to throwing the ball far ahead of her—that kept Baby Bear safely in the forefront.

"Dad. I wanted to say something about Jo letting up on dance. I don't want you to worry about that, and I don't want you to worry Jo about that. Jo is trying to figure out which direction to go in. If she can't be a dancer, who's she going to be?"

I was recovered enough from the bullet hole so that I could jog and talk at the same time—it was cool weather, or it wouldn't have mattered how fit I was.

"See, Merrie, Jo took her rejection too personally—so much of this is subjective. Some teacher decides she likes an apple-polishing—"

"No, Dad." Merrie picked up the spit-slicked ball and faked a throw. Baby Bear went tearing off. "Your hundred and ten percent speech, Dad? What if you're giving a hundred and ten percent, and it's still not enough?"

I focused on keeping my breathing even, my steps high through the dried, crackling weeds on the levee.

I thought about Merrie's question.

"What you have to do, Merrie, is buck—"

"Dad, no matter how hard you 'buckled down' for UT, you didn't grow three inches taller, and you never weighed more than two hundred seventy. And that wasn't enough, was it Dad? Not for the pros."

"Dance doesn't have those kinds of physical limitations, and—"

"Of course it does, Dad. Do the physics. The way your body is built, the length of your limbs, how long your legs are compared to your height? All that impacts how fast you can spin, how high you can leap. Jo worked her guts out. She worked harder than she ever has in her life, and it wasn't enough."

Merrie was jogging easily—not winded. I threw the ball for Baby Bear, buying myself some breathing time. Merrie scooped the ball up without slowing her pace.

"Here, you hold it. Ick." She wiped her hands on the seat of her shorts. "Jo doesn't think there were politics involved. The girls picked to stay were the girls she would have picked if she'd been in charge. Those dancers were better, that's all. You can be the best in high school, Dad, and not rank in college, or, you know, that ballet school. And it doesn't mean you aren't trying."

We jogged in silence. I wasn't going to win the argument. Besides, she had all the air she needed for rebuttals. I could barely keep up with my daughter. Now, there was a time when I could run the forty in five seconds. I should have been jealous that Merrie could outrun me now. But I wasn't. She was so beautiful, no makeup, sweating, and wearing ratty Texas Tech workout clothes, she was so dang beautiful running in that effortless lope, that my heart nearly burst with pride. When we passed another jogger, I watched them to see if they appreciated the sight of my lovely daughter. When we passed a guy, I watched to see if he appreciated the sight *too* much.

I managed to get out, "Is she going to be all right?"

"Of course she is, Dad. Have a little faith. It's not the end of the world to change plans, Dad. You don't have to know at fifteen, or even nineteen, what you're going to do for the next ten years. Tell you what—with the ballet disappointment and all the angst she's wasting over whether or not she could have helped Phoebe, Jo could use a change now. What if I took her back to school with me? For a couple of days? We could leave Thursday night after Thanksgiving dinner and I'd put her on the plane Sunday night. She'll be at school Monday."

I stopped to squirt some water into Baby Bear's mouth. I squirted some on his head and worked it into his coat.

"Let's head back," I said, "Baby Bear has had enough." Baby Bear has never in his life had enough.

Long-legged Merrie didn't call me on it. She tightened the band on her hair and turned around. Baby Bear watched us for a while, refusing to turn back when there was so much more of the levee that needed to be explored.

"You going to let me take Jo?"

"I don't think so."

"Why not?"

"Your friends are too old for her."

When he saw he couldn't change our minds, Baby Bear galloped ahead of us and waited, tongue out, for us to catch up.

"Dad, they'll be nice to her."

"That's what I'm afraid of."

"You think I'd let a guy hit on my baby sister?"

What I thought was I didn't want my fifteen-year-old daughter going off with her nineteen-year-old sister to a college campus where there would be a lot of athletes, all of whom would be drinking, twenty-one or not, and almost all of whom would be happy to cheer up a depressed, pretty girl who might look older than she was. "I don't think it's your responsibility to cheer Jo up."

"Uh-huh. I'm going to ask Mom."

"Not after I've already answered, you're not. Or if you do, you better tell her I've already answered, and then you're going to be in trouble with both of us."

"Ohhh, Dad," she said. And then she left me in the dust.

———

Friday after Thanksgiving, the girls invited all their friends over. We saw kids we hadn't seen since high school graduation. Nobody looked depressed. It was a good night, an extra thanksgiving.

Baby Bear and I made it a point to walk past the Pickersleys' home every couple of weeks, in case someone was out working in the yard. I wanted to know how things were—that's all. We never saw anyone but yard men outside.

Merrie came home for Christmas break and said she wasn't going back to Texas Tech and she didn't want to run track anymore. She wanted to take a semester off and get a job and live at home. I convinced her to see her sophomore year out and promised we could revisit the question over the summer.

I should have seen it coming.

Twenty-two

On Saturday, January twelfth, I got a call right before dinner. It was a nurse at Methodist Sugar Land Hospital. She had a patient there, very distraught. His name was Mark Pickersley. He was asking to see me. There had been a car accident and his passenger was dead. Could I come?

The seven-minute drive took me five minutes. I gave a prayer of thanks for the ample parking Methodist had built and checked in at the front desk. They gave me room number 5371. I tried to relax. It wasn't going to happen. I hate hospitals. I hated them before I got shot. I hate them more now. It's a problem because ministers visit hospitals all the time. It's part of my job. The elevator doors were closing when a man yelled "Hold!" and I caught the door before it could close. Wanderley stepped into the elevator.

"Mr. Wells."

"Mr. Wanderley."

"Detective."

"Detective Wanderley."

"You are here because . . . ?"

"I got a call. Part of my job."

Wanderley showed me his teeth. "Me, too. Got a call. Part of my job."

The elevator door slid open on the fifth floor and we both stepped out.

"After you, Bear."

"After you, Wanderley."

We set off together in the same direction, passed the small waiting area before the faces I saw in the alcove registered. I retraced my steps to the two old people who sat huddled next to each other like children trying to stay warm.

"Mr. and Mrs. Pickersley." I took their hands.

"It's Mr. Wells, isn't it?" asked Mark's grandfather. "Don't let us keep you here. Go on to Mark. He needs you. We'll be fine, and Mark's folks will be here as soon as they can."

Mrs. Pickersley raised her hands. "Those two motherless children! What will Mark ever do?"

Um. I guess that answered my unspoken question regarding who Mark's passenger had been.

I asked the elder Pickersleys where they were coming from and if they would like to spend the night at our house, but they said no, when they left the hospital they would be relieving the housekeeper and taking care of the twins until Mark's mom could get in from New Orleans.

Wanderley was with a nurse outside the hospital room. She was standing between him and the door.

"He's with his doctor," she said like she was saying, "He's with the Pope."

I asked the nurse, "How is he?"

"He broke his collarbone and fractured his right leg. He tried to go on and walk on that leg and that didn't help matters. He has some cuts on his face. He'll be okay."

"But Lizabeth got the worst of it? Was anyone else involved?"

Wanderley said, "It wasn't the crash that killed Lizabeth, Bear."

I looked at the nurse.

"No, they were out picnicking, and Mrs. Pickersley-Smythe

had an allergic reaction. Her husband panicked and grabbed her up and got her in the car. They had the accident on their way here."

"Unfortunately, in his *haste*"—Wanderley gave every word an emphasis that implied he meant the opposite—"Mark left everything behind at the picnic area, food, drink, *cell phones* . . ."

"It was so awful for the man," said the nurse. "He was all to pieces when he got here. But there wasn't a thing to be done. She was long gone. If it hadn't been for that farmer coming along on his tractor, they would be out there still, and it's supposed to get cold tonight."

Here Pickersley's door swung open and a young, bald, doctor stepped out. He sized us up and faced me.

"Are you Mr. Wells?"

I was.

"My patient has been asking for you. I've given him some sedatives, but he's lucid. You know he's lost his wife? He tried to hike out for help on a broken leg."

"Very devoted," said Wanderley.

"Yes. Are you with Mr. Wells?"

"I am," he replied before I could answer.

"Don't keep him too long. I gave his grandparents fifteen minutes. I'll give you ten. And sanitize your hands." He was off in a flurry of hyperefficiency. We used the squirt and rub self-consciously while the nurse watched.

I pushed the door and stepped into the dim room. It smelled of antiseptic and plastic and metal. I'm sorry, but I was glad it wasn't me in that bed. I'd spent my time there and I don't want to do it again.

Mark lay half inclined, his eyes closed. He was pale and thinner than the last time I'd seen him more than two months earlier. His left arm was in a sling and his chest was wrapped in white tape. He had stitches trailing from his chin to his cheek and one eyebrow had been stitched together. Mark being Mark, though, the eventual scars would probably make him look rakish.

"Bear." He reached out for me and I took his hand. "And Detective Wanderley?" Mark sounded gruff and sleepy. He patted his bedclothes, looking for something. He gave up. "Why are you here?" He was asking Wanderley, not me.

"Sorry for your loss," said Wanderley, not sounding sorry. His eyes were bright.

"I *have* had a loss. A terrible loss." Mark opened his half-closed eyes and gave Wanderley his stare back and added interest on it.

"Mark," I said, "tell us what happened."

"I'm going to want to hear, too, Mr. Pickersley," said Wanderley when Mark hesitated. "Why don't you tell your story now to both of us?"

Mark fumbled for his plastic water jug and knocked a menu card and folded tissue to the floor. I poured him some water and bent to retrieve the card and tissue. Couldn't find a trash can so I stuffed the tissue into my pocket.

Mark drank from the cup, put it down and lay back again. He winced with the movement and closed his eyes—that doctor should have been more generous with the pain meds. "It's all my fault. All of it."

"I was wondering if it might be," Wanderley said. I gave him a warning elbow nudge. He stepped away from me.

Mark opened his eyes. They were clear and focused.

"I meant the picnic was my idea—if we hadn't gone on this picnic, Liz would be here now."

Wanderley said, "Strictly speaking, she is here. She's downstairs waiting for her last trip to Galveston. You know, for the autopsy."

I knew what Wanderley was on about. I knew he was insinu-
ating that this hadn't been an accident. I thought he was acting
pretty callously since he couldn't possibly be sure it wasn't an
accident.

Mark hitched himself upright and grunted.

"Wait," I said. I found the button on his remote control unit
and the bed hummed as it inclined Mark to a sitting position.

Mark said, "Are you calling for an autopsy? If you are suggesting there may have been . . . if you think this was anything
but an accident, then, please, yes, order an autopsy. I'm sure you
could explain that to your superiors."

Wanderley nodded his head, acknowledging Mark's point.
Autopsies are expensive. "Tell us about the 'accident.'"

Mark kept his eyes on the detective a moment longer, and
then let his lids drift closed. "I don't think she suffered."

That was a mercy, then.

Wanderley put his hands on his hips. "That right? Don't
you suffocate when you have an allergic reaction? Your throat
swells, right? And she would feel that happening, it getting
harder and harder to take in air, until finally her throat closed
tight. It takes three to five minutes to lose consciousness when
you can't get air—all that time she knew no help was coming
because *you* managed to lose both cell phones *and* her EpiPen—
did I get that right? That's what I heard at the station. That's,
whoooo, I'd say that's a long time. I'd call that suffering."

Mark's eyes were open and as bright as Wanderley's. He
didn't turn his head away from the detective's gaze. "The doctor said she was almost certainly in shock and not conscious."

"Well, yeah." Wanderley nodded and smiled, his eyes slits.
"When I meet the victim's family, in the course of duty, I mean,
I always say they didn't suffer, too. So go with that if it works
for you."

"What is wrong with you?" I asked him.

"Nothing. Nothing. Let's hear the story."

"It's not a story, Detective, it's what happened."

"Tell it, then. I'm interested. I really am." Wanderley yanked a straight chair over, spun it around, and straddled it backward. He was wearing beautifully detailed black-cherry cowboy boots.

"Liz and I went for a picnic. I thought that would be a good idea—things have been tough since . . . after Phoebe died . . . we haven't had time for the two of us. Margot, she's the new housekeeper, agreed to watch the boys and I packed a lunch and we went for a drive. The weather has been so nice."

The Houston area had been enjoying sunny days in the low seventies for a week. Today *would* have been a good day for a picnic.

"We went out George Ranch way. There was a private road and Liz wanted to see what was down there."

"Liz wanted to," said Wanderley.

"Yes."

"It was her idea?"

"Yes."

"Her idea to pass up Brazos Bend State Park—you would have driven right past it. Five-thousand-acre park—she didn't want to picnic there? Where there would have been medical help at the park center? That didn't have any appeal?"

"She wanted us to be off on our own, not picnicking with hordes of Boy Scouts and families. We left our own boys at home—we wanted time on our own."

"Down a private road, you said? So, technically, you were trespassing?"

Mark gave a cough. "Uh, yeah, Detective Wanderley. Technically, I guess we were trespassing. You want to charge me with trespassing?"

Wanderley waved away the suggestion. "Hell, no. Not me."
A beat or two passed. "We'll see what the farmer has to say."

I said, "Wanderley, what is—"

Mark said, "What if I tell the story to Bear and he can tell you later?"

"No. Go on. I won't interrupt." Wanderley folded his arms over the back of the chair and rested his chin on them.

"You're sure?"

Wanderley nodded and gestured for Mark to continue.

Mark lifted his paper cup, found it empty, crushed it and tossed it in a pail in the corner. Nothing but net. "Liz found a good place to stop and we spread a quilt out. Yes, *Liz* found the spot—*she* chose it." He watched Wanderley for a reaction but the detective stayed quiet.

"Right where we spread the quilt, there was a line of pecan trees alongside a stream—that's why Liz wanted to picnic there. We walked the line of trees until we saw the farmhouse and then we turned back. Liz was taking pictures with her phone, you know, the bare tree branches, the way the light hit the stream, and she got careless and dropped her phone in the stream. I went in after it, got my shoes wet, but it was dead. She didn't get too upset over that, but we didn't know we were going to need it, either."

She must have been due an upgrade then. Liz didn't seem likely to take a three- or four-hundred-dollar loss calmly, even if it had been her fault.

Wanderley said, "And where was your phone?"

"At home. Last night, when I bathed Toby and Tanner, I dropped the phone in the tub. I ordered a new one this morning. We only had Liz's phone."

"Perfect storm, huh?"

"A lot of things went wrong, yeah."

There was a long, uncomfortable silence while Mark and

Detective Wanderley stared at each other. I pulled the recliner over so I could sit down, too, but that put me too low to see Mark's face so I ended up perching on the arm of the chair.

"I didn't mean to stop you," said Wanderley. "Go on."

"We walked back to our quilt and everything was fine. Liz was in a good mood. I mean, it meant two new phones in a week, but—"

"But it's not like you couldn't afford it, right? Liz had you set up pretty good, right?"

I said, "Wanderley—" but Mark put up a hand.

"Yeah. Liz made a lot of money. We're comfortable. Oh, and then there's that extra bonanza we got."

"Tell me about it."

"Turns out Liz had taken out a life insurance policy on Phoebe. Term. You know, the one that rewards your estate when you die. She did it a month after we married. When Phoebe died, we got a million dollars. Yeah. We're comfortable." He said "comfortable" like it was a curse.

Mark gave us some time to take that in. Wanderley patted his breast pocket, identified what he wanted, and slipped two fingers in to draw out a clear Lucite guitar pick. He put it in his mouth. Wanderley maneuvered the pick to the back of his teeth and said, "Well, for sure *you* are—you'll get everything now, right?"

"We had new wills drawn up after Phoebe died. See, after we got married, I took out a life insurance policy, too. For Phoebe, in case I died. The twins would be taken care of if anything happened to me. But somehow I didn't feel all that confident Liz would take care of Phoebe. You know that 'your people will be my people' business in the Bible? That didn't work for Liz. She didn't consider Phoebe 'her people.' I wanted to know Phoebe could go to school, or get some training—something. It was only a hundred thousand because I couldn't afford more. Not on the salary Liz was paying me. Not with the contributions I had to make to our living expenses.

"Liz came across the policy when she went through my desk looking for the papers on that trailer. She wanted Phoebe's grandfather to pay six hundred dollars a month to live in that trailer. I kept telling her the trailer wasn't ours, it was Phoebe's. Jenny got it in the divorce, then Phoebe got it when Jenny died. If Phoebe hadn't made a will, the trailer would've been mine. Not that I want it. But she *did* make a will. She'd filled out an online will form. There's not much to it, but it's legal and Mitch DeWitt has a place to lie down drunk for as long as he can make the two-hundred-dollar-a-month rent on the trailer space." He looked at me. "I paid the space rent up to Christmas. I don't want any more to do with Mitch." He touched the stitches on his forehead.

"He'll be able to make it, I guess. What with the money he got from the policy he took out on Jenny. The money from Jenny's insurance policy? That went to Phoebe? That went to him, too." He was telling this to Wanderley. He'd already told me. "Phoebe left it all to him. Liz wanted me to fight Phoebe's will."

"You wouldn't have done that, would you?" I didn't like Mitch DeWitt but for two people with so much, to fight one poor old guy for so little, that was small.

Mark flashed his perfect teeth at me and dipped his head in approval. Nothing of the grieving widower in his face. He was grave, but not grieving.

"Anyway. Liz found the policy I took out for Phoebe. By going through my drawers. She was comfortable going through people's drawers, because they were really her drawers. Her house, her piece of furniture." He pinched the bridge of his nose.

"She set up appointments with our lawyer and my insurance guy, Manny Alvarado. I played ball with Manny in high school. Her guy has offices at The Galleria. Liz wanted me to make her the beneficiary of my policy. I wanted to make it over to my grandparents first, and if they died before me, to my parents, because what was Liz going to do with an extra hundred thousand? She said, how would I feel if *her* policy went to *her* mother? I said I hadn't taken out a policy on her, Liz seemed like the kind of woman who would live forever, but if she took out a policy on herself, then yeah, she should go ahead and name her mom as the beneficiary. This was all said in front of Manny. We compromised and I listed the boys. She probably did the same. I don't know." Mark touched the stitches on his face. "I'll be okay. Even if she left everything to her mom, I'll be okay. So will the boys. Heck, we'll be okay even if she found a way to take it all with her. And she might have, Detective. Money was very important to Liz."

Wanderley snorted and ran that pick over his teeth with his tongue.

"I still want to know what happened," I said. Mark looked confused. "At the picnic today," I clarified. "You went for a walk and Liz dropped her phone and then what? How did she have an allergic reaction? She was so careful. All those hard-and-fasts."

"Oh!" Mark thought for a while. His face grew heavy. When he started speaking again, he spoke slowly, carefully.

"Liz set out the lunch, she said how great it was to have strawberries in January. I'd bought strawberries at Whole Foods because Liz loves them, along with a double-cream Camembert to go with them. I opened a bottle of wine and she liked what I'd chosen. She doesn't always, but she liked this one. I can't remember what it was. A sauvignon blanc—some kid at Whole Foods picked it out for me. I don't know anything about wine. It was cold and I liked it. White, because she was having chicken and that kind of thing was important to Liz, the right wine with the right food.

"We toasted the day. There was pâté and those tiny French pickles you're supposed to eat with pâté." Mark wasn't looking at us. He was looking back at the picnic. "I'd gotten so many of her favorites, I wasn't even sure she would eat her sandwich. Maybe save it. But it was the first thing she bit into. She never got to the strawberries. She didn't eat any of the strawberries at all."

A last meal. That's what it sounded like. All her favorites.

Mark's face twisted. It was the first sign of grief I had seen. He took a breath to start speaking and stopped. When he began again, he was talking to me, all his attention on my face. This is what he'd wanted me here for—whatever was coming, I thought, *This is it.*

"I went to the car to get Liz her sweater. It had clouded over and she was cold. She had gooseflesh on her arms. When I came back, the sandwiches were unwrapped and half a sandwich was in her hand. She dropped it on the quilt and she looked up at me."

Tears pooled in Mark's eyes. His free hand picked at the edges of the tape that crisscrossed his chest. "Her lips and eyes were swelling. It happened that fast. I had no idea it could happen that *fast.*

"She dumped her purse out, searching for her EpiPen. We couldn't find it. We turned the purse inside out but it wasn't there. I helped her up and before we could make it to the car, she collapsed. She couldn't walk. I had to carry her to the car. All this is less than five minutes, less than five minutes from the time I got back from the car with her sweater.

"I started the car up and realized we'd left her purse and I ran back, scooped everything in it, everything I could find—I was thinking about the phone, Liz's phone, and I got to the car and realized her phone was dead—from the water. We couldn't call out. I was in a blue panic."

Mark gripped the side bars of the bed and his knuckles were white. He was in real distress. He wasn't putting this on—I would have been able to tell. I hoped Wanderley was taking this in.

"I said, 'Liz, we passed a hospital on 59, I'm going to get you there, you're going to be okay.' She shook her head. She couldn't answer me. She was having trouble breathing. She pulled at her seat belt, the shoulder strap, like it was pressing on her, choking her. So I held the strap away from her with one hand. I'm driving with the other. Her eyes got so puffed up she could hardly see—looking out at me through these slits. She clawed at her throat. Then my damn seat belt alarm set itself off. I couldn't buckle up, I had one hand on the wheel and one holding the shoulder strap off her neck and that alarm is going off *bong, bong, bong* like a countdown. I let go of the shoulder strap and tried to buckle up and I hit a tree. The air bags exploded." Mark leaned his head back on his pillow and closed his eyes on tears. Wanderley didn't say anything snotty.

After a moment, I asked, "Can I get you anything, Mark?"

"There's some pills on the tray."

I didn't see any.

"On a napkin."

I remembered and pulled the tissue from my pocket and unfolded it to find two white pills. I gave them to Mark and he took them, drank some water and leaned his head back down again on his pillow.

"She was dead." Mark's eyes stayed closed. "When I came to."

Wanderley waited as long as he could. Finally he got off the chair, put it against the wall with a whack and stood next to the head of Mark's bed. He examined the man's face.

"But you hiked out for help anyway, and on a broken leg," said Wanderley.

"Yeah."

"Even though you thought she was dead."

"I had to do something. She was so still, and covered in powder. There's powder in the air bags."

"You think the sandwich caused the reaction?"

"Yeah. The tuna sandwich."

Wanderley and I both did a double take.

"She ate tuna? She's allergic to fish and she ate tuna?" Wanderley said at the same time I said, "What about the hard-and-fasts?"

Mark nodded. "A bite. That's all it took."

"How do you think *that* happened?" Wanderley was incredulous. I was feeling some of that, too.

"I think she got the sandwiches mixed up."

"Tell me about that."

"She had chicken salad. I had tuna. I think she got them mixed up."

Wanderley shifted his weight. He danced the guitar pick between his fingers. "Let me make sure I have this straight. You went for a picnic with your wife—"

"Yeah."

"Way the hell out there by the George Ranch, down a private road no one hardly uses—"

"Yeah."

"And you brought tuna sandwiches, despite knowing your wife has a life-threatening allergy to fish."

Mark opened his eyes. "The tuna was for me. She had the chicken."

I said, "Mark, you're telling us you knew you had a tuna salad sandwich in that picnic bag?"

"Oh, right," said Wanderley. "So then your wife somehow mistakes tuna salad for chicken salad."

"They look alike, but they were marked."

"They were clearly marked yet she ate tuna anyway."

"You know, I didn't stop and check out the sandwiches," Mark said in frustration. "Liz was having a reaction. I was trying to get her to the hospital. For all I know, a bee stung her."

"She was allergic to bees, too?"

"Not that I ever heard of."

The dancing guitar pick stilled. It went back in Wanderley's mouth and I heard it click against his teeth as his tongue worked it back and forth. I had long since given up worrying about James Wanderley's tooth enamel.

"Mr. Pickersley, if I were a suspicious man, do you know what I'd think?"

The door to Mark's room slammed open so hard it smacked the wall. Liz's sister, Sue Ellen, burst in like all three Furies. I was standing in her way and she pushed me to get at Mark. With one foot she shoved the recliner I'd pulled up to the bed so hard it bounced against the wall. She had her fingers around Mark's throat before I knew what she was up to.

He screamed. I grabbed Sue Ellen around her waist and picked her up off her feet, moving away from the bed. She held on to Mark, nearly yanking him out of the bed before she had to release him. Once her hands were free, she reached back and clenched them in my hair. She dang near pulled my scalp down to my chin. I gently bumped her into a wall to get her to let go. She let go of my hair when her head clunked against the wall, reached between her legs and fumbled for my crotch. I found the door and threw her out and got it closed right before she flung herself at it. I braced my back against the door, all 230 pounds of me, and she still managed to pop it open an inch each time she threw herself against it.

Mark was moaning, curled over himself, cradling his arm and shoulder. Wanderley, stalwart lad that he was, was talking on the phone.

"You want to lend your weight here?" I asked him.

Wanderley held one finger up, letting me know he'd be done in a minute. He mouthed "security." The door popped open again behind me.

"Now?" I said.

Wanderley came over, not hurrying any, and put his shoulder against the door.

"That's a nice healthy woman you've got on the other side of this door, Bear." The door popped, only half an inch now that there were two of us struggling to hold it closed. "Is she a random nutcase or someone special to you and Mr. Pickersley?"

"Liz's sister, Sue Ellen. Dang!" She took another run at the door.

There was a scuffle in the hall. I looked out the narrow window. Two good-sized orderlies had hold of Sue Ellen. I waited until I was sure they had a firm grip, then opened the door. A nurse hurried into the room to tend to the groaning Mark. Sue Ellen was struggling like a demented warthog. The stream of words from her mouth was foul but unimaginative. She tried to spit at me but spattered her own shoes, black cotton Mary Janes with flimsy rubber soles.

"This lady is Junior League. All the way," commented an orderly.

Wanderley pulled something out of his jeans pockets. "If you gentlemen will hold her still a moment longer, I'll cuff her."

"What you going to cuff her with?" I asked.

Wanderley held up some plastic strips.

In terms I won't repeat, Sue Ellen inquired into why she was being cuffed.

"I'm arresting you. I'm expecting some uniforms here in—there they are! Hey, Craig! Who's your friend? Ah. Officer Khan. Thank you for coming so promptly. Will you please cuff this good citizen for me? You're better with the plasticuffs than I am. It's assault. Put me and the preacher here down as your witnesses." He turned to Sue Ellen, who was trying to head butt anyone in reach and instead caught the wall for a much more solid clunk than I had given her. "How's that? When you go to trial, you'll have a cop and a minister testifying against you."

Sue Ellen let fly with another gob of spit.

"Whoa! Is that nice? Is that nice? Craig! You got a muzzle or something? This is a very nasty subject." Wanderley took a roll of paper towels off a cart and wiped the front of his shirt. "I'm giving this shirt away. Tide can only do so much."

I ducked my head in Mark's door. "Is he okay?" I asked the nurse.

"No. That collarbone is pulled out of whack again. His doctor is on his way." She seemed mad at me personally.

I said to Wanderley, "Did you hear that? Mark has to have that collarbone set again."

Wanderley said to his officers, "Can you cuff her feet together, too? Hey, Sue Ellen, that's your name? On behalf of myself and my officers, we want to thank you for choosing the Chinese house shoes over your biker boots this morning. You do have biker boots, don't you?"

Sue Ellen lowered her head, exhausted and finally subdued, and then with no warning, thrust herself forward at Wanderley's upper thighs. I snatched him back a fraction of a second before he would have had to give up the idea of fathering brothers and sisters for Molly. Sue Ellen crashed to the floor on her face. Craig and his fellow officer made another attempt at the flailing legs.

Wanderley bent down to look in her face. "Sue Ellen, right now you're looking at assault and battery and attacking an officer and resisting arrest. If you keep this up, I'm going to ask Craig to go get his Taser and I'm not going to be too picky about what mode he uses. Are we clear?"

Sue Ellen, her ankles tethered together, struggled to her feet with Craig and the other officer helping her. I was watching her mouth. They hadn't done anything to disarm those teeth.

She shook her lank hair from her face. Sue Ellen was going to have a bump on her forehead. I couldn't decide if her nose was beginning to swell or if it had always been that shape. Okay, I take that back. I'm being mean. But keep in mind the woman did try to neuter me.

"You're arresting me, not him?" UNCLEAR ON CONCEPT lit up and blinked on her forehead.

"You. Are. Under. Arrest." Wanderley was calm and smiling and, I swear to you, seemed amused.

Not me. I wasn't amused. I had never in my life seen a woman behave that way, and keep in mind that as a University of Texas football player, I had, in my days, dated a good number of Zeta sorority girls. But, my word—nobody like Sue Ellen Smith.

"You're gonna arrest *me*, but not *him*." She tipped her head toward the room where the two helpful orderlies were moving Mark to a gurney. His doctor was very cross about having to reset that collarbone.

Wanderley hesitated. "What would you have me arrest him on?" The orderlies wheeled Mark to the door. "Hey, Craig, let's move on down the hall so Sue Ellen here isn't tempted to add to her list of violations."

"You're not going to arrest him for murdering my sister?"

She yanked herself away from Officer Khan. He'd been unprepared, let her go, and because her feet were bound together, she fell into Officer Craig. They would have both fallen to the ground if one of the passing orderlies hadn't grabbed Sue Ellen's elbow and steadied her. Once she was on her feet, the orderly slipped a card into her jeans pocket.

"When this mess is over, you give me a call. I like feisty women." He winked and went on down the hall. Sue Ellen and I both watched him go with open mouths.

"Do you have proof that Mark Pickersley murdered your sister?" Wanderley sounded hopeful, but I could have been reading that into his tone of voice.

"I have the good sense God gave a goose!" Sue Ellen hadn't thought through her last sentence.

"I don't doubt that, Ms. Smythe—"

"Smith."

"But if you have evidence that your brother-in-law murdered your sister, the thing to do would have been to call the police. Nine-one-one? You can still do that. You have a ride ahead of you with Officer Craig and Khan. They'll be glad to hear anything you have to tell them and they will report to me."

"Let's see what the autopsy finds out," Sue Ellen countered. I'd say she spat the words out, but I'd seen real spitting in action from the woman.

Wanderley gave a regretful sigh. "Unless Mark Pickersley requests an autopsy, there's not going to be one. There isn't any question about the cause of death. You sister had a history of allergic reaction to fish, Mark says there was tuna fish at the picnic, and your sister apparently displayed all the signs of anaphylaxis. There was no indication of a struggle or altercation."

"And you believe that? You must have a baboon's bottom instead of a brain."

Big grin from Wanderley. "That's a colorful turn of phrase,

Sue Ellen. I hope you won't mind if I borrow it. There are so many occasions when I'd find it useful."

"Where was her EpiPen? Huh? She always carried an EpiPen in her purse. She's done it for years."

"I don't know. Maybe it fell out. Maybe she changed purses and forgot to switch the EpiPen over to the new purse."

"How do you know Mark didn't take her EpiPen away from her? Fling it off over in the woods? How do you know he didn't trick her into eating that tuna fish sandwich?"

"I don't know. It's possible he did just that. But, Ms. Smith, how do *you* know he did? Because in America, we don't arrest people on suspicion. We arrest them when we have evidence. I don't have any evidence here." Wanderley put his hands in his pockets. "I'm going to let these officers escort you downstairs, now. I'm sorry for your loss. I am. But if bereaved people were allowed to attack any and all, funeral homes would have to install wrestling rings." He leaned in close to her. "Normally I would have cut you some slack—I'm not happy with Mark Pickersley, either. But spitting? That's nasty. That's a no-no."

―――――――

Wanderley and I walked out to the parking lot together. It was evening and a cold front had come in while we were in the hospital. I can remember when the night sky in Sugar Land was blanketed with glittering stars. Now, between the mall and theater and hospital, and the hundreds of new homes that had been built since I was a kid, the sky was bright with neon light and the stars had receded. It's handy having the mall and hospital so close. But I do miss the stars.

Wanderley beeped his car and pulled out a coat. He shut the door to the car and shrugged on a long, camel-hair coat that looked like it was from the fifties. It smelled of pipe smoke. This would be another of his grandfather's hand-me-downs.

"James," I said, "do you think Mark Pickersley killed his wife?"

He laughed mirthlessly. "Oh, yeah. Definitely. We're not going to be able to touch him for it, though. We couldn't touch Liz for what she did, and unless Pickersley did something really stupid—like if, when I look into it, I find out his cell phone isn't broken and he hasn't ordered a new one—if he hasn't made a mistake like that, then your God is going to have to handle this one. Probably even if he did make a mistake. That happens sometimes."

"You don't think it could have all happened the way he said it did?"

Wanderley rested a booted foot on his bumper.

"It could have. But I don't see a loving husband bringing a tuna salad sandwich on a picnic with a wife who is allergic to seafood. I mean, tuna salad and chicken salad do look the same. But we don't convict men for not being loving husbands.

"And I could see the EpiPen somehow getting left behind. The car accident? Even a cold-blooded man could be shaken at the sight of a person having an allergic reaction like that. They're bad, I've seen it—we had a prisoner once try to commit suicide via peanut butter sandwich. We got epinephrine in him before he could die, but it was close. It happens fast and it's not pretty. So if you're driving a country road and dealing with an anaphylactic attack on the seat next to you, yeah, I could see the accident being legit.

"Now, both phones going out? That was pushing it. That was a step too far."

Wanderley rubbed his jaw and I heard the scritch of his whiskers. "You know what really creeps me out? That picnic. Him going through all the details about the food and the wine and the strawberries. What did that make you think of?"

I knew what he was thinking. I wasn't going to say it.

"A last meal, that's what he said. I think he had gathered up all her favorites, because this was going to be her last meal."

"But it *could* have happened the way he said."

Wanderley put his foot down and leaned against the hood of his car. "Bear, yes. It could have. That whole awful sequence of events could have been coincidence. If Pickersley hadn't added one more coincidence on top of it, then, maybe."

"You lost me."

"The date, Bear. Today is January twelfth. Lizabeth Pickersley-Smythe died on January twelfth."

"I don't get it."

"Today is Phoebe's birthday. She would have been nineteen. Her stepmother, the one who got caught on tape doing everything she could to get her stepdaughter to kill herself, because let's not pretend that's not what we heard—the woman your daughter exposed to the world, died on Phoebe's birthday. And that last 'coincidence'? Well, I'll accept Dan Brown's albino, self-flagellating, assassin monk before I'll accept that one."

Twenty-three

I was sick about what had happened. I was sick about what part I, or my daughter, or my family, or my church, had played. I should have reached out to Mark and Liz as soon as they joined the church. Rebecca warned me something was off—I should have listened. Liz had told me there were issues with Phoebe and I'd handed her a phone number. I passed the problem on and I hadn't followed up. Jo had cut Phoebe out of our family, and I hadn't been sorry—that's the truth. It had been wearing having Phoebe there all the time, and I was relieved when it stopped. And my daughter had made a very, very public scene between Liz and Phoebe that probably precipitated Phoebe's suicide. And that may have precipitated Liz's death.

When I returned home, Jo was out with Baby Bear and Rebecca's pugs, whom we were sitting for yet again. Annie greeted me at the door and put her soft arms around me and hugged.

"Sit down, Bear. I'll get you a beer." Annie said she had kept my dinner warm for me, and I could have it on a tray. I took my tray into the family room and sat in my good chair.

Annie let me eat in peace. She waited to ask me what had happened until I'd come back into the kitchen and rinsed my plate and put it in the dishwasher. Before I could tell her, Jo and the dogs made their entrance. Jo confirmed for Annie that all the dogs had done their business, got their leashes untangled and refilled water bowls, and then came over to give me a kiss.

Her lips an inch from my cheek, she stopped and drew back, looking at me.

"What's wrong?"

I shook my head. Baby Bear put his front feet on the chair arm and gave me a big slobber and I wiped my face off with my sleeve.

"What's wrong, Dad?" Jo insisted.

Annie patted the sofa next to her. "Sit down if you want to hear about it. Daddy was just going to tell me."

Tommy jumped onto the arm of my chair and scrambled onto the chair back. He liked that perch. From there he could see out both the front door and the kitchen door. Baby Bear commandeered one of the pug beanbags until Mr. Wiggles rumbled a complaint. Baby Bear looked at Mr. Wiggles and Wiggles looked back—unrelenting. Baby Bear groaned and got up, circled and plopped down on the rug. Mr. Wiggles continued grumbling until he had kneaded the bag into the right shape, then sank into it.

"Dad?"

So I told them. How Liz had taken out a life insurance policy on Phoebe, how she wanted the trailer and money Phoebe had left to her grandfather, how Mark had planned what turned out to be a deadly picnic. I didn't elaborate. I didn't have to.

"Do you think Mrs. Pickersley is dead because of me?" Jo said. Her face was white and still.

"Jo, no. I don't. I don't know why Liz is dead. I don't know exactly what took place today and you don't, either. Don't take this on yourself. I mean . . ." How could I know if what Jo had done had played a part in all this? I wasn't going to put that on her. "There are some things you have to leave in God's hands. We do the best we can, and maybe we make mistakes—"

"You think I made a mistake posting that recording."

I was silent. I thought Jo had appointed herself judge, jury, and possibly executioner. But I wasn't going to say that.

Jo said, "Tell me again how Phoebe died."

"She drank Dilaudid. I told you. She wasn't forced. She made that choice."

"She drank it? You never said she drank it. How could you drink it? Isn't it a pill? How do they know she drank it?"

"Well, Jo, they think she drank it because that's what she had to hand, left over from her mom's throat cancer and because her stomach was full of diluted sugar syrup, and her mouth and lips were stained with it."

Jo sat there, her eyes wide and thoughtful. Annie put her hand over Jo's.

"Dad and I are going to pray together and then your dad is going to bed. He hasn't been sleeping well. Do you want to pray with us?"

She unfolded. "No. I'm going upstairs." She curled her fingers and Baby Bear ambled to his feet and followed her up to her room. The pugs stayed tight. We heard her door click shut.

After prayer, I read my chapter in the Bible, showered and got in bed. Annie brought me a sleep-aid tablet. Over the counter. Not the serious stuff. I took it gratefully and fell deeply asleep.

———

Two A.M., I woke up next to Annie, who was wearing my Bose noise-canceling headphones to mute the pugs' snores. It was like sleeping with an air traffic controller. I'm not sure what woke me, but once awake I got up to empty my bladder and having done that, made my way into the kitchen for a bowl of cereal. That's when I realized what was missing.

No one had joined me for cereal. I set the milk down on the counter and went back to the bedroom to make sure the pugs hadn't died in their sleep. I couldn't think what else would keep them from a midnight nosh. It was too dark in the room to see whether two fawn-colored pugs were sleeping in their fawn-colored beanbags. I unplugged my phone and clicked it on, used the light.

No pugs.

I climbed the stairs and quietly opened Jo's door.

No pugs. No Baby Bear.

And no Jo.

I checked the rest of the house. Slipped on jeans and a shirt and sneakers. Debated waking Annie but decided against it. Jo had clearly taken the dogs with her, wherever that was. My bet was she had gone to meet Alex, crept out to the levee and walked down to the Avalon Community Center. That's where the two of them used to meet before we found out about the nighttime forays. As she had taken the dogs with her, she clearly didn't sneak out the window this time. She must've disarmed the alarm system, or else we would have heard her leave. At least I would have. Those Bose noise-canceling headphones work.

A cruise around the neighborhood and I'd locate her. How far could she get with three dogs?

I took my jacket from where I'd left it on the back of a kitchen chair, got my car keys and opened the kitchen door to the garage.

Annie's car was gone.

The tom-toms in my chest pounded. I called Jo's cell number and got routed directly to voice mail.

"Jo, this is Dad. I don't care what it is. I don't care what you think. I don't care how important this might be. Wherever you are, stop right now and call me. I mean it. Right now, Jo."

No point in waiting for a response.

I got in my car and plugged my phone in. Lesson of the day—bad things happen when you can't call out. Technology is good. Stupid is bad.

I put the car in reverse and let the car roll silently down the driveway.

Where was Jo?

There were a hundred places she could have gone in her mother's car. There was only one place I could think of that she absolutely, positively, could not, should not, be.

I put the car in Drive and headed for Telephone Road.

Two o'clock in the morning and traffic is not a problem. That's not to say the streets are empty. On the outskirts of Houston, there is always a steady stream of traffic. The colored lights from the car dealerships, the strip centers, the Vietnamese, Indian and Cajun restaurants slipped past.

Who could she have gotten to drive her? Not Alex. He had more sense. Truth be told, he had more sense than my daughter. And if she had talked him into it, he would have taken his truck, not Annie's car.

Cara, then? Cara could drive.

Yes, she can. Better than— That's what Alex had said. Right before extolling the virtues of teaching someone how to drive when they were underage. Better than *whom*?

I had a baboon's bottom instead of a brain.

Better than Jo, of course. Alex had been teaching Jo how to drive. It was Jo driving Annie's car.

So why had she taken the dogs? Baby Bear, that I could see.

Baby Bear was some protection, and he would have protested at being left behind and that might have woken us, plugged ears or not—but the pugs? Why the pugs?

I laughed. It wasn't funny, but I had to laugh. Jo took the pugs because they, too, would have protested long and loud at being left behind. I wanted to call Alex and see if he knew where she was. Surely she would have tried him first, tried to bend him to her will. But if Jo hadn't tried Alex first, and he found out where Jo was headed, where Jo *might* be headed, Alex could well do what I was doing. Because there was every indication that Alex was in love with my daughter. Whatever that means at his age. And I could not put someone else's child in this situation.

I thought about calling my brother Tucker. Tucker owns handguns. He and his wife Lee bought a huge old house in a part of town that is being slowly gentrified. They've been reclaiming that house for six or seven years now. The second time the house was broken into, Tucker and Lee were home. The intruders made Tuck and Lee lie facedown while they ransacked the house; the whole time Tuck and Lee were praying none of their kids woke up and startled the thieves. Before the burglars left, they stole Lee's wedding and engagement rings right off her hand. After that, Tuck and Lee bought handguns and took lessons. They go to the range regularly. Their kids can shoot, too.

I'm not a gun guy. I'm no hunter—not because I think there's anything wrong with it, I just don't like being cold and wet and getting up early in the morning and I don't like to sit still and be quiet for long periods of time. I get bored—and I've never felt the need for handguns. We live in a safe neighborhood. Besides, when Merrie was a toddler, her investigative talents were phenomenal. There wasn't a child lock made that she couldn't figure out. Where exactly would I have hidden one? It would have had to be secured in such a way as to make it useless for home protection.

But right now, I wanted a gun and the know-how that went with it. I gave my head a shake.

Wanderley answered on the second ring.

"Are you kidding me?" he said into the phone.

"Are you awake?"

"You better be calling me to make sure I don't miss the Rapture, Preacher. Anything else isn't going to be good enough."

"Jo is gone."

There was a rustle of bedclothes and a woman's sleepy voice complaining.

"Just a minute," Wanderley said. Seconds later, "Okay. What's up?"

"I'm probably overreacting."

"If it's not the Rapture, you definitely are."

I told him what I knew. I asked him if I should call the Houston police.

"How sure are you that that's where she's gone?"

I wasn't sure at all. I was headed that way because it was the only dangerous place she could have gone to that I could think of. So it was all good. Jo had an amiable Newfoundland and two spoiled pugs to watch over her and keep her safe as she drove to a trailer that housed a gun-toting drunk with a chip on his shoulder.

"Bear, we're going to have to put an ankle monitor on that girl. Hope you're okay with that."

I told him I thought we should put one on both ankles.

He breathed into the phone. "You know, Bear, I *was* spending the evening with the mother of my child, trying to convince her she could have a normal life married to a cop."

I didn't say anything. I could apologize tomorrow. Right now, I wanted my Jo.

He gave a long, exasperated sigh. "Where are you?"

I told him.

"Pull off the next exit and park in the nearest parking lot. Wait for me. I'll come get you."

"James. I'm not waiting for you. I'm ten, fifteen minutes away. You're thirty, easy. I'm not waiting."

"Don't be a cretin. Wait for me. I'm almost dressed."

"I'm almost there," I said. I hung up, turned my phone off, and began to pray.

The Lord will rescue me from every evil attack and will bring me safely to his heavenly kingdom. To Him be glory forever and ever. Amen.

I prayed for my child. I prayed that the God of Heaven and Earth would cover her with His hand. I prayed that He would remember the faithfulness of her parents, and grandparents and great . . .

I know that my God allows terrible things to happen.

I drove faster.

———

Telephone Road swept past me, overbright with fluorescence. There was a really good chance that this wasn't where Jo had gone. In fact, hardly any chance at all that I would find her here, I told myself. What could she hope to accomplish? She knew, now, that the trailer was occupied, and occupied by a crazy guy with a gun. And Jo wasn't stupid. She wasn't academic, but that's not the same thing as being stupid. There wasn't a stupid bone in her body.

One sweep through the Green Vista mobile home park. That's all I needed to do. Once I saw that Annie's car wasn't there, I could call Wanderley back, apologize up one side and down the other and go back and cruise the likely haunts of Sugar Land. My tires crunched over the loose gravel as I turned into the Green Vista entrance. I rolled my windows down to let the cool air fill the car and my lungs.

Green Vista was set back from the strip centers and three-story apartment complexes. It had resisted the new trend to pave entire mobile home parks—surely a merciless upkeep decision once the summer sun arrived. Green Vista had kept its trees—mature, overhanging oaks, still heavy with leaves in early January. That made the park darker than the street. But I knew my way. I crept along and passed the trailer I remembered as belonging to Lacey Corinda.

And there was Annie's car, a white Accord, parked behind Phoebe's green-and-white mobile home. Three furry faces were pressed against the passenger-side window. They barked when I rolled past, but the windows were rolled up and the sound was muffled. I put my finger to my lips and all three dogs ignored the signal. Jo was nowhere in sight.

I kept the car steady and drove slowly past Phoebe's trailer. Circled through the park and pulled in next to a vintage Airstream near the front entrance. I turned my phone on, noticed I had missed a number of calls from Wanderley, and texted him the exact location of Annie's car and DeWitt's trailer. I put my phone on vibrate and it buzzed right away.

Wanderley again. I knew what he was going to say. He knew I wouldn't wait.

Patches of grass grew through the gravel in places. I tried to stay on them to mute the sound of the gravel under my sneakers. There were windows open in the trailer. That made me feel hopeful—if you were holding someone at gunpoint, you wouldn't be likely to open a window, right? When all the person would have to do is scream? There wasn't any screaming going on. When I got closer, though, I could hear talking. Some of the tightness around my heart eased up. Jo would be sitting at the table, just like last time, only this time Jo and Phoebe's crazy granddaddy DeWitt would be sitting at the table, sharing iced tea and telling Phoebe stories. I could go right to the door and knock, and DeWitt would let me in, and this time I would get the chance to tell him how sorry I was for his loss . . .

Fifteen feet away from the trailer, I again texted Wanderley. I said I was going to call him, and I wanted him to answer, but I didn't want him to speak as I would be close to, or inside, the trailer. That was so he could hear what was going on.

I called his number and snapped my phone into the holster I wear on my belt, then made the last fifteen feet in a crouch. I ducked beneath one of the open windows. The trailer felt cool and dusty under my hands. From inside, I could hear Mitch DeWitt maundering on about Liz and Mark getting theirs—my heart seized up again. Slowly, I raised my head high enough to see through the dark window over the kitchen sink. Between the Palmolive liquid bottle and two Jim Beam empties, I saw Jo.

Mitch sat across from her, drinking something the color of tea, but it was in a shot glass. The trailer was completely dark. My Jo was there, sitting at the table, just as I had imagined her.

Well, not *just* as I'd imagined her. Hot rage poured into me, filling me so completely, I could have taken that trailer apart like the crackerbox Liz had called it. I wanted to lift that trailer up over my head and shake that drunken sot out on his head— Jo would be safe when I did that because *that son of a gun had taped my daughter to the table!*

Duct tape had been wrapped round and round the kitchen table, pinning Jo's arms, wrist to elbow, flat against the surface. Another piece of duct tape was across her mouth. DeWitt held his shot glass in one hand and a pistol in the other. A brand-new bottle of Jim Beam was down four or five inches and working its way toward joining the empties on the kitchen counter.

Jo's eyes found mine and glided past. But she knew I was

there. She knew I had found her. She knew I would save her. And I would.

But I didn't know how.

Oh, God, I prayed. *I've never asked You for a miracle, but I'm asking for one now.*

I scurried back to the plastic flower garden—the three dogs bounding from window to window to watch my progress—and I picked the heaviest gnome I saw, tucked him under my arm and leaped from grass island to grass island back to the trailer. I didn't give myself a chance to think. I didn't give myself a chance to doubt.

We don't do Hail Marys in the Church of Christ, but I threw one in anyway.

The garden gnome hit the back of Mitch DeWitt's head so hard, it forced his head forward with enough force to smack it against the kitchen table before breaking. The gnome, not DeWitt's head, thank you, God. My feet hit the kitchen floor about the same time Mitch hit the table, my fingernails scraping at the duct tape binding Jo down. Useless. Then I remembered. In a flash, I had Annie's worthless anniversary knife open and slashing the tape on either side of my daughter's arms. As soon as I had freed her arms, I grabbed her around her waist and yanked her from the booth. She came but her feet didn't. I ducked under the table and sliced at the tape binding Jo's ankles tightly to the table base. Mitch must have happened upon a duct tape special at the local Sam's Club. I finally got her loose and I rose up from under the table to find Mitch's flat, cold eyes staring at me, wanting me dead.

I looked for my gnome but he was beyond help himself. De-Witt stood slowly and I tried to put myself between him and Jo but she elbowed me hard and that's when I saw that Jo, her mouth still duct taped, was holding DeWitt's nasty little snub-nosed pistol about a foot and a half from his belly.

"Give me the gun, Jo," I said.

She shook her head, her hair flying loose from its band. She held the little gun in two hands like a movie cop. I didn't know if that would help her accuracy but I thought it would be hard to miss from less than two feet.

I held my hand out for the gun. "You don't want to accidentally shoot him, Jo—"

She nodded her head so emphatically, it was hard to miss her intent.

"Honey, he's an old man, and he's harmless and unarmed—"

Mitch DeWitt reached across the table and snatched the gun from Jo.

My mouth fell open. Without saying a word, DeWitt raised the gun and shot me, then half spun and fell across the table, faceup. Jo looked down at her blood-splattered hands and arms and her eyes screamed at me. I snatched her up, put my shoulder to the door and burst through it, stumbled over a stick in the grass and the world exploded.

———————

A long time later, when the world came right and my ears stopped ringing, I tried to sit up. I couldn't. A great suffocating weight pinned me to the ground. It was hard to breathe and the air was hot and humid and it smelled like garbage. I opened my eyes. Baby Bear gave my face a lick and shifted his weight so most of it was on my belly and groin. I pushed him off and took in a deep breath. I could sit up now, now that I didn't have 180 pounds on my chest. I brushed gravel off my face. I could hear Wanderley swearing long and evenly and without any appearance of taking a breath to fortify himself for more cursing.

"Where's Jo?" I said. "Is she okay?"

"She's okay." He added something that I'll leave off.

"Where is she?"

He flung out his arm, pointing toward the trailer I had stolen the gnome from. On one of the webbed chairs sat Lacey Corinda. Jo sat in the woman's lap, her arms around the woman's neck. The woman held her tight and rocked back and forth. The bloody T-shirt was gone and Jo was wearing a plaid flannel shirt, three sizes too large. The two pugs were planted in the garden among the gnomes, wondering when refreshments would be served. As Jo was out of range of Wanderley's cursing, I let him vent.

"How bad am I shot?" I asked.

"You're not shot." He kicked the side of the trailer and Baby Bear barked at him. At that, a tall young woman appeared at the door of the trailer. She was backlit—all the trailer's lights were on now. I peered up at her. It was Chloe, Molly's mom.

"Was that you?" she asked Wanderley.

"Sorry."

"Chloe?" I said. "What's Chloe doing here?" Baby Bear climbed the steps to the trailer door but Chloe pushed him away.

"She wouldn't stay behind, that's what she's doing here and don't you dare say a word to me about it because none of your women listen to you."

"They listen to me."

"They listen and then they ignore what you say."

"When will the cops be here?" Chloe said.

And far off, we heard the whoop of the siren.

"Soon," he said. "Will he live?"

"Long enough to die of alcoholism."

"Thank God," I said. "If Jo had killed him—"

"Jo didn't shoot him, you idiot. I did. You stood there like a moron and let her hold that gun a foot away from the man—he took it from her, don't you remember? She hadn't even cocked the pistol, for God's sake, don't you know anything?" Wanderley was mad.

"Oh." I got to my feet. Even though Wanderley had told me I wasn't shot, I pulled my T-shirt up and checked to be certain. I wasn't bleeding. "Did you shoot at me, too?"

"No, Bear. I didn't shoot at you. Though if you hadn't been carrying your daughter, I'd have been tempted. Do you want to tell me why you saw fit to bring a pack of dogs with you?"

I ignored him and looked around. We had again gathered a crowd of interested onlookers. "*Someone* shot at me."

"No one shot at you. I shot DeWitt through the kitchen window. He had the gun. I had to take the chance. On your way out, you tripped over a shotgun and the shotgun went off. Some moron laid a shotgun right outside the front door."

"Hey," I said, "that must've been a different moron. I didn't do it." I got one of Wanderley's unibrow stares. "I didn't bring the dogs, either. Jo did."

"That would be a detail you forgot to mention."

"It wasn't topmost in my mind."

Baby Bear at my heels, I walked over to Lacey Corinda and gathered my child up. Jo was crying so hard I don't know that she noticed. I stuck half my hand out to the woman, the rest being needed to hold Jo.

"We haven't met properly. Walker Wells," I said.

She shook my hand then held on to it as she hefted herself out of her chair. "It's a pleasure to meet you, Mr. Wells." She had a soft purr of a voice. "I'm Lacey Corinda. Your daughter tells me Hilliard gave his life to save hers. He would have liked that."

Oh, dear God. I'd gotten someone else killed. "Hilliard?"

"The gnome."

"Oh."

A cop car followed by an ambulance followed by two more cop cars screamed into what space there was in Green Vista. The pugs leaped to attention and started that yapping they do when they want to alert you to new arrivals. Baby Bear felt remiss, so he added his voice, too.

I said, "Miss Corinda, I'm going to excuse myself. But I owe you a gnome. I'll see that you get it. I'll get this shirt back to you, too." I patted Jo's flannel-clad back. The pugs hopped out of the raised flower bed and joined me as I made my way back over to Wanderley. I was kind of hoping that he could keep me out of a jail cell this time. I was determined that he would keep Jo out of one.

A uniformed officer came up to me, his police baton at the ready. "That your dog?" He pointed the stick at Baby Bear, who was staying close to my side.

"Jo?" I said, "Let me put you down. You're too old for this. *I'm* too old for this." I put her on her feet. The flannel shirt hung to her knees. I lifted her face to mine and examined it. I turned her around, squeezed her arms and patted down her legs.

"*Dad*," she said.

She seemed okay to me.

"Sir! Is that your dog?"

"He's mine," said Jo. "He doesn't bite."

"Leash him, please."

I reached down and caught Baby Bear's collar. "I don't have a leash. Not on me."

Before the officer could call me a moron, an onlooker stepped forward.

"I'll getcha some rope—got some back of the trailer." The young man was back in a minute with a thin rope looped over his arm. He pulled a pocketknife out of his pocket and cut off three lengths. He dropped to his knees in front of Baby Bear, hesitated and said, "He won't bite me?"

Jo said, "He won't bite you. He only bites bad guys."

The guy paused a moment more and then searched through Baby Bear's heavy coat for his collar. "Beautiful boy. What is he?"

"He's a Newfoundland. He's mine," she said.

The young man smiled at her. "I heard. He always know the good guys from the bad?" He tied the rope to Baby Bear's collar and passed the end of it to Jo.

"So far." She smiled at him and nudged the pugs forward with her toe. The man must have had something savory for dinner because the pugs crawled right up into his lap in their eagerness to smell his shirt. He got them secured, too, and gave all three makeshift leashes to Jo.

Jo and I watched as the EMS squad gingerly hoisted DeWitt out of the trailer on a stretcher. When they had him secured in the ambulance, and the ambulance had backed out of the park and sped away down Telephone Road, I said to Jo, "I'm thinking about sending you to a military academy. You know that, don't you?"

She sat on the gravel and pulled Baby Bear against her. The pugs fought over her lap. "No you aren't, Dad."

"I am, too."

"You'd miss me."

"I'll miss you more if you go off and get yourself killed." I had to cover my eyes. It had been too close. This time, it had been way too close. If I had gotten there five minutes later—if Wanderley had gotten there five minutes later.

Jo put her small hand on the middle of my back. "It's okay, Dad. I'm okay."

I wanted to tell her that it wasn't okay. It was *too close.* I couldn't talk.

Chloe, freed from taking care of DeWitt, sat down next to Jo. "Let me see your eyes, Jo." She shone a tiny flashlight into

Jo's eyes, approved of what she saw there, took Jo's arm and pushed the sleeve up and put two fingers on her wrist. She nodded.

The inspection had given me some time to pull it together. "Are you a doctor, Chloe?" I asked.

"I'm a physician's assistant."

I helped her to her feet. She had been pulled from bed in the early hours and she wasn't wearing any makeup. She wore a pair of jeans, a jacket that was too big to be hers and loafers on her feet. And she was still beautiful.

"Huh," I said.

"What?"

"Nothing. Only, you and Wanderley are both in the business of saving people. I think that's interesting, is all."

Chloe opened her mouth to respond but closed it. Wanderley had pulled himself loose from the Houston police officers.

"You owe me, Preacher."

"I know I do."

"We're all going to the station. Um, the dogs are a problem. They'll call animal protection for the dogs."

Oh, no. Not for my dog. Not for Rebecca's pugs, either.

I took the leashes from Jo. "Wait a minute."

Lacey Corinda was still watching from her trailer. I took the dogs over to her and explained about animal protection.

"You want me to watch them for you?"

"Would you, please? It won't be more than a couple of hours," I fibbed, knowing it would likely be more than a couple of hours. "I'll pay you."

"You're a preacher, aren't you? That's what that boy called you?" She was talking about Wanderley.

"I am, yes."

"You don't have to pay me. I'll do you the favor. Maybe you'll do me a favor in return."

Ah. "What would that be?"

"We'll talk about it. Go on, they're waiting for you."

I gave the dogs some love, told them to stay, and started off. The pugs had a meltdown. Baby Bear wasn't too happy, either.

"You know what Miss Lacey has in the house?" I heard Lacey Corinda tell the dogs. "Miss Lacey has some ham bone and beans. You like ham bone and beans?" All three were sure they would. I should have warned her about the beans.

Twenty-four

It was four o'clock in the morning when I called Annie Laurie to tell her that Jo and I were on our way to the police station. Again. If Annie hadn't fallen asleep holding her phone while playing Scramble on her iPhone, I never would have woken her. The Bose headphones are that good. The iPhone's vibration woke her.

"Are you serious?"

I said I was. I told her where the dogs were and heard her swing her legs out of bed.

"I'll go get them," she said.

I explained that she couldn't do that because I had taken my car and Jo had taken hers. I told her the dogs would be fine.

"Are you serious?" she said again. "Jo took my car? Jo can't drive."

"She can apparently drive well enough to get to Telephone Road," I said. "Call Brick and tell him he's the pulpit minister this morning. Three services. Tell him he has my prayers and he'll do fine. Tell him no jailbird preacher jokes."

"Bear," Annie said. "All this? This is from your side of the family. Stacy and I never gave our folks a minute's worry."

James Wanderley was right. I owed him. If Jo and I hadn't been accompanied by a police officer, albeit a Sugar Land police officer, I'm sure I would have gotten to know a whole new cell full of strangers and Jo—well, I'm not going to go there. The idea of my girl behind bars . . .

As it was, an officer herded Chloe, Wanderley, Jo and me into a room with a big table and lots of hard plastic chairs. Someone brought in a tray with a thermos of hot water, cups, plastic stirrers and an offering of instant coffee, hot chocolate packets, and tea bags. I made Jo some tea. She sat with her legs tucked under her. Even with the heavy flannel shirt, she gave a shiver now and then. After a good while, two plainclothes detectives came in. The tall, beefy one introduced himself as Detective Gustav Ruiz and the thin, weedy woman who looked like she should be teaching economics to college freshmen told us she was Detective Bianca Dabriel.

Ruiz said, "Where do we start? Mr. Wells, you first called Detective Wanderley at . . . what time would that have been?"

I took my phone out, pulled up my call history and told Ruiz, "Two twenty-eight this morning."

Wanderley took over, relaying the gist of my phone call and the story behind it. I was glad he did. He was concise and clear and I wouldn't have been. I was tired and aching and the cop coffee I'd drunk was sitting in my stomach like a cup of pickle juice.

Ruiz and Dabriel asked few questions. They both took notes. When Wanderley had finished, Ruiz looked down the table at Jo.

"Tonight's story starts with you, Miss Wells."

"Jo."

"Jo. Want to tell us what happened?"

Jo uncurled her legs and sat up straight. She twisted her hair into a rope, tied it in a knot and pushed it behind her shoulder.

"Mrs. Pickersley, Phoebe's stepmother, died today. Yesterday. And Dad came home and told us, and he said how Phoebe's grandfather got all Phoebe's money and the trailer, too, when she died, and I remembered how her grandfather was so mad at Phoebe's dad and said that Phoebe's dad would get his and he did."

Dabriel said, "Can you please be more clear?"

Jo sighed. "Mr. DeWitt, Phoebe's grandfather? He blamed Phoebe's dad for Phoebe's mom dying. She was Mr. DeWitt's daughter. And then Phoebe died—so Mr. Pickersley did 'get his' if you saw things that way, right?" She looked up at us to see if we were following and everyone nodded. "Then when I asked Dad again about how Phoebe had died, and he said she drank the Diloudid but the thing is, I don't think she did, you know?" Jo gulped the last of her tea and put the cup on the table. "But Dad, remember how I told you that Phoebe's grandfather would make her his disgusting power punch? That Phoebe made it for me and Alex, and it totally stains your mouth? I started thinking about how if someone said those bad things to me like her stepmom said to Phoebe, and I wasn't the kind of person who would kill herself—and Phoebe wasn't—then I would want to go be with someone who liked me. Phoebe thought her grandfather *loved* her. Only I don't think he did, which is really sad." She looked up again and we all nodded, less certainly, but still, we were with her.

"On the video, Mrs. Pickersley said she had some of the medicine, that stuff that killed Phoebe. She didn't say she had it all. So some of it could've still been at the trailer and Phoebe's grandfather could have made her power punch and put that stuff in it and when Phoebe was in my room she didn't know she was dying, she only wanted to prove to me that the bad things she said about her stepmother were true and that's why she left me her phone only she got too sick to leave. I looked it up online and that stuff can make you hallucinate. Right. It makes you itchy and hot, too, if you take too much—I think that's why she took all her clothes off." This time only Chloe nodded.

"Go on, Jo."

"So I wanted to know. Even though I still think Mrs. Pickersley really did want Phoebe to kill herself, she really did want her dead, and that's the same thing as killing someone."

"Not in a court of law, it isn't," said Ruiz.

"It is in the Bible. Ask my dad." Five heads turned my way.

"She's paraphrasing, but, yeah. First John, three fifteen—'anyone who hates his brother is a murderer.'"

With her thumbnail, Jo prized half-moon chips from her foam cup. She did this methodically, with concentration, her head down. "I didn't want Mrs. Pickersley dead, though. For what she did."

Detective Dabriel said, "Tell me why you broke into Mr. DeWitt's trailer again, Jo."

Jo's head came up. "I didn't break in. Not the second time." Her brow creased. "Oh, wait. Not the third time."

I said, "What?" and Wanderley made a slicing motion with his hand. I shut up.

"So, the first time I used Phoebe's key which she said I could, so that wasn't breaking in. And tonight, first I used the key and I went in and got his gun and put it outside so he wouldn't shoot me . . ." Meaning that Jo was the other moron Wanderley had referred to—I gave Wanderley a smile so he would know there were no hard feelings. ". . . and then I locked the door behind me and I knocked on the door. So that can't be breaking in at all, since he let me in. Really, it never was because I used a key the other two times and that doesn't count."

Jo used the side of her hand to sweep the cup chips into a pile. "Did you know it's seriously better for the environment to use those cardboard paper cups with little handles on the side? Plastic foam is a total Earth-killer. It won't decay. Five hundred years from now you could pull any of these cups out of a landfill, wash it out and use it all over again."

Ruiz gestured to the pile in front of Jo. "Not that one, you couldn't."

Dabriel put her hand over Jo's, stilling the sweeping and flattening and mound-shaping Jo was doing with the chips. "A man was shot tonight, Jo. You directly precipitated that shooting—"

I said, "Hold on, now—"

Dabriel cut her eyes my way. "Be quiet, Mr. Wells." I shut my mouth. She gave her attention to Jo. "We're taking that very seriously. I want you to stop waffling and give us an answer. Why did you go to Mr. DeWitt's trailer tonight?"

Tears leaked out from under Jo's lashes. I said, "Come here, honey," but Dabriel pressed her hand down on Jo's and kept her in her seat.

"I wanted him to tell me," Jo said.

"Tell you what?" Dabriel let go of Jo and picked her pen up. Wanderley uncapped his pen and stuck the cap in his mouth.

"I wanted him to tell me if he had killed Phoebe." Jo closed her eyes.

The three detectives put on smug, adult smiles.

"He said he did," she continued.

The smiles vanished. "What did you say?" Dabriel asked.

Jo opened her eyes. Her mouth was twisted. "He said he did."

Ruiz pushed his chair closer to the table and the chair screeched on the floor. "Start at the beginning and tell it to the end."

Jo nodded. "After I moved the gun outside, I knocked on the door and Mr. DeWitt took a long time answering but I knew he was in there because I'd already heard him snoring and, anyway, he smells bad and I could smell him. But finally he comes to the door and he opens it and he stares at me like he's never seen me before and he says 'What the hell do you want?' and I introduced myself because I didn't think he remembered me from the first time. Probably because he was really drunk. But I introduced myself and said, 'Remember, I was Phoebe's friend.' Which I was once, but not a good friend. She wasn't, either." Jo looked around at us again. "I'm only saying. Dying doesn't make you all perfect." She shivered.

Chloe got out of her chair, slipped Wanderley's jacket off her shoulders and draped it over Jo's. She sat down next to Jo and put her arm across the back of Jo's chair. I glanced at Wanderley, but looked away. He was watching Chloe, and his eyes were heavy with love and longing. It was a private look and I was sorry I'd intruded.

"He wanted to know what I was doing there, and I said I thought he knew because I saw that in a movie. He said he was going to call the police and I said, 'Call them, then,' because I knew he wouldn't and he just stood there holding the door open with one arm and pouring down underarm odor all over me but I didn't make a face and he said, 'Come in, then,' and I did because I knew his gun was outside and I'm stronger and faster than he is—"

Ruiz thumped the table and we all jumped. He got up and leaned over the table, putting his face right into Jo's. I stood up and said, "Back off." Wanderley stood up and put a hand on my shoulder and said, "Bear." Ruiz barked, "Sit down!" I didn't move. Ruiz moved back a foot. I waited and he waited and we sat down together.

He said, "I'm going to interrupt you for a minute. You're from Sugar Land, aren't you? Lotus-eater land. Maybe your daddy thinks life is so safe out there in outer suburbia he doesn't need to teach his girl how to protect herself." He lowered his

black brows at me. "I'm here to tell you that you aren't anywhere near as strong as Mr. DeWitt—"

Jo interrupted, "I'm a dancer. I train every day. I can—"

"No!" Ruiz didn't get out of his seat but he leaned as close
to her as he could without getting up. "You are a hundred
pounds of nothing. You know what strength is in a fight? It's
weight. It's mass."

Jo said, "Yes, but—"

"I'd be hard-pressed to find a single guy in this whole building, and I'm including all the skinny little white guys, who
couldn't take you down. And your self-confidence, your self-
delusion, is stupid and dangerous. Bianca, tell her."

Dabriel said, "First, let's—"

"Would you *tell her*?"

Dabriel made a *tchh* noise with her teeth and put her pen
down. She faced Jo. "I'm trained and I'm trained well. If I have
to, I fight and I fight hard. But the number one rule is, don't get
in the fight. A man held a gun on you and you went back for
more. Alone and at night. What you did was criminally stupid.
I'm embarrassed for you."

Jo was scarlet and her eyes flooded. My heart felt for her but
Dabriel was right. She just was. I was going to let Jo take that
one. Chloe didn't like it one bit, though. She dropped her arm
from the back of the chair to Jo's shoulders, looking daggers at
Wanderley who said nothing.

"Okay," Jo said, "then I'm stupid." She tried to control the
tremble in her voice. "Do you want to hear, or not?"

Dabriel said, very controlled, very patient, "I didn't say you
were stupid. I said you had behaved stupidly. Everyone in this
room has behaved stupidly. Don't do it again. That's the message you should be hearing. Now. Tell us what happened."

But Jo was lost in tears now. She started to talk twice, choked
on her tears and buried her face in her hands. I picked my chair

up and put it down behind Jo's. I turned Jo's chair around until
she was facing me. I took Jo's tearstained face in my hands and
I kissed her forehead. Found my handkerchief and gave it to
her and she gave her nose a good blow.

"Josephine Amelia," I said, "Here's the thing. Right this second, I do not give a dang what you did. By the grace of God,
and by that grace alone, you are here and you are safe and right
now, that's all I care about. That's all. You want to go home and
I want to go home and all these good people have homes to go
home to, as well. And Baby Bear and the pugs are at a stranger's
house and they probably want to go home, too. And no one *can*
go home until you tell us what happened. So take a breath, and
ask God for strength, and tell us the rest of your story. Can you
do that?"

Jo took a long, shuddery breath, and nodded.

"Okay, then," I said, "let's turn your chair around." I turned
her chair around. "And you hold your head high, and you tell us
what happened."

Jo gathered herself and began again. "Mr. DeWitt let me in
and he told me to take a seat. I sat down on that booth seat at
the kitchen table and he said to tell him straight why I was there
and I said it was because he was the one who killed Phoebe and
he did it by putting Phoebe's mom's medicine in a power punch
and I knew it because Phoebe had left me a message on her
phone and I was going to tell the police. All that was made up,
but, see, I thought that if he got all upset and started crying and
said he would never, ever hurt Phoebe, that he loved her and
couldn't get over her dying, then I would have told him I made
it all up and told him how sorry I was and that Phoebe really
loved him and always said such good things about him. But he
didn't say any of that. Instead, he said why hadn't I, then, called
the police, and I said because I wanted to know *why* he'd killed
her. And he said he was going to get a drink and he went to the

sink, and when he turned around he had a gun in his hand. And that was when he taped me to the table and I knew he meant to kill me, too." More tears but she wiped them away. I reached my arm around her and took her hand.

"He said it was Mr. Pickersley's fault that he lost his daughter and now Mr. Pickersley's daughter was dead, too. I said I thought it was so he could have Phoebe's trailer and all her money and that she'd trusted him and loved him and she had come to him when something bad happened to her and instead of helping her he had killed her and he would go to Hell for that and the fires of Hell would crisp his skin and that's when he taped my mouth shut."

Where the heck had that come from? My daughter talked like a 1930s backwoods evangelist. Crisp his skin? Not that I disagreed with the gist of what she said.

"He said he was going to kill me and drive Mom's car to the Houston Ship Channel and push the car into the water and that people would be eating crab at Pappadeaux's Seafood Kitchen and that crab would be fat off my flesh . . ."

Yeah. Mitch DeWitt was going to Hell and getting his skin crisped. Yes sir.

". . . and he said everyone would just think I was a runaway. But he didn't know about the dogs in the car and Baby Bear would have torn his throat out."

Or Baby Bear would have been killed, too. Along with Rebecca's pugs.

"And then Dad and Detective Wanderley came and that's all." Jo wasn't crying anymore. She was relieved to have it done.

Ruiz said, "That's quite a story, Jo. We can't use it, of course. It's interesting, but we don't have any proof. It's your word against his." He looked deflated. Dabriel capped her pen and put it in her breast pocket.

Jo reached into the flannel shirt and fumbled with her bra. I said, "Jo . . ." She pulled out her cell phone, clicked and scrolled and laid it on the table.

"It's the Smart Recorder app. It was four-ninety-nine, Dad, it goes on your card. I'll pay you back, but you have to use a credit card and you won't let me have one even though Cara has one. I borrowed yours." She touched the screen. First there was her voice, traffic noises in the background, an occasional yip from an excited pug. She set out her plans and the recorder shut off. Jo touched the screen again.

This time we heard Jo knocking on the aluminum screen door, Mitch DeWitt answering. And then everything. Just the way Jo had told it. When DeWitt told Jo he was going to kill her and dump her body in the ship channel, I jumped out of my chair. Walked to the door and leaned my back against it. Walked to the other side of the room. Back to the door. Checked the change in my pockets. Bowed my head and thanked my God.

I wanted to hit someone.

From the recorder there was the sound of breaking glass, the struggle, the explosion. Jo touched the screen and the recorder shut off.

Chloe, Wanderley, Ruiz and Dabriel sat staring at Jo's phone. At last, Dabriel picked the phone up.

"What was that app, again?"

Ruiz put his fist in his palm and cracked his knuckles then cracked the knuckles on his other hand. He blew a stream of air out his nose.

"That recording wouldn't have been worth anything on the bottom of the ship channel, Jo," he said.

"I set it to upload to the Internet. Automatically. Alex will get an alert."

"Ah, well. That's all taken care of, then. Of course, you could still have been on the floor of the ship channel. On your way to becoming some crab's dinner. And from there to being served with drawn butter at Pappadeaux." He made smacking noises with his mouth.

"Detective Ruiz?" I said, "Could you not? Please?"

Jo pushed back from the table and stood up. She spoke to Detective Dabriel. "Can you use it? Can you get him for killing Phoebe?"

Dabriel didn't mess around. "Yes, Jo. I think we can. I think we've got him."

Jo dropped to her knees and burst into tears.

Twenty-five

There was a FOR SALE sign in front of the Pickersley house. I called several times. Each time, Mark's mom or dad answered. It was never a good time for me to talk to Mark.

The seventh or eighth time I called, Mark's dad said, "Preacher? Don't call no more. He ain't coming to the phone. Mark and the boys, they're trying to put all this past them. They're coming up to New Orleans with us and we'll keep an eye on them. If Mark feels the need to talk to you, he's got your number. So don't call, okay?"

Somehow the gnome-as-weapon story got out. Monday morning I went outside to get the paper and there was a garden gnome on my front porch. He held a solar light lantern aloft. I put him in the garage. Tuesday morning there were six of them—two on the porch, the other four scattered over the lawn. Baby Bear peed on one of them before I could get them all picked up. On Wednesday there were more than thirty and I hollered at Jo to get her butt out of bed, this was all her fault and she could get them picked up and stored away. I made a NO GNOME ZONE sign and stuck it next to the front porch.

By Thursday morning we had forty-two gnomes, and when I unfurled the weekly local paper, *The Fort Bend Sun*, there was a picture of our gnome-bedecked front yard with the caption

"No Roam—Gnomes' Home" on the front page. Friday morning the gnomes spilled over into our neighbors' yards.

By Saturday morning, we had collected 388 garden gnomes. We boxed them all up and stuck them in the back of Alex's truck. He wouldn't let me drive but he said it was okay if Baby Bear came, too. Jo sat in front with Alex and Annie and I clambered into the backseat and made sure our seat belts were buckled. Baby Bear squeezed in as best he could.

We dropped most of the gnomes off at the East Fort Bend Human Needs Ministry Resale Shop. They were tickled. From there we headed out to Green Vista.

Lacey Corinda was also tickled to see us. She laughed out loud as we unboxed the forty garden gnomes we had brought her and stroked Baby Bear's head—best buds from the time they'd spent together. She hauled some chairs out of her trailer and made us sit there while she made hot cider. Jo and Alex lined the gnomes around the base of the trailer—it looked like a battalion of gnomes was guarding Miss Lacey's trailer.

We filled her in on the rest of the story and she wagged her head and clucked her tongue. Miss Lacey wasn't any older than me, but she had the mannerisms of my grandmother.

We ran out of words and Miss Lacey said, "I want to thank you for doing your best to make up for the loss of Hilliard." So, uh, Hilliard was too personal to be replaced. Even by forty gnomes? Oh well. "Now," she said, "let's talk about that favor."

Oh, yeah. She had refused payment when Annie and Stacy had come by to get the dogs, telling her, "The preacher and I have an understanding." A week later, I was about to have that understanding explained to me.

"What I want," said Lacey, "is for you to come out here and hold services. I want songs and communion and a sermon. Make it twenty minutes or so. Too long and I'm gonna fall asleep."

"Lacey, I'm in the pulpit over in Sugar Land every Sunday morning."

"Doesn't have to be Sunday morning. Doesn't even have to be on Sunday. Every day is the Lord's day."

I thought for a while. Yeah, I could fit that in. "Okay. I can do that next week."

"Every week. I'm going to ask some friends, too."

"Every week?"

"That's right." She nodded.

"I don't think I can do it every week, Lacey, I've got responsibil—"

"Tell you what. You commit for a month. Then we'll talk. How's that?"

The young man who had supplied the rope to leash the dogs the week before stepped out of his trailer. He saw us and smiled. Lacey waved him over, introduced him as Max and he joined us for hot cider.

You know what? My daughter was alive. Both my daughters were alive. I had a beautiful wife and I loved her. Baby Bear was luxuriating in the cool November air and I had returned Rebecca's pugs home to her safe, if flatulent (the ham bone and beans had been, no surprise, a colossal mistake—Annie and Stacy had driven home with the windows open weeping from the smell and their own hysterical laughter). I thought Jo could do worse than Alex. He wasn't that bad.

I looked around me at the rows of trailer homes, some of them neat and tidy and cared for, some of them not. I looked at the woman who had held my weeping daughter on her lap, a stranger's child drenched in blood, who'd brought who knew what troubles with her. Lacey had not hesitated to take Jo into her arms. The day was bright and darkness was past. God had been good to me.

"Okay, Lacey. You've got me for a month."